TRUTH

OR

BARE

TRUTH

OR

BARE

A NOVEL

RICHARD CAHILL

KÜNATI

LARGO, USA

TRUTH OR BARE

For information, contact Kunati Inc., Book Publishers in both USA and Canada.
In USA: 6901 Bryan Dairy Road, Suite 150, Largo, FL 33777 USA
In Canada: 75 First Street, Suite 128, Orangeville, ON L9W 5B6 CANADA,
or e-mail to info@kunati.com.

FIRST EDITION

Designed by Kam Wai Yu
Persona Corp. | www.personaprinciple.com

ISBN-13: 978-1-60164-016-1   ISBN-10: 1-60164-016-1
EAN 9781601640161   FIC000000 FICTION/General

Published by Kunati Inc. (USA) and Kunati Inc. (Canada). Provocative. Bold. Controversial.™

http://www.kunati.com

TM—Kunati and Kunati Trailer are trademarks
owned by Kunati Inc. Persona is a trademark owned by Persona Corp.
All other trademarks are the property of their respective owners.

Library of Congress Cataloging-in-Publication Data

Cahill, Richard.
  Truth or bare : a novel / Richard Cahill. -- 1st ed.
      p. cm.
  Summary:"Fictional account by an industry-insider explores sex-trade and
the seedy underbelly of society"--Provided by publisher.
  ISBN-13: 978-1-60164-016-1
  ISBN-10: 1-60164-016-1
  1. Sex oriented businesses--Fiction. I. Title.
  PS3603.A378T78 2007
  813'.6--dc22

                    2007028105

D E D I C A T I O N

To the memory of my brother, Greg Cahill, 1962-2001.

Acknowledgements

The author wishes to thank Alan Ackoff, Matt Cahill, Bobby Day, Jenifer Johnson and Sky Wyttenbach for being his original readers and encouraging him to keep at it when other encouragement was hard to come by, and all those people who over the years gave him night jobs so that he could write days, in particular Dennis Smith, currently of Anchorage, Alaska.

My thanks also to James McKinnon at Kunati, without whose help more mistakes would have been made.

Chapter One

It seemed to me, in this sunny state, in this most favored nation, in this abundant century, in the middle of a career in a lucrative field like the law, completely ludicrous that a man like myself, nearly halfway to ninety, should have to bother with clients like Marvin Maeger. Yet there I was, on a perfect September afternoon, bracketed in my windowless office, face to face with the X-rated visionary who had brought the latest wrinkle in adult entertainment to town, and managed to get himself busted for it. His eyes rolled with exasperation as he laid out his legal predicament, and he jabbed at the air with one finger, fencing with my questions as if they were a physical opponent.

You may have heard that I was a sleazy lawyer, but that wasn't true. I was an honest lawyer who specialized in defending people who had sleazy businesses. Some were perfectly legal. Some were less than perfectly legal.

If you were a pimp or had a peep show, you were a dancer or a streetwalker, had a topless bar or an escort service and you got yourself a legal problem, I was the counselor for you. I hollowed out that niche for myself when I re-entered the law field. Kept me from sucking on some insurance company's teat or springing carjackers for a living.

You were a dope dealer or an alien smuggler, I might have taken your case, too, but I probably would have passed you along to my friend Illegal Search and Seizure Izzy.

The man was a genius. You could accidentally offer a kilo of Mexican brown to the police chief's wife, and Izzy would find that you had a reasonable expectation of privacy. You got pulled over for a DUI, I'd take your money, although all I could really offer you was the assurance that you wouldn't get screwed deeper and more meaningfully than any other slob with a bad-news breathalyzer result. Nobody walks on a 502 anymore, now that MADD's a bigger operation than the United Fund.

Wasn't always that way. I started out as an eager defense attorney. Public defender hired me the day after I passed the bar, but I put out a private shingle as soon as I could, to separate myself from the dolts in the office who couldn't get a guy with no prostate off on a rape charge, and the cynics who cut deals while they golfed with DA's minions.

Then I ran into the repeat customer problem. Armed robbers who walked because I demolished their sobbing victims on the stand were calling me from jail when they'd been caught sticking another gun in another clerk's face at midnight. Rapists went loose because I humiliated the women they stabbed with their weapons. I confused children so their molesters could go free to entice again. Then there was the Willy Washington fiasco and I stayed out of lawyering for a year. When I went back to the courthouse, I kept to my principle of defending only those accused of so-called victimless crimes, although it's not the most profitable corner of the law.

And business was drier than usual on that day when Marvin Maeger and, later and more importantly, Angel Pisaro, entered my life. Any interruption in trade was bad for me because of my financial style. I didn't have any. What I had was an ex-house and an ex-wife, both of which I was still making payments on, and a teenage son with a nose for high-dollar trouble. Not only was my bank account down to the low triple figures, but I had just been served a notice that could mean I would not be earning any more money, at least by being a lawyer, in the immediate future.

Visa hates me. MasterCard has canceled me, and American Express doesn't want to know my name. I repeated that, like a mantra, to myself as I endured my moments with Marvin. He looked like he was about to start hating me, too, and I really needed his business. It's what everyone in the trade calls it, but when I uttered the nickname for his shop, Marvin Maeger acted like he was about to get up and leave. Marvin owned Phantasy Photography. Phantasy Photography had nothing to do with photography and everything to do with fantasy.

"Don't call it that," he said. "I don't even let the girls call it that."

"Sorry." The one word apology struck even me as being less than heartfelt. Marvin's glare went up an F-stop. Lack of attention and sympathy for the client always cost me more business than actually losing cases, and Marvin was a perfect client for me. It was not his fault that he had come by on the day that the City Attorney's office had shown its fangs. "What do we want to call it, then?"

"It's a fantasy parlor."

"And what happens in this fantasy parlor?"

"My customers come in, they see a girl they want to photograph, they pay to go into a private studio."

"With the girl?"

Always ask a stupid question. People love to answer them, and it puts them off their guard.

"Of course," Marvin said suavely.

"And when they get into this private studio, does the girl disrobe?"

"Yeah, sure."

"Completely?"

"Sure. They can. I mean if the clients want them to."

"Do the clients ever not want them to?"

"Mostly never, no."

"Do the clients bring their own cameras?"

"Sometimes, yeah."

"Are they allowed to use them?"

"No. They all bring digitals. Or those fucking cell phone cameras. I hate those things. None of them in here. We have regular cameras for rent."

"What's renting an obsolete camera cost?"

"Fifty bucks."

"Does that include film?"

"No. Film is extra."

"How much film do you sell, compared to how many cameras you rent?"

"Whaddya mean?" Marvin asked, gingerly.

"Do guys usually buy just one roll of film? Or do they buy two or three?"

"I dunno. I don't keep track of things like that."

Marvin, I guessed, was being one hundred percent untruthful at this point. If I read Marvin right, he was the kind of businessman who knew to the nickel what the coin-vended tampon machine in his ladies' room was bringing in.

"Mr. Maeger, they can subpoena your books."

If I had told Marvin he was about to be probed on the spot with a dry sigmoidoscope, he could not have looked more distressed.

"Relax, Mr. Maeger. They're not the IRS. These are simple-minded vice cops."

Lackeys of Danny Akami. City Attorney. DA in waiting. Prick extraordinaire.

"So, how many rolls of film do you sell for each camera you rent? Just one?"

"Not that many."

"Less than one? What, these guys are renting empty cameras?"

"Maybe they bring their own film."

"They're not allowed to bring their own cameras, but they can bring their own film?"

"I said maybe. I don't check their pockets."

"So a guy goes into a room with a naked girl and an empty camera. What happens? What does he do?"

"He fantasizes."

I loved that answer, but it would be difficult to seat a jury that would.

"When he fantasizes, does he touch himself?"

"I don't know. Fantasy is a very private thing."

"Because it would be illegal for him to touch himself. That would be masturbating in a public place."

Marvin snorted. "Yeah, that's one of the things I don't get. How can a private studio be a public place?"

"Because it's open to the public. That's the law, Mr. Maeger. You sell admission to the public, it's a public place."

"I don't sell nothing," Marvin said stubbornly. "I rent cameras."

Best to keep Marvin off the stand. Besides the injured air he cultivated, which a jury was going to hate, he looked the part of the sex merchant. Black hair swept horizontally and gelled over a bald spot, translucent cheeks sprouting five o'clock shadow even though it was not yet two, loud striped shirt stretched tightly over a little round belly.

"How long you had Phantasy Photography, Mr. Maeger?"

"Three years."

"Before you bought that business, what kind of business did you have?"

"Video rentals."

Great. Try and find twelve jurors that hadn't had to pay the late fee.

"Why did you switch trades?"

"Video business sucks. Clerks were robbing me blind. And you don't know how many people walk off with their videos."

"But you charge their credit cards for them. Usually around eighty bucks."

For a disc that cost twelve dollars. I knew people that hated Blockbuster more than the IRS. No point in reading further on Marvin's résumé. Probably he sold time-share or used cars to get the seed money for the video store. Some people just have a knack for unpopular trades.

"Retainer is a thousand dollars, Mr. Maeger."

"A grand!" Marvin's pale cheeks flushed.

I doubted it was embarrassment. Hypertension, most likely. Long hours of sitting at his post, munching on high cholesterol snacks, wondering which of the customers flitting across his closed-circuit screens were undercover vice cops. Enough stress to make anyone's arteries harden. Plus word on the street was that Marvin was a type A personality. A hard man to work for. The Mussolini of muffs.

"That's just the retainer, Mr. Maeger. It's a hundred and sixty an hour once the retainer is exhausted. We're likely looking at a jury trial, both for you and your employee."

"Fuck her. I told her to wait until they pull it out of their pants before mentioning money. She just waltzes over and grabs the cop's glands. I got the whole thing on videotape."

Marvin was just a little excited. Surely when he calmed down he would realize that the vice squad would be happier to find Marvin's in-store tapes than Jimmy Hoffa's final chauffeur. I, of course, could not advise him to destroy the tapes. Technically, as an officer of the court, I was required to inform the City Attorney, my colleague Danny Akami, of their existence. I didn't know a single defense lawyer that would publicly castrate his case like that, but it was a day that had been suddenly given over to technical questions of ethics. And Marvin.

"You leave her hanging, the city will surely offer her a deal. To testify against you. Who knows what she'll say? Right now, you're looking at a misdemeanor."

"Yeah? And loss of my business license? Board of Health is talking about shutting me down, too. Lot of grief, just for a misdemeanor."

"Racketeering rap would be a lot more troublesome. And the feds discovered a long time ago that judges'll let them paint almost any criminal act involving more than one person as racketeering. The girl, is she from here?"

"She's from Oregon. Lotta my girls come from Oregon and Washington. Ain't no economy up there."

"So you invited her to work for you?"

"One of her friends already was working at my place. My girls make good money."

"So she crossed state lines to perform an illegal act while in your employ. Couple of homies pulled ten years for bringing some girls in from Minnesota and turning them out. Sounds like almost the same thing you did. Federal time, which means they get to serve it all."

"Yeah, but they're black."

"Think maybe Uncle Sam would like to prove that had nothing to do with it?"

Marvin contemplated ten years in the federal pen. "Jesus, that ain't fair," he said, as if the concept of a universal standard of justice had just occurred to him.

"That's why we don't want it to happen to you. So we take care of your girl, too. That way the City Attorney won't boot it over to the Roosevelt Building."

That was pure bluff on my part. Getting a raw ribeye out of a hyena's mouth would be easier than getting Danny Akami to give up a splashy vice bust. But I didn't want to see Marvin's girl get hammered while he walked. Besides, a thousand bucks was only twenty camera rentals for Marvin. And he had the tax-free end, too, whatever he made the girls kick back.

In the most satisfying moment of a day that had been notably short of them, Marvin paid in cash. Despite his squawking, he knew what my retainer would be. He had it all in one of his business envelopes.

"What did the Board of Health cite you for?" I asked, by way of breaking the tension, as I recounted the stack of twenties.

"Claimed they found semen on my floor."

"Could happen, huh?" I stuck the money back into Marvin's envelope and put it in my pocket.

"Hell, no. That, for one, is a bum rap. I got a guy sponges it up."

"So you got a spooge sponger?"

"I run a clean business," Marvin said, annoyed again. I kept quiet as I made out the receipt. Could be I would need Marvin more than he needed me someday. Someday soon. Day after the Bar Ethics Committee met, if Danny Akami could keep his witness in line. The Notice of Hearing was still sitting in my In slot, a legal warhead in a heavy bond artillery shell.

I wondered how Marvin's janitor had begun the downward spiral that led him to become a mop boy in a fantasy parlor, or, in street parlance, a spooge sponger. In a whack shack.

I work alone. If my caseload got too heavy, instead of not nearly heavy enough, which is what it was the day I signed up Marvin, I dumped the surplus cases off to Branster and Schuckelgruber, my office neighbors. Branster hardly ever came in, preferring to supervise Schuckelgruber, the junior partner, from afar. We shared a secretary, too. Back then we had Amy, a brunette with big green eyes. I didn't think Amy was going to last long, because even as I went out to check any calls I might have gotten while I was closeted with Marvin Maeger, I saw Schukelgruber massaging her shoulder as he was standing behind her, and a look on Amy's face of wishing that at least one of them was somewhere else.

"Calls?" I asked. Schukelgruber's hand left Amy's shoulder. He brushed a bead of sweat from his forehead. Having a hand on Amy was really raising his core temperature.

"Mikey."

"Mikey with the topless bar or Mikey with the escort service?"

"Tit bar."

Mikey Armando owned Terrifically Titanium. He had some kind of national franchise deal where he had to remodel and change the name of his place every four or five years. It started out as Gorgeously Gold. Then it was Perfectly Platinum. Terrifically Titanium was his latest stop on the Table of Elements. I wondered what it would be next. Kompletely Kryptonite?

I personally was rooting for Sensationally Silicon. The place was steady work for me. One of Mikey's dancers had stepped over the six-foot line, or put a little too much friction into a table dance while the vice were in the house. Mikey was one of my favorite clients, because everything he did was legal. That meant he didn't have secret video cameras and flashing warning lights like Marvin Maeger had installed in Phantasy Photography. This made him an easy target for the vice, who swarmed through the door anytime they felt like it and popped his help for technical violations. The girls didn't even have to pay fines in most cases, but Mikey was looking at a hearing before the Alcoholic Beverage Commission every time one of his bare-breasted attractions scampered off the stage without fully fastening her bra, if the vice tagged her for it.

A bar owner standing before the ABC by himself has about as much chance as a third string quarterback on fourth-and-eleven. You needed the deftest of attorneys just to keep from being buried by the rush. Lucky for Mikey he had me.

The phone rang again.

"It's for you," Amy said. "You want to take it in your office? It's a Detective Sergeant Pennofrio."

"No, I'll take it here."

Pennofrio was in Homicide, last time I ran across him. I hadn't had anything to do with him in ten years. Couldn't think of anything he had to say lurid enough that I needed privacy to listen to it.

Amy looked grateful. Schukelgruber was staring judiciously at the bound legal volumes on the shelves, making sure number XV followed XIV, killing time until he could be alone with Amy. Schukelgruber was sixty. Amy was nineteen. I lost a case where a twenty-three-year-old client got a year for statutory for screwing a girl only six years his junior. He was Mexican and the girl was white, was his problem.

"I need a favor," Pennofrio said. I couldn't even remember what he looked like until I heard his voice. Big Italian, bald. He was mixed up in a couple of my wins and losses, but there was never anything personal between us.

"What's that?"

I figured a DUI. Cops get them more often than you'd think, especially when they're out drinking in another jurisdiction. Not that they can't get in worse trouble; few professions are so tightly bound by the law and simultaneously presented with so many opportunities to break it. Lawyers are one of them. But Pennofrio's reply surprised me.

"You remember where the cooler is?"

"Been ages."

"Yeah. Well, it's not like we miss you."

"The favor?" I was not in a philanthropic mood. I didn't need to be insulted on top of making a trip downtown. Afternoon traffic would snarl up tight on the way back.

"Meet me there."

"ID? Doesn't he have any relatives?"

"None that want to admit it. Come on. I get to close this file, you know him. I'll owe you one."

Nothing made a cop happier than closing a file. I had made so many cops unhappy, though, I doubted my reputation among the ranks could be much improved by my helping out the sergeant. Only curiosity made me agree. One of my ex-clients had apparently kicked the oxygen habit.

Whichever one it was, the world was no doubt better for it.

Chapter Two

The atmosphere of the morgue, fumes of industrial antiseptics overlaying the cold molecules of decay, was already tickling the back of my throat when Pennofrio slid open the drawer. Two things I became aware of right away. I did know the corpse. And he had been dead for quite a while. I stumbled back to the door and sucked clean air in from the corridor to keep from retching.

Stay out of a place for ten years and you're apt to forget the most elementary things about it, like how much cops enjoyed playing their little jokes on casual visitors. While I was trying so settle my stomach, a figure in surgeon's robes walked by.

"Hey, Vampire," Pennofrio greeted him.

"Odd nickname for a doctor."

"Vampire Eddie's not an MD. He's an organ harvester. Strolls these halls looking for spare parts. How's business?" Pennofrio shouted after him.

Vampire Eddie only returned a glum wave.

"Pick up on the weekend," Pennofrio said. He turned his attention back to me. "What about the cold guy?"

"About a quarter of the people in this town could've identified him," I said.

"Regulations. First we gotta ask relatives. Then known associates. You were known to associate with this guy."

"I was his lawyer."

"So the association is documented."

"Why didn't you call the president of KSUN down here? I'm sure he remembers him."

"Guys who run TV stations are busy, important guys. We don't bother them, we don't have to."

It was apparently assumed by the police that I had more unstructured time in my schedule. "I live in East County," I said.

"Traffic is shit today, too. Us cops got that two-way radio thing, so we know before anybody else, even Eye-In-The Sky Channel Four News. Better ID the remains and get a hop on it."

"You know as well as I do who he is."

"You ain't really in a hurry, are you? You're probably staying downtown for the big lawyer barbecue and beer bash at the Radisson."

"Not me. I was heading home."

The Jefferson Day dinner, the blowout of the year for the criminal defense bar, was that evening. I wasn't planning to make use of my invitation, even before I got the Notice of Hearing. Which might already be the main buzz during cocktails, and guaranteed to be the number one topic if I showed up.

"Speak the magic words, then. Identify the contents of the city's Tupperware and win a hundred dollars."

"He's Frank Fernando."

"Whoa, we're done."

Frank Fernando. Otherwise known as Chessie the Clown. Had a really successful kids' TV show during the administration of Bush One. He wore an outlandish costume with a huge orange nose. If a kid got to beep his nose, a trap door in the ceiling would open and the kid would get showered with toys from a sponsoring toy store. Kids loved him. And he returned the favor. I got my name in the paper nearly every day during the trial.

I couldn't get Chessie the Clown off. One little girl's testimony that Chessie told her he had another clown nose, between his legs, was pretty devastating. I nonetheless considered Frank Fernando one of my success stories. I got him probation and a heavy fine. He quit drinking, back then when people didn't consider getting sober an act of saintliness next to managing your own leper colony, and never touched another child, except probably in his dreams.

I was sorry to see him dead. If I had any say about the order of expiration of my clients, Frank Fernando would be far from the top of the list.

"How did he die?"

"Didn't take a lingering look, huh? There's a bullet wound in the middle of his forehead. Did the job himself. Want to see?"

"No."

"It's a nice centered shot. Powder burn around the wound. Probably held the gun an inch away."

"He leave a note?"

"No note."

"Then how do you know it was suicide?"

"Gun found by the body, .22 caliber Derringer. Registered to the victim. Residue on his right hand. Hollow point bullet in his brain somewhere, if it's like the one that was left in the gun. Good choice of weapon. Not quite enough zing for an exit wound, but plenty of power to turn his noodle into creamed corn. Patch up the little hole, you've got a good-looking corpse. That is, if someone notices before he goes ripe."

"So someone could've shot him and planted the gun."

"I'm sorry I made your day more difficult, Counselor, but stop trying to return the favor. You hold still and let somebody pump a bullet into the middle of your forehead? Not unless you're immobilized, and Chessie the Clown wasn't. Wasn't even wearing clothes, as a matter of fact. Hole would be on the side of his head, or the back. Plus a killer would've used both bullets. Not your most devastating handgun, a .22 Derringer. Plus he was found alone, in his apartment, with the door locked."

"He got naked to commit suicide?"

Pennofrio shrugged. "People do stranger things. This file is closed. God knows he had plenty of reasons to hit the off switch."

"All that stuff was years ago."

"So? Maybe it was preying on his mind. Or maybe he couldn't stand to live another day without running his fingers around some ten-year old ass. Who knows? Who cares?"

"He wasn't that bad of a guy."

"Maybe you can do his requiem, huh? 'He wasn't that bad of a guy.' That's a good start. Good finish, too. Keeps argument down to a minimum. He was a baby-fucking piece of crap, that's another point of view. Didn't have money enough to hire a smart-ass lawyer, he would've done at least five as some cellblock daddy's cornhole boy. Which would have served him right."

A good smart-ass lawyer always has a retort. "He wasn't a recidivist. He reformed. Started dating grown-up women."

When they would have him. God knows his life would've been easier if he'd left town. A native of this balmy little corner of the country, Frank Fernando couldn't see himself waking up anywhere else. Lot of people get the surf and sand in their blood like that.

"How do you know? You double date with him?"

"I keep track of my old clients."

"I'm doing you a favor, then. You're the first to be able to cross Chessie the Clown out of your address book. Next time folks ask you to bring your child-molester friend to one of their cookouts, you can politely decline. On the grounds that Frank Fernando finally put a nice clean bullet through his dirty little mind."

So much for making the cops happy. I left Pennofrio grinding his teeth at Frank Fernando's remains. It wasn't unheard of for a cop to carve a finger or an ear or another unremarkable digit off an especially detested corpse.

Preserved in formaldehyde, they formed the basis for good stories, and even better practical jokes. Pennofrio was too mature and ranked too high in the department to do such a thing, would be my guess. The coroner would be dividing up Chessie the Clown's remains soon enough.

I decided to go by Mikey Armando's place. It was only a half-mile out from downtown, underneath the flight path for the airport. A 757 passed two hundred feet overhead as I handed my keys to the valet parker. Mikey had to keep the volume on his system turned up pretty high, so the customers would assume it was the music shaking the building, not air traffic.

I hadn't returned Mikey's call. No emergency, I figured. Some liquor code violation relating to the topless bar business. Plus if I saw him in person, I could pick up some cash. Mikey's violations were great meatball law. A hearing, a conviction, a reversal on appeal. No matter how bloodthirsty the bench was in this town, no matter how rabidly pro-prosecution, they still had to pay some attention to the Constitution and the rules of evidence. Not so the ABC. Political appointees all, usually minor league city councilmen or ex-school superintendents that had run into electoral woes, the finer points of the law were beyond them. They had their hands on the reins of power for the last time in their political lives and they rode the steed of justice like Napoleon rode into Russia, heedless of risk and hell-bent for disaster. I had never won a hearing before them. I had never lost an appeal.

The ABC imposed hellacious fines, usually at least ten grand. This for a violation like a single pubic hair springing out from underneath one of Mikey's girl's G-strings when she backflipped away from the vice cops. Lot of cash for even a profitable business. My fee cost Mikey half that. I tried to persuade him every time he got popped that this was the one we should take to the Supreme Court. Get all the rules thrown out. Lift the burden of oppression off the spike-heeled and g-stringed of the nation.

Mikey always resisted. My fee for a simple hearing and one appeal was high enough. The Supreme Court case could be won, but I would own Mikey's bar by the time it was completed.

Kompletely Kryptonite would finally come into being. I would insist my doormen bear at least a passing resemblance to Lex Luthor.

The interior of the place sparkled with lasers and spots but it was not really bright. I had to look carefully for Mikey. He jumped around the place continually, from the DJ booth to the dressing room to the bar, making sure the girls were ready to toe the six-foot line, the music was the proper brand of brazen rap and the bar backs were not spitting in the blender. Lot of work went into maintaining the atmosphere at Terrifically Titanium. I spotted his back in conference with a couple of his customers.

"Speed," he said when I tapped his shoulder. "I'm glad you came down in person."

"No problem," I said. Mikey was one of my oldest and best customers. "What's the deal?"

"First let me take care of you." He snapped his fingers at a waitress, rousing her from an inspection of her lipstick in one of the mirrored walls long enough to bring me a bottle of beer. "Close enough to five," he told me. He led the way back into his office. The business used to be a restaurant and Mikey's office was once some kind of pantry. It was long and narrow and overstuffed with filing cabinets that were themselves overstuffed. Ends and corners of tax forms, job applications and inventory sheets bulged out of drawers that refused to close. The walls were hung with photographs of feature acts who had graced Mikey's stage, porn actresses between stints before the camera and girls who were just surgical miracles.

The only decoration in the room that wasn't cheesecake was the picture of Mikey's three kids. Mikey's children did not resemble each other much, owing to the fact that they had three different mothers, all dancers that had worked for him, one white, one black and one Asian. He was just that kind of guy. He's probably tried every flavor at Baskin Robbins, too. I knew the kids and their moms cost Mikey plenty, and I also knew that that did not keep Mikey from owning a Jaguar and a condo in Rosarito as well as a big place in the valley. Mikey also dressed well and ate well and offered his dates cocaine that had not been stepped on as many times as the dance floor at Hussong's.

Mikey lived large. That meant almost as soon as one of his customers slapped a five on his bar in return for a frosty one, the fin was out the door, on the way to the mortgage company or MasterCard or one of his kids' orthodontists. He paid everything in dribs and drabs and late as well, including his legal bills, a financial style I completely understood. But this time he pulled up the corner of rug that concealed his safe and withdrew a stack of twenties.

"Business good, huh?"

Mikey shrugged.

"How's the kids?" I was just making noise while I counted.

"Good, except for Aaron. He's still crapping out in school. Teacher wants to put him on Ritalin. Fuck that, I say. Last thing the world needs is another pill-popping seven-year-old. His mother wants him to see a kiddy psychologist."

Too bad. Another eighty-five bucks an hour heading out of Mikey's till.

"But Luke is doing real good." Luke was the oldest, the hapa one, half Korean. "He comes in around here on weekends and helps me clean up before the place opens. Think maybe he wants to get into the business with me, he gets old enough."

"That'd be great, Mikey." Luke would be fifteen or sixteen by now. I glanced up at all the 8 X 10s of breasts and asses on Mikey's office walls and doubted his kid's interest in the business was purely vocational.

I stopped counting when I got up to twenty-six hundred. "How much is here, Mikey?"

"The whole five grand."

The most money Mikey had ever given me at one time before was a thousand. As badly as I needed the money, nothing arouses my suspicions faster than someone being overly generous, especially a friend.

"What's this about?"

It was true that I always cost Mikey five grand, but I would not send him the whole bill at once. Maybe I'd win a hearing before the ABC someday. Not likely, but it would cut Mikey's costs in half. A hearing and appeal took time, too. If Danny Akami convinced the ethics panel I'd suborned a witness, and since the witness was going to testify that I had, the chances looked at least even that he would, my shingle would be on the shelf when the appeal was heard.

Schuckelgruber would have to handle it for Mikey. Could work out. Maybe he'd give Mikey a discount for letting him give his patented shoulder massages to some of Mikey's stable.

"This one I want to move on."

"Why?"

We didn't get too excited over Mikey's busts. The vice unit in town was large, active and under pressure at all times from the City Attorney's office to produce cases that Danny and his team could prosecute. Mikey got nailed all the time, mostly for nonsense like a g-string not having three square inches of material in the back or one of his girls pumping out more than three pelvic thrusts in a row.

"Here's the paperwork." He slid a sheaf over to me.

All I had to do was glance at it.

"You don't want me for this."

With a poignant sense of loss, I shoved the money back at him.

"You're the only lawyer I got, Speed."

"Time to get another lawyer, then. I can recommend a couple."

"You're the only lawyer ever got me off anything."

"What I get you off, Mikey, is pissy little vice busts. Shit that nobody cares about. The Alcoholic Beverage Commission helps me out by treating them like they were war crimes, so they look even more ludicrous when we appeal. This is way out of my league. Who is this girl?"

"She used to work for me."

"Doesn't even work for you now?"

"Naw. Worked for an outcall company. Private parties, mostly bachelor, a little acting out…"

"Acting out?"

"Scenarios. S&M stuff. All they do is buy the costumes and whip their customers a little. You'd be surprised how many guys go for it. Big names, too. Pols and execs."

"I believe that, Mikey. Fact is, I never had any welders or plumbers tell me that they wanted to find the right girl to whip their asses. But it doesn't have anything to do with this, or you. Why do you care?"

"I dated her a little bit."

"Aww, Mikey."

"It's not what you're thinking. I don't go for that. It was just straightforward sex with us. She needed it, after all that play-acting. Plus the business, the girl she was in it with. Lotta times they got paid a lotta money to do it together. She needed straight sex with a straight guy more than any woman I ever met."

"She was a switch hitter? And the girl that died was her lesbian lover? I'm just guessing here, Mikey, because that would be the worst possible case to defend. Better she accidentally strangled one of her customers, but I see from this preliminary, which the public defender's office handled, that the victim was named Evelyn, so my bet is not."

"No. It was her business partner."

"So she had a sexual relationship with the victim. A financial relationship with the victim. Lot of pressure can build up between two people, they depend on each other for money and orgasms both. And she only stabbed her…" I looked at the papers, "three times. Allegedly."

"It was self-defense. You got to hear her story." The money was still sitting between us. Mikey pushed it back toward me.

"I'll listen to her, Mikey, but it won't cost you five grand. I'll listen to her and recommend another lawyer. But how about we both save some time, and I'll tell you her story right now? She was having a little fight with her girlfriend, and her girlfriend picked up the knife—the victim always picks up the knife first in these kinds of stories. They struggled for possession of it, and somehow poor Evelyn got stabbed. Three times."

"That's not how it went. That wouldn't be self-defense."

"No, but it could be manslaughter. Get her a sentence of eight to twelve. Luck and good behavior, and no priors, she could end up doing three."

"She can't do any time, Speed."

"You got a room full of other girls out there, Mikey."

"Just get her side of the story. Self-defense."

"Self-defense is a long road. Especially when you stab someone three times."

"She wanted to make sure she was dead, Speed."

"That's the kind of statement we want to avoid making in open court."

Not that I planned to go to court on behalf of Mikey's girl. I hadn't defended a murder case in more than a decade.

"What would you do if you found out the person you were sharing your life with was a killer?"

"Are we talking about the deceased Evelyn?"

"Say you found out. And she knew that you knew. How secure would you feel, sleeping under the same roof as that person?"

"Not real secure, but there's a lot of things you could do before you stick somebody three times. You could move out. Straight across the country, if you had to. You could change your name. You could join a cult with communal sleeping quarters. You could shack up with a rougher, tougher lesbian. Above all, you could call the cops and let them deal with it. Why didn't she do that?"

"I think it was a sudden thing. Where she was going to be the next victim."

"Better be an accurate impression, your girl wants to walk on this. The DA is going to want to know why she just didn't light out."

"She didn't have a chance."

"She better not have. Because self-defense is a hard defense to prove. That's why you don't hear it much. Prosecutors don't believe in self-defense. Nobody moves up in the office letting people walk away from corpses. Even if you got a case for self-defense, it's likely the DA is going to offer you a choice to plead to manslaughter and get a sentence you'll live to see the end of, or go to trial for Murder One. Most people take a deep breath and go for the deal."

"That's not justice."

"Mikey, you're in an honest business. Your girls show an honest breast for an honest buck. It's hard for me to explain what the law is like to someone in such a straightforward trade, but let me tell you that the law has damn little to do with justice. And even less with truth. It's more like a pickup basketball game between a bunch of eighth-graders, with a referee who's either completely useless or malignantly aligned with one side or the other. Winning is everything, and the DA has everything he needs to win this one. Your girl is going down for at least three years, no matter who you get for a lawyer. Save yourself a bundle and let the public defender do it."

"She'll never forgive me if I don't get a hired lawyer."

"Then I'll find you one." I happened to know where they all were right at that moment. "It's going to be a lot more than five grand, too."

"Take it for now. And take the case yourself, Speed. I trust you."

"Thanks for your confidence, Mikey, but no thanks. You wouldn't hire a pediatrician to take your gall bladder out. You want a guy that's tried a first-degree beef since disco died."

Chapter Three

I bought a paper but there was no mention of a stripper murder. Probably happened yesterday, or in the small hours of the night before. No chance of getting yesterday's newspaper, so I would have to walk into the Jefferson Day dinner knowing just what was on the report of the preliminary hearing about the client I was going to foist off on the first of my colleagues that would take her.

I'd gone into trial knowing less. The downtown Radisson was a great green-glass heap lined in golden metal. It was only a few years old and sat incongruously among the brick and mortar of the older downtown buildings. Some marketing genius had decided that the spirit of Radisson needed to be represented in the inner city, so they had tossed up this giant greenhouse that looked as though it ought to dominate a golf course and a ten-acre parking lot. Instead it was crammed into a single block on a diagonal from the courthouse.

Convenient for members of the criminal bar. Unlike other lawyers, we actually spend time there. Or maybe the downtown Radisson just gave us a rate. Lot of us needed to watch our cash flow; the PDs had to live on government salaries and the rest of us had to split up what few people got themselves accused of criminal conduct who actually had assets. The tort guys had their dinner out in the valley. Consumer Recovery Advocates is what I believe they're calling themselves this year. Expense not a worry for them. Their only problem was to stop stuffing money in their pockets long enough to eat.

The flow of downtown nightlife had adjusted nicely to the perimeter of the Radisson. I watched as a weather-beaten woman rooted around in one of the potted plants that fronted the lobby, hoping to add a discarded empty to the collection of cans in her shopping cart. She wore a black T-shirt with You Make My Snout Wet printed across the front. She glanced up at me and her mouth cracked open. I hurried inside before she could pan-handle me.

Hadn't I done enough by making her snout wet?

I pinned on a name-tag like everyone else, although most of us didn't really need them. The beer at Terrifically Titanium had given me a thirst for another lager. I gripped a bottle and ventured onto the floor.

"Speed! You come solo?"

"Yes, Desiree."

Desiree Mason stood before me in a brocaded dress with the kind of vague flower print on it that most people reserve to cover sofas. What might cover a sofa would not necessarily cover Desiree, though. She had a white wine in one hand and a plate brimming with hors d'oeuvres in the other.

"Having trouble with your social life?"

"Decided to come at the last minute."

"You must not be dating anyone anyway. They would have insisted on coming along, or else not let you go by yourself," she said shrewdly.

Even at a respectable weight for a lineman, Desiree still had a woman's confidence that she knew exactly what any other woman was thinking. "How's your son?"

"Fine."

"And you? Still getting hookers off the hook?"

"In the idyllic suburbs of the law, it is still my own special little subdivision."

I watched fascinated as Desiree raised the plate to her mouth and tongued a Swedish meatball off the edge.

"Very sensuous," I complimented.

"Thanks. I was trying to turn you on. At my size you have to be a complete slut in order to get any sex at all. How about it?"

"Got plans for later."

"Now is fine. This is a hotel, you notice."

"Before dinner?"

Desiree refused to acknowledge the slight.

"Dinner I can miss. Chicken cordon bleu. Same as last year. Probably left over from last year." She reached over and tugged the end of my belt. "I want something new this year."

"Scandal would dog us."

"I worry about my reputation?"

"Don't you have some interns or rookie associates you should be molesting?"

"Been through the crop. And in record time, too."

Desiree actually ran the public defender's office, although officially she was only a deputy. She was going to cost the city a fortune in a sexual harassment suit one of these days, and the beauty of it was that she just didn't care. If she hung out her own shingle, she would have to be a lot more discreet. With the taxpayers' wallets to back her up, she went through all the tender young male attorneys the office hired like a turbocharged John Deere through a ripe field of winter wheat. Those who refused to unroll her plus-size panties got stuck defending endless unwinnable DUIs. Only the gays and the girls didn't have to pay her tribute.

"I still want you, Speed."

"I got to network here."

"You? Even Schuckelgruber says you're a moody bastard."

"All that's changing. I'm turning into a social animal."

"I love that kind of talk. Especially the animal part."

"I got to mingle."

"You know I'm on the Ethics Committee?"

Fat lady could drop a bomb like a B-52. Didn't keep her job just because she was another pretty face.

"Didn't figure you had the time."

"Don't, but I have to. One PD has to be a member at all times. Wasn't able to duck it this year. I see you're coming up before us."

"A misunderstanding."

"The City Attorney worked long and hard to create that misunderstanding."

"The City Attorney has a great big hard-on for me."

"Danny doesn't have a big hard-on under any circumstances. Trust me on that."

"I was speaking metaphorically."

"Didn't come here to find a guy that could do it metaphorically."

"Sorry."

"One vote on the EC goes your way, you can walk." Desiree winked.

There was a tiny globule of gravy on the end of one of her eyelashes. It waved haphazardly, like a specimen of marine life caught in a rushing tide, as her eyelids fluttered.

"Thought you needed three to get off."

Four to convict. I had read the bylaws of the EC the minute the notice had arrived.

"But any individual member can block any witness's testimony. If a member is possessed of knowledge pertaining to the credibility of a witness, he or she may bar that witness from testifying. Saving the time and patience of the Committee."

"That's a hell of a loophole, Desiree."

"The law is always easy on lawyers, Speed. All you need is one friend on board. Got one?"

The makeup of the Ethics Committee changed from year to year. No one wanted to spend more than the minimum term passing judgment on his fellow lawyers. The problem was it could rotate around until it got out to the asteroid belt before a friend of mine was on it. About the only people in the room that could be counted on to let me off the hook, besides Izzy, were Schuckelgruber and Branster, but they weren't on the committee. Not that they liked me, but they needed my third of the rent and Amy's salary. I could see Schuckelgruber on the far side of the reception room, gabbing away at some PD fresh out of school. Man's tastes were consistent. She looked only a few years older than Amy.

And these people were my fellow members of the defense bar, my putative allies. God knows I wouldn't get any mercy from the rest of the committee. They would be from the DA's or the City Attorney's office. Couple guys from the civil bar were always on the committee, too, but they would follow the lead of the others in matters of ethics, knowing it was a field in which they lacked any experience.

"Guess I'd better make one."

"Now you're talking, baby."

"But not tonight. More than a week before the hearing, right?"

"Speed, that was cruel. And dangerous. What if I got permanently *miffed?*"

"I really do have business to take care of," I pleaded. "Who's handling the lesbian murder?"

"Don't talk shop. Talk smut. What do you care?"

"Accused's got a friend with cash."

"Tell him to save it. DA might let her cop to manslaughter. Miracles sometimes happen. She's not going to do any better than that. What, you're back in the big leagues?"

"Hell, no. I'm here to farm it out."

"Could be tough."

"How so?"

"The victim. She had a lot of friends."

"Here?"

"Here, there, everywhere. She was a party girl. Regular at those disgusting stag things you guys go for. If you got out more, you'd have known her. Clientele was all top-shelf. Used to do one-on-ones, too, with plenty of kinky icing. Bondage. Dressing up like a schoolgirl. I hear a couple guys pretty high up on the food chain are plenty pissed their sex toy got stuck by her girlfriend. They're ready to fry the little bitch."

"PD's office wouldn't let that happen, though. And now she's got a white knight. So who's handling her defense?"

Desiree looked embarrassed. Odd, because Desiree didn't do embarrassment.

"Over there. Talking to your office mate."

Schuckelgruber was still chatting with the baby PD. He was using the hand-on-shoulder technique he employed with Amy to keep her from slipping away.

"The rookie? On a first degree?"

I stared at Desiree in amazement. The happy glow from the glasses of wine and pillow talk had vanished. She wouldn't look at me. The gravy sphere fluttered into stillness.

"These big boys, they got to you, too?"

"Taking this case is not going to help you in the popularity polls."

"I told you, I'm here to sublet it."

"Market's going to be down, let me tell you."

"What's the big deal?"

"Told you everything I know already. Just leave it alone. Vainglorious bastards will forget about it, we get a couple continuances and they get themselves a new playmate. We'll cop a plea on the QT after Christmas.

You push on it, they're liable to toast her."

"I already took a fee."

"Find an excuse to give it back."

"How old is your colleague, anyway?"

"Twenty-eight. She just looks younger."

"It's her first year in the office, right? I haven't seen her."

"She's a sharp one, though. Little political. Wouldn't be surprised if she defected to the other side, eventually. She can handle the deal, especially with me walking her through it."

"I'd better have a talk with her anyway. Obligation."

"If I had a twenty-five inch waist, you'd take my advice, Speed."

"Besides, Schuckelgruber drools on her any more, he's liable to dehydrate. Collapse. Can't pay all the rent on the suite myself." I moved away.

"And your problems with the EC would be over," Desiree called after me.

I plowed through the party. Luckily, most of the revelers were happy to turn their backs on me. Getting tapped by the Ethics Committee was like contracting a potentially fatal and possibly contagious disease; no one really wanted to be exposed to me. They forced grins, murmured greetings, and made little gestures towards their mouths, indicating that they were too busy stuffing themselves to speak. Judge Barry Appenzeller, nicknamed Broad Appeal Barry, was the only non-member of the defense bar I could see present. Barry hadn't acquired his nickname because of his popularity. It was because when you argued in Barry's court, you always had broad grounds for appeal. Also always a chance to serve an afternoon in jail for contempt. Barry had a slow cancer that meant he would expire before his term of office. He had chosen to spend his remaining years torturing his fellow members of the legal profession, just as his own cells were tormenting him. Some people claimed that if you knew what kind of chemo he was taking that day, you could predict whether the prosecutor or the defender would suffer from his Mad Hatter brand of justice. I regarded them as being as reliable as astrologers. Broad Appeal Barry attending on Jefferson Day was like Himmler organizing a ball at Buchenwald. He did it only to observe his next victims.

Search And Seizure Izzy held out a hand.

"Speed. Hear Akami got one of your ex-clients to roll over on you."

"I hear that too, Iz."

"It's your own fault."

"Almost always is."

He was big, too, nearly as wide as Desiree, but with a handsomely fleshy face, a full head of black hair, and a salesman's charm. He could make a jury identify with almost any client. *Suppose, ladies and gentlemen, that you were crossing the United States Border. And suppose your doctor had told you it was necessary for your health for you to carry certain vials in a suppositorial fashion. And say you were instructed by a customs official to bend over so he could remove those objects. Would not you feel entitled to refuse, on the grounds of health maintenance and privacy?*

He had actually gotten a mule off with that argument. Didn't hurt that he'd managed to impanel an entire jury out of San Ysidro, where almost everyone made their living in border trade, legal and otherwise. It was said that the Customs bulls had quit doing rectal searches for a month out of sheer discouragement when that one walked.

Izzy made the world a better place. There was no doubt about it. I acknowledged his rebuke humbly.

"You should have given Danny a break years ago," he continued. "All he wants to be is DA."

"Not my fault he's not. Blame Jimmy Donnelly."

Jimmy Donnelly was our Reaganesque District Attorney. Had been voted into office so many times and was thought so kindly of by the voters that no matter how many high-profile cases his office botched, no blame was attached to him.

"Man wants to die with his boots on."

"He'll die in a nice nursing home, with his teeth on his nightstand, if Danny has his way. All Mr. Clean needs to do is rid this town of every topless joint, peep arcade and dirty bookstore. Then he'll have a record of accomplishment that'll beg for electoral recognition. And guess who's standing in his way?"

"My clients run legitimate businesses. They're entitled to the protection of the law."

"What about the hookers? You spring enough of them for a chorus line every year. What they're doing ain't legal."

"You know most of them I just plead down to disorderly conduct."

"Man does not get to be DA by winning a mountain of disorderly conduct cases. Let a couple get convicted of actually soliciting. What's wrong with that?"

"I regard it as a Constitutional issue. If a woman is not free to sell the pleasure of her vagina, then how can she be said to control her own body?"

"That's logical, Counselor. Make the connection with Roe vs. Wade and the Supreme Court just might buy it. Unfortunately, you don't appear to have looked at a map, lately. Supreme Court is about twenty-four hundred miles east of here. You got almost as much support for legal prostitution in this town as you have for changing the name of the place to East Beijing."

"We all have our dreams to chase, Izzy. Mine is to free the vagina; yours is to make impregnable the rectum. Either one's worth the seven years of college, don't you think?"

"Let the pussies and the assholes of the world run free!"

He clinked his brandy against my bottle in a toast.

"In the spirit of that sentiment, I've got a client I'd like to pass along to you."

"My plate is full, friend Speed."

His glass was, too, but not for long. He swirled his snifter around and drained it. I hoped my colleague Search And Seizure Izzy wasn't planning on driving himself home. Wasn't a cop in town who wouldn't love to lead him in the Breathalyzer Two-Step.

"Client? Let me tell you about a client," Izzy said expansively.

"Mine's got him or her beat."

"Funny you should put it that way. My boy's got him or her on the brain. Homie by the name of Jerome Putnam. Only he doesn't go by that handle much. He prefers to be known as Double Delicious Didi."

"The transvestite armed robber?" Some of the sociopaths on Izzy's client list were so spectacular everyone had heard of them.

"That's the one. Double Delicious has two hobbies. One is dressing up like a woman, and the other is small-time armed robbery. He likes to combine the two. Every time he slips on his nylons, it seems, he can't help but stick up a gas station. Might work for him, disguise-wise, except that Double-Delicious usually panics and starts discarding his feminine accouterments as he makes his getaway, leaving the odd wig or scarf to mark his trail. So the cops catch him more times than not, they answer the call before some bag lady starts scooping up Didi's wardrobe in order to gussy up her own ensemble."

"I seem to recall Didi was multiple-strike loser. You'll be pleased to know your future client has no previous-felony issues."

"Let me finish. Last time they were following Didi's droppings, though, they must've taken time out for a cruller, because they don't catch up to Didi before the he-she is holed up at home, over in the projects with one of his aunts. Cops waltz right in and find Didi with the swag, about seventy-three dollars and a display case full of control-top panty-hose.

"Of course, a man's home is his castle, even if the man is not really a man and the castle is subsidized by the Department of Health and Welfare. No warrant, even though it would've taken about nineteen seconds to get one, with the evidence the cops had in hand. I get the case on one of those hundred-an-hour farm-outs from the PD's office.

"I don't feel like wasting my time, but before I can move for suppression, the DA's office comes begging for a deal. Says they'll give Jerome six months home confinement if he pleads. All he has to do is wear one of those electronic anklets and he'll be able to avoid the big house, stay at his aunt's, catch up on his reality shows and work on base, blush and eyeliner combinations for the next time he's ready to dance. No reason for me to deal down Didi, but the DA says if I do, they'll give me some slack on a paying client I got with more serious evidentiary problems. Totally unethical, but that's the town prosecutor for you.

"So I sign on the dotted line. Didi does what he's told, the judge formalizes the deal, and I explain to Jerome that I've got him six months of sitting pretty at his auntie's instead of a third strike and life at Chico. Well, Jerome goes berserk. Turns out there's nothing he wanted more than Chico. All of his best clothes are there. Plus his favorite asshole bandit is going to be staying there until the guy in the White House has been an ex-president for about twenty years. His lover Rolando. Rolando's in for attempted murder with mutilation in a gang thing. Carved an "R" on his victim's forehead after crushing his spleen with a post-hole digger. Where do you find a post-hole digger just lying around in East LA, Speed? Also, why not a "Z?" At least make the cops guess.

"Jerome's screaming like we've set fire to his panty drawer. 'Rolando is Spanish! You know how those fucking Mexicans are! In six months he will have had every piece of ass in Chico! How will I ever get him back?'

"He threatens to kill me, the judge, everybody. Picks up twenty days for contempt. After that, though, the only thing that keeps him from going on a murder spree is an electronic anklet. Oh, and he'll probably have to put together an outfit for it. Something in velveteen and pearls would about do it. He-she wants to kill, he ought to dress up like Agatha Christie, you think?" Izzy snorted at his own joke. "I'm a damn effective advocate, aren't I, Speed?"

"The best, Izzy."

"So what you got for me?"

"The lesbian murder."

"Oh. Her." Izzy's grin disappeared, and suddenly he wasn't looking me in the eye. Easy for him, since he was at least five inches taller than me. "Can't cover that one for you. Comes with heat like August in Yuma. You stay away from it, too, is my advice."

"Why doesn't anyone want to defend this girl?"

"PDs will do it. It's their job."

"Desiree's assigned her to a first-year intern."

"Doesn't surprise me."

"Okay, Izzy, I'll be straight with you. I don't know anything about this homicide. I didn't even read the paper yesterday."

"Wouldn't have learned anything about it from the paper."

"So tell me about it."

"Mostly it's about the victim. She had a lot of fans in this town."

"High up on the food chain, too, it's been said to me."

"This guy owns the food chain."

"What? The mayor? Donnelly? One of our distinguished representatives in Congress?"

"They probably all had a shot at her, but let's face it, she turns up dead, they're probably breathing a sigh of relief. Only a private citizen can afford to love anyone other than his wife. Try Frankie Manus."

Frank Manus had owned the entire valley before it became its current candyland of high-end hotels and pricey malls. Replacing his family's dairy herd with an equal number of cement trucks had made him a prince among princes in the California real-estate boom. He was referred to as the Father of Mission Valley in the gushy texts of his company's own press releases.

"And?"

"You name 'em, Speed. She did 'em all. Did 'em well, and left them sighing for more."

"Personal nostalgia there, Izzy?"

"Just saw her play a couple times. Invited by the upper crust. Those guys like to keep me sweet, they accidentally wipe out a pension fund or pave over an endangered species, they might need me someday. Got to be quite a tradition. Pig roast in the spring, barbecue in the summer, cocktails at Christmas. Manus put on the party. Him, couple of guys like him that got cured in real estate, not necessarily the mayor or Donnelly, but a whole slew of their aides and advisors. Boys' night out. Fantasy would be there every time, knocking 'em right out of their monogrammed socks."

"Fantasy?"

"Stage name. Real name was Evie. She'd pass out her business cards and you'd almost get sick watching those rich old farts drool. Course, that end of the business was strictly confidential. No one knew who wanted to get whipped, who wanted her to dress up like a sixth-grader at St. Bernadette's, who wanted to watch her and her dyke girlfriend eat each other's sushi."

"Still, she's just a stripper. Talented one, maybe, but the woods are full of 'em. Why all the heat?"

"Coming from the top. You ever tell a rich bastard he can't have what he wants? I have. They fire you. Maybe hire you back after a couple other attorneys have told them the same thing. Manus wants the accused to fry. Donnelly doesn't want to get fired. All Manus has to do is put one of his cash-pumping stations in Akami campaign headquarters and instead of dying in office like the last gunslinger, Donnelly gets tossed out on his ass as a senile hanger-on." Izzy snagged another brandy off a passing tray. "Take this case, and you'll have both the DA *and* the City Attorney trying to kick you in the nuts. You ever take the bar in any other states, Speed?"

"No, but I figure they'd be easy compared to this one."

"May have a chance to find out soon, huh? Especially if you sign on with this girl."

"Told you, I'm just here to lend-lease her."

"Good luck with that," Izzy snorted. "My advice is, go to LA or Springs or even Sacramento for some out-of-town talent. Someone who won't even know they're being bushwhacked until they feel the edge of the tomahawk under their scalp. They'll go for first degree on this all the way."

"Can't get it. No evidence of premeditation, no time to form intent, from what I see."

"They'll be looking for some. Your client ever talked about killing her girlfriend because she didn't pay her half of the cable bill, or sharpened the cutlery sometime before she stuck her, they'll find out and introduce it as evidence. You're looking at both barrels, Speed."

"I wish you'd quit calling her my client."

"You argue like she is."

"I'm just looking to make a gift of her to someone."

"No one in this room. Lots of lawyers left in California, though. Must be a list somewhere. Find it and start dialing."

"I'm contact-poor."

Result of my isolation in my own little corner of the law. Shit, I didn't know half of the lawyers at the dinner.

"Can't help you, Speed. Hey, Pete!"

"Israel!" Pete Winam embraced Izzy as fervently as he could without causing him to drop his drink. "Mr. McKeon! How's your dad?"

"He's dead."

"A great man, your father," Pete said, as if he had not committed a social foul at all.

It was true my father had not made a lot of headlines when he died, the political tide having run strongly against him for the last part of his life, but the society columnist, of all people, should have known he was deceased. I wondered what Winam was doing here. The defense bar in this town is a rather shabby lot. Years of Republican control have left us with judges that don't grant us too many newsworthy victories. Maybe Pete was hoping Dan Horowitz would show up, to shine his light among his poorer brethren.

I read Pete's column every day, mostly because it was printed at the top of the funnies page. Society columnists are the opposite of tabloid journalists. Mere celebrity is enough to insure the kid-glove treatment. Anybody with a famous name passed through town in a public way, he or she was mentioned reverently by Pete. Any antics by the well-known, like wife-beating or a string of divorces or an unfortunate indictment were treated with broad amusement by him, in the relaxed, tolerant way of a man who has just had an excellent dinner and several drinks. Which was Pete's usual condition. I wanted to get over to where Schuckelgruber was still bore-assing the greenhorn PD, but Pete kept a hand on my arm as he gabbed away at Izzy.

To pass the time, I dreamed up a few phrases for Word Around Town by Winam. I hoped for his sake that he had another banquet to cover besides the Jefferson Day affair. What to write about here? *Desiree Mason, sturdy champion of the public defender's office, was seen molesting meatballs sans knife and fork. Ms. Mason, dressed in enough brocade to tent over a used-car lot, had her horns out their usual mile.*

No. Lacked Pete's literary tone. How about *Ernie Schuckelgruber pressed his claim to be Legal Old Goat Of The Year by shoulder-squeezing an attorney thirty-five years his junior until her collarbone needed X-raying?* I tried to make eye contact with the PD, but her eyes were glazed with ennui. Schuckelgruber does a lot of tax law. Tax evaders by definition have cash, but they don't necessarily have interesting cases. Listening to Schuckelgruber recount his legal triumphs was like trying to stay awake through an evening of viewing The Committee Channel. He gulped at his drink hurriedly as he recounted some Tax Court drama in which he had outwitted the IRS.

Cocktailing was the high point of the party so far; no one seemed anxious to press on to the chicken. Criminal lawyers drink a lot more than the tort guys. Consumer Recovery Advocates stick to bottled water and Diet Coke. Can't have their hands trembling when they're trying to count their money. Maybe Pete could take his lead from the bag lady's T-shirt. *Many a snout was wet at the Jefferson Day dinner…*

"So you're going to be defending the lesbian killer?" Pete asked.

"You talking to me?" I was nonplused.

Izzy was grinning like he had just clipped his toenails into the punch bowl. Nobody loved a hot rumor more than Izzy, even if he had to start it himself.

"That's going to be a tough one to win. But it's good to see you playing in the majors again."

Everyone is ashamed of my legal specialty but me.

"It's not a done deal."

"You've got to let go of the Washington William thing."

"It's Willie Washington."

Was Willie Washington. The late William Washington, whose manner of death was as spectacular as his life had been drably, if criminally, ordinary.

"Nobody felt more for you than I did, that day."

Pete had been a beat reporter then, before some talent spotter at the paper had decided that his goateed picture would look perfect above the society column. Also he was getting a little too thick around the waist to be chasing around town after fires and bank robbers. Maybe it was true. Maybe he was my number-one source of empathy that day. I hadn't known it until now, because no one asked him how he was feeling. Almost everybody, including him, wanted to know how I was feeling. They mobbed me right outside my office—microphones, cameras, TV lights—all asking the same question, all beginning with *How does it feel?*

Felt just awful. Still does. My determination to farm out Mikey's girlfriend burned brighter.

"I gotta mingle," I said, brushing off Pete's arm.

"Good to see you out and about," Pete said.

The fresh PD was within striking distance. Schuckelgruber saw me coming and spun her around with his ferrous grip so that her back was to me.

"Ernie," I said. "You remember to turn the lights off?"

"Is this your partner?" the PD asked.

"No," Schuckelgruber said hurriedly. "This is Ted McKeon. Everybody calls him Speed. We share office space with him. Ted, this is Jill. From the public defender's office."

I reached out to shake her hand. Schuckelgruber had miscalculated. In order to let me reach her hand, he was going to have to either let go of her shoulder or let his fingers drag across her breasts. He let go. I pulled her towards me, effecting her rescue while shaking her hand. "Very nice to meet you."

She nodded, not seeming the least bit more enthralled with my company than she was with Schuckelgruber's.

"My last name is Congliaro."

"Italian?"

"Ex-husband was. An electrician. He put me through law school." The rookie PD was serving notice, I believe, that she was not here to be taken advantage of. She was attractive, though more from being youthful-looking than classically beautiful. She had the pug nose of a young girl and creamy skin with just a hint of freckle, in which time and care had furrowed no wrinkles.

"I was telling Jill about the opportunities in our office. When she starts her private practice."

Schuckelgruber was promising out partnerships in return for satisfaction for his horny old fingers? I wondered what he was offering Amy. Put her through college on a Schuckelgruber Fellowship?

"Nothing's going to be bigger than tax law in the future. With the IRS capable of performing more and more audits each year, the number of contested amounts and criminal indictments is bound to grow." Schuckelgruber prattled on. His hand made useless, grasping gestures now that it had been detached from Jill Congliaro. "Of course, we all got our start in the Public Defender's office. Mine was in Ventura County, though. Speed did his stint here, didn't you, Speed?"

"You bet."

"Did you graduate here?" Jill asked. The interest of one recently graduated. Law school seems like a life ago to me.

"No. UCLA."

"But you're from here?"

"No, Los Angeles." Not wanting to explain that I moved away so that I wouldn't have to conduct my career under my father's supervision, either actual or by proxy, I changed the subject around to business.

"Desiree says you have the lesbian case."

"It's so white male to call it that."

"Pardon me?"

"Characterizing the accused by sexual preference. I supposed if it was a gay guy in the box you'd call it the fag murder."

Schuckelgruber shook his head resignedly, as if to suggest that he'd been doing great with Ms. Congliaro with the clavicle massage and tax chat approach before I had wedged myself into the conversation.

"I might, I suppose." No point in denying the obvious. Not unless you can get at least one juror to go along with you.

"The defendant has a name."

"It's Angel, isn't it? Angel something Spanish."

"Pisaro. It's Portuguese."

"Angel has a friend who asked me to help her out."

"The Office of the Public Defender is capable of handling this defense." The PD glared at me, a perfect stranger horning in on her first first-degree case. Schuckelgruber looked at me with disgust, as it was apparent that I had pissed off Ms. Congliaro more in two sentences than he had in a half-hour of heavy breathing.

"I'd really like to be able to tell Ms. Pisaro's benefactor that," I said.

"Then please do."

"I'd like to be a little more familiar with the case."

"Read the indictment."

"Especially in terms of projected defense strategy."

She sighed. "All right. You've got to make the appointment with me, though. I'm still counselor of record."

"I anticipate that you will so remain." Unless I recommended to Mikey that he pay for some out-of-county talent. The mood among the remainder of the freelancers in the room was no doubt as anti-Angel as Izzy's. I held out my hand.

She tried to put a squeeze in her response, like a jock. "We'll be talking then, Mr. McKey."

"It's McKeon. Everybody calls me Speed."

She looked me up and down, and then I suppose she just had to ask.

"Where did you get a nickname like that?"

"In high school. I was the slowest guy on the track team."

I skipped the chicken cordon bleu. The caterer served it in heaps in giant pewter chafing pans. The entrees looked like a pile of skinned rodents, oozing ham and Monterey jack for entrails.

The Consumer Recovery Advocates always had lobster. Desiree, forgetting her earlier disdain for the main course, had already stacked her plate with the cheesy breasts.

Out of a healthy fear of the Ethics Committee I pressed her hand between mine before I had my car brought up.

"Speed," she said, looking wounded.

"Got to be in Vista tomorrow morning." Standard lawyer excuse for leaving anything early. The North County courtroom was thirty-five miles from anywhere, in traffic. All the attorneys that begged out of boring parties ever actually showed up there, they'd have to put on a new wing. "We'll talk," I added, as the look on the PD's face clicked over from hurt to anger.

"Dinner, then," she said.

"Fine," I agreed briskly, then walked bravely away, before I had any time at all to think of the prospect of spending the night, or at least a couple of hours, in Desiree's arms *after* watching her eat, just so I could stay a lawyer.

Not that there aren't many, many better things to do besides lawyering. The question for me is, can I do any of them?

The valet parkers brought up my car, a Cadillac, a mid-range lawyer's car. I had to have the thing detailed every other week so that people wouldn't notice it was ten years old.

I took the Reverend Doctor Martin Luther King Jr. Freeway out east. The bad neighborhood freeway. Any one of the exits would drop you off in a neighborhood of barred windows, used car lots and pawnshops. Peep shows and X-rated arcades, pimps and whores as well. Crime hummed along the boulevard. It was the heart of industry for guys like me and Izzy.

My exit was out toward the foothills, where a single premature hill elevated itself above the valley. The ramp curved off into a neighborhood of view homes and swimming pools that rose a thousand feet and several social strata above the flat terrain. Scattered among the ranchers, like dandelions in a bed of roses, were a few two-bedroom shacks like mine.

As soon as I started the climb, the temperature light went on. The height of American technology, at least the height of it ten years ago, and they couldn't even put in a proper thermometer. The engine had no doubt been heating up on me the whole gradual climb east. Either the thermostat or the radiator's shot, Hector at the garage had said, and he'd already put in the thermostat. I pulled over in a turnout and locked up, taking what papers I guessed I needed for the night.

Crime comes up the hill, not often, but when it does it makes the papers, since it is proper tax-paying citizens that get preyed upon up here, not the welfare lumpen of the flatlands. I huffed around the uphill curves. I was almost in sight of my home when I heard the metallic rasp of a shotgun being pumped. I closed my eyes and cringed.

"Kenny!" I called out. "Is that you?"

"McKeon?" A figure, dressed in camouflage, dropped onto the road beside me. "What're you doing walking?"

"Car overheated."

Kenny did a quick once around, checking all the approaches. "Quiet tonight," he commented. "Lucky for you, McKeon." Kenny always addressed me by my last name, military fashion, even though I'm fifteen years older than him. We used to have Neighborhood Watch up on the hill. Kenny was its earliest and most enthusiastic member. Too enthusiastic. A cell phone and a

T-shirt was not kit enough for a proper crime-fighter, in his opinion. He took to prowling the hill as he was now, camouflaged and armed, a violation of the group's bylaws. In a meeting filled with rancor and accusations, Kenny was expelled. He formed his own organization, Neighborhood Extreme Watch, of which he was the only member. The two protective associations existed uneasily side by side for a few months, and then the members of the original group decided it was madness for them to be roaming the hillside along with Kenny armed with only the T-shirts and the cellular phones. They gradually abandoned their vigilance, rather than be accidentally shot by him.

Of all his neighbors, I am the one that Kenny would most like to shoot accidentally, I expect, being a criminal lawyer and therefore an ally, although a legal one, of the sea of slavering scum that Kenny imagines will one day surge up our hillside.

"Where's your night vision goggles, Kenny?"

"Busted," he said shortly.

"I'll be okay from here, I expect."

"Wait. Something I want to show you." Kenny moved closer. He broke the shotgun and extracted one of the shells. "Rubber pellets," he said, showing me that the shell was filled with little Super Balls. "Non-fatal."

"Not necessarily."

"But if someone died, no intent."

"I'd argue that, if I was your lawyer."

"You think I don't listen to you, but I listen."

A few conversations I've had with Kenny have turned on the trouble, criminal and civil, he could get in if he managed to fulfill his lifelong dream of putting to rest a marauder, let alone injuring an innocent. Lot of people think that Kenny keeps to his schedule of day job and night watchfulness with the aid of illegal stimulants. The shotgun does tend to go off at the most hallucinatory times of night, four AM to first light. Kenny always says it was a snake when questioned about those nighttime blasts, even in February, when the snakes have been coiled up since Thanksgiving.

"Israelis use rubber bullets. Nobody sues them."

"Can still kill, Kenny. Can still do a lot of damage. Break bones, obliterate nerves, crush organs."

"We can't be totally defenseless."

"What about the cops?"

"Cops have all the fun." He laughed briefly.

"You're right about that." He produced a flashlight and shined it right into my eyes. "Good night, McKeon."

I was surprised he didn't add "dismissed." I stumbled along in the dark, impenetrable now that Kenny's flashlight had made my pupils contract to day-at-the-beach size, something I was sure he did to increase my feelings of helplessness and dependence on Neighborhood Extreme Watch.

The light at my house was out. I hadn't anticipated coming home after dark. I flicked on the porch light and the inside switch simultaneously. The mismatched clutter of my home flared into view. The place screamed for a garage sale. That was one thing I liked about being married; I'd had color-coordinated furniture. All of the stuff I currently owned had been given to me by clients instead of cash payment. That was why I had four fax machines, for example, only one of which was hooked up, and probably all of which were hot. Two sofas, one leather, one a clashing velour. Some of the payments in kind had been really spectacular. Above the fireplace was a javelin, given to me by one of my ex-classmates in high school, a fellow member of the track team, whom I had gotten off on a post-graduate domestic violence beef.

There was an acrid smell in the place. The cat had no doubt shit someplace inconvenient, as punishment for my staying out too late. I looked around for the damage, but couldn't find it. Too tired. Cleanup would have to wait until morning.

I opened the bedroom windows so I could have fresh air for sleeping and lay down on my bed, a perfect Sealy Posturepedic, donated by the owner of a hot-sheet motel who I kept in business for years despite his being targeted by Danny Akami as a public nuisance. He swore it had never been spotted by trade. I flicked on the TV, even though I could already tell that I would never stay awake until the news came on. Above the bed was a pair of silver hand-axes, said by the pawnshop owner who had given them to me to be the ceremonial ones used to cut down the first sapling to make way for the original town square of Springfield, Illinois.

Or was it Springfield, Missouri? I believe he had been purposely vague, in order to puff the value of the axes, which he foisted off on me in lieu of a grand he owed me for getting him found innocent on a charge of distributing child pornography. Didn't know what was on those tapes, he said, and the jury believed it. Knew a lot more about the axes, apparently.

They looked old enough, the silver long gone to tarnish. People used to tell me I shouldn't keep them over my bed. Old Uncle Richter sends a big enough earthquake, they could decapitate me. I yawned. Didn't feel like earthquake weather.

The next thing I knew the TV had decided it was already tomorrow. I disagreed by clicking it off and nodding back to sleep.

Chapter Four

The phone rang while I was still in bed. I croaked a greeting into the receiver.

"What's the difference between a lawyer and a vulture?"

"What?"

"Lawyers get frequent flyer miles."

"Hello, son."

"Did you hear that the Post Office recalled their latest stamps?"

"No."

"They had pictures of lawyers on them. People couldn't figure out which side to spit on!"

"Shouldn't you be in school?"

"I'm ditching Phys-Ed. I told my counselor if they gave me Phys-Ed for my first class, I would never go. Who wants to jock around first thing in the morning? What's black and brown and looks good on an attorney?"

"A pit bull."

"I already told you that?"

"Somebody did."

"Mom's pissed about the tuition. It was due last week."

My son ditches Phys-Ed at an expensive private school. At first he went to private schools with academically challenging standards. When he was not up to the challenge, he transferred to public school, where he could be with students of his own ilk, that is, tenth graders who did not understand fractions. After he was caught dealing pot out of the trunk of my car, which he swore he needed to help transport handicapped classmates on a field trip, he had to start attending another private school. This one was for the aesthetically gifted. My ex-wife thought I was stupid for not realizing he should have been there all along. A kid as lousy at math as mine had to be aesthetically gifted.

I thought I was an idiot for falling for the handicapped classmates' story.

Now he studied things like abstract sculpture and white rapping. Also he got his own car. I bought it for him, just in case he planned to keep the pot business going. An attorney sure looks like a dumbass when he gets his car confiscated under some zero tolerance law.

I had to buy his and mine in the same week. It was then that my tastes in cars went from new to classic.

My ex-wife told me that my son was far more socially successful at his new school, instead of being regarded as a cranky and mentally suspect loner, as he had in public school. Didn't surprise me. Those aesthetes need a reliable and reasonable dealer of the weed. I wondered how he made money at it. Drug dealers I defended were always talking about halves and quarters and eighths.

Guess he had picked up on fractions after all. Between the shifting around between schools and the semester he had to skip on account of the pot bust, he was going to be nearly old enough to drink legally by the time he was ready for junior college, if my ex-wife could find one whose standards were high enough for him.

"I had to pay your car insurance last week."

"Hey, not Mom's fault when the bills come due. Don't try and blame everything on her."

"They're going to have to wait another week for the tuition."

Fifteen hundred a month. All I had on me was Marvin Maeger's grand. Plus Mikey's money, a dime of which I spent meant I had Angel Pisaro for a client.

"Or else your mom's going to have to cover it."

"Never, Dad. She knows she lets you slide once, it's going to be a motherfucker to get you to pay every month."

"Since when are you allowed to say 'motherfucker' in front of me?"

"Get off my cloud, Dad. I'm a fucking adult now. Hey, better dress up warm. It's cold today."

I frowned. The breeze through the bedroom window felt balmy enough.

"How cold?"

"So cold I saw a lawyer with his hands in his own pockets! Haw! Gotta go, gym's almost over."

"What's next?"

"Study hall. Hey, pay the tuition, huh? They start giving me creepy looks if I'm late."

Get set for a semester of creepy looks. Wonder how long the school would let my son attend if my income dropped to zero? Not long enough to graduate, I imagined. Since public school wouldn't have him back, he could end up being the most expensively educated dropout in the state.

The smell of cat crap grew stronger when I opened the bathroom door, but I didn't locate the offending pile until I was almost waving a bit of it under my nose. The evil little mammal had gone to the trouble of climbing up on the cabinet and shitting all over my toiletries. There was a pungent chunk of cat turd on the toothbrush I almost stuck in my mouth.

"You hairy little fuck!" I screamed, but naturally he had lit out.

When my cat decides to punish me, soiling the rug or the sofa is not enough. He likes to dirty something I'm going to have to put my hand on. He's hit the TV remote and the silverware drawer, and now my toothbrush.

No amount of rinsing would be enough to let me put it in my mouth, so I just showered. The phone rang again before I could leave.

"Visiting hours started fourteen minutes ago."

"Mikey, I have an office."

"I know. I already called there."

"Didn't they tell you I was in court?"

"Yeah, but I decided to take a chance. You gotta go see her, Speed. She's going to pieces in there."

"What do you want me to do, Mikey?"

"Have 'em set bail."

"Bail's already been denied. And it'll stay denied. Murder Numero Uno. Judge isn't going to see her as having strong community ties, no matter how many aldermen she's fucked."

"That was her girlfriend." Mikey sounded hurt. How could I forget he was in this for love?

"You want another lawyer for this one, Mikey. I'm still working on finding you one."

"No one else wants it." He said it as a matter of fact.

"Who says?"

"Your big Hawaiian buddy, for one. Him and a couple of his friends came in here after the attorney shindig at the Rad last night. They were bombed enough to be loud. Are you really going to have to bang some fat broad lawyer to stay in business?"

I didn't mind Izzy blabbing about the Ethics Committee; it was the talk of the local bar, without a doubt. But he should leave my putative sex life out of it.

"Don't worry about it."

"How could you get yourself in that kind of trouble?"

"Doing what everybody else does."

"That's the worst way to get in trouble, doing what everyone else does. You gonna pull out of your spin in time to save my girl?"

"Doesn't make any difference. The Secretary of State couldn't negotiate a deal for your girl less than eight years, Mikey. But I'm doing my best to stay a lawyer, if that's what you want to hear."

"Good. That's brutal though, having to fuck somebody to keep your deal. Didn't think that went on, in the attorney business."

"Don't think that it's going to."

This kept up, the tryst between Desiree and myself was going to make the tabloids. Or at least Winam's column. *Professional Misfit Mates with Horny Mammoth.*

"I understand, if you got to take care of that business, why you can't go down and see Angel."

"Nothing's going on right now. I'm alone at home."

Practically putting cat shit on my molars. Then I realized Mikey had cornered me.

"All right. Soon as I get out the drive."

"You're a rock, Speed."

"I still haven't spent a dime of your money."

"Put it in the bank."

"A friend of mine works out of Indio, he might take it. I'm just remembering him now."

"No strangers. You know this town, Speed."

Only a guy that ran a nudie bar would think that. I was their liberator, the sleaze operator's Constitutional Avenger. Adversary number one to Danny Akami, the Japanese-American Comstock, the keeper of the public panties. Mikey could never imagine what a raw stranger I was at the District Attorney's office. I left a message for Jill Congliaro, asking to be permitted to see the public defender's client, Angel Pisaro. I hiked down to where I had left my car to cool off. No sign of Kenny. Wasn't Neighborhood Extreme Watch aware that eighty percent of burglaries occur in the daylight hours?

I drove the Cadillac up my drive and filled up the radiator with the garden hose. The cat, in a rare miscalculation, stuck its face out from underneath the porch while I had the hose in my hand. I let it have a shot right in the ear.

Fortunately the women's jail was in East County and for the most part downhill. The temperature light only flickered once on the way over. I gave the sheriffs my name and the name of the prisoner. I half expected to be turned away, but Jill Congliaro must have passed the word down the line. I was ushered into the conference room, where I got to wait for fifteen minutes while the deputies rounded up Angel Pisaro.

She looked plain in jail garb, petite and small-breasted. Short hair and brown eyes. A discerning eye would notice the muscles in her calves and the supple shoulders, clues that the body underneath the smock was formed well enough so that its owner could make a living from displaying it.

"Mike sent you," she said dully. "Are you going to be my lawyer?"

"I'm Ted McKeon," I said, avoiding answering the question directly. "Everyone calls me Speed."

"Took you long enough to get here. When is the trial?"

"We don't know yet."

"Because I'm sick of this place. All the other girls are black or Mexican."

Somehow she managed to convey the impression that this was a sexual inconvenience. Or that was just the way I read it. She was not entirely gay; I had Mikey to vouch for that.

"We may not want to go to trial."

"They're not going to let me loose without one. I know that much. Let's get going with it."

Great. She wanted to push the trial along just as badly as the DA's office. Ten years out of the bigs, and if I weren't careful I'd be marshaling arguments in a death penalty phase by the end of the month.

"Let's talk about what happened."

"Evie was going to kill me."

"How did you know that?'

"She said she was."

"Lot of people say that. It's a common expression to use, when you're angry. You did kill her, though."

"I had to."

"She was coming after you with the knife?"

"No. She was sitting on the couch. I stabbed her in the chest."

"Three times, right?"

"The first two times, it didn't feel like it went all the way in."

"Did you tell the police that?"

"They made me."

"Did you call the police?"

"After I was sure she was dead."

"Did you tell the police *that?*"

"They made me."

"Did you ask for a lawyer at any time the police were questioning you?"

"They weren't really questioning me. They just wanted to know what happened."

"Did you ask for a lawyer anyway?"

"No. I knew Mikey would send one."

"Did they read you your rights?"

"Yes. Just like on TV. When can I get out of here?"

"Not for a while."

"Mike said maybe you could get me out on bail."

"It would be very unusual for a judge to grant bail in a capital case like this. The defendant would have to have very strong community ties, and considerable assets. Are you from here?"

"No. Missouri."

"Do you have any family here?"

"Don't have any family anywhere."

"Bail is set as an assurance that a defendant will show up for trial. What kind of work would you be doing, between now and the trial?"

I assumed that the sex-for-show business with the late Evie had closed its doors.

"Just regular dancing."

"Mikey would give you a job?"

She made a face. "I wouldn't work for Mike."

"Where, then?"

"I don't know. I'm sick of this town, though. The whole thing kind of spoiled it for me. I get sad thinking about Evie, too. An agent said he could get me a job dancing in Osaka. That's in Japan."

"I know where Osaka is."

Angel was the princess of wrong answers. Let her on the stand, might as well have the lethal injection gurney waiting in the bailiff's quarters. Save the government time and money.

"I almost have enough money to get implants."

I just sat and stared. Many people looking at a capital murder charge would let it distract them from the prospect of augmented breasts, but not Angel.

"What are you looking at?"

"Nothing."

"My tits are small, but they're nice. You just can't appreciate them in these clothes."

"I wasn't looking at your chest."

"Yes, you were." She smiled, so broadly that it was a caricature of invitation. "Evie already got implants," she said bitterly. "Our biggest customer bought them for her, but not for me."

"Let's talk some more about Evie," I said, businesslike.

What was Mikey doing mixed up with Angel? I knew he satisfied his appetites with a steady string of dancing girls, but there had to be better company than her stepping across his stage.

"Were you fighting with her?"

"No."

"You just up and stabbed her?"

"I told you, it was because she was going to kill me."

"She would have stabbed you?"

"No. She would have made it look like an accident. Nobody would ever have known. It makes me shiver, thinking of dying that way."

"How would she have done that?"

"I don't know. She did it before, though."

"To who?"

"Guys. Guys that deserved it."

"How do you know this?"

"She told me."

"You never saw her do it?"

"No!" Angel shook her head, affronted.

"You see her coming home with blood on her hands, or all scratched up, like she'd been in a fight?"

"No."

"Ever show you a body, or tell you where one was buried?"

"No. I wouldn't look, or want to know. Anyway, I'm trying to tell you, she never did it like that. She always made it look like an accident. The cops always cleaned up after her. She used to laugh about it. Said men were so stupid they couldn't even tell that someone was picking them off."

"Why did she tell you about it, you think?"

"To impress me. She was like a guy that way. She was like a guy in a lot of ways."

I wondered if I could work the sexual oddity of the murderer and the victim around to convince a jury of Angel's innocence. It was useful that the late Evie took the masculine role in the relationship. Maybe I could paint a picture of Angel as the battered wife, so psychologically cowed that she could've stuck her lover in her sleep and get acquitted on the grounds of self-defense.

"Evie ever hit you?"

"No. I mean, not for real. Once we were doing a gig for a bunch of leather lesbians, she chained and gagged me and whipped me. That was all for show."

"You only did that once?"

"Evie said there wasn't much of a market for it. Not many leather lesbians around."

"She never threatened you? Did she tell these stories about killing men to try and keep you in line?"

"No. She wanted to impress me, just like a guy. Guys will always tell you stories about fights they've won."

"Only she had murder stories to tell."

"I didn't like hearing about them. I told her that."

"Do you consider yourself a lesbian?"

"No, of course not. Ask Mike."

"How about what you did with Evie?"

"That was for show."

"How about what you did at night? When you weren't working?"

"That doesn't really count."

"Why not?"

"Evie said only what you do with guys counts."

"Was Evie a lesbian?"

"No. More than I was, though."

"What do you mean?"

"She only did it with guys when she was paid to."

"When was that?"

"When we did a little girl act. When you do a bondage act, you don't have to have sex with the guy. They come anyway. But when you do a little girl act, you always have to fuck the guy. And pretend you're scared and it hurts you, too. That way they come right away."

"You did these acts?"

"Evie taught me how. It was hard for me. Sometimes when they pulled out their little peters I just laughed. They would get mad. Evie would have to do them for free, then, to keep our clientele. That was the only time she ever got mad at me, when I would screw up on a gig. So she did most of them, most of the time. She had to use me for the doubles, though. I didn't mind that. The guys wouldn't even touch you. They'd just jerk off."

"Evie taught you that?"

"Yes."

"And Evie handled all the business?"

"Oh, yeah. I wouldn't want to even talk to most of those guys. Just a bunch of hard dicks to me."

It was apparent that Angel had downplayed her involvement in the business to Mikey. Angel was a nasty, lawless little bitch even before she knifed her roommate.

But Evie was her mentor. Try the victim. It was one way of winning over a jury. At least there would be plenty of ordnance if I wanted to attempt that strategy. The problem there was that if I got to naming the names of the men who had enjoyed peeling the Catholic school uniform and the Tweetie Pie underwear off the late Evie, I might as well tape a pair of antlers on my head, throw on a fur coat and go for a hike in the hills during deer season.

On the other hand, Angel would probably keep me from committing professional suicide by not recognizing any of her clients. From her brief description of her average working day, it seemed unlikely she had looked at any of them above their navels. She wouldn't be ID-ing any of the gentry of the town as long as they took the ordinary precaution of wearing pants on the witness stand.

"Okay, Angel, that's all for now."

"What about getting me out of here?"

"I've got to talk to another lawyer before I can do anything."

"What about bail?"

"I told you, it would be highly unusual for the court to set bail in a case like this."

"Then what about the trial?"

"Sometimes it's not a good idea to rush into trial."

Mental evaluation was the solution for Angel. Jill Congliaro would go along, if she hadn't thought of it herself already.

"Sure, if you're guilty."

A month in the state hospital was the ticket. A cooling-off period for the bluebloods who wanted her shoved onto Death Row, and thirty days for Angel to get used to living in a structured setting, because that's where she was going to be for a while.

"But I'm innocent. Once I tell my story to the judge, he'll set me free."

The woman had great confidence in her idiot wiles, as misplaced a confidence as any she had put in her Evie. Innocence didn't look right on Angel, like curb feelers are wrong on a Humvee.

"Sometimes it takes a little more doing than that."

Angel scowled. "Mike said he would send me a good lawyer."

A deputy moved in. "The man said that's all for now."

Angel didn't resist being led away. An orderly followed her with a glass of milk and a small wedge of hard-crusted pie.

"Since when do inmates get a coffee break?" I asked one of the sheriffs.

"When they're pregnant, they do," she replied. She looked at me quizzically. "Don't get around the ladies' jail much, Counselor?"

"Jail at all," I admitted.

There were four messages from Mikey on my cell. I ignored them all. I coasted the Cadillac over to the garage where Hector let me know that a new radiator was going to be six hundred dollars, *mas o menos.* I grabbed my briefcase and had Hector drop me off at Low Rate Auto Rentals. My cell rang while I was plugging it into the cigarette holder of an Asian econobox that was barely newer than my Caddy.

"Well?" Mikey said.

"She's going to go down, Mikey. My specific advice is for her to take any deal that the DA will give her. If she goes on the stand she's going to barbecue herself."

I frowned. My temporary wheels appeared to have been exported by accident. The controls for the air conditioner were marked in what looked like Korean.

"Speed, the girl is innocent."

The call-waiting tone bonged in my ear. Ordinarily I would let the phone dump the new caller over to voice mail, but at that moment I couldn't think of a single diplomatic phrase that would convey to Mikey my opinion of Angel's innocence, without insulting him, so I said "Just a minute," and hit the flash button.

The second I heard Marvin Maeger's voice I regretted it. "Hey, I want my grand back."

"Why, Mr. Maeger?"

"I hear you're not even gonna be a lawyer by the end of next week."

"That's not necessarily true."

"So what? I give up a grand, I want someone who's going to be a lawyer by the time they finish spending it."

No sense mentioning to Marvin that I was already spending it. Hector needed four hundred just to pick up the radiator.

"If you have another attorney in mind I'll be happy to send your file over to their office."

Marvin was nonplused by my bluff. "Don't you have to find me another lawyer?"

"If I was unable to continue with the case, due to circumstance…"

"Like getting kicked out of the lawyer clubhouse?"

"That would be one circumstance, yes. Then I would be obligated to find an equally qualified attorney and turn over your case and the remainder of your fee…"

"Remainder! I gave you a grand!"

"A bill would be prepared."

I didn't hate myself for sounding like an attorney when I said things like that to Marvin. Look long enough, you can find something good about everybody. One of my father's favorite epigrams.

Dad never knew Marvin Maeger. Or Willie Washington.

"A bill for what?"

"Interviewing the client. That's you, Mr. Maeger. Preparing possible lines of defense." Because the I-just-rent-cameras defense was going to be tough to sustain in court. Especially if Danny Akami leaned on your spooge sponger.

"You get paid just for thinking?" Marvin spluttered.

"You get paid just for renting cameras."

"Those cameras cost me money! Sometimes I don't even break a hundred rentals, on a Monday or a Tuesday. I still got all kinds of overhead to pay."

So Marvin didn't gross more than five grand a day until the weekend. Compared to that, getting paid just for thinking was a lousy racket.

"That's too bad, Mr. Maeger. We lawyers get our offices and our office help for free, because people like us so much."

"You're kidding." Marvin hesitated. "Hey, you are kidding. Are you charging me for this?"

Hundred sixty an hour. *Phone convs. with client—.25 hour.* Forty bucks. Adds up. I knew how to write up those lawyer bills, too. Let Marvin decipher the invoice when it came, though. "The lawyer jokes are free," I said. "I got a source."

"So what you're saying is, you're not going to give me my grand back?"

"Not all of it."

"But if you get tubed up the ass, I don't get fucked with you?"

"Not at all."

Thankfully. Sodomized in tandem with Marvin; that was a mental image I could let dissipate without regret.

"If I shitcan you, I got to start from scratch with another lawyer?"

"That's about right."

"He'll charge me another grand?"

"Probably. At least."

"If you get reamed, what lawyer would handle my case?"

"Guy I've known for a long time. Ernie Schuckelgruber."

"I like his name. Sounds like a real lawyer name. Your name sounds like you ought to be a cop. Or a priest."

"Often I wish I were."

"Maybe you'll get a chance, huh? If they bust your stones for being a lawyer."

Marvin Maeger, the Saddam of snatch. Better he stick to that than become a career counselor. I took a shot in the dark. "Marvin, you ever have a girl work for you named Angel Pisaro?"

"That little bitch?"

"That a 'yes,' then?"

"Unreliable little cunt. Worked a week then quit without notice. On a Saturday, no less. Saturday afternoons are big for me."

I could see that. Cut the grass, watch the game, get bored when the score got too lopsided, head over to the local whack shack.

"Found out later she was passing out business cards with her dyke girlfriend's picture on them."

That would be Evie. The deceased had a mind for business. Marvin Maeger hated Angel. That was the only thing I decided I liked about her.

Mikey was still on hold. I made a mental note to charge Marvin Maeger a half hour for the phone conversation, got him off the line, and clicked back over to Mikey. It was almost eleven and I was still in the rental car parking lot.

"You heard her story?" Mikey said, as if he had never been on hold.

"Enough of it."

"That other girl was the real murderer."

"Unfortunately, Angel's the one got caught with the knife."

"She didn't have a choice, Speed. It was kill or be killed."

"You said that. She said it, too. But some of the other things she said were not so helpful to her case. Like making sure Evie was stiffening up before she called the police."

"What about the other murders?"

"What other murders? She was real vague about them. No names, no places, no corpses, no evidence. I figured her girlfriend made up the stories to keep little Angel's panties wet."

"There's names. Well-known names, too. Deaths the cops attributed to accident. I can't believe you didn't ask her about them."

"Angel's a little tough to question, Mikey. Ask her something directly, and she'll spin the conversation around until she's talking about her most passionate desire in life, which is to have silicon boobies."

"When these people died, it made the papers."

"Probably where Evie heard about them, and decided to paint a picture of herself as a mysterious murderess. Maybe she thought Angel would tongue her rug deeper, she thought she was eating out a gun moll."

Mikey was silent. Probably deeply offended. I couldn't do much more damage to this particular client relationship, so I just asked. "You think she's carrying your kid, don't you?"

"It was one of the things we talked about, that night."

"That night?"

"The night it happened. She came by the bar and told me everything."

"She told you she was planning to stab Evie?"

"No. I told her to go to the police. She told me about Evie's victims. She knew the places, the circumstances of each death. I checked the newspaper files on my computer, and she was right about each one. Now how's a girl like Angel going to know that, unless Evie told her?"

I couldn't answer that. It was a dead lock Angel didn't read the paper. And she struck me as the kind of person that would switch over to a fifteen-year-old sitcom rather than watch the local news.

Mikey went on. "I told her to move out. I offered to go with her, but she said no. She said she would be safe, that Evie wouldn't kill her unless she could think of a way to make it look like an accident. Then something happened while she was over there, and she decided it was either Evie or her."

"What happened?"

"Are you still on a cell?"

"You know that. You called me."

"All right. I don't know what to think, here. How about you come over? I'll tell you in person."

"I got some other things to do. It'll have to be later."

"Speed!"

"Mikey, relax. Angel's as safe as she'll ever be. They're even giving her pie and milk to keep her strength up."

Mikey's main concern had to be his unborn kid. I couldn't think of any safer place for number four, as long as he was tucked inside his mother's body, than his mother being locked up. No drugs, no booze, no private doubles or bondage or little girl acts to put him at hazard. Once he got out of the womb, I could see his mother being a serious threat to his chances of growing up sane and well, whether she had to raise him in the Central California Women's Facility or not.

"I'll come see you before the sun goes down."

"I'll be at the club."

I climbed into the rental car and flicked the lever nearest the AC back and forth. Nothing happened.

"Don't hang up yet. You going to talk to Luke's mom today?"

"Probably sometime. Why?"

"You think of it, ask her what's Korean for 'Maximum Cool.'"

Chapter Five

I steered the Hyundai off at one of the intermediate exits on the Dr. Martin Luther King Jr. Freeway. The asphalt curve dropped me onto a four-lane avenue lined with slum businesses, bars, check-cashing joints and used car lots. Red and green lights twinkled above one of the lots; an incongruous billboard bore the likeness of Santa Claus and a sign proclaimed It's Always Christmas Here!

Underneath a furniture store where painted windows screamed of halved prices was a dim neon sign for a basement bar. *Nubie's*, it read, along with the name of an extinct lager. I parked behind a lavish Mercedes, trimmed in gold plate instead of chrome and equipped with tiny flat performance tires. All the cars in the Santa Claus lot put together wouldn't be worth what it cost to paint the Mercedes. My rental car disappeared from view behind its bulk as I took the stairs down to Nubie's.

The place was deserted except for the bartender, a massive black man with a shaved head. He made no move to serve me, but instead put down the glass he was drying and folded his arms. He wore a sleeveless shirt. On one of his shoulders he had *Soledad 1979* tattooed. On the other he had every subsequent year up to 1998 inked in. My guess would be that he was still on probation for whatever crime had put him in the pen. He stared at me with the impassive look of a man who is used to being fucked with, and had at long last learned to measure his responses.

"I'm here to see Bandit," I said.

"Dat your Hyundai?" he asked. I nodded.

"No salesmen," he growled.

"No," I agreed.

"Might be out back."

The bartender gestured towards a filthy curtain.

I brushed through it. The poolroom was little brighter than the bar. Bandit was wearing thick gold sunglasses despite the gloom. He was emptying the coin box on one of the tables. A shining heap of quarters lay on the felt.

"Surprised to see you," he admitted. "I din't even tell Sully not to let you back."

He frowned, as if the oversight might be the first sign that his empire was fraying. Bandit was an old-line pimp. His longevity in the field was nothing short of astonishing. The girls of his first stable were dandling grandchildren on their knees by now.

"Why are you doing me down, Bandit?"

"Shit. You allowed to be here? Ain't they some lawyer rules against this? Intimidatin' a witness, or some shit?"

He stood up. The huge bartender would barely come up to his armpit.

"Nothing they could make stick," I said.

"I don't wanna see you, Speed."

"No surprise there, I guess."

"And you ain't gonna get me to retract nothin' I already said. It a done deal."

"What kind of deal?"

"Deal kind of deal. Your ass for mine."

"What did they have on you? That I couldn't get you off of?"

"You! 'Member, you quit bein' my lawyer."

"I didn't quit. I just didn't take the ag assault."

"Why not?"

"Like I told you then, it isn't my specialty."

The girl Bandit had whipped in the street with a bicycle chain had nearly died. Izzy had walked him after every single one of the twenty witnesses to the crime had abrupt amnesia regarding the beating. The victim moved back to Flintlock, Kentucky, with marks of the links still embedded in the skin of her jaw.

"I hated you dumpin' me off like dat."

"I gave you to a better qualified attorney."

"Waddn't even white," Bandit groused.

"You the racist now?"

"Fuck you, Speed, you knows what I means. Man walks into a court where everybody is white 'cept the bailiff and a couple churchy niggers onna jury, he want a white man on his side."

"You walked."

"More my doin' than his. It was serious work. Don't need no second strike. I got to set up in another state, and you know I ain't ready for that."

I knew. I didn't know who held formal title to Nubie's, or the Santa Claus lot, or the furniture store, but I would be willing to bet that Bandit would have a tough time cashing out his equity in them.

"Another strike and I ends up like Sully, only with dis century tattooed on my arm."

"So you dumping on me because I gave you to a better lawyer?"

"Fuck no. That wouldn't make no sense. But you shoulda defended me in the ag assault."

"Wasn't anything I promised you. Told you, I'd only cover business-related charges."

"Was business related."

"Was a damn pimpish thing to do," I admitted.

Bandit grinned, exposing incisors rimmed in gold.

"You all right, Speed. I sorry about snitching you out, but I ain't got no choice." His paranoia flared right after the apology. "You ain't wearing no wire, is you?"

"I'm a lawyer, not a cop."

"I guess. You sure it ain't no beef, me talkin' to you?"

"Well Danny Akami wouldn't like it, but not everything Danny Akami doesn't like is illegal." Although it would be if Akami won enough elections.

"It a RICO thing."

"The Racketeering Influenced and Corrupt Organizations Act," I said. "That one?"

"That it. I never heared of it, before. Thought Rico was the back half of Puerto. It a federal beef. Ten years a fuckin' count, and the jap-boy explain they got more counts on me than they got in a Tijuana boxin' match."

"Bringing in girls from Kentucky to work the street for you is interstate commerce."

"As right. An' the little bitch can set all pretty in Flintlock, where my influence ain't so good, just waitin' for her jaw to heal so she can start flappin' it to the feds."

"And Danny Akami pressed this investigation?"

Exceeding his authority by about the distance to Borneo.

"He come to me wit' it all laid out."

"Personally?"

The picture of Danny Akami bringing his personal politicking down to Nubie's was one I would love to share with the voters.

"Hell, no. Vice cops arress' me an' all of a sudden I'm chinnin' up with the head man hisself. Lays out the big RICO picter. You know the feds can take away everythin'?"

"Yes."

"Onna grounds that it a fruit of a continuin' criminal enterprise? Ain't that shit?"

"We in the defense bar certainly think so."

"We inna defense bar. Shee-it. You don' have to talk like that here."

"We in the defense bar talk like this because it makes the car payments."

"From the looks o' you car, that ain't much."

"It's a rental. So Danny Akami is going to walk you over to the federal building if you don't cooperate?"

The state had its own version of RICO, but that would mean giving up Bandit to Jimmy Donnelly and the DA's office.

"S'what he says."

"And in return for letting you stay in trade, all he wants is my shingle?"

"It a good deal from my pointa view. They not only gonna tag me for pimpin,' but they take away Nubie's an' everythin'. What am I supposed to do? This here my retiremen' fun."

He poked a huge finger at the pile of quarters. I caught a glimpse of Bandit's eyes over the tops of the sunglasses as he bent low and saw the lines in their corners. I tried to remember his age and failed, but he had to be at least in his mid-forties. It was hard to think of Bandit becoming infirm, but apparently he had thought about it. Someplace in that impregnable-looking body was a hurt or a shiver that whispered to him of impending age.

"Didn't it strike you as a lot to give up for one lawyer's ass?"

"Dem people hate you, Speed. Back when you was my attorney, it made me nervous, how much they hate you."

"So you going to appear at this hearing?"

"Gots to."

"How long do you think the City Attorney is going to leave you alone after you snitch me out?"

"It ain't really snitching. All I gots to do is say that you tole me to deny any panderin' onna stand."

"Like you would be stupid enough to admit it."

"Or even stupid e-nough to take the Fifth. But that's all it take, the little

Jap tell me, for them to take away your law books. Hard for me to believe. Lawyers got some fucked-up rules they gots to follow."

"We don't follow them. Suborning witnesses is probably an attorney's number one job. But as you and I both know, I didn't have to tell you to deny anything."

"What we know ain't necessarily what the Jap want to hear," Bandit pointed out diplomatically.

"You didn't answer me. How long do you think Akami is going to leave you alone for doing me?"

"Forever, he say. And I ain't gonna be inna trade much longer. Gonna get Nubie's fixed up, maybe put inna DJ booth. Already I tole the girls none o' them is allowed in here."

Urban gentrification swallows another pimp den.

"What makes you think Akami won't come back at you with the RICO thing? Like maybe under the state RICO, if he gets his wish to succeed Donnelly?"

"Man will leave me be."

"He's gone after every pimp and working girl in this town, every peep show, every topless bar, every X-rated bookstore. What makes you think you're going to be the exception?"

"He already been after me."

"He'll be after you again. And I won't be around to help you."

"I will be fine."

"You heard of Hitler, Bandit?"

"Sure, man. I ain't stupid. I watch all them swastika war movies."

"Hitler tried to exterminate every Jew in Europe. He said that after he was finished with the Jewish race there would only be enough of them to fill one streetcar, which he would personally drive around the streets of Berlin."

"The point bein'?"

"The point being that every Jew in every concentration camp in Europe thought he was going to be on that streetcar. You're just like them."

"Man, I ain't no Jew. Ain't Muslim, neither."

Arguments fail. If I could see behind Bandit's glasses, I would no doubt observe the look I'd seen in a jury's eyes as reasonable doubt was being frittered away. While we were talking he had stacked the quarters into piles of forty. Before he began poking them into coin wrappers, he picked up a TV remote and flicked on the tube in the corner.

"My movie's on this afternoon."

The face of Burt Reynolds, chattering in a makeshift Southern drawl, and looking younger than I am now, glowed on the screen.

Bandit pulled a chair up to the pool table where he had stacked the quarters.

"I took my name from this movie. I digs Burt Reynolds. Most white man ain't close to smooth. But when they smooth, they the coolest. Like Mr. Burt."

I was being dismissed. I picked up the briefcase I hadn't opened. Bandit looked over the top of his shades again, this time thoughtfully.

"Too bad you ain't smooth like him. You wouldn't be inna shit."

It was noon before I made the office. I pulled the Hyundai into one of the client spaces instead of my own. I waved off Amy as she tried to hand me a sheaf of messages. Schuckelgruber was nowhere to be seen; maybe he had a week of appearances in Tax Court on his calendar.

I put in a call to the City Attorney's office. I asked to speak to Danny Akami.

"Regarding?" said the secretary.

"Marvin Maeger."

She put me on hold. The city had invested in light background music for their telephone system. I listened to "Karma Chameleon" being played by a thousand strings while I awaited the courtesy of my worst enemy. He had to respond to my call, just as I was a slave to his subpoena. The law is as formal a combat as two knights meeting to settle a score with lance and sword in a medieval glen. When law was practically unknown, it was war that was ritualized. Now that the law has swelled to a huge bovine that requires a million lawyers a day to milk its teats, war has become an anarchic blood sport where the combatants are relatively safer than the innocents. Lawyers issue challenges and count coup; soldiers secure buildings by leveling them.

If I was a guerrilla, I could disembowel Danny Akami with C-4. Instead I was a squire petitioning a lord for battle.

"Mr. McKeon?" The voice was unfamiliar.

"I asked to speak to Mr. Akami."

"The Maeger file is on my desk. I'm Terence Chichester, associate City Attorney."

Danny Akami could send his seconds into combat, though.

"Is Mr. Akami in the office?"

"Not at present."

"Have him call me back."

"Mr. Akami has assigned me to this case."

"As of when?"

"That is hardly relevant."

"Let me make a guess, then. How about five minutes ago?"

While I was on hold. I imagined Bandit was concerned enough about his deal that he had called Danny Akami the minute I left Nubie's. Looked like Danny didn't want to talk to me directly until I had some time to distance myself from the emotions I was experiencing from finding out the kind of witness and evidence he was planning on offering the Ethics Committee at my hearing.

"The internal workings of this office are not a matter of public speculation."

"The speculating public is wondering why Danny Akami is not directing the prosecution of Marvin Maeger personally, since he is the exact sort of high-profile slime unit that the City Attorney craves to obliterate."

"I repeat, Mr. Maeger's file is on my desk."

"Terry, babe, are you an intern?"

"I told you I was a full associate. Please do not address me as 'babe.'"

Likely that promotion also occurred while I was listening to the city's Muzak cover Boy George. I had never seen Terence Chichester identified in court, which meant up until very recently he had merely held the hem of Danny Akami's robe in court, one of the grim-faced interns who shuffled papers and passed notes to the City Attorney while he dueled. Doubly grim-faced because they were not quite sharp enough to make the District Attorney's or the Public Defender's staff. When a law school disgorged a class of fresh barristers, those twisted enough to interest themselves in criminal law had three places to intern. The DA took the brightest and the most ambitious. The PD took the smokers and drinkers, anarchists and thinkers. The City Attorney took the rest. The City Attorney's office handled all the civic matters of the city, sued when it needed to sue, defended it when it got sued, and issued opinions on the legality of the city's actions when asked. Almost as an afterthought, it prosecuted all misdemeanor cases.

Almost all the violations that my clients made in the law were punishable as misdemeanor offenses.

"I want to deal with the boss on this."

"You would think you'd prefer to be countered with a less experienced attorney."

"I've had some success against Canny Danny, hard as it may be for you to believe."

"The evidence is very solidly on the prosecution's side on this. Unfortunately for your client."

"I like to think I've single-handedly kept your boss from pushing the DA into early retirement."

"Your obsession with defending sexually aberrant scum has been noted by this office."

"I bet it has, Terry old boy. So what about Marvin Maeger, since you're the attorney of record? I see him as a typical small businessman, providing a perfectly legal service."

"Renting cameras to photograph naked girls is not what we would regard as typical."

"Constitutionally protected freedom of expression. My argument, hands down."

"But what really goes on there, as we both know, is that the naked girls gyrate while the customers masturbate."

"Sheer speculation."

I tried to form a mental picture of Terence Chichester. Pasty-faced, earnest, dogged after the main point. Deputy defender of the public morals. Just the kind to relieve the after-work tension by dropping his pants at a whack shack.

"And besides, the criminal acts in that situation, if any, are committed by the customers, not the naked girls. Or Mr. Maeger."

"The allegation here is that one of Mr. Maeger's employees—"

"Contract workers. I'm not going to let you get away with calling the girls employees in court. And they are very nice contracts, too, with stiff penalties for the contractee—that's the naked girl, babe—if she performs any illegal acts."

"—handled an undercover vice officer in the groin area."

"Groin-handling? Whose groin was grabbed?"

"A Detective Pullman."

I laughed so loudly that Amy looked through the doorway.

"His name is really Pullman?"

"You wouldn't be so juvenile as to make an issue of that?"

"I'll have the jury smirking all through closing. Tell you what. I'll plead the girl to disorderly. Marvin walks. In return, I let the Board of Health have his ass for no more than ten days."

"No deals."

"You've got nothing on my client, except some alleged semen on his floor. And we'll be discussing how that particular inspector knew it was semen. And if they don't have the semen pressed between glass, with an unbroken chain of evidence leading directly back to Mr. Maeger's floor, then that semen might as well be oatmeal as far as I'm concerned. And how close was Detective Pullman's groin to the girl's hand before she allegedly grabbed it? I think we're going to say that he was waving his engorged manhood inches from her face while she attempted to entertain him with an interpretive dance, and she was trying to push him away, so as to have sufficient distance for her art, when she accidentally brushed her hand against the groin area."

"Mr. Akami has familiarized me with your style of argument already, Counselor. Save it for the trial."

"Trials. Separate. First motion I'm going to make. Last offer. You're not even going to get the DC, you don't take it."

"Office policy is to no longer deal down sexual miscreants."

"Since when?"

"Merely because these crimes are misdemeanors doesn't mean they aren't serious offenses. Establishments like Mr. Maeger's are magnets for all kinds of criminal activity."

"Like what? Couple guys walking out without remembering to zip up?"

"The Phantasy Photographys of the world will no longer be winked at on Mr. Akami's watch."

You can't get to be DA by winning a mountain of disorderly conduct cases. Izzy had it right. I stared up at the ceiling as I contemplated his wisdom. Danny Akami would sweep the boulevards of the city clean of sleaze on his way to elective office. It was a year and a half until the voters went to the polls to pick a DA again. I wondered how long he figured it would take to close up a few of my more prominent clients.

"When you're through not winking at the Phantasy Photography file, how about sending it over?"

"Of course."

Terence Chichester hung up. Six months, maybe. About what the Ethics Committee would suspend me for if Danny could find five votes against me. And despite his pimp witness and the blatantly trumped-up charge, he might be able to do it. It was obvious that Akami had timed out his plan a while back.

I should be flattered at being thought important enough to scheme against, but my ego wouldn't swell to the occasion. All I could think of was that it was fifty-fifty I was still in the shit. And still broke. If I had dealt Marvin and his girl, I could at least have sent Phantasy Photography's proprietor a final bill.

Amy came at me waving her sheaf of mail.

"And Mikey's in the office."

"Mikey with the—?"

"Tit bar."

"I told him I would see him later."

Amy gave me a shrug. Some tasks were beyond even the most inspired secretary, which wasn't Amy. Keeping obsessed clients from showing up at the door was one of them. "Send him in?"

"Make him wait."

I was cornered, but that didn't mean I couldn't manufacture a few tasks to avoid Angel Pisaro's benefactor until after lunch. With any luck, Mikey would have a topless-bar related emergency; one of his staff would take a spill and squash an implant, maybe, and he would have to go back to his club.

The mail was the usual collection of bills, notices and services by mail, except for one heavy handwritten envelope. The return address was unfamiliar, but by its looks it was some beggar after a legal favor. I nearly tore it in half without opening it, but some inner yearning for punishment compelled me to read it.

It was from a Gladys Bernheim. Gladys Bernheim lived in the same complex as the late Frank Fernando. Chessie the Clown's suicide had not proved convenient for her. She was agonizing over the disposition of his effects. Reading between the lines, and influenced by the name Gladys, I imagined her a portly lady in support panty hose, neglected by her own children, clucking and fawning over the bachelor with the dark secret next door. Now that he had abruptly ended his own existence, her final chance to meddle in his affairs was represented by me. She didn't want to see the Fernando possessions swept away by their landlord, as was his legal right once Frank Fernando's last rent payment expired. Perhaps there was a will directing the disposition of the Fernando spoils. Wouldn't I be so kind as to look? Frank had always spoken well of me. The extra weight in the envelope was the key to Frank Fernando's apartment.

I doubted there was a will. The police would have found it while they were investigating the suicide. You had to think well of Gladys, though. Most neighbors with time on their hands and a key in their pocket would have done their own investigating. I threw the envelope haphazardly on my desk and made a mental note to have Amy compose a formal letter to Gladys Bernheim explaining that in the absence of heirs or legal instructions, the state had the rights to the material excrescence of Frank Fernando's life, and if it chose not to exercise that right over his cups and plates and sticks of furniture, then his landlord might as well have them. And I would have Amy enclose the key back, so that Gladys could pick Chessie the Clown's gear over first.

I could hear the phone ringing in the outer office and Amy answering it with a prim "Law Offices." A moment later the intercom buzzed.

"A Jill Congliaro," Amy said.

I picked up the phone.

"Since the preliminary has already been held, this office is in possession of all files including discovery," Jill Congliaro said without preamble. "I'll have them delivered by messenger, if you're going to be in your office to sign for them."

"I am in no need of files from the PD's office."

"The prosecutor will not supply a second copy of discovery without being compelled by the court. Save yourself some effort."

"You may be under the impression that I have taken over the defense of Angel Pisaro. That is not necessarily true."

"You interviewed her this morning."

"With your permission."

"Not. Didn't arrive in the office until eleven. Had to take my cat to the vet," she added, as if I suspected her of lying in with a boyfriend or a hangover.

"Somebody let me in."

"Must have been the aura and majesty of your presence. Anyway, a decision has been made. You're welcome to Angel Pisaro."

"Made by who?"

No real need to ask. Desiree Mason was the guiding light of the PD's office.

"The people who tell me what to do. Are you going to be in this afternoon or not?"

"Not," I replied. I didn't want to gladden Mikey's heart by signing for the Pisaro file while he was waiting in the outer office. Somewhere in the vast width and breadth of the state of California there must breathe a barrister who wanted Angel Pisaro for a client. I planned to find that attorney if Mikey had to wait outside all afternoon.

Mikey would have no part of my plans. He stuck his face in the door behind Amy and caught me hanging up on Jill Congliaro.

"Just ten minutes of your time," he asked.

"I told you I would come to your place."

"She's calling me every five minutes. Collect."

"How did you ever get mixed up with Angel Pisaro?"

"Told you, it was a sex thing."

"Why her? You have fifty girls working for you."

"Lot of times it's not such a hot idea to bang the girls that work for you. You're banging one, the other girls treat her like crap. You bang more than one, they start comparing notes. At first when she came into the club, I thought she was recruiting for her business. That was before I knew what a close-knit little two-girl act it was. I nearly eighty-sixed her. Instead we got to talking."

"Talking? About what? Angel's not the sharpest tool in the shed."

"Sex mostly, I guess."

"How did she end up pregnant?"

"That was a mistake. She was changing over to a new kind of pill."

"You going to take care of the kid while she serves out her time?"

Mikey recoiled. He had never married any of his kids' mothers, or even lived with them. He was probably the best dad in the world who had never changed a diaper.

"Speed! A baby needs its mom. You got to get her out of there. What about bail?"

"If I could manage to get bail set, which is unlikely, and if it is not such a stupendous amount that you could raise it by re-mortgaging your house and your club and any other assets you might have, which is even less likely, then her freedom would still only be temporary. She has no defense."

"What about self-defense?"

"Self-defense is no defense."

"What about battered-woman syndrome?"

"So far it's only worked for women who have killed their men. Another itsy problem is that the late Evie never laid a finger on Angel in anger, except when she was getting paid for it."

"Psychological torment. She was convinced that Evie was going to kill her."

"I could maybe do something with her state of mind. Convince the jury that since Angel sincerely believed she was going to be killed, she was not capable of forming an intent to murder. It would be the longest of long shots, though. I'd take any deal the DA offered me before I ran that one out on the track."

"What about the dead guys? The guys Evie killed? They're real, Speed."

"I'm sure they're real. And I'm sure they're really dead. But what I'm really, really sure of is that the deceased Evie had nothing to do with them. She just claimed to have rubbed them out in order to impress or intimidate her little Angel, who, having used less brains in her whole life than get into a can of Spam accidentally, was suitably impressed or intimidated."

"That's where you're wrong. I can tell you how Evie iced two of them. In detail. Because Evie told Angel and Angel told me. You haven't even asked about them."

"I haven't asked about the tooth fairy, either."

"The first one was the priest. Father Howard Canto. You've heard of him?"

"Monsignor the molester? Got caught with his fingers under the altar girls' robes?"

"That's him. Your friend the big surf nigger got him off without prison time. What kind of a career is that, helping child molesters roam the streets?"

"What kind of a job is selling guys booze while your employees give them hard-ons?"

"It ain't even in the same league."

"It isn't making the world a better place."

"Okay, I'm no saint. And neither is your buddy. And neither was Father Canto, even though he was a priest. You remember how he died?"

"Car accident, wasn't it?"

"He was in his car, but accident had nothing to do with it."

"Didn't the cops rule it an accident?"

"Yeah."

"He drove off a cliff, didn't he? Last winter?"

"April 13, this year. And it was more like a mountainside. It was up on 76, way up past avocado country. Blood alcohol was in the low thirties. Valium in his system, too. Kind of a puzzle how he managed to drive up the mountain far enough to fall off. Should have been unconscious."

"Some people have a lot of tolerance for the grape, Mikey. You know that."

"Yeah, maybe. Or maybe it was just like this. The fallen priest finds himself a little hooker that's willing to act out his secret fantasies for him. Maybe she finds him, really, but he's so happy to get his ashes hauled in the special way that makes his consecrated dick hard that he doesn't worry himself much about that. They head up into the mountains together, because they need privacy for their little act. On the way, the hooker's driving, because the good father is so excited about getting his sacred boner squeezed he's popping tranks and slurping Seagrams just to stay calm enough to keep his pants on.

"They pull off on 76, which is a damn quiet highway. Not much traffic between Rainbow Valley and Brawley. They do their little act. The hooker gets her Catholic school uniform and a bicycle out of the trunk. She goes off behind the pines to change, then comes riding toward the priest like a fifth-grader lost on the road. This apparently is the fantasy Father Gonads has always had, so he gets a chubby the size of Vatican City. They do the bump in the deserted glade. Afterwards the priest passes out, as is any man's God-given right to do after a fifth of booze and an orgasm. The hooker starts up the car, slips it into drive, and lets the priest ride over the side in a state of mortal sin. After, she rides her bike back to Rainbow Valley, it's all downhill, and takes a cab back to town."

"That's a nice story, Mikey. Totally lacking in supporting evidence, though."

"There's evidence if the cops would look for it, the lazy fucks. What about the cab driver? How many cabs you think work the avocado groves? What about the bicycle? She must have ditched it somewhere."

"Don't imagine a bicycle in good condition would last long with all the illegals camped out up there. A stolen bike represents good, reliable transportation to them. Probably been swiped and repainted a dozen times since then. If it ever existed at all."

"Evie was plenty worried about it being found. Also about the cabbie. She was muttering about doing him. That's one of the things that scared Angel."

"I read Angel right, she's probably scared of being kidnapped by aliens, too, or having Elvis come back and catch her in a mismatched bra and panty set. She's tabloid all the way. Evie just told her ghost stories to keep her in line."

"You haven't heard the other one yet."

"I don't want to hear it."

"Speed, look at me." Mikey was all pleading eyes and placating hands. Sweat banded the silk of his shirt. "Do you really think Angel is capable of murder? Real murder, premeditated?"

I thought of Angel as I had interviewed her, her dull consciousness resting always on the present line. "Probably not. Probably not capable of premeditating lunch."

"But they're going to lay her out. I know what kind of clients Evie had."

"Weren't they Angel's clients, too?"

"Evie handled all the business. Angel told me she thought most of the clients didn't even like her."

"Not hard to believe."

"She's carrying my kid."

"No matter what happens, they're not going to harm your kid."

Could be the most famous unborn kid in the state, if Angel was convicted by the time she started to show. Which would be just about right. And he would be about six, seven by the time his mother's appeals were exhausted. He'd have *People* magazine in his face while they strapped her into the gurney.

"Harm him? They execute his mother, it's not going to harm him?"

Since the kid's mother was Angel Pisaro, it was a question that required some thought. I was mulling when Amy opened the door to admit the legal messenger. He was a pimply pre-law student, stocky despite his job of pedaling a bike between law offices all day. "Got something for you, Mr. McKeon. Sign here."

The box had "Angel Pisaro" scrawled on the side, in big, ugly, *foreboding*, for Christ's sake, black marker.

"Ms. Congliaro said take a chance, bring it on over."

"Thanks, Ruben. I guess."

Mikey looked deeply and meekly grateful.

I signed and got both of them out of there. I snuck out to the Hyundai through the back door and steered it over to my son's school. The five grand had been an uncomfortable lump in my pocket since yesterday. As long as I was stuck with Angel, I might as well pay my bills.

The "campus," as the brochures advertising the place liked to call it, was located in the back half of an industrial complex. The warehouses had been sectioned off into areas for art, theater, and white rapping. The brochures mentioned that tuition would be considerably higher if the school wasn't located in the low-rent neighborhood. Also the industrial noise drowned out the screech of electronic instruments being inexpertly played, and the howls of performance artists in training.

Despite the grimy setting, the brochures extolled the place as a fine school, a stark contrast to the public system. Here they didn't drill their students in standard American propaganda, turning them into oversocialized dolts capable of only standard American careers. They taught them to think for themselves, to catch the absurdities in life and to have a cynical disrespect for every form of endeavor. They turned them, in short, into sarcastic little leeches. You get what you pay for.

My son was stretching his legs out front, sitting on a parking block. He didn't recognize the Hyundai and so didn't flick his cigarette into the bushes until I was almost on top of him.

"Mom got to you, huh?" he sneered.

"A talent she seems to have passed along generationally," I answered. "Don't you ever have to actually go inside your school?"

"Hey, man, I got to work all weekend besides go to school. I didn't ditch once in a while, I'd never get outside."

I thought about asking the headmaster for a copy of my son's schedule so I could figure out what class he was ditching, but the only person in the office was a receptionist. She wrote out a receipt for the cash. On the way out I offered my son a ride.

"Nah," he answered. I could tell he wanted me to leave so he could light another cigarette, so I paused.

"Sure?"

"I got my own car. Not that it's much."

"I was having a bad week when I bought it for you, trying to get my car back from the cops."

"Which you never did."

Thus I had to assume the blame for my car being the property of the state, since I was not lawyer enough to get it back from them. Those zero tolerance laws are a bitch, and the Supreme Court is fine with them.

"Guess you won't have to worry about handling your own cases much longer, though. Mom told me about the Ethics Committee."

He gave me only a beat to wonder how Mom had found out. He clutched at the pack of Marlboros in his shirt pocket, an addict's reflex, and said, "That must really hurt, Dad. That you're not even ethical enough to be a lawyer."

Chapter Six

I took stock of the day and decided that enough had been done with it, professionally speaking. Time to turn my attention to social concerns. I dialed the general office number for the Public Defender on the car phone and made my request of the receptionist. After a two-minute delay, in dead silence, the city not having seen fit to install Muzak on the phones of the Public Defender's Office, Desiree came squealing onto the line.

"Speed! You called!"

I couldn't think of a reply to that statement that would not involve pointing out the obviousness of it, so I kept my mouth shut, concentrating instead on the speedometer of the Hyundai. The machine required an extra touch on the accelerator when I charged my cell phone, I noticed. The minuscule power drain was enough to affect the performance of the tiny four-banger.

Performance was on my mind. My sex life had been lately lacking. I had even lost the habit of masturbation, since I hated to do it in front of the cat. Not that my night of heat with Desiree would have to set any kind of sexual record in order to swing her vote on the Ethics Committee. The most perfunctory of stabbings, even, with any luck, a premature drooling, would be enough to content her, I was certain. But there had to be some kind of act, and I was not sure there would. Even with my tanks topped off, hormonally speaking, the sight of Desiree nude and breathing hard might cause penile thrombosis.

Certain crucial veins would snap shut. Just thinking about it could exacerbate the problem, so I tried to put it out of my mind.

"I know just the place!" Desiree chortled. She mentioned an overpriced fish house in North County.

"Kind of far," I objected.

"Been there?"

"No."

"Stunning view. Awfully..." She hesitated on the verge of the word "romantic" and stumbled, concluding lamely, "awesome."

"You drive," I said. It wasn't that I didn't want to be seen in the Hyundai. I would prefer it, actually. Needed to get all the sympathy factors working for me. But I was planning on drinking heavily. It would either render Desiree desirable to me, or give me a ready-made excuse, should I fail at the critical moment.

"No problem, Speedo," she crowed. "Can you meet me at the sewage plant?"

The PDs had that nickname for their suite of offices. They were situated under the jail floors in the municipal building. The prisoners, from the moment of the building's dedication, had realized the advantage of having the higher ground. They would routinely plug up the toilets so that waste flowed down the walls. The offices, which were originally scheduled to be occupied by the prosecutor's staff, were quickly reassigned to the public defenders, on the theory that the incarcerated would be less likely to crap on the defenders than the prosecutors.

The inmates would have none of it. In the way of the criminal, they blamed everyone but themselves for their predicament, and everyone in the courtroom especially, judge and jury, bailiffs, stenographers, prosecutors and defenders alike. Human waste still dripped from the ceiling several times a week. If I was unlucky, and considering the way the week had gone that seemed likely, there would be a few drops of dried shit in the file I had yet to open on Angel Pisaro.

If I was really unlucky, it would be wet shit.

"My car's at the shop," I said. Didn't want to be paraded in front of the PD's staff like a trophy marlin. "Can you pick me up at my office?"

I went back there. Schuckelgruber and Amy had both departed for the day, even though it was before five. I spent an hour warily pulling random papers out of the Angel Pisaro file, hoping to find a loose brick in the wall of the prosecution's case. It was an astonishingly short file, even for a standard household homicide. No DNA, no fiber evidence, no defensive wounds on the victim, no reports from the neighbors of screams or fighting. Angel must have walked up from behind and made her three swings with the blade so swiftly that Evie didn't have time to react. A description and a picture of the knife, a carbon-bladed, wedge-shaped number. Designed to hack a turkey or a roast apart with just a few easy strokes. Set you back eighty bucks if you picked it off of Nordstrom's bridal registry. No doubt a gift from one of the girls to the other on an occasion—a birthday, Christmas, or the anniversary of their first date. Thick-bladed and wickedly sharp. Practically unused. One of the pages was a catalogue of the household trash. Fast food wrappers and wine bottles were the primary components.

The medical examiner's report was equally mundane. Only one of the stab wounds was fatal, or "immediately life-threatening," in coronerspeak. That third stroke was a beauty. Must've been like a golfer discovering his swing. It tore through both the auricle and ventricle of Evie's heart on the right side, stilling both chambers instantly. It would only have been a second or two before the entire muscle collapsed. Even the look of surprise in her eyes would have gone dull almost instantly, as her blood pressure went down to zero and her optic nerve and brain were deprived of oxygen.

Evie had bubbled up and died almost the second her heart had been opened up to the air. Lucky for me and Angel. Lot of people get stabbed twenty, thirty times before they stop moving. Just from my one interview with Angel, I had no doubt that she was capable of swinging that knife as many times as she needed to. Prosecutors always point to multiple stab wounds as proof of the savagery of the perpetrator, but in most cases it just points to their prudence. Once begun, homicide is an act best finished. There's always a witness to attempted murder.

The other wounds, as Angel had surmised, were inconsequential, although one had put a scratch in Evie's aorta. The other had merely punctured the implant that had been installed under Evie's left nipple. The coroner had noted the scar from the plastic surgery seemed fairly recent, in his initial examination. No silicon had oozed into Evie's open heart in her final moment, though; the implant had been saline. Evie had been about eight when Dow-Corning quit making silicon enhancements. There was the usual picture, taken prior to Evie being sliced up like a rack of lamb on Easter so that the examiner could find the secret of her pierced heart. Apart from the collapsed breast and the gelatin that death laid over her eyes, she made an astonishingly good-looking corpse. She had lived fast and died young, and so had come in under the wire on that measure of a successful life. Evie had been a month short of her twenty-third birthday.

That, and Evie's occupation, listed as "dancer," was about all the biographical data the report contained. Evie's remains had been released to her mother, who had an address in the county.

The interview with Angel was just as she had described it; short, sweet and incriminating. I deciphered the signature at the bottom and discovered it had been taken by my buddy Pennofrio. It was probably why he had still been in such a scintillating humor when he pulled Frank Fernando's drawer out under my nose just a few days later. It was an excellent piece of detective work. Enough to put the perp away for life, maybe even get the lethal injection needle filled. Angel had to have premeditated long enough to at least grab the knife.

The perils of premeditation. I had them to think about, while I waited to peddle my ass, in order to prove to my son and Marvin Maeger that I was still ethical enough to remain a lawyer. I had a four-cubic-foot refrigerator in my office. I opened it and found I had four beers in there, along with some tomato juice and a packet of Kona coffee kept cold for freshness. I palmed a beer can but put it back before I snapped it open. I checked the device's tiny freezer. There was a bottle of Belorussian vodka behind its plastic door, unopened, a rare brand, given to me by a client who had bought it at the source. I replaced the beer and poured three fingers of slushy fire into the only glass I had, a souvenir mug from Knott's Berry Farm. I sat and watched the door like Scrooge on Christmas Eve, in imminent expectation of being haunted.

My specter did not disappoint. She even arrived in chains, or rather a dress that seemed to my vodka-blurred eyes to be made of a profusion of tiny metallic ringlets. A vast profusion. There had to be a significant hole in the mountain out of which miners had extracted enough ore to make that dress. She had painted her meaty features with lip liner and eye shadow. She looked like a battleship topped off with a smiley face instead of a gun turret.

"Your lair," Desiree said. "I've never been."

"Such as it is." I waved a hand deprecatingly around. The vodka was already rendering me inarticulate. "Drink?"

"Not yet."

"Not much to see here. I would show you the Schuckelgruber Suite, but he keeps it locked up when he's not around. Afraid I'll swipe some of his tax evaders. Get going?"

"We have reservations."

Meaning they'd hold our table. Desiree settled herself into my vis
chair. She ran a hand along her throat in a motion meant to
slid it across her shoulder, nudging the strap of her dress.

average size the movement would have popped the strap off her shoulder but Desiree's was held fast by her bulk. She pushed at the strap a couple of times with her fingertips but it refused to budge from the valley it had made in her flesh. She settled for a smoldering look and jutting her gallon-size breasts aggressively across my desk.

"I'm starving," I said hurriedly.

"Wouldn't want that to happen. Deprive you of your strength." She gathered her purse and her keys. "We have all night."

Jesus, what a frightening thought. I allowed myself to be guided out to Desiree's car, a mid-range Buick, a civil servant's automobile, full of trepidation, like a freshman girl going to the senior prom and wondering what she was going to have to put out in return for the night of glamour. Desiree had her hand on the inside of my thigh so fast it was caught under the seat belt as I strapped it on. She had to extricate it in a hurry, and was too embarrassed to replace it.

"Why am I all of a sudden welcome to Angel Pisaro?" I asked.

"Speed, let's not talk shop."

"It's a long drive. Share it with me."

"She's better off with you as her attorney rather than some rookie PD, right?"

"Don't know. I'm a little rusty."

"Mama'll have you oiled up in no time." Desiree reached over and squee̶̶̶̶̶̶ ̶̶̶̶̶̶eading it as if it was the organ she planned to grope

e subject. "Why not let an experienced battler for the accused? Such as yourself?"

at kind of caseload I'm already carrying. Besides, l a private attorney is welcome to one. The PD's rite burden."

"Or else you're under pressure to collapse on Angel. That is what you just about admitted to me yesterday."

"So I faced the heat. Wisely I let her case pass from an untried counselor to a veteran attorney. The case is unwinnable, anyway. What's your strategy?"

"I plan a creative defense."

"Really? Way the office looked at it, we were going to move for continuances until after the holidays, then take anything short of life without that the DA would let us have."

"Delay is part of my scheme as well. ME, to start."

"Mental evaluation? That is good, Speed. Already the girl is in better hands, I can tell. Little Jill would never have thought of that one."

"Little Jill. What's her story?"

"It is unbearable enough that you insist on talking law on our date. Now you want me to fill you in on other women. I thought you were a gentleman."

"That's a prerequisite?"

"Naturally not. But it doesn't hurt."

"Why me, anyway?"

"You're perfect. To be seen in public with. I can buy my little interns dinner, but you can always tell other people think the relationship is completely professional. But with you, it looks like a date. Or even a relationship." Meaning I was old enough to have a partner that had gone completely to seed. No need to spare feelings here.

"Back to Jill."

"You're going to end up a slobbering old goat like Schuckelgruber, you don't learn to train your tastes for more mature women."

I gave up on the subject. No evidence Jill was interested in me in the least, on the face of it. I had already stolen her first big case and now I was getting set to prostitute myself with her boss to save myself at hearing. I was

Jill, I'd leave me alone, too.

"How were you planning on keeping Angel out of court until after the holidays?"

It wasn't even October. And I knew, heat or no, that Desiree would never let herself be rushed to trial if she could cook up any scheme to delay while she negotiated a deal.

Desiree looked uncomfortable. "Well, with you involved…"

"Nice to know I was part of your strategy."

It was a day for revelations. First I found out that Danny Akami had been all the way to Kentucky and back as part of his plans for me, and cruising with Desiree I find that I'm part of the PD's long-term thinking.

"Let me guess. With my shingle hanging by a thread, you get enough members of the Ethics Committee to call in sick so you can't dispose of my case unfavorably for a few months. Then with me looking for another career, Angel Pisaro gets bounced back to you with a built-in reason for continuance."

"The girl doesn't deserve to fry, Speed."

"And I do?"

"You were pretty curt Jefferson Day."

"So everyone who resists your advances deserves to lose their livelihood? Excuse me, but that's got to be a lot of unfrocked lawyers."

"I'm going to pretend you didn't say that, because someone has to stop escalating the level of antagonism. And it's not going to happen now," Desiree said. "Don't ruin a perfect evening by being surly about it. Your troubles with the Ethics Committee have vanished. And don't suppose it would be as easy as you think. The government members of the committee can't sick out. Me or the DA or CA's reps are unable to attend, we have to send a substitute. And mental evaluation is the perfect solution for Angel. You have saved both yourself and her, barely trying. You are *good*, Speed," she added, putting enough emphasis on the word so that it came out that I was both morally superior and professionally perfect.

I kept a cold silence. It was convenient.

"What psychiatrist you think would play ball on Angel?"

"Hadn't progressed that far yet." I said shortly.

I maintained my insulted air as we were valet parked and ushered to our table. I kept to my drink, chilled vodka, when Desiree tried to order a bottle of wine. The view was quite nice. The lights of one of the North County marinas were displayed before us. Berthed sailboats sparkled prettily as they jostled against their piers and the tide. A one-lane road ran next to the docks, on which an occasional vehicle discharged passengers bearing wrapped twelve-packs and bottles, heading for a party on one of the boats. Something about seawater compels people to add alcohol. I had already finished my shot.

"Isn't it beautiful?"

"Great," I said shortly.

"Don't be so moody."

"As you mentioned before, moodiness is one of my personal flaws."

"It isn't going to work if you're going to be this way," she warned.

I slurped at the shot. Vodka number three tasted velvety smooth. I didn't let out an unseemly gasp when I polished it off. The fire that poured from my throat to my belly seemed much diminished, as if the heat of the liquor had been banked back. I asked the waiter if they had anything in a higher proof.

"Speed! Such a boozehound."

Desiree leaned forward and tried to grasp my forearm. I looked deep into the canyon of her décolletage. Parts of Desiree seemed to move independently of other sections, I observed. A shifting on one side of the metallic dress took a discernible time to ripple to the other side, where it might collide with the aftershock from the previous movement, either stilling or doubling the fleshy oscillations under the gray. The whole effect was fluid and fascinating, in the scientific sense. It was like observing a giant ball of mercury. In the corner of my mind that hadn't yet been distilled, I realized what a booze-soaked thought that was. Perfect. I summoned Vodka Four with a snap of my fingers.

We ordered. Both of us ignored the seafood. I had the lamb. Desiree ordered the baby back ribs with extra barbecue sauce and a loaf of onion rings. She had a thing for finger food, apparently, not wanting the cold tines of a fork to come between her and the palping of her morsels.

Desiree didn't so much eat as she harvested. Each rib was picked to the bone, each onion ring devoured to the final crumb. She emptied the basket of rolls and scraped every foil clean of its butter. Only the barbecue sauce was wasted. It flecked the tablecloth and the chain mail of her dress as she dolloped the ribs in the tangy pool and sped them to her mouth, like blood shed in her one-sided victory over dinner.

"A lot of women of size pretend they don't eat at all," she said, in one of her few conversational forays while the meal was underway. "Take 'em out to dinner and all they order is salad. Then they go home and eat a bag of Doritos. Not me."

"Not at all," I said, although I doubted a bag of Doritos would be safe from Desiree when she got home. The sheer industriousness with which she dipped, picked and swallowed her dinner made me wonder if she would ever stop. Either the view or the vodka was destroying my appetite. I paused midway through the rack of lamb to order another beverage.

"I have to freshen up," Desiree said when her campaign against her entree had been completed. "They wheel that dessert cart by again, make sure they stop here."

I watched the view of Desiree wending toward the ladies' room and tried to convince my pickled brain that it was in some way libidinous, but my mammalian urges would have none of it. Outside, the view had become clouded by a coastal drizzle, just enough rain to dampen the asphalt of the marina's alley. A taxi crept along the path, looking for the right dock number for its passengers. The sign on the side read *Rainbow Valley Cab.*

Long run from the interior of the county. Then I remembered Mikey's murder story about Father Canto. There couldn't be too many hacks working the avocado groves. Nor could there have been that many young female pedestrians looking for a ride back to town last April thirteenth.

"Tell the lady I'll be right back," I said to the busboy who had charge of the dessert cart. I walked out into the rain. It had turned cold as soon as the sun went down. The rain was little more than a thick fog, but it still made me shiver. I paced the docks toward the end, where the cab had stopped and let a couple out at their yacht. With a bit of luck, the cab ahead of me had been the only one in Rainbow Valley the day Father Canto had met his premature end. He wouldn't have picked up any mysterious, shapely cyclists, and so he could demolish Angel Pisaro's story once and for all. I could treat her case in a straightforward, lawyerly fashion, and beg the DA's office abjectly for a deal. I waved it down as it began its reverse journey up the tarmac.

"Can I ask you something?" I asked.

The driver was a fleshy white man, longhaired, with a sunburned arm, no doubt from hanging it out the window of the cab. He was dressed in woodsman's green. He wore a cap, also green, in which a profusion of fishing lures had been stuck. Not just flies, but plastics and mechanicals as well. I recognized a Rappel. He had a beard and a mustache. He looked like a fat Jesus under a crown of hooks.

"Only talk to passengers," he said.

I slid into the back seat. He flicked over the meter.

"Been driving for Rainbow long?"

"I am Rainbow."

"Anybody else ever drive for you?"

"By the time I'm ready to quit, ain't much cab action up here."

"Were you driving this cab last April thirteenth?"

"I guess. I drive it every day. This is a lot of somethings."

"Did you pick up a female passenger, young, maybe wearing a dress or cycling gear, last April thirteenth, and take her for a long ride back to town?"

A horn honked behind us. Someone else wanted access to the one-way road.

"I gotta get moving."

"You don't remember anyone like that, do you?"

"Sure, I remember her. You want to go somewhere?"

I looked inside the restaurant. Desiree hadn't returned to our table. "Drive it around the block."

The cabbie backed up past the waiting car, a limousine driven by a Hindu chauffeur. "Fucking dotheads," he growled. "That's why I drive up here, so I don't have to deal with the dotheads and the sand niggers and the wogs that drive cab in town. Now they're all over the coast up here. Pretty soon they'll be clear out to Bonsall."

"Yeah." Great. An upcountry Nazi. "The girl, you remember what she looked like?"

"Yeah, sure. She had a nice body." I waited for him to go on, but he didn't. He swung the cab left, under the freeway.

"That's all?"

"All you could tell. She had on one of those stretchy bicycle suits, like you said. And a helmet."

"She wore her helmet in the cab?"

"What's wrong with that?" He turned around to look at me, and the lights of opposing traffic gleamed on the barbs in his hat.

"Did you ask her where her bike was?"

"No. Probably stolen by Mexicans. Mexicans'll steal anything."

Should rename his vehicle Militia Cab. But I didn't want to antagonize him by telling him something stupidly liberal, like a lot of my best friends were minorities, even though it was true, or at least had been true. My father was so steadfast a Democrat that he sent me to public school in East LA in order that the underprivileged could edify themselves with my company. Lot of my best friends had been minorities. All my worst enemies had been as well. Gave me a more well-rounded view of the human condition, which had been my father's intention. Also taught me to walk around with my head up, and gave me a chance to be the slowest guy on the track team.

"Where did you pick her up?"

"On 76."

"What were you doing on 76?"

"Just dropped a bunch of wetbacks off in Temecula."

No need to ask what the cabbie and the illegals were doing in Temecula, or why they had gone up 76 instead of the freeway. The Border Patrol checkpoint was on the freeway. In Temecula the illegals were free and clear, only a bus ride away from LA.

"You think I'm nuts, helping a bunch of Mexes slip past the checkpoint when I hate 'em, don't you?"

"Everybody's got to make a living."

"I don't care, because LA's ruined anyway. When it cracks off into the ocean, I'm gonna stand up and cheer."

The size of that earthquake, I doubted anyone was going to be standing up. And my survivalist buddy was going to quit cheering when he discovered that Rainbow Valley was located on the same side of the fault as the big town. He'd better start driving cab in 29 Palms if he wanted to be on the mainland instead of LA Island.

"Where did you drop the girl off?"

"Are you a cop?"

"No."

"Didn't think so. Your breath stinks, for a cop."

So much for the kisses-but-never-tells theory about vodka-drinking.

"This meter's only up to about four bucks."

"I got a fifty, you remember where you dropped the girl off."

"It was in the valley."

"What address?"

"I can't remember that." He paused. "But I can take you there."

Deserting Desiree in the middle of dessert. That would tear the heart out of our date, and be a hideous mistake, career-wise, as well. I thought of the backside view of her shuffling away to the ladies' room. The grain helped me decide as well.

"Go ahead," I told him.

I had all the way to town to think of excuses for my behavior toward Desiree, but no plausible ones came to mind. The fix would not be in when I went up before the Ethics Committee. I wondered if Desiree would recuse herself on the grounds of our disastrous social life. Probably not. She would decide she retained enough professional distance to see me disbarred. I would have to defend myself in a free and open hearing. I was so busy thinking up vodka-flavored lines of defense, I barely noticed when the cab jolted to a stop in the valley.

"Right here," the cabby said.

It was the Manus Building. Right where Frankie kept his offices. The meter tab was seventy-nine sixty. I paid it without quibbling. Eighty dollar cab rides were currently the least of my worries. Even the Ethics Committee hearing had been bumped into second place. Angel Pisaro's case was taking the worst of all possible turns. Not that Angel Pisaro was telling the truth; I assumed that all along. But that there was some truth to the tales her Evie told her.

The ride had sobered me up enough to realize I wanted another drink. There was a white-collar bar in the hotel next door. It had probably been roaring at happy hour, when the office buildings emptied and traffic gave everyone an excuse for an hour's worth of cocktailing while the freeways cleared. It was deserted now, except for a couple of tourists and transients waiting for the night-long fun that the hotel promised in its brochure to begin.

And Jill Congliaro, drinking by herself at the corner of the bar.

"I'll get that," I volunteered as the bartender slid her drink across the wood.

"Mr. Speed," she said.

The bartender looked at me inquiringly. It was time to get off the straight vodka binge if I wanted to repossess my faculties before noon tomorrow.

"Bloody Mary," I told him.

"This is a surprise," Jill said. "Didn't think you were the type to go out drinking unless you had a social reason."

"I thought the same about you."

"I've got an excuse. I was on the date from hell. Guy showed up bombed, so I had to drive. He insisted that I smuggle a pint into the movie theater for him in my purse. He chugged most of it before the Coming Attractions were through and spent the next half-hour burping and groping. I escaped by telling him I had to go to the restroom to take my pill. I came straight over here. How about you?"

"Just out and about," I lied. No sense magnifying Desiree's social woes by carrying tales to her underlings.

"The fucker's on the Mayor's staff, believe it or not. Guess I've closed off that career path by keeping my knees together. Fucked being a career woman."

She said the word "fuck" with a peculiar intoxicated enjoyment, as if it was a freedom that only booze allowed her. Jill Congliaro had been sitting at the bar for a while.

"Your white male career path isn't strewn with these kinds of obstacles."

Lucky for me I had the Bloody Mary to stick in my mouth by this time, otherwise I might have told her. I took a big gulp and frowned.

"No good?"

"Okay, I guess. I just always assumed these things tasted lousy because you had to drink them first thing in the morning. I wish you'd get off the white male thing. Why are we alone to be blamed for the condition of our birth?"

"Because you're goddam responsible for everything else."

"We white males don't get everything we want."

"But everybody who does get everything he wants is a white male. With some exceptions for professional athletes."

"Aren't the rest of us in the same morass as anyone else?"

"Don't ask for my pity. You at least had a shot at the top."

"So those of us that don't scheme and steal our way to individual pinnacles are deserving of contempt? And the few who do deserve loathing?"

"Are you cross-examining me?"

"Sorry."

"Don't be. I think you found an inconsistency there. I heard you were quite the advocate, in your day."

"In my day?"

I wasn't too drunk to be insulted by that. I was nearly twenty years younger than Schuckelgruber.

"You know. Before you became a pimp lawyer."

"Not all of my clients have been accused of pandering."

"You know what I mean. Pimp lawyer, whore lawyer, topless bar lawyer. Same thing."

"Surprised you know so much about me."

"You were the buzz, Jefferson Day. The Ethics Committee. Lousy rap, from what I hear."

"None lousier."

"You going to beat it?"

"Consider it already beaten," I lied.

She frowned. I'd forgotten she was probably privileged to her office's master plan for Angel. She was counting on getting her back.

"If the dinner was today, you'd be the buzz again. For taking the Pisaro case."

"I've had it more or less shoved on me."

"People would be damn surprised anyway. Of course, you probably know what you're doing. No chance of you springing Angel like you did that Washington guy."

"Like as not."

"You know I was only in high school when all that went down."

"Luckily you were engaged in the pursuit of hard knowledge rather than glued to the TV that afternoon."

Unlike every other person in town.

"No. The teacher stopped class and flicked it on."

It couldn't have been so long ago that standoffs with hostages taken were a novelty. Jill's teacher must have merely experienced the warm human yearning to see someone else's brains get splattered all over their yard.

"What did he say that made him famous?"

Desiree was right about little Jill. She was probably on her way over to the DA's staff. She had all the empathetic qualities of a flash flood.

"He said 'I want to thank…'"

I want to thank. Like he was holding an Oscar in his hand, instead of an automatic pistol.

"'my lawyer…'"

Myself.

"'for giving me this chance…'"

Just doing my job, Willie.

"'To make my life come out right.'"

"That's it!" Jill said gleefully. "I couldn't remember it for dick, the other day. Me and some of the interns were talking about it. Then he shot his wife and her kid, right?"

"His girlfriend. She wasn't even his common-law wife legally. And it was his kid, although Willie didn't think so. He only killed the child. SWAT bullets killed the woman. Wound that Willie put in her was superficial."

"To make my life come out right. Can't believe I'd forgotten it."

Hard for me to believe, too. Even the cops used it for a couple of months after Willie was laid to rest.

"Spread 'em," they would tell suspects, "Or your life is going to come out right."

"What was the whole background?" She leaned forward, all blonde hair and painted lips. For the movie she had worn slacks, but her blouse cut low across her breasts. From the new angle I could see creamy swellings disappearing underneath the outline of a black lace underwire bra. The drinks I had put back did not make her look any less desirable. My sex drive was recovering from its encounter with Desiree at a cosmic pace. All that little Jill wanted, in return for keeping me company, was the story of my greatest professional trauma, a career transformer. It was like asking a paraplegic about the accident put him in the chair. With a little help from vodka, and a fresh look at her cleavage, I told it to her.

"Willie Washington was an ex-con, two assaults, one aggravated, and an armed robbery on his rap sheet. He'd done plenty of time in bits and pieces. That didn't keep him from getting a job as a security guard, carrying a revolver around a Brink's warehouse every night. Nowadays it'd never happen. Willie'd be three strikes and out, but back then, there were some people who still believed in rehabilitation and weren't afraid to say so out loud. Plus Willie no doubt lied to Brink's to get the job. It was before the cops had all their computers wired together, so Brink's had no way of checking.

"Willie had a girlfriend, Dolores Buea. Before he went upstate on his last conviction, he knocked her up. Dolores presented Willie with a bouncing baby boy named Desmond two years later when Willie made parole.

"Willie put his life together. He moved back in with Dolores and Desmond. By all reports he was a good enough father to his kid. At least he didn't leave any welts or cigarette burns on him, which is about the best you can expect for a dad that got most of his education in Chico. He didn't marry Dolores, of course, because that would've meant an end to her welfare, but between her check and the eight-fifty an hour he earned keeping an eye on Brink's fence every night, they were doing pretty good.

"Willie had to sleep most of the day and was away all night, so I guess that left Dolores feeling unsatisfied. She took up with a neighborhood boy named Sonny Mackle. Sonny ran numbers and did other minor bag jobs for a couple of the local entrepreneurs, so he had plenty of free time. Sonny was only twenty. Willie's schedule was pretty regular, so five nights a week Sonny and Dolores played naked Twister while Desmond slept and Willie guarded.

"The inevitable happened. One of the other guards came back early from his vacation and wanted his schedule back. They bumped Willie out of the yard. Sent him home early. Found Sonny on top of Dolores, ass cheeks flapping. Put all six shots from his revolver in him at close range. I get the case farmed out to me.

"Willie's story is that he thought Dolores was being raped. Dolores isn't arguing the point. And Willie didn't know Sonny, so that checks out. But Willie's got plenty of problems. His criminal record. And it turns out that Sonny is called Sonny because he's the bastard boy of a police lieutenant in East. I want bail. DA's office opposes. Little wiseass junior prosecutor, immigrant father just finished spending the family fortune to put him through Stanford, bets me a c-note I can't get Willie sprung.

"That just fires me up. At the hearing I got Brink's, I got Willie's pastor, I got maybe sixteen other members of Willie and Dolores' congregation testifying what a reformed young man he is. I got to put Willie on the stand, even though the prosecution screamed like I'd poured acid into their wing-tips, for state-of-mind testimony. He was great. 'All I want to do is make my life right,' he said, and the churchgoers chanted 'Amen.' Actually did. Not only did I get bail, I got it at seventy-five grand. The congregation broke open their piggy banks and Willie's on the street.

"First thing he does is buy a clip of 9mm ammo at one gun store. Then he goes to another and asks to handle a Glock. He slips the clip in over the counter. Now, robbing a gun store is a risky proposition. The owners are, by definition, armed. There are two of them in this particular shop, and as soon as Willie goes to flee, they open up at him. They're not sharpshooter enough to hit him, but the bullets spraying on the street alert the cops, who have SWAT on Willie's tail the minute he makes his homecoming.

"The rest of it you saw on TV."

Including Desmond taking one of the huge slugs in his two-year-old back. Camera didn't cut away quite fast enough. And Danny Akami, holding a hundred-dollar bill high in the air at the prosecutor's press conference after the fact. Saying it represented my fee. It was the start of his rise in the public's awareness.

"That's when you decided to become his personal Joker?"

"No. He's only been City Attorney for five years. Been working my corner of the legal plantation for over ten now. Plus I took a year off when Willie and his family died. Worked as a liquor salesman. One of my best accounts got popped, for serving a minor. I handled the case as a favor to the owner. Won. I picked up a couple of big orders after that. I picked up a couple of other nightclub cases, too. Easy law. Vice cops weren't used to having an adversary back then. Procedures were full of legal errors. Racked up quite an unbeaten string. That's when the pimps and the whores and the peep shows started showing up with retainers. It was Danny that moved in on my turf, not me on his. Kept me busy ever since. Not rich, but busy."

"You want me to buy a round?"

"Richer than working for the Public Defender. I got it." I didn't have to throw all of the rest of Mikey's money to the Visa wolves.

"The Defender's just a stop on my resume. I don't plan to end up like Desiree Mason."

"You won't," I assured her. Rather walk off the Million Dollar Spin than leave Jill stranded. Chivalry inspired the thought, but reality intruded. I was the one who needed a ride. We slurped the rest of our drinks in silence, hers apparently thoughtful, mine inflamed, then, when there seemed nothing else to do but ask, I asked.

"My car broke down. I wonder if you could give me a lift? It's directly east of here."

"I shouldn't be driving."

Prudence there. The valley was known to be 502 territory. CHP loved the high density of hotel bars and nightclubs.

"Besides, I live only a half mile from here. I was going to take a cab."

Too bad Rainbow Valley Cab had already faded back into the hills.

"I'll get you a cup of coffee at my place." I said, laying my whole scheme bare. "You'll be fine to drive."

"All right."

She had a sparkling little Honda, nearly brand new. How can all the secretaries and junior account execs and rookie public defenders of the female white-collar world afford these beautiful little Japanese machines? I made three times what she did and could barely afford to detail the Cadillac and rent the Hyundai.

I drove slowly and smoothly, keeping my blood alcohol content in mind. No red and blue lights flashed on in the rearview, so I must have passed for sober. Climbing the hill, I thought I saw a flash of camouflage in the bushes. Kenny spooking the neighborhood. Jill saw it too.

"Possum hunter. They're nocturnal."

"I'll say."

The porch light was off again. I staggered up the steps. I always feel drunker in the dark. I flicked the electric on.

"Some place," Jill said, eyeing the mismatched furniture.

"Bachelor, you know."

"Smells like cat."

Not too badly, I thought. Residual from yesterday's soiling. I hoped the miserable little mammal was constipated as hell. I rattled the coffeepot and dug around in the cupboard for the grounds.

"I can't drink coffee now."

"Thought you kids could drink coffee all hours of the day or night."

"Rather have what you're drinking."

The vodka was located more conveniently. I sat next to her on the couch, the velour one, for warmth. I forgot to flick on the stereo for background music. I always do. As soon as she put her glass down I kissed her.

"I like that," she said. "I hate the preliminary chatter. Pretending to be interested. Pretending not to notice the edging closer."

"I hate preliminaries myself."

We'll go right to the trial. Trial by flesh. Trial by jury of Jill.

I slid a hand between the lace of her bra and her flesh; her nipple rose into the fondling of my fingers. With my other hand I tugged at the back of her blouse. She leaned forward so that I could slip underneath it and unfasten the bra. It fell away together with the blouse when I unbuttoned it. Her breasts sloped gradually downward into a sizable swelling south of the nipple. They looked and felt bigger when Jill was unclothed. I licked one nipple in a circular motion. She wet the fingers of my hand with her mouth and placed them on the other. I favored it with the same rhythm as my tongue.

I tugged at her slacks and she helped me, easing them over her hips and letting them drop unheeded to the floor. I let my mouth work over the slight protuberance of her belly and then eased her back on the couch. I pulled off her panties by hooking them by the back with my fingers and sliding them down her legs. I licked the tendons that connected the inside of her thigh to the base of her mons. I ran my tongue in an encompassing circle around the pink circumference of her center.

"Go ahead," she said. "Go ahead now."

I feathered the bump and the hood with my tongue until my chin muscles were cramped. Finally she arched back and pressed herself deep into my mouth, the salt and the sweat and the musk so sweet, as her chest blushed pink with the bloom of orgasm.

"Are you hard?" she asked, grasping me so that it was not necessary to answer her question. "From behind," she said. "On the floor."

There was no question who was running the room. I held her by the angle of her pelvis and pushed myself inside her.

"Don't come inside of me," she said. "I was lying about the pill."

Her back was long and white and perfect. The muscles of her shoulders tensed as she threw herself against my hardness. The lips of her vulva shrank in and pushed out as they formed themselves to me. The unmatched vista and her breathy outcries brought me past the point of self-control. Obediently I withdrew and pumped my sperm manually. It ran in a frothy stream between the globes of her ass.

Afterwards she ran her fingers around my neck and I absentmindedly fondled her thighs. I led her upstairs to sleep. "Not under those things," she said when she saw the Springfield, Illinois hand-axes in their place over the headboard. I removed them and placed them haphazardly on the kitchen counter downstairs.

At four AM she woke up without need of alarm. "I have to go."

"What? Now?"

I had never been able to get a public defender on the phone before eight-thirty.

"I've got lots of repair work to do. With my own makeup, in front of my own mirror. Before I can face the world of men."

"Tonight? Tomorrow?"

She laughed. "I wouldn't have slept with you if it was going to be ongoing."

"That confuses me."

"I don't sleep with men on the night I meet them if I'm going to have a relationship. And I don't have relationships with guys I meet in bars. It's simple. Any guy with the potential for long term, I wouldn't want him to think I was a tramp. But a guy I'm never going to be with again, I might as well enjoy the sex. It's a matter of compartmentalizing."

I thought I had solved the problem of my sex life at least through the weekend, if not longer. I was flattened.

"I'm having trouble with that," I began, but she interrupted.

"Sorry. But don't worry. It's not just you. The mayor's ass-boy fell into the same category. He would've gotten what you got last night, if he hadn't been such a rude little snot. I was planning to be spontaneous."

She kissed me on the forehead. "I'll see myself out. Don't worry. In a couple days, you'll feel lucky about this."

It was too early even to have a morning erection. I fell back into the daze of sleep. I dreamed that the baby in Dolores Buea's arms had Jill Congliaro's face, right before the bullet tore out its spine. I woke up as dawn was filtering around the hill and realized it was just a nightmare.

I felt lucky already.

Chapter Seven

"When are you going to get me out of here?"

Angel was the same. Same shapeless jail smock. Same dull stare. Same preoccupation. I looked at the well-formed forearms and calves, the only flesh Angel exposed, and felt a keener appreciation for her body that morning. Going one round with Jill Congliaro had only tuned up my sexual engine. The attentions I hadn't had a chance to pay to her waited impatiently to be transferred to another woman.

I felt no more appreciation for Angel's conversation, however.

"We're just getting started. Mikey told me the story about Father Canto. There seems to be some independent corroboration."

"What does that mean?"

"It means we may have the beginnings of a defense. Not an easy defense."

"Evie would have killed me if I didn't kill her. What more of a defense can there be than that?"

"It's a perfect defense, if I can satisfy a jury that Evie killed someone. I want you to tell me the story about Father Canto. Everything that Evie told you."

"Evie hated him."

"Did she know him?"

"Not really. Somebody she knew knew him. That's how she got in touch with him."

"She called him out of the blue?"

"No. She ran into him. A girl can always meet a guy if she wants to. Even a priest. They have to go to the supermarket like everyone else."

"And then what? She told him she had a thing for fallen priests?"

Angel shrugged. "I don't know. She didn't tell me everything."

"Did you even know about him, before he died?"

"Sure. She went out with him a couple times before she did it. She used to make fun of him. He had a big, rumbly voice. Evie used to mimic it. She would do it when we were eating. 'Pass the holy fucking salt,' she would say, in this priest's voice. It was hilarious."

"So you met him?"

"Sure. We partied. And he'd call. When he got drunk, he used to sing these old church songs. Songs that weren't even in English."

"Latin?"

"I guess. It sounded like Mexican."

"Did he call often?"

"Plenty. Evie would make me shoo when she took the calls. I knew she was helping him jerk off. I couldn't figure it out, because we never did anything with guys except for money, and I knew she wasn't getting paid for it. That's when she told me about the little girls."

"The altar girls?"

"Yes. It used to make Evie mad. 'Little girls in church,' she used to say. 'Little girls praying to God to make them pure. And he fucked them.'"

"Did you get mad, thinking about it?"

Angel shrugged. "Naw. I got fucked when I was their age. When you're born a girl, it just happens. Sometimes sooner than others. I thought it was kind of funny, these churchy girls, scampering around in robes like they're little Virgin Marys. I guess that priest showed them. Guess he helped them figure out that they were just a bunch of little twats."

"So you knew Evie was going to kill him?"

"I knew she was going to do something bad to him. I didn't know she was going to kill him. I thought maybe she was just going to get him drunk and leave him naked, on the steps of the church, maybe. When Evie told me she did it, I got scared."

"Was Evie scared?"

"No. A little nervous, maybe. She got the chance and she did it."

"But he never did anything to her? Except get free phone sex?"

"No, she fucked him. She had to have."

"He paid her?"

"Maybe. He didn't have much money."

"Why would she kill him?"

"I told you. She hated him. He was a child molester. A father molester. Evie's father molested her. He was another father molester. Evie said they all deserved to die."

"Why did she think that?"

"For ruining us. Evie thought she was smart. She could've gone to school. Instead she started dancing when she was sixteen. Because of the money. And because it was better than what she was doing before that."

"So? The fact she was molested, that didn't make her a dancer."

"Yes it did. It made us all dancers. And worse, whores. Because men will always pay us money to be naked. A regular girl, she's too scared to get naked in front of strangers, no matter how much money there is. She's afraid that something bad will happen. But a girl that's been fucked by her father, she's not afraid of being naked. Because the worst thing has already happened."

"So you were molested?"

"I told you, we all were. All the dancing girls, all the peep show girls, the bondage girls, the streetwalkers. Wouldn't do it if we hadn't been."

"And Evie took revenge for all of you?"

"I guess," Angel said listlessly. "Didn't ask her to."

"You said she was nervous after she killed Father Canto."

"Yeah."

"Just excitement, you think?"

"No. She left something in the car. She was afraid the cops would find it."

"What was that?"

"A dream catcher."

"What's a dream catcher?"

"It's a necklace. A piece of jewelry."

"Why is it called a dream catcher?"

"It's an Indian thing. You wear it, and when you sleep, it's supposed to make you catch good dreams. Evie used to say powerful dreams. She was really into being Indian."

"She was Indian?" The corpse in the morgue photograph had been blonde.

"One eighth. She used to say Cheyenne, but one time she admitted to me it was one of those Eastern tribes that no one's ever heard of. She used to dream of killing molesters. An Indian would do what she dreamed of, Evie said, so she did."

"She left her dream catcher in the car?"

"The priest made her take it off. Said it ruined the effect. It wasn't something a little girl would wear. I guess he was right. Evie said he was afraid of it, that he knew it was powerful magic. I don't know. She left it in the car, and then when it was over, she could hardly go get it, could she? It was a thousand feet down."

I rummaged in my briefcase until I found a piece of scrap paper, along with a pen. "Can you draw me a picture of the dream catcher?"

Angel scrawled out a loopy oval with radiating tines. "When is the trial?"

"We don't know yet."

"Who is we?"

"You and me."

"What about Evie's rich guy? He hasn't tried to pay you off, has he?"

"Nobody's paid me off but Mikey."

"Mikey's a sweet guy," Angel said, a trifle absent-mindedly, I thought, for speaking of her only benefactor. "Those rich bastards wouldn't care so much about Evie, if they knew how much she hated them. What about bail?"

"I can only ask for another hearing if I can present evidence that the court has not yet considered."

"The lawyer I had at the first hearing wouldn't even let me talk."

"Angel, you ever see a psychiatrist?"

"I think so. One of our customers was this big headshrinker."

"No, I mean as a patient."

"Why? I'm not crazy."

"I'm going to try and get you moved to another place. There'd be psychiatrists there."

"Oh, no. I'm not going. You're not going to put me with a bunch of crazy girls. Rather be with the sistahs and the Mexicans here."

"It wouldn't be permanent."

"I said I'm not going. I'll get Mikey to get me another lawyer if you try some shit like that."

How could this idiot, murdering woman pull Mikey's strings so deftly? I had that to wonder after the guards led Angel away for her pie break. She couldn't be lying about being pregnant. The standard medical exam performed on all prisoners would have revealed that. The question I wanted to ask Mikey was, how was he so certain that the child was his?

Probably mere overconfidence in his own fertility. Didn't want to believe Angel got knocked up on one of her commercial transactions.

Amy was waiting outside in her car.

"I picked up your voice mail from a pay phone," she said as I clambered into the passenger seat. Like Jill Congliaro, she drove something nearly new and snappily Japanese. I looked about the interior for clues to the make, but the manufacturer had not included any. My rental had "Hyundai" in bold cursive on the steering column, like the mark of the beast.

"Anything from Desiree Mason?"

"No."

That was ominous. Chances are, Desiree was permanently miffed.

"Anything else?"

"A Mr. Frank Manus."

Angel was prescient. A talent that did her no good at all, I was certain. Cassandra was the epitome of credibility when viewed through the same glass as Angel.

"What did he want?"

"He wants to see you at his office, at two. Seemed to think you'd show up, too."

"Anything else?"

"Marvin Maeger. Said if you wanted to interview his little bitch—his expression—you'd better hurry up, because he was about to fire her. And Mikey, half a dozen times, as usual."

"Mikey with the tit bar?"

"Of course. The other Mikey calls, it'll be an occasion, from my point of view."

"You're doing a nice job, Amy."

"Thank you. I try," she said tersely.

Not looking forward to an afternoon of Shuckelgruber's shoulder-kneading, I imagined. Nice little break for her, having to pick me up at Las Colinas. Pleasant for me as well. The car was a manual. Amy's shortish skirt rode up high on her thighs as she engaged the clutch and stepped on the gas and brakes. The night with Jill had plainly left me sex-starved. I wasn't careful, I'd end up exactly as Desiree had predicted, a drooling old fart like Schuckelgruber.

The Hyundai was still occupying one of the visitor stalls. Damn things were almost never stolen, I recalled reading someplace. Schuckelgruber raised an eyebrow when Amy and I arrived together. He immediately monopolized her, handing her a sheaf of papers and a list of phone calls. I waited five minutes while he played the office orchestrator.

"As for me," I said, when Schuckelgruber mercifully got a call he couldn't ignore, "just a couple things. Call Marvin Maeger back and tell him I won't be able to see his girl until at least tomorrow. Also, tell him that if he fires her, he might as well go to county and pick out something nice in a corner cell, because he's going to go down for at least six months, once she turns over on him."

"You really know how to dish out joy, don't you?"

"I'm learning as I go. From Marvin. Tell Mikey I'll see him later. Possibly much later, but today. Also tell him not to come by or call, because I'm going to be out. You remember that cop called the other day?"

"Sergeant Pennofrio?"

"That's him. See if you can track him down."

"And Mr. Manus?"

"Depends if Pennofrio calls back."

Pennofrio had not been located by two, so I decided I might as well go see Frank Manus. The mogul's flagship building shone in off-white and bronze in the afternoon sun.

A security guard stopped me immediately inside the entrance. I didn't think that happened to everyone who had business at the Manus building, so I guessed it was all part of the process of being leaned on. The guard looked like he wanted to frisk me, but he settled for making me stand at attention in the foyer while he mouthed security jargon into an internal phone line.

"You can go up," he said finally.

"Up where?"

He looked at me pityingly, as if not knowing the location of Frank Manus' office rendered me utterly aboriginal.

"Top floor. Ocean corner. Wear this." He handed me a laminated card with a safety pin attached. *CLEARED* had been stenciled on the front.

I felt a dim pride. Would that it were always so easy.

I came to a foyer, lit brilliantly enough for brain surgery. A blue-haired secretary looked at me as if I was a toilet that needed to be unstopped.

"Wait here," she told me and disappeared.

There were no books or magazines. The room's only entertainment was a fish tank, devoid of fish. It was not empty, though. Along with a loop of water hyacinth, the tank was infested with a profusion of snails, a hundred or more, creeping along the sides and bottom. Frank Manus' subtle way of letting his petitioners know what he thought of them, I supposed.

After fifteen minutes the dowager receptionist told me I could go in, in a tone that implied she thought that her boss granting me audience was a reckless and hasty decision. Hate to try and see the guy if I hadn't been invited.

"Mr. Manus has just been released from the hospital," she said, as if I had been responsible for putting him there.

Frank Manus sat behind a desk that encompassed more square footage than my office. The file photograph that the newspaper always used when some doing of his merited coverage was taken maybe five years ago, the result being that while he looked like he was escaping age in the newspaper, Frank Manus looked shockingly older in person. His sparse white hair was razor-cut like a TV anchorman's, his nails had been buffed by a manicurist and the suit that hung at precise angles over his meatless old frame probably cost more than the Hyundai, as if he believed minute attention to the details of his grooming might stave off the advancing years.

He didn't look at me at first; he concentrated on his perfect fingernails splayed across his desk, which was empty except for a single telephone.

"Mr. McKeon," he said finally.

"Mr. Manus," I replied. So far the exchange wasn't taxing my wit or powers of cogitation.

"Your client," he said, and stopped.

Apparently he was so used to being waited on that his audiences were expected to finish his sentences for him.

"Angel Pisaro."

"I knew her."

"She hasn't spoken of you."

"I never liked her."

I waited for him to tell me why. From my acquaintance with Angel, I knew he had a plethora of bad qualities to choose from.

"I never liked her," he repeated.

I wondered if Manus was suffering from a touch of dementia. Then he looked up at me and I saw his eyes were as focused and clear and cognizant of the present moment as a pilot's attempting a touch-and-go. They were hard blue eyes, white trash eyes. The same eyes had no doubt belonged to his ancestors while they fomented the Whiskey Rebellion, had peered into the setting sun the night before the Oklahoma land rush destroyed the Indian Nation, had guided Manus' father into California to escape the Dust Bowl. They were eyes that could look without pity at a trapped animal or a gut-shot Seminole.

I had heard Frank Manus' business philosophy expressed by a few of the people he had paved over to become concrete king of the county. What he had was his. What he could get of yours was his, too.

"Do you like her?"

"Hardly relevant," I said.

"Don't talk like a lawyer to me."

Like summoning the occupant of an igloo, and ordering him not to talk like an Inuit.

"I knew the girl she killed, too."

"I did not."

"I liked her. She was a performer who genuinely enjoyed her work. She added something valuable to life."

"I heard she was quite talented."

"Talented doesn't begin to describe it. She was one of a kind."

"She was a stripper. And that's the most charitable way you could describe her. There's two hundred of them on stage in the city right now, working the late lunch crowd."

"Don't call her that!" Manus ordered.

"An ecdysiast, then."

"She was a performer without peer. Dancing girls have been around since the Stone Age. Many cultures have revered and respected them. Ours is not one of them, but that doesn't mean that a gathering of men cannot enjoy what nature designed them to enjoy."

"No disagreement there. In fact, I've argued in favor of it many times."

"It is my concern, in the trial of your client, that Fantasy's good name be preserved."

"I am obligated solely to the interests of my client."

"Don't recite legal formulas at me." Manus looked annoyed. "I know that, in the world of lawyers, a common strategy is trying the victim. What I want from you is assurance that you will not employ that strategy."

"My defense has not yet been formulated. Not even in my own mind."

"Fantasy would not hurt a fly."

"That's because they don't make whips, gags and leather underwear in fly sizes."

I was getting weary of the go-around. Manus snapped upright like he'd discovered a thumbtack on his seat.

"I don't know what you've heard about her, and from whom, but what that girl did, she did out of generosity."

"For people who were damn generous in return."

"A professional deserves to make a living. You're a young man," he said, seemingly at tangent to his argument.

"I'm forty-four."

"Exactly. When I was your age, I required no special conditions to assert myself as a man. But as you grow old…"

He let the sentence trail off, and his cracker eyes went bleak. I got the message. In all likelihood Evie had taken his final erection to the grave with her. I wondered what made the withered Manus member soar; the bondage act, the lesbian combo, or having Evie's ankle socks up around his ears.

"Who's paying you?" he suddenly snapped.

"That's privileged," I lied.

By paying me to represent someone else, Mikey was actually standing over one of the cracks in attorney-client privilege, but I wasn't about to give him up to Frank Manus.

He slid a drawer open with his left hand and produced two crisp sheets of paper out of it. On top of the cover sheet was my name. He pulled a pair of reading glasses out of his inside pocket.

"You're behind on a few payments," he noted.

"I don't recall applying for credit from you."

"One of my holding companies has the lease on your office," he replied.

"A professional deserves to make a living," he said again. "Your reputation is good, even though your finances are lousy. I think you've been picking up bad clients."

"I'm a criminal lawyer. Bad people are my business."

"I've got a project up in Oxnard. It's hit a little snag. Two, three months work in situ by a capable attorney ought to straighten things out."

"Development and property statutes are mysteries to me."

"It's not so complicated."

"I've got more than enough to handle here."

Frank Manus put my credit report back in the drawer. He folded his hands in front of him and stared at me over the silver crescents of his spectacles. I wondered what he was going to try next. We'd already been through bribery, intimidation and humiliation. Plus he had tried to jerk a few tears over the loss of his sex life. The guy really knew how to play a room.

"I want to show you something."

With his right hand he pressed an unseen button. A high-def TV descended from the ceiling to his right, and the room darkened automatically. He pressed another button, and the screen flashed as a tape was rewound. He directed it to play by flicking a remote.

It was a short feature, in black and white. A drunk in a sport coat stumbled out of a cab. His hair was disheveled and his eyes were intoxicated moons. He looked up, right at the camera practically, and mouthed the words "Manus Building" stupidly. Then he hopped off across the parking lot, short-cutting across the asphalt.

To his night of bliss with Jill Congliaro.

Rainbow Valley Cab was clearly visible on the side of the taxi as it pulled away.

I winced. Manus had decided on a second helping of humiliation to close out the show. "Security brought this to my attention this morning."

"Great sport coat, don't you think? Mervyn's, thirty-nine bucks."

"I will not even ask you what you were doing on my property at nine-fifty-five PM."

The video was time-stamped.

"Cabbie thought it was the Mission Hilton. I was looking for Wednesday Night Jazz in the lobby bar."

"You looked like you'd already seen quite a few bars."

"I was supposed to play flugelhorn."

"Smart-assing me is not improving your chances to succeed in this town."

"Somebody who knows jazz and can blow a smooth flugelhorn will always be able to find work."

"It's apparent to me that you deserve your problems with the Ethics Committee."

That took me aback, but I remembered that Manus contributed to both Danny Akami and Jimmy Donnelly.

"I haven't done anything unethical since I've been in here," I reminded him. "And I've been offered the chance."

"Been a good ten minutes for you, then," he sneered. "Mrs. Ambergast?"

The blue-haired heavy led me to the elevator, watching me closely all the way, as if she suspected I might start stealing the furniture or spray-painting graffiti on the walls if she left me unsupervised.

"Possibly you don't know how sick Mr. Manus was," she hissed as we waited for the elevator. I guessed she had been monitoring our conversation over the intercom.

"Possibly I don't care," I replied.

She gave me the backed-up plumbing look again.

"You wouldn't be so glib if you'd been through what he's been through. I doubt you'd even be out of bed. Five days ago he had a kidney transplant."

"Up and about in remarkable time, isn't he?"

"Mr. Manus never lets anything stop him."

In the parking lot I saw the Rainbow Valley cabbie. He was adjusting the lures in his hat in the glass that fronted the lobby. Wanted to look organized for his interview with Manus.

All unaware that he was about to get the fare of his career. The direction my defense was tending toward would be obvious to Frank Manus after the cabbie had served his time in the snail room. I really needed to know if Pennofrio had called back.

I called the office when I got in the Hyundai. To my surprise, Schuckelgruber answered.

"Where's Amy?"

"She's out of the office right now." Schuckelgruber sounded nervous.

"Doing what?"

"I'm on another call."

"Well, I need my messages."

"She'll be back in five minutes."

"Now."

"I really can't keep this person on hold."

"Just one then. Anything from Pennofrio?"

There was a hurricane of paper rustling as Schuckelgruber destroyed the organization of Amy's desktop, then he said. "Pennofrio," and read me a number.

"Thanks Ernie. And stick to counseling, is my advice. You haven't got the dulcet tones for secretarial work."

"Bye, Speed," he said, breaking the connection.

Schuckelgruber must have picked up a client with oodles of concealed income to get as excited as he sounded. When the feds caught you hiding greenbacks, Ernie's rule of thumb was that you gave up half of the lucre to them, to get them off your back. The other half you gave to him. Ernie felt he had a half-interest in every mattress stuffed with cash in America.

I moved over to an adjacent lot before I punched in Pennofrio's number, to be out of Manus' surveillance range. He answered on the first ring.

"Remember that favor you owe me?" I asked.

"I don't think I even remember you."

"Frank Fernando's lawyer."

"Oh, yeah. What do you need?"

"When a car's been totaled in a fatal accident, what happens to it?"

"That would depend on whether it's been a good car, or a bad car."

At least I'd caught Pennofrio in a jovial mood. His day's catch of corpses must have been neat, undecomposed kills with suspects conveniently at hand.

"Does the state keep track of where they end up?"

"The state keeps track of where all vehicles end up. Your tax dollars at work. You have the vehicle ID number?"

"No. I expect it's in the police report."

"And you want me to extract this police report?"

"Please."

"Date and location of accident?"

"April 13, this year. State Highway 76. In the pass."

"That's sheriff territory. Out of my jurisdiction."

"So you can't find out about it?"

"Sure I can. We got XP now. Eastbound or westbound?"

"Off-bound. He fell off the mountain."

"Number of fatalities?"

"One."

I could hear Pennofrio tapping a pen or pencil on his desk as he waited for it to come up on the screen.

"Hey, this guy wasn't even yours," he said.

"I know."

"Another corpse that meant the rest of us could all breathe a little cleaner air, though."

"The vehicle ID?"

I Ic read it to me. "Chevy Caprice, black."

A priest's car. Father Canto knew the importance of maintaining a clerical profile.

"Now, just a little more help from your flying fingers."

"I already punched it in." Again the pen played percussion. "Otay Auto Salvage."

"Anything left of it?"

"There's limits to what computers can tell you, Counselor."

"Another favor?"

"Not likely. Happy Hour at Bennigan's starts in fifteen minutes. I plan to be planted at a corner table, on the far side of the two-drink minimum, when the secretarial flesh starts flowing through the door at five."

"Just a little lift to Otay."

I didn't expect the operator of the junkyard to cooperate much with one lonely lawyer, but a police sergeant would have him snapping to attention.

He snorted derisively. "Secretaries-Bennigan's. Greaseballs-junkyard. Where do I want to be at quitting time? The scales are not tipping in your favor."

"But you owe me a favor."

"I just paid it back."

"Tapping a couple keys? I had to run across town to ID your corpse."

"So I'm a wicked old policeman and don't always pay the favors that I owe."

"How about I cover your DUI next time you pull out of Bennigan's twisted, and the CHP on your tail?"

"The CHP knows and loves Pennofrio."

"Transferable, then. The drunk driver of your choice."

Pennofrio paused. "How long is this going to take? And by the way, what the fuck is it all about? Some insurance deal?"

"Tell you on the way there."

Pennofrio pulled up in an unmarked Crown Vic. The ride to Otay was one of the briefest I had ever taken to South Bay. Pennofrio threaded the lanes at about ninety. I kept my mouth shut, until we were well past Chula Vista, but when I heard brakes squeal behind us and horns blare for the fifth or sixth time as Pennofrio decapitated yet another driver's right of way, I made a suggestion that I thought had some merit.

"You're going to drive like this, shouldn't you put on the lights?"

"Against regulations," Pennofrio said calmly. "Getting back to Bennigan's in time to pick up the last lonely receptionist at the bar does not qualify as an emergency in the opinion of the Department. Don't need one of the professional butt-chewers who okay my paycheck to catch me lighting up traffic for no discernible reason. So what kind of deal is this?"

He barreled between the guard rail and a rumbling produce truck heading back to the border for a fresh load of Mexican mangoes, then had to screech to the inside to avoid clipping the tail of an old Dodge Polara. The geezer operating it apparently thought the speed limit applied to the left lane.

"You took Angel Pisaro's statement, didn't you?"

"You bet. And a piece of work it was, too. Lotta times your perps come across with a lot of weepy crap before they finally admit they sunk the blade, but not Angel. Why do you ask?"

"You think she deserves to die?"

"Everybody deserves to die." Pennofrio made it seem likely we would both meet the same fate soon by executing a four-lane sweep to the exit. "That's the way God made us. Who are we to argue?"

"You know what I mean. Go down for Murder One."

"I think we ought to execute them all. First, second, third murder, every degree of manslaughter. Let God sort them out. Bet you didn't know I had such a religious bent."

"Only because I'd never ridden anywhere with you before." My eyes were tearing up with fear. "Let me rephrase the question."

"Wish I had a hand on a woman's thigh for every time a lawyer's said that to me."

"Of all the perpetrators you've put the cuffs on, where does Angel Pisaro fall?"

"On the guilt line? Ninety-eighth percentile."

"On the deserving to fry line."

"Well, further down than that. You got your cannibal murderers, your serial murderers, your kid killers, your rape-murderers, your other murders committed in the course of a crime. Your cop killers. Maybe some others I can't think of right now. They'd all fall in ahead of Angel in the lethal injection line, in my opinion."

"So you think she shouldn't have to die, just because somebody with a lot of bananas wants to see it?"

"And who would the Big Monkey be?"

"Frank Manus."

"One of this burg's fiercer fossils."

We were spinning up a crumbling asphalt road, nominally two lanes, but with shoulders deteriorated enough so that Pennofrio had to keep to the middle. A tow truck hauling a smashed sedan came straight at us. The driver was honking the horn aggressively. Pennofrio punched up the blue and reds.

The tow truck driver panicked when he saw the lights flash and spun into the dirt, the wreck at the end of his chain jackknifing into the manzanita. Pennofrio grinned at the chaos in the rearview.

"Once in a while you got to say fuck the regs. I hate tow truck drivers," he said. "What the little bitch do to piss Frank Manus off?"

"Her girlfriend was the last person on earth who could give Frank a woody."

"Well, that makes sense." Abruptly he pulled the Crown Vic to the side of the blacktop. "What doesn't is why I'm here. Are you Angel Pisaro's lawyer?"

"You're a hell of a detective."

"Get out."

I clicked the door latch open but stayed in the car. We were in the immediate vicinity of Otay Salvage. That was obvious from the heaps of rusted wrecks that vied with the sere hills for possession of the skyline, but there were several junkyards that competed for the auto-salvage dollar down here, so close to the border you could smell the smoke from Tijuana. I didn't feel like wandering from one to the other, begging for a glimpse of any squashed Caprices they might have. Also, it was a hell of a place to be stranded.

"Otay Salvage. Right around the corner. Drop me there, we'll call it square."

"Goddammit, I can't believe I'm here helping some defense lawyer. Mouthpiece for my own perp."

"Just trying to keep her out of the lethal injection club. Leave some room in there for the cop-killers and the Jeffery Dahmers."

"She's little. She won't take up much space. Can probably see St. Peter on half a shot of potassium chloride, too."

"Should Frank Manus be able to dish out the death penalty?"

"Some real estate salesman has his paws all over my receptionist right now. I can feel it. Psychically."

"Ten minutes more, you'll be on your way back. With the look of eagles in your eyes, fresh from the field. One glance at you, the receptionist's panties are awash. The condo pusher gets shot down like an Iraqi jet."

"Close the fucking door. Might as well get this over with. I'll be lucky to get back to civilization in time to grab a six-pack and look for something with bare tit on HBO."

Otay Auto Salvage was painted in red on the side of a '58 Rambler that had been welded to the top of two poles to serve as a billboard. The mother of all junkyard dogs, looking to be half Rotweiller, half velociraptor, threw itself madly against the fence, pressing its drool-flecked maw against the rusting metal, barking to the smoky skies its desire to sink fangs into flesh. I noticed Pennofrio locking the unmarked car carefully.

"Someone around here might be just stupid enough to try and steal it."

He put the keys in his shirt pocket.

Manning the office at Otay Salvage was an overweight man of indeterminate Middle Eastern ancestry. He had a huge florid mustache and teeth like miniature marshmallows. Puttering around the yard were a couple of grease-stained Mexicans, who no doubt did the actual work of unbolting used parts from the wrecks. The office manager didn't look any too happy to see Pennofrio's badge. He pointed down one of the haphazard lanes between the wrecks, so thoroughly oil-soaked that they were practically asphalt, as the direction in which we might find the Caprice. He didn't offer to send one of the Mexicans to guide us.

"These guys sell vehicle IDs and titles all the time. One way to make a stolen car legit. If I'd showed him a Department of Motor Vehicles badge, he'd've shit out a camel," Pennofrio said.

It was Pennofrio that identified the Caprice. It was bent like an "L" so that the junkyard had it stored on its side. It looked like hardly anything had been removed from it. It looked like there were very few usable parts left on it. And the Chevy Caprice was a huge, monstrously ugly model. Probably very little demand for replacement parts. If the cops hadn't found Evie's dream catcher, and it hadn't been spun out of the car as it crashed down the mountainside, it was probably still in there. I climbed in carefully through the hole where the windshield had been. Dangerous-looking ridges of cracked safety glass still bordered it.

Gravity would have dragged anything left in the wreck toward the driver's side, which lay at my feet. I hunched over and felt carefully around the shards of glass and metal shavings that had accumulated around the door and the seat cushions.

"What are you looking for?"

"A dream catcher."

"What the fuck is a dream catcher?"

"Looks like this." Glad of the excuse to straighten up, I produced Angel's drawing. "Want to help?"

"Fuck, no. What is it, a piece of jewelry?"

"Yeah."

"Looking for a little piece of twisted metal in a big piece of twisted metal. Who says you legal eagles don't know how to have fun?"

I opened the glove compartment, which was at my eye level. No necklace tinkled to the ground, but a piece of paper fluttered to my feet. I picked it up. It was a credit card receipt from Suds 'n Sparkle Auto Detail. Dated April 12.

Father Canto had wanted the Caprice clean for his date. I folded the paper away.

"You got about two minutes and your police escort is leaving."

"What do you have on Angle Pisaro, besides the confession?" I asked, wanting to distract Pennofrio away from clock-watching with a little conversation.

"Read the discovery files, Counselor."

"I get to ask you on the stand anyway. You got physical? Fingerprints? Fiber?"

"It was a home grown stabbing, Counselor. We don't need any of that shit."

"DNA?"

"For Chrissakes, they were lesbian lovers. They probably got each other's DNA all over each other's cervixes, you want to bother looking."

Everybody loves to answer a stupid question. I was barely listening to Pennofrio, though. Underneath the front seat, draped up in the springs where the centrifugal force of the accident had flung it, was a handful of silver. I unhooked it carefully from the springs and held it in my hand while I fingered the kinks out of the loops and feathered out the tines. A dream catcher.

I felt like Oppenheimer at Alamogordo. The whole world was about to change, and I alone knew it.

"Here it is." I showed it to Pennofrio. He took it in his hand.

"Well, that's worth the drive," he said sarcastically. "Precisely what does this do for your case?"

I was so excited and grateful, I told him. About Evie and Father Canto. About Rainbow Valley Cab. About how the state's whole case against Angel Pisaro was about to go down like a hang glider in a wind shear.

He listened without any reaction. When I was done, he simply smiled. Then he tossed the dream catcher high behind his head. It flashed silver in the lowering sun before disappearing with the tiniest of tinkling noises into the metal chaos of the junkyard.

"Enough of favors," he said.

I must have looked like a kid who's been told Christmas has been canceled. Pennofrio laughed so hard he closed his eyes and threw his head back.

I snatched the car keys out of his pocket and tossed. I put more mustard into my throw. The second minuscule clink on a heap of rusting auto parts sounded much further away.

I wasn't ready for Pennofrio to punch me. I doubt I could have stopped him if I was. He delivered a perfect right cross and suddenly I was on my hands and knees, wondering if I would ever move my jaw again. He kicked me, but half-heartedly, and right in the flesh of the buttocks.

"Goddam," he said. "Goddam."

I scrabbled over in the direction he had thrown the dream catcher and started pawing at the steel wastes.

"I find the keys first," he warned, as he walked in the opposite direction, "I'm leaving you to the dog."

I spent five minutes looking for the dream catcher in the ravines of rusted metal, passing with foreboding over long, deep cracks between crushed vehicles where it easily could have fallen and reluctantly overlooking heaps of screws and wires that could conceal it by providing a perfectly camouflaged background. Just when I had resigned myself to searching until dark, and maybe again when the sun came up, I found it. It had fallen precisely on the center of an upturned hubcap, appearing to my grateful eye like a party favor on a doily.

I pocketed it, then went over to where Pennofrio was having less luck with the keys. "Split a cab?" I mumbled. I was trying to talk just using my lips and teeth.

"Fuck you."

"Okay, I'll pay for the cab."

"You know what kind of shit I'm in, I have to tell the watch commander I lost the keys to one of the department's vehicles? Not to mention the one-in-a-thousand chance it could last overnight here without getting stripped."

"Quite the quandary for you, then."

"How about you help me look for them?"

I settled myself on the cracked vinyl of a discarded bucket seat. "Why did you toss my dream catcher?"

"It was a whim. I was disgusted with myself for wasting my Happy Hour digging through a junkyard looking for exculpatory evidence in as slam-bang a murder case as I've had all year."

"Could be construed as obstruction of justice."

"Only if you found the thing again." He looked up. "You did?"

"Easy. You don't have the arm you used to, obviously."

"Goddam." Pennofrio squinted at the sun setting over the horizon of junk. "No good now, though. The chain of evidence has been broken."

"By you chucking it over your shoulder? You think I found *another* dream catcher in this junkyard?"

"Could be. Could be a very popular piece of jewelry. Could be every hippie chick in town doffs her dream catcher before she spreads her legs in the back seat. Probably at least one in every other wreck in here. Least that's what I would argue, were I the DA."

"So you're mustering arguments while I'm looking for evidence? Who is the cop here, and who is the lawyer?"

"What do you want?"

Pennofrio was not talking to me. I looked around to see one of the Mexicans standing a respectful distance away.

"*Senor*, it is time for the yard to close."

"Fuck that."

"*Senor* Haddad has told me to let go the dog."

"The dog comes anywhere near to getting released, I shoot it. And you. And him," Pennofrio added, pointing to me. He drew his jacket aside so the Mexican could see the gun there, a short-barreled automatic. Even Homicide detectives, who rarely draw a gun, don't carry revolvers anymore.

The Mexican shrugged, with what I imagined was a Third World indifference to life, especially mine. "I will tell *Senor* Haddad."

"Tell him I want to see a clean title to every Honda in this yard, too," Pennofrio shouted at the Mexican's back. "That ought to keep him from bothering us again until at least midnight," he said to me.

"And here I thought I didn't have a prayer of getting a date for tonight."

"I repeat, fuck you. You getting comfortable there? Maybe you ought to search out something in leather, with independently adjustable comfort settings."

"This is fine. Very cozy. A great spot to sit and philosophize. One of the questions I've been pondering is why you, as a police officer, have such a problem with justifiable homicide."

"Ain't no such thing."

"Except when a cop does the killing."

"Cop draws down on a perp in the line of duty, there's no reason he should face a firing squad."

"Only cops don't always draw down on perps. They don't even always draw down on people with guns. They shoot people with screwdrivers. Hell, anything metal. Didn't a cop shoot somebody a couple years back who was holding a stick of gum with the foil still on it?"

"I don't remember that."

"Didn't the DA rule it justifiable?"

"You got no idea of the pressure cops work under, is your problem. We were getting shot up like the French Navy that year. Little extra quickness on the trigger was advisable, you didn't want to come home in a coffin."

"So cops understand the problems of cops. And the prosecutor understands them, too, because without cops making cases he's out of a job. Anybody else kills someone defending their own life, though, they get no slack, from cops or prosecutors."

"As it should be."

"So one hundred percent of the time, a police officer guns someone down, he's justified. And one hundred percent of the time, a civilian kills another individual, he's guilty of homicide in some degree. Does that strike you as likely?"

"It's getting dark. You going to pitch in here, or not?"

"I would say, not likely. I would say there's at least one cop out there who got away with manslaughter when he popped a fatal cap. And I'd say there has to be at least one accused murderer who was completely justified in the act, because it saved their life. And from the evidence we've found today, I'd say it was my client, Angel Pisaro."

"I don't think I hit you hard enough. Otherwise you wouldn't be so fucking long-winded. Save it for court. As for Angel, fuck the little bitch. She did it, and she's going down."

"You got no idea of the pressure of being Angel Pisaro, is your problem. You got a lesbian roommate who runs your whole life. Turns out she has a habit of murdering older men, which she confides in you, then decides you've got to be eliminated because you know too much. To deal with this enormous personal problem you've got an eighth-grade education, the IQ of an algal bloom, and the only trade you know is slipping out of your panties automatically when people start giving you money. I think she was damn restrained in only stabbing her victim three times."

"Save the state of mind crap for court."

"I'm giving you the chance to be on the side of the angels, which, coincidentally, is Angel's. I want you to tag that dream catcher as evidence and sign for it."

"No fucking way. How do I know that it wasn't Father Canto's?"

"A Catholic priest? With a pagan religious symbol around his neck?

Wouldn't sit well with the parishioners."

"Keeping peace in the parish wasn't concern numero uno for the good father, if you recall."

"His secret lust's all the more reason to behave impeccably in carrying out his other duties. Besides, I'm not asking you to testify it was his. I'm just asking you to say you were with me here, when I found it, and identify it for the court. I'll take it from there."

"Sign what?"

He had me for a second. Then I remembered I was still carrying around Marvin Maeger's money in his business envelope.

"You going to help me look if I sign?"

"You bet."

"Phantasy Photography?" he said distastefully.

"Only envelope I've got."

"Here." He had another envelope. It was even marked EVIDENCE. My case was getting stronger all the time. I dropped the dream catcher in. Pennofrio signed.

"You going to start looking now? Going to be time to go back to the car and get a flashlight, soon."

"No need." I handed Pennofrio his keys.

He looked as surprised as if I had just given him an all-day pass to Heaven.

"I threw my keys," I explained, "I palmed yours. For certain, Low Rate Rentals has another set. Don't hit me again," I added, when Pennofrio balled his fists.

"Give me that," he demanded, speaking of the dream catcher.

"I'll hold on to it for now." I started walking toward the fence.

"You're going to have chain-of-evidence problems, you don't give it to me."

"What problems? I'm an officer of the court. And it's not like it's a pee test, or something else I could adulterate."

"That's evidence in a potential murder case."

"Father Canto's? You'll reopen it?"

"Not up to me. That's Sheriffland, out there. I could recommend it to my colleagues in that department."

"And you would?"

"Fuck, no. They like reopening cases almost as much as they like incurable, contagious cancer of the balls. Especially cases involving people whose croaking was an event the whole world welcomed."

"What are you going to do if I give it to you, then?"

"File it."

We had reached the office. Pennofrio unlocked his car.

"Where?"

"Somewhere I never have to look at it again. Lot of a cop's job is figuring out how to file stuff so that nobody ever has to look at it again."

"Thanks, but no thanks. I'll hang on to it."

"Suit yourself."

I reached over to open the passenger door, but Pennofrio kept it locked.

"It's a one-way ride, then, counselor."

I nearly picked up a rock and threw it at the Crown Vic as it reversed away, but I thought better of it. Pennofrio was still my best witness, and I had the double pleasure of knowing he was the DA's star as well. No sense making him any angrier than I already had. A cab ride back to my office couldn't be as expensive as last night's fare. I turned to face Mr. Haddad with the intention of having him phone one for me.

Mr. Haddad wore the irate glare of a man who is an hour late for his dinner. The Mexicans backed him up with sullen stares of their own. The mega-dog barked lustily at the end of his chain. My police escort had publicly abandoned me.

I put on an insincere smile. "So," I said heartily, "What've you boys got around here that runs?"

I pulled in to the valet parking line at Terrifically Titanium behind the wheel of a 1986 Buick LeSabre that had already started smoking ominously during the comparatively short ride up from Otay. Mikey was supervising the line. It was the time of evening when his place started to get busy. He smiled faintly at the car.

"At least you're driving American," he said.

"Beauty, huh? Six hundred bucks. It was either that or walk north from the border. I've had a hell of a day."

"Me, too."

"Tomorrow I'm filing for an emergency hearing for bail for Angel. I think I've got a pretty good chance of prevailing at it. I need Angel free, too. To assist at her own defense. I got the dream catcher. And Frank Manus got the cab driver. On tape. Even if he pays him enough money to take a year's vacation in Bavaria, I can subpoena the tape. And him. He can help get Angel off. I need to get that subpoena issued tomorrow, before he realizes I can cut his balls off with that tape and erases it."

Unfortunately, Angel's jury was going to get to see me stumbling drunk, too. I was thinking as I was talking.

"Also, I need Angel to testify, so I need her to stop referring to her sister females as 'twats.' Are you following me?"

"Want to come inside?"

"Not necessary. I've got plenty to do. I've still got to read Angel's discovery file. I don't even know who the presiding judge at bail will be. I'm just letting you know I'm on it. I thought you'd be happy to know. Angel's got a chance."

"Speed, I've got to let you go."

The curb felt like it was crumbling beneath my feet. I leaned back on the filthy flank of the LeSabre.

"What, worried about the fee? I wasn't going to ask for more until after the bail hearing."

"Nah. Keep the money."

I didn't want to have to say it, so I said it fast. "It's not your kid?"

"No, it is. But I got three other kids. Expensive kids. With expensive moms. The only way I get to see the kids is if I keep shelling out every time their moms hold out their hands. Going to be tough to do when they bulldoze this place."

"You're losing your property?"

"Whole block's going down, is what they say. A course, that's just me and the rental car company, and the rental car company can just find another parking lot to work out of. Me, I got a liquor license. A non-transferable liquor license. I'm not here, I'm selling Dr. Pepper and fruit smoothies to my customers."

"What, they're condemning the block? To put up what?"

"Ten story parking structure. Airport needs the parking."

"Airport needs a flight path, too. What town would be dumb enough to put up a hundred-foot obstacle in it?"

"This one, if Frank Manus wants to."

"Manus is behind it? Openly?"

"Not openly, but his fingerprints are all over it. Why did you tell him it was me?"

"I didn't."

"You told somebody. Somebody told him."

"I didn't tell a goddam soul."

"I'm sure it was an accident, Speed. I'm sure you just let it slip. Anyway, it's over. I'm as sorry as I can be about it, but I've got no choice. All my law money is going to fight this parking structure thing. It's self-preservation, now. Maybe I can at least delay it. You want a drink?

"No, I'm still busy."

"You got nothing to do now, Speed." Mikey spoke the words firmly, as if he granted himself the authority to make me quit.

"When the five grand is wiped out, I'll hand it back to the Public Defender."

"Hand it back now. Keep the rest as a tip."

"I got to move on, Mikey."

I climbed back into the LeSabre. The ancient springs of the seat squeaked harshly as they adjusted themselves to my weight.

"No motions, Speed. No hearings. No anything."

"And you're going to quit taking Angel's calls?"

Mikey rolled his eyes unhappily. "Just enjoy a night off, okay?"

I gave a little neutral shake of my head as I pulled away. Mikey could interpret it as acquiescence if he liked. The LeSabre did not betray me by throwing an axle or blowing a gasket on the way to my office, but I kept a paranoid eye on its dials and lights, fearful of mechanical treachery. The smoking seemed to have abated a little. The rest at Terrifically Titanium had done the engine some good.

I thumbed through the Angel Pisaro file, looking for the ruler of the courtroom in which I intended to argue her bail, all the while feeling depressed and trapped into betraying Mikey. What I could maybe make him understand was that my obligation was to my client, Angel Pisaro, not to the man that paid her bill. I couldn't fool myself, though. At this point I wouldn't give up Angel to save myself. Angel was a killer, but she was innocent of murder, first or second, and of manslaughter in any degree. She had killed to preserve her own life, and as small and repugnant as that life might be, she was entitled to retain it.

The Report of Preliminary Hearing was in my hand. The presiding judge was Barry Appenzeller. Great. Broad Appeal Barry. At least he was erratic toward the defense and the prosecution alike.

I began to outline the standard arguments for a bail hearing on a yellow pad. The detailing of special circumstances would have to wait until my mind was less of a jumble. Who had ratted out Mikey to Frank Manus? I knew I had not. I reviewed all of the lawyers I had talked with at the Jefferson Day dinner and afterwards, when I was still trying to farm Angel out and knew I hadn't mentioned her benefactor's name to any one of them.

Who would know? It came to me as I read his name. On the door of his office, right opposite mine. *Ernest Schuckelgruber, Esq.* The bastard.

I lay down on the couch in the office, hoping he would show up in the middle of the night. I'd beat him to death with the fax machine and claim I thought he was a burglar. With the reassurance of that plan in hand, I was relaxed enough to go to sleep.

Chapter Eight

First light was just slipping through the mini-blinds when I woke up. I gave myself a sponge bath using a sopping gob of paper towels in the bathroom and shaved with the emergency razor I kept there. I put on a shirt of dubious freshness I found in the coat closet.

By 8:30 neither Amy nor Schuckelgruber had showed up. I put off my plan for grilling Schuckelgruber about Mikey's woes. It promised to be a very unlawyerly, fists-on-the-table, edging-towards-violence interview, and while I was in the perfect frame of mind for it, I had to be at Broad Appeal Barry's courtroom at nine.

I tapped the gist of yesterday's findings into Amy's computer and let the machine put it into the proper legal format and print it out. I had a bad moment when the LeSabre let out only an ineffectual slow grinding when I turned the key then, as if it had been slapped awake, turned over briskly and started. I pushed the air-conditioning level over to Maximum Cool. Nothing happened, so it was at least the equal of the Hyundai in that department. Nothing on the machine had started smoking yet, so I guessed it needed to warm up. I used the moment to transfer my gear from the econobox to the Buick. Could be a while before I got out to Low Rate to get that extra set of keys.

I pushed the DC plug into the hollow where the cigarette lighter used to be and miraculously, the cellular lit up. I was really starting to favor the LeSabre. It had a ton of room, even more than my Seville. The ride was pleasantly pillowy, and the acceleration was adequate. In the rearview I could see a jet of black smoke appearing every time I stepped hard on the pedal. I imagined that gave the car a rather racy, jet-propelled look to an outside observer. It had power windows and locks that still worked. I had been getting tired of cranking the Hyundai's windows up and down because the air conditioner wouldn't translate.

The smoking from the engine compartment still wasn't apparent. It was probably just residue burning off from the V-8 not having been run in a while. I put the phone to my ear. People see a guy driving a six-hundred-dollar car, they might be tempted to fuck with him, but they see a guy driving a heap while wearing a suit and talking on a cell phone, they think maybe he's some kind of ultra-undercover homeless cop or an eccentric millionaire, so they leave him alone.

I guided the Buick into attorney parking at the courthouse at nine exactly and offered the nominal buck they charged us to the attendant. He looked at the car leerily. Except for it, the lot looked like it belonged to a dealer who carried top-end foreign models exclusively. It was a phalanx formed of perfect Porsches and gleaming Beamers, massive Mercedes and luxurious Lexuses.

I pressed the dollar into his hand. "What, you got something against American cars?"

I must have looked a little wide-eyed that morning from not being able to release my hostility on Ernie. The sponge bath and the office shirt and shave didn't make me appear excessively socialized, either. The attendant decided that he wasn't making a big enough hourly to argue with me.

No one was in Barry Appenzeller's court except his clerk, which suited me perfectly. I filed a request for an emergency bail hearing for the following day. Any other judge would at least make me wait through the weekend just for having the nerve to make such a request, and if I was unlucky, Barry's chemo would be giving him hot and cold flashes every time he saw a defense lawyer and I would be denied entirely, but if it was the DA that was pissing him off when he read my request, he might just grant it, just to see the office scramble like a kicked anthill to oppose it. I also filed a request for a subpoena for any and all security tapes owned by Frank Manus, The Manus Building, any persons employed by same, et al., etc., for the date of night before last.

I was back in the car by ten. Time to work on what had abruptly become my only paying case. I got the number for Phantasy Photography from cellular information and had them dial it automatically.

"Phantasy," Marvin Maeger answered.

"What time are you open?"

"We're open now."

Ah, yes. Pick up the morning hard-on crowd. I spread some papers across the front seat and read a name.

"Raquel Bumgarden working today?"

"Ain't got no Raquel Bumgarden here."

The Nazi of nude photography had fired her. Fine. Appealing Marvin's conviction would be more lucrative than getting him off in the first place.

"All our girls just work under first names."

"Right. Raquel, then."

"Ain't got no Raquel. You sure she ain't working under another name? Come in anyway. You'll recognize her if she's here. If not, maybe you'll find another just as good."

"Mr. Maeger, this is Ted McKeon. Your attorney. I'm looking for the girl whose given name is Raquel Bumgarden. Is she in today?"

Criminal lawyers are used to dealing with the perpetually paranoid.

"She's in. For now. Get over here quick, is my advice. Somebody told her she's got me by the short hairs with this court case, so she's acting like she's the Queen of Bush. She may not last past lunch."

"I'm on my way."

I discovered I was almost there. Phantasy Photography sat conveniently between two of the freeways that funneled traffic downtown, in a strip mall, appropriately enough, that also housed a number of mundane businesses— a fast food joint, an H&R Block office, a beauty salon. I berthed the Buick in an empty slot by the salon. When I headed toward Phantasy Photography, a chirpy matron wearing a T-shirt that read *Security* barred my way.

"You can't park there," she said. "You have to park in one of the studio stalls."

She pointed out the spots reserved for Phantasy Photography, which were painted Chernobyl pink to set them apart from those designated for the non-sex trade.

"I won't be long."

She snorted. "Who ever is? I got a tow truck on call."

"I'm here on business. Legal business."

"I doubt that. I hear the city's working to shut this place up tight. The tow truck's right around the corner. He'll yank your car before you're finished yanking your…"

"I get the picture."

I moved the LeSabre over to one of the Phantasy spots. Last one. Business, apparently, was throbbing at the whack shack.

A sign on the awning read *Eighteen And Over Only*. The entrance was a double glass door that opened outward, with the glass painted over, then an appropriately seedy curtain, black velvet, then another set of glass doors. The second set opened inward. Calculated to slow any raids of a vice cop nature. Inside it was cool and clean, but dark, especially for an alleged photography studio. Music played, just a notch above background, not overt porno-film music but nearly so, a seductive blend of bass and low horns and a female vocalist singing scat that was tight with desire.

Three girls, one black, two white, lounged in a pair of sofas, all dressed in filmy teddies, all with wantonly spread legs and round breasts rustling against the gauze. The black girl ignored me. Waiting for some homeboy trade, maybe. Both white girls were brunettes, one with straight hair, one with permed. Curly jumped up like a used-car salesman skating the driveway line and put both hands on my forearm.

"Welcome, stranger," she purred.

"I'm looking for a Raquel Bumgarden."

The statement, made like that, with my new and nearly nude acquaintance tugging me toward her curves of breast and thigh, struck even me as being stupidly formal. She giggled.

"Nobody goes by two names here. I'm Amber." Then, as an afterthought, "Are you a cop?"

"No, I'm a lawyer."

"Oohh. I love professional men."

"I really have to see Raquel."

"Who is Raquel?"

She asked the question of the other girls; the black one stirred and said "Blondie."

"You mean Hope? Or Opal?"

"Opal."

"She's with somebody right now, baby. You sure you don't want Amber to pose for you? Variety is the spice, and all that."

"Amber, what the fuck are you doing with that man?"

Marvin Maeger's voice, coming over a background speaker, suddenly blotted out the background music, like a security announcement at the airport.

"My job."

Amber addressed the ceiling, but Marvin made that unnecessary by charging in through a door painted to blend in with the wall.

"Leave him alone."

"You ain't gonna charge me with no walkaway, are you? We got to pay Marvin ten bucks for every customer walks away," Amber complained bitterly.

"I ain't gonna charge you with no walkaway," Marvin said, mimicking her tone. His back was to the black girl. She flipped him the bird.

"You charged me for one last week, and the guy was really here to take pictures."

"You can't get him in the studio, you pay."

"That ain't *fair*, Marvin," Amber whined.

"And you been wearing the same fucking nightie three days in a row."

"I told you, Marvin, I got kicked out of my apartment. All my stuff is still there."

"What kind of a loser excuse is that? Get another apartment. And for fuck's sake, buy another negligee. Come on," Marvin said to me. "They'll bitch instead of work all day, if you show them the least bit of sympathy," he added after we had gained the security of his concealed office.

As I suspected, it was dominated by TV monitors. They were of the nine-inch, black and white variety. The screens switched from one camera to another at ten second intervals, so it was like watching one ghostly gray nude postcard after another. One screen did not vary; the entrance and the lot were outlined in the glare of the sun. Marvin's eye out for trouble. The tiny figure of the Security woman could be seen directing another Phantasy customer in the direction of the proper parking zone.

"You gonna tell her what to say?"

"We're going to review her testimony."

"I like what you said to me, that she was just dancing and the cop tried to put his dick in her face and she pushed him away. I would never have thought of that in a hundred years."

"My expertise is what keeps me in business."

"A course, she wouldn't have thought of it in a million years. While you got her attention, mention to her that I'm still paying the bills around here."

"I'm a lawyer, Mr. Maeger. I'm not here to improve workforce morale."

"Including yours."

Another quarter of an hour was going on Marvin's bill for that remark.

He peered at one of the screens. "She's done," he said. He clicked a mike open. "Opal, stay put."

The figure on the screen paused in the middle of re-holstering her teddy, and let the garment lie in her lap. "Take a camera," Marvin said to me, handing me a cheap 35.

"What for?"

"Don't worry. It's on me."

He led me down an aisle between cubicles brocaded off from each other by heavy silvered curtains. The music got louder, probably to conceal the stertorous breathing of Marvin's customers. Marvin counted the cubicles and stopped at the fourth one. He pulled the curtain aside. "Go ahead."

I sat down in the single armless chair provided. Unsure of what to do, I pointed the camera vaguely at Raquel Bumgarden.

"Please, no pictures," she said wearily.

She was nearly as tall as I. No fat on her, but willowy instead of muscular, with a long flat stomach that dove towards a postage stamp–sized pubic patch that gave the lie to her hair color. Her face was set in professional indifference.

"You can take your pants off now."

"Just a minute."

"Or you can wait. We expect a bigger tip, though, if you wait. There's tissues next to you, when you're ready."

"Ms. Bumgarden, I'm your attorney."

"How do you know my name?" She frowned. "Marvin must've told you."

"I'm here to discuss your court testimony."

"Shouldn't we be in your office?"

"It's important for an attorney to be aware, sometimes, of the layout where the incident took place."

"Yeah. Well, don't forget about the tissues. What do you mean, incident? Do you mean when the cop came in?"

"Exactly."

"He was so cute. Most of the guys that come in here..." She shuddered. "You're not so bad," she added.

"Thank you. So, the vice cop, he was an attractive man?"

"A dreamboat. I just gave it a little squeeze. Just to say hi. Just to say, kind of, thanks for being a good-looking guy and coming to a place like this. The judge will understand that I wasn't doing anything criminal, don't you think?"

Like Angel, she counted on the implicit sympathy of the court, and also on its maleness.

"I'm not sure what the court is going to do."

"Anyway, he turned out to be an asshole. Writing me a ticket and shit. I wished I hadn't touched him at all."

"Marvin feels the same way."

"Fuck Marvin. He would have fired me by now, except for this court thing. I know it. Probably will fire me the minute it's done."

"The important thing is that you don't get convicted of a crime."

"What should I say?"

Suborning a witness. Danny Akami would be so proud.

"Let's start from the beginning. How close was Officer Pullman to your person when you made contact with him?"

"He was on the chair, like you are. Not close. That was one of the reasons I did it, to loosen him up, get him friendly."

"Think back on it. Couldn't he have been a little bit closer?"

"He could've been, I guess."

"Like maybe even standing up?"

"He was standing up when he came in."

"And what if he started crowding you?"

"He didn't."

Another line of questioning was needed.

"Do some customers crowd you?"

"Ye-ess." Raquel Bumgarden emphasized her answer. "Sometimes they try to get right on top of you. Then their stuff'll get on you."

"What do you do then?"

"Oh, shove them off."

"That works?"

"Most of the time."

"If it doesn't?"

"Call Marvin. That always works. No one stays hard with Marvin around."

"Where do you shove them?"

"Anywhere."

"You mean, you don't pick a particular spot?"

"Fuck, no. I don't even look."

"So you could accidentally brush their genitals?"

"Oh, yeah. Oh, wow," she said, as comprehension dawned. "So I could say the whole thing was an accident."

"I think it probably was, don't you?"

"Yeah. It was." Raquel Bumgarden beamed. "You really are a good lawyer."

"Thank you."

"I really mean it. You can go ahead and, you know. If you want."

"That's all right."

"You don't even have to use the tissue," she said selflessly.

"How long have you worked here, Raquel?"

"Oh, forever. That's why I'm so pissed that Marvin's going to fire me. For one mistake."

"You remember any girl ever working here named Angel Pisaro?"

"Naw. What was her work name?"

"Angel, I think. What about a girl named Fantasy?"

"I remember Fantasy. Everyone hated her. It was like the place was named after her. She and her girlfriend were weird."

"Her girlfriend Angel?"

"If you say so. I don't think I even knew her name. She wouldn't talk to anybody except Fantasy. I'm serious. If you asked her something, she would whisper the answer to Fantasy and Fantasy would tell you. They didn't last long here. Marvin caught them trying to do business on their own."

"They ever mention wanting to kill someone? Even if you thought they weren't serious, you ever hear them talk about it?"

"They hated somebody's father."

"You sure it was somebody's father? Couldn't it have been a priest? Father somebody?"

"Maybe. You work in a place like this, you hear all kinds of stuff. Don't pay any attention to it, most of the time. All these girls in here hate somebody."

I remembered another of Angel's statements, and decided to test it.

"Were you ever molested, Raquel? As a child or a young girl?"

"Are they going to ask me that in court?"

"Probably not."

"Because I would say no. I don't even like to think about that."

"But you were?"

"My brother. When I was twelve. When these were just starting to grow."

She held her breasts absentmindedly. "He was fifteen. Every day for nearly a year. Our mom was at work when I came home from school. He was in a different school. He would already be there. He'd do it to me, anywhere he could catch me. If I didn't come home from school, he would beat me up the next day before he did it. My mom got laid off from work one day and came home and caught us. She sent him off to live with my dad. Otherwise it would've never stopped.

"You were raped by your brother?"

"Every day."

"Did he use condoms, or pull out, or try to make you take birth control?"

"No. He just did it. I think I was too young to get pregnant."

"Where is he now?"

"Back east. He's got a wife and a couple kids and an aluminum siding business."

"Do you talk to him?"

"No. He wouldn't want me talking to him. Or his wife, especially. What's to say?"

"How do you feel about him?"

"How do you think? I hate him. Look at him. He's got everything. Look at me." She ran her hands over her flanks with a certain professional flair. "Working in a whack shack. I'd like to kill him." Then she had a doubt. "I make really good money, though. Are they going to ask me all of this?"

"Depends on what kind of defense I organize."

Already I was thinking like a major-league lawyer again. A state-of-mind defense for lewd touching? A psychological profile of a public masturbator? I would get laughed out of court. A simple misdemeanor requires a simple defense. Major crimes get major justice. Meatball crimes get meatball justice.

"The most important thing is that now you remember you touched

Officer Pullman by accident."

"Yes I did." She smiled at the secret of our shared lie.

Marvin Maeger looked angry. "What was all that shit about?" he demanded when we were back in his office.

"All what shit?" I responded precisely.

"This." He hit a button.

My voice always sounds so adenoidal on tape. I choose to believe that it's a flaw in the recording process, otherwise I would never have the nerve to speak in public.

"You're the Richard Nixon of the stroke hut industry, Mr. Maeger. Recording everything that goes on in this place is going to bring you down."

Lucky for me Danny Akami had impatiently picked Bandit to roll over on me. If he'd waited a week, he could have gotten his puritanical paws on Marvin, and instead of relying on black pimp testimony, have me on Memorex suborning a witness.

"Am I getting charged for that advice? Like I'm getting charged for the half-assed psychological shit I hear you spouting on this tape?"

"That was damn cogent legal advice, Mr. Maeger. What I said to you, not her. Of course you're paying for it."

"I told you Angel Pisaro only worked a week for me."

"You also told me you fired her for not showing up, not for running a business on the side. And you didn't say anything about Evie working here."

"So I didn't want to speak ill of the dead. And what was all that crap about Opal's brother fucking her? So she's West Virginia to the bone. Who cares?"

"Just testing a theory I'd heard. That all of the girls in the sex trade were molested by someone in their youth, otherwise they'd never have made the naked career choice."

"That's stupid. My girls are in it for the money."

"Why don't you do a little survey for me, Mr. Maeger? See if I'm right?"

"See earlier statement. Who fucking cares? It's hard enough running this business with these flaky whores. You want me to start them *thinking* about why they're letting strangers cream on them?"

"You're right, Mr. Maeger. I'll do the thinking. It's what I get paid for, anyway." I handed the camera back to him. "Thanks for the freebie."

The parking for Phantasy Photography was in the direct line of the sun. The interior of the LeSabre was hot enough to fuse deuterium, but I barely noticed the pain of sitting in it until the engine cranked over and I could roll the window down. I was thinking, hard enough that if I was billing Marvin for it I could sit in Phantasy Photography with a comp camera for a week. If all the dancing girls of the world had been molested, it was a sexual Holocaust, and an unreported one at that. Was it so unlikely that one of them had decided she was justified in taking her revenge? And wouldn't one of the perpetrators of the crime serve as well to pay for it as any other? Father Canto had just been unlucky enough to have his name in the paper.

I was so occupied with thought that I failed to notice the process server sitting on the steps of my office, although he was so obvious a bearer of a writ that he should have had *Process Server* tattooed on his forehead. I even vaguely knew him, a sheriff's deputy from East County, one of my home neighborhood cops making a little extra cash serving notices on the side. He stuck the papers in my hands without me making any effort at all to avoid.

"Shit." The top sheet, as mandated by law, had YOU ARE BEING SUED in the required capitals. "What now?"

"Don't read 'em, Mr. McKeon. Just serve 'em. This is for you, too."

BY ORDER OF THIS COURT the second document began. What court was ordering me to do what? Both documents trailed off into small print. I needed my reading glasses, a gift to myself for my forty-third birthday. I usually kept them in a corner of my desk and made an effort to wear them in front of no one. I tried to brush past the deputy. He stepped back, but directly blocked my way.

"Better read that one, Mr. McKeon."

I peered at the print. If I squinted so hard that my eyes teared up, I could just make it out. "Wait a second," I said. The deputy crossed his arms.

"Legal order of the court. Sorry, Mr. McKeon."

"They can't do this. All of my work, my documents…" I let the statement trail off when I noticed the boxes stacked neatly by the doorway.

"Your secretary and your partner packed them for you."

"I need to talk to them."

"They're not in right now. What this says is you can't talk to them, or go in there right now," the deputy explained patiently, as if the mechanics of a restraining order were as unfamiliar to me as they were to the average guy who got nailed with one because his wife needed some space to screw the neighbor while they settled their divorce.

"Goddammit, I had no hearing on this."

"Papers are dated yesterday, six PM."

When I was in the junkyard with Pennofrio. Late for court to be sitting. Who had enough crank in this town to persuade a judge to work through Happy Hour? The answer was obvious to me, although I doubted his name would appear anywhere on the papers.

"What's the basis?"

"Probably in the lawsuit," the deputy said, again patiently. I was reacting like anyone else who just got hit with a legal blitzkrieg. The deputy was accustomed to it. Didn't even occur to him that as a lawyer I ought to be better prepared for it.

"I'll help you with the boxes."

The trunk of the LeSabre was easily commodious enough for them all. The deputy didn't even blink at the car. Just assumed I'd been sued before, I expect.

"I've got files on my secretary's computer."

"They told me to tell you they'd transmit any working files at your request. Request by Email only."

Didn't want to hear the sound of my voice.

"Any communications you get will be transferred to a location of your choice."

I sat down behind the wheel and began to leaf through the papers.

"Technically, you're allowed to remain on this street, but I would move. The order can always be expanded, if the court feels you're not complying with the spirit of it."

"What are you, the high priest of restraining orders?"

"It's kind of a hobby, yeah."

Figures Manus would know the specialist in any field.

I parked the LeSabre in the lot of Lucky Liquors, having a presentiment that I'd soon make a blip in their afternoon trade. The boxes had been packed haphazardly, no doubt with one of my tormentors keeping an eye out for my return while the other crated. My reading glasses were wedged unceremoniously beneath a pile of files. They fitted my face rather more crookedly than before.

Amy was suing me for sexual harassment. Amount of damages, unspecified. She was being represented by Ernest Schuckelgruber, counselor at law. Along with the bare bones of the suit was Amy's deposition, which formed the basis for it and the restraining order. I glanced through it.

Repeatedly uses the word "tit" in my presence.

Forces me to associate and communicate with persons employed or active in the sex trades.

Requires me to drive him back and forth to the office so he can force me to be alone with him.

Makes crude remarks, audible to me, under the guise of communicating with his so-called clients.

So-called? What was the implication there, that I was a heavy investor on the pimp business frontier?

Refers to female breasts as "tits" or "boobs."

You already said that, Amy. It was a goddam thin lawsuit. The "emergency" nature of the restraining order was likewise bogus. *Issued without opposition.* Like anyone had really tried to get hold of me. Even if they had the misfortune to contact me, I would have had about fifteen minutes grace to formulate an opposing argument.

Argument opposing this order will be granted hearing by this court at such time when the court is in session and parties to the dispute have been suitably notified.

So Schuckelgruber could keep the order in force merely by avoiding service. Which he was no doubt prepared to do. That *court is in session* line was foreboding, too. A restraining order issued *ex parte* only lasted for seventy-two hours under normal circumstances, but a particular judge could retain jurisdiction over the case at his discretion. The order was signed by a Judge Rheinhart. Acting on a grim hunch, I dialed the courthouse and asked to be put through to the judge's chambers.

"Judge Rheinhart's," a female voice cooed.

"May I speak to His Honor?"

"Judge Rheinhart is on vacation. All messages will be retained by this office until he returns. Would you care to leave one?"

"Yes. Ask him for the number for the Manus Travel Bureau."

"I beg your pardon?"

"Never mind. I'll just look it up in the Yellow Pages."

Why had I been so flip with Frank? The ancient developer knew how to negotiate an obstacle course. Every hotel and shopping center in the valley was a testament to regulations being overruled and easements being granted. That meant he knew how to set up hurdles, too, and now he had me running his oval. And I had always been the slowest guy on the track team.

I went into Lucky Liquor and noticed right away they now had my favorite flavor, the Belorussian stuff. With all the bad tidings I had endured in the past twenty-four hours, it was small comfort to know that Belarus was getting its export act together. I paid twenty-three dollars for a liter. I needed a freezer to throw it into.

The LeSabre backfired explosively when I gunned the engine. The clerk in the liquor store ducked instinctively, I noticed. I thought briefly of exchanging the LeSabre for the Hyundai, then realized my stuff would never fit in the Hyundai. Also under terms of the restraining order I was forbidden from entering the lot where it was parked, so Low Rate Rental Cars was making a guaranteed twenty-six bucks a day from me as long as the order was in effect. Little silver lining action for them.

The LeSabre was more accustomed to the highway; the engine throbbed and threatened to quit on me several times in the downtown traffic. I pulled into the parking structure attached to a nondescript, blue glass tower about twelve stories high, taking the vodka with me. The elevator hummed me up to the tenth floor. I had never been here before. I had to look for the office number in the directory.

Israel Kahauolopua, Attorney-at-Law. 1001

He was in. His office was heavy with potted plants and early fifties travel posters for Oahu. He looked up from a computer screen.

"Speed," he said, surprised. "What brings you over here?"

"I need a freezer, Izzy. Also a lawyer."

Chapter Nine

By the time the vodka had chilled, Izzy had suggested that I set up temporary quarters in his office. We arranged a conference table to serve as my desk and hooked up a spare phone and my computer onto one of his lines. Izzy had real crystal in which to pour the vodka. I gulped while he sipped and listened to my problems. Half the bottle was gone before he got past conventional sympathizing. Then he went for the point.

"The temptation to say I told you so is nearly overwhelming."

"Thanks for restraining yourself."

"For Christ's sake, why didn't you just let the PD do it?"

"PD gave her away. Part of their long-term plans for her. I'm supposed to go down in flames before the Ethics Committee and they'll get her back."

"But now you don't want to give her back."

"The girl seems to have as compelling a reason for justifiable homicide as any."

"What about the Ethics Committee?"

"Still trying to think of a way to keep them from carving up my career. Thought I had it whipped, but turns out I didn't have the stomach for the solution."

I gave him a thumbnail sketch of my date with Desiree. He stopped me at my description of her in the dress.

"Don't let the vodka make you too vindictive."

Izzy was a mountain of brown flesh himself. Even with the top button undone, his neck still bulged at the inside of his collar.

"The lawsuit is a petty annoyance."

"I agree. Hurts my feelings more than anything else." I had always thought of myself as Amy's protector against Schuckelgruber's horny intimations. Apparently I hadn't been more wrong about anything since I took the local team and the points a couple Super Bowls ago.

"Did you really use the word 'tit' in front of her?"

"Of course I did. Do you think I refer to my client's business as a 'female breasts bar'?"

"Still not sexual harassment in the orthodox sense. Maybe Ernie'll come up with something creative."

"Ernie wouldn't be able to find his ass in a real courtroom without an acre of spreadsheets and a couple CPAs to help him out. The lawsuit is just to justify the restraining order, which is just a device to keep me from best defending Angel Pisaro and, incidentally, myself, until that bright shining day when I get disbarred. Ten days from now, which is probably a week before the judge that issued the thing gets back from rafting the Amazon, or wherever it is his abrupt vacation took him."

"You're digressing, Counselor."

"I'm getting a little angry here. Wouldn't you be? In fact, why aren't my fellow attorneys up in arms about seeing one of their own abused in this manner? At least my fellow members of the defense bar?"

"You're not the most popular member of the courthouse club, Speed."

"I realize that. I have been told that. Not only by you. But I fail to understand it."

"It's because you think you're better than them."

"That is not part of my professional billboarding. On my office door, I do not have 'I am better than them' inscribed under my name. Where do they get that impression?"

"The misdemeanor cases, Speed. You are too good to defend felons."

"I bury myself in the business of pimps and whores and people think it elevates me?"

"They think you think it does. If you would only let the jail doors swing open for a couple rapists or grand larcenists, you could be part of the fellowship."

"I've got an admitted killer on my docket right now and I'm swinging for the fences on her behalf. Doesn't that rehabilitate me?"

"Somehow, not. Don't ask me to explain the logic of it."

"Why do you like me, Izzy?"

"Because I am a man of principle myself."

"Nobody walks more felons than you."

"That's the principle. I throw my entire strength against the bars of the jail. Everyone deserves to be free. No one is a criminal in their own mind."

"That just goes to show how deluded the minds in question are."

"Or perhaps I am just punishing the white man for his rape of my island home and my people's heritage, by freeing the members of his society that are living nightmares, so they can prey upon him again and again."

"Jesus, Izzy, you really think that?"

"When I have enough of this stuff, I do. Time to stop. I have to go home."

"Me, too."

"You do not. Finish off the bottle. That car you're driving screams *Pull Me Over* to the police. There's a gym in the basement of the building. Shower there in the morning and buy a new shirt before you go about your business. While you were taking a leak a message was forwarded to you. Your bail hearing is on for tomorrow. Nine o'clock."

Barry Appenzeller had long ago lost all of his body fat to his disease, along with his hair and any empathetic qualities he may have once had. The loss of the subcutaneous layer underneath his eyes gave them an ominous bulging quality. His veins stood up in great puffy knots on the impossibly skinny forearm that jutted out from beneath his robe.

His skin was dry gray leather, its suppleness destroyed by chemotherapy. He had a distinct twitch from the neck up this morning, I noticed. His whole head bobbed leftward and shuddered back about once every ten seconds, at the bidding of some pharmaceutical metronome.

"What do you have here, counselor?"

"Evidence of the truthfulness of my client, Your Honor. May I introduce?"

"Objection." Jimmy Donnelly himself.

Why I had been surprised to see him, instead of one of his deputies, I don't know. He formed a startling contrast to Broad Appeal Barry, even more so because they were about the same age. The approach of his seventieth year had only made him handsomer; his full head of hair was now snowy white and contrasted to photogenic effect with his ruddy complexion. It wasn't a boozy redness but the windburnt glow of a weekend sailor.

"Naturally."

"The matter of fresh evidence should be reserved for trial. Not that my office won't object to its introduction there."

"Again, naturally. Why should the defense be permitted to introduce any evidence at all?" Barry asked sardonically.

Tactical mistake by Donnelly, I thought, showing up himself. The judge had to resent time having treated them so cruelly differently.

"Why don't we just haul the defendant up from downstairs and hang him in the foyer?"

Donnelly kept quiet. Nothing would suit him better, and if any judge was capable of carrying out such a whim, it was Barry Appenzeller.

"The defendant is female," I pointed out. "She's not downstairs, she's in Las Colinas."

"That's damned impertinent of her."

"Also she's pregnant."

"Counselor, you've made your point. There'll be no hanging today. This is a bail hearing anyway. What've you got for me?"

I held the dream catcher in its envelope. "This piece of jewelry, found yesterday by myself …"

"Objection."

"What are you objecting to, Mr. Donnelly? Mr. McKeon finishing his statement?"

"There is no basis, in the evidence at hand, for considering the piece of jewelry to be material to the case. Also, the attorney for the defense cannot serve as his own witness. Also, why shouldn't we believe that Mr. McKeon did not just purchase this piece of so-called evidence, which is so stunningly useful to his case, at his convenience?"

"Consider carefully what you are saying, Mr. Donnelly. You are accusing an officer of the court of manufacturing evidence. That's a very serious charge. If it were made on an emotional rather than a factual basis, action might have to be taken against you."

Jimmy and I could be up before the Ethics Committee on the same day.

"Now I am going to ask Mr. McKeon a few questions, and I trust you'll not interrupt a sick man by screaming 'objection' arbitrarily every few seconds. Mr. McKeon, the only merit I can see so far in the District Attorney's argument is that you, as counselor, cannot be your own witness. Shouldn't you recuse yourself, in the interests of your client?"

"I was accompanied at all times in my investigation by Police Sergeant Donald Pennofrio, already listed as one of the District Attorney's witnesses. He'll serve to introduce the dream catcher."

"The what?"

"The piece of jewelry. I won't be in the position of forcing the District

Attorney to cross-examine me."

"That's fair enough. What about the sustainability of the evidence?"

"In my client's confession…"

"Which my office will steadfastly oppose any attempt to suppress."

"Mr. Donnelly, just because you did not preface that remark with the term 'objection' does not mean it didn't irritate me very much. Mr. McKeon has not asked me to suppress your confession."

"Nor will I, Your Honor. It is intrinsic to my defense. In the confession, my client clearly states that she killed the victim because of a clear and cogent threat to her life. She stated that the victim was a murderer, and had killed two men to her knowledge. This is evidence that she is being truthful about the deaths of one of those men."

"Your Honor, there is no link. It is true that the defendant described the victim as a homicidal individual herself. There were no names of alleged victims mentioned."

"The defense cannot be expected to address the flaws in the procedure the police used to interrogate the defendant. If I may be permitted latitude for a personal observation…"

"Objection."

"I do not wish to make an electoral martyr of you, Mr. Donnelly, which is the only reason you are not going to spend the rest of the afternoon in jail. If you interrupt Mr. McKeon again, I will grant his bail request summarily."

"The defendant is the sort of person who will not answer a question until it is posed to her directly."

"Mr. McKeon is no psychologist."

"And therefore he knows nothing about the mind?"

"I move to bar the introduction of this evidence, on the grounds that the defense has not linked it to the crime."

"Denied. Merely because the defense has not demonstrated a linkage doesn't mean that they cannot, even if it means putting the defendant on the stand. I trust you'll welcome a chance to cross-examine, Mr. Donnelly?"

"The confession makes the case cut and dried, Your Honor. I doubt the people will find it necessary to cross-examine the accused. Especially if the court follows the request of my office to limit the evidence to that pertaining to the homicide in question, not some other death, a death ruled accidental, by the way, and closed by the Sheriff's Department..."

It was my turn to interrupt. "Why is it no one wants to hear my client's side of this story?"

"I assume that question was rhetorical, Mr. McKeon. The court cannot answer it, in any case."

"Since the new evidence has been admitted..." Which Donnelly had apparently failed to notice, from the content of his last outburst, "...and arguably makes the case seem much more complex than the District Attorney would have the court believe, release of my client from custody would help immeasurably in her defense. I move that bail be granted."

"Denied."

There went a solid morning's work.

"This is a capital murder case, Mr. McKeon. The accused has no job and no relatives in the county. Why wouldn't she pose a flight risk?"

"Angel Pisaro believes she is innocent, sir. She welcomes trial."

"One misplaced piece of jewelry is not likely to win a verdict of innocent, Mr. McKeon. Not in my courtroom," the judge warned.

"Further exculpatory evidence will be forthcoming," I bluffed.

"You bring me some and we'll reconsider this matter."

"In the matter of the subpoena, then?"

"Objection."

"You are fined one hundred dollars for contempt of court, Mr. Donnelly. Pay the bailiff."

"Your Honor, the defense is engaged in a fishing expedition. What specifically do they expect to find on these tapes?"

"Five hundred. And the check had better be good."

"I'll be happy to address the prosecutor's question."

"No need. The subpoena is granted. Any other business, counselors?"

"Nice try in there, McKeon."

Jimmy Donnelly slapped me on the back in the courthouse hall. What did he want, my vote?

"Haven't had the pleasure of opposing you in a while," he added.

"Sorry about the five hundred bucks."

"Oh well." He grimaced. "Barry Appenzeller's court is always a bit of a minefield."

"Why not leave it to your deputies, then?"

"The people deserve the best representation possible, especially in a case as serious as this one."

Exactly why Donnelly should have left it alone. He was good at winning elections, not court cases. The dimpled chin and white hair looked great on TV. The set of his jaw was stern and unrelenting as he talked about how tough he was on criminals, but he was often at a loss for words when representing the people in court. The DA's office had its pick of the graduating law classes, though, and somebody in Donnelly's office could spot talent.

"Just a household homicide, Mr. District Attorney."

"Call me Jimmy." The capped teeth flashed.

"Not a multiple murder, not a torture-murder, not a murder committed in the course of another felony, not a child murder. Just a garden-variety living room stabbing. What's so heinous about it?"

I doubted I could make Donnelly admit that Frank Manus was pulling his strings, but I wanted to make him sorry he started in with the small talk.

"All murder is heinous. I'm surprised you haven't requested mental. From what I hear, the girl isn't quite all there."

"Perhaps I hadn't thought of it."

Easy enough to deflect that clumsy probe of my strategy. Maybe Donnelly would figure out that it wasn't in my interest to sow doubts about Angel's mental stability, since I was going to ask the jury to believe the story about Father Canto. And I doubted mental evaluation would show that Angel wasn't all there. There just wasn't much there, period.

"My office would oppose, of course."

"From the way the hearing went, I imagine you would oppose me opening my fly to piss."

"God, that sense of humor! We've missed it, over at the shop. How's Danny Akami, by the way?"

"Don't know. Can't seem to get hold of him lately."

"You've tied him up in knots a couple times."

"Doubt I can keep him leashed up forever. He'll have your job, one of these days."

"Over my dead body."

Exactly, considering the difference in their ages. Donnelly was insensitive to the implication in his own remark.

"Don't know where those people get off, thinking they're fit for a position like mine."

"Those people?"

"My eldest brother was killed on Guadalcanal."

"Akami is American, counselor."

"He'd have you believe that. That's the way they insinuate themselves. Trying to act more American than a real American. More Christian than a Christian. And in Akami's case, more Puritan than a Pilgrim. But he's a black-hearted Buddhist at the core. They all are."

Jimmy had apparently written off the Asian vote. And forgotten whose son I was. God knows my father's liberal notions have fallen out of favor. From what I've seen of human behavior, deservedly so. But I've never been able to bring myself to register Republican. I get a special pleasure out of opposing Danny Akami for my own reasons, not because of World War II.

"Care to join me for lunch? I've got a campaign thing. The caterer's got a few extra plates, I'm sure."

Donnelly was famous for his ability to pack away political lunches and prayer breakfasts. Even if his job involved no power or fame, he'd be in it for the food.

I demurred and made an excuse to split off at an adjoining corridor, leaving Donnelly to ruminate in solitude over his own personal yellow peril.

I drove out to Las Colinas. I was gaining great confidence in the LeSabre; on the highway it accelerated past the speed limit as if it had rolled off the line yesterday. It took the sheriffs only a few minutes to find Angel.

"Well?" she said.

"We had a bail hearing this morning."

"I'm still in here."

"The judge still refuses to set bail. A few positive things have happened. I found the dream catcher. Right where you said it would be."

"And they still won't let me out?" Angel wailed.

"Not yet. We will be able to use it at trial."

"So what?" she said bitterly.

Couldn't really expect Angel to understand what a legal triumph that was. Probably the only trial she'd ever seen was of the movie variety, where a last-minute discovery of additional evidence either convicts or frees the accused. What the movies don't show is the weeklong spat over the admissibility of the miracle evidence, with the jury out of hearing that would inevitably follow such a discovery.

"I've had a subpoena issued for other evidence we're going to find useful."

"Don't you understand," she said, speaking slowly but with anger in her voice, "that I'm innocent? I don't belong here. Why won't you just believe my story?"

"I do believe your story."

Even though it required a leap of faith like getting baptized in the river. I felt vaguely purer after the words had been spoken, like the freshly saved must feel.

"Concrete evidence of its truthfulness will be helpful in convincing the jury, though. You said Evie killed two men."

"No I didn't."

She hadn't, I remembered. Mikey had told me that.

"She killed three. One of them was supposed to be her own father. She would never talk about that one much. It was a long time ago. Got run over by a riding mower and bled to death on somebody's lawn. I think maybe it was actually an accident. She took credit for it, though."

"What about the other one?"

"Forget about that. She did a good job on that one. Everything is under the ocean."

"Who was it?"

"Some guy named Big Daddy. You ever hear of him?"

"Big Daddy O'Toole? The musician?"

"Yeah. I never listened to old music much, but Evie said he was famous once."

"She's right. Angel, he drowned."

"He had help."

"They found him after he'd been in the water a couple weeks. His boat sank. No one else's body was found. What did Evie do, sabotage his boat?"

"No. She was with him on it."

"And she swam to shore?"

"No. She said that was impossible. Something about the current. She surfed."

"From the middle of the ocean?"

"She said it was a long way. She said it was scary. The scariest part was when he woke up and started swimming after her."

"Why don't you tell me from the beginning? The way Evie told you."

"She met him like she always did, because she planned to. It wasn't like Father Canto, where she had to have a couple dates with him. Guess he just figured because he was famous, it was natural for a pretty girl to want to fuck him, in the special way he liked. It was his idea to go out on the boat."

"And her idea to take a surfboard?"

"No, there was one on the boat. He was famous for singing surfing songs, Evie said, so he always had one. Evie said she always used the weapons at hand. That's the way she said it, 'weapons at hand.' She would never use a gun or a knife that could be traced to her. Men are so stupid, she said, they've always got something dangerous lying around.

"He got drunk, like they always do. He had some drugs, too. Evie pretended to take them with him. Then she did the little girl act. He passed out after the sun had gone down. Evie could still see the lights on the shore, so she knew which way to go. She went down into the boat and unbolted some bolts. They held the motor on. Just enough so that the boat started leaking. Then she switched off the pump that pumps water out of the boat. I didn't even know there was such a thing. I thought if a boat leaked, it just sank.

"Then she went to get the surfboard. It was bolted to the side of the boat. She barely got it off in time. The bolts were rusty, she said, like it hadn't been unbolted in a while. She thought she was going to have to use the raft. That would have been a dead giveaway, her floating around the ocean in a life raft when the sun came up. She nearly switched on the pump again. But she got it off. She had a wet suit in her costume bag. Always did. Evie loved to surf. She was born here, you know.

"The boat took a long time to sink. It began to turn over. Then she dove into the water with the board and started to paddle. Guess he woke up when he felt the water. She heard him splashing after her, screaming. Finally she heard him suck water and die. The boat was gone. She rode the first wave in around daybreak."

"What day was that?"

"I don't know. August sometime."

"Were you worried when she was out all night?"

"Nah. We were a lot, when we went on dates."

"Were you jealous?"

The DA was very short of providing a motive for Evie's stabbing. I wanted to make sure they couldn't manufacture one out of Angel's own words.

"Of course not. It was just business."

"Turned out to be a little more than business."

"Yeah."

"When did Evie tell you about it?"

"When they found the body."

I remembered that; it had been Labor Day, so that put Evie's midnight paddle right in the heart of August, just as Angel had said. The corpse had bobbed up on the Silver Strand, just north of Imperial Beach. The papers and the TV news had made quite a fuss over it. Holidays are slow news days. The body had floated right into a combination Labor Day-family reunion picnic that about a hundred people were attending, at the height of it. Fashionably late. They hadn't identified it as Big Daddy's body until the working week was well underway. Two weeks at sea makes a dead person unrecognizable as human, let alone as a specific individual.

But it would be a lot better for my case if Evie had told Angel when she was fresh from the kill.

"Why Big Daddy?" I asked Angel.

"He was another child molester."

"I can't remember that."

"It was a while ago. A fourteen-year-old girl was caught with him by her parents. The law was going to get involved, but they let him take her across the border to Mexico and marry her. Just because he was famous. A year later they broke up."

Jesus, Evie had a long memory.

"That was years ago. How did Evie even know about it?"

"The girl worked with us. At one of the parties we worked at. Somebody brought it up. She cried. Just another stripper turned out by a horny old guy, now."

The revenge of the statutorily raped. Evie was consistent. Angel had something else on her mind.

"Why won't Mikey talk to me?"

"Mikey's having some problems."

"If I lose Mikey I won't have anybody."

She was ready for tears. It was the first emotion I had seen Angel display other than petulance. It was only self-pity, but then it was obvious Angel didn't have much of an affective range.

"You got me, Angel."

"Thanks, Mr. Speed. Can I get bail, too?"

"Not unless we can crank out some more exculpatory evidence."

"Well, get cranking. On whatever you just said."

Now it was Angel that was ending the interviews. Suited me. I had no further questions. The story of Big Daddy's death promised little help for my case. I forgot what category the police had finally decided fit the circumstances of his death. I thought it was one of those catch-all categories like "misadventure at sea." When he and his boat had first turned up missing there was little fuss; his fans said obviously he had decided to set sail for Hawaii to surf the North Shore. I remembered they had located the boat after they found the body. A sonar sweep of the near shore had turned up the new wreck. It was a case the police were even less likely to re-open than Father Canto's.

I left Angel gulping her pie. I took a detour by my house, left out some food for the cat and grabbed a change of clothes. I drove by my office and thought about scaring the crap out of Amy and Ernie by lurching up to the door with the tire iron in my hand, but decided I was in enough trouble legally. At least now they had solitude for their shoulder massages. I berthed the Buick in Izzy's spot and awaited his return.

He was in by three and listened to my story contemplatively.

"Two things, as far as I can see," he said when I was finished. "The first is the board. Where is it?"

"Abandoned it, I guess. Just like the bicycle."

"Can't count on someone stealing a surfboard. Do you surf?"

"No. East LA, we didn't do much of that. Dad didn't want me hanging around with surfer types. Too Caucasian a sport for his tastes."

"A board washes up on the beach, the assumption is that there's a surfer in trouble. Evie couldn't afford that."

"Maybe the board just drifted out to sea."

"Unlikely, with the prevailing waves and currents. And even more suspicious. A floating board deep at sea is sure to bring Coast Guard attention. No, she would have to get rid of the board. The second is the boat. Where is it?"

"Sitting in the kelp, I'm sure."

"Depends on how much it was worth, and if it was insured. Could be it's all dredged up and ready to be introduced as Exhibit C."

"And how do we find that out?"

"Leave it to your Brother Izzy. I have some insurance contacts. Do a little work in that field."

"I never knew."

"Don't think less of me for it. Sometimes I run short of felons with assets. And the white man has afflicted my island soul with greed. Is this boat your last gasp?"

"The deceased Evie has a mother somewhere. I suppose I could look her up, see if I can get her to say something nasty about her daughter."

"A sublime task. Wish I could do it myself. I wouldn't mention you were Angel's attorney."

"Sometimes your guidance is overly intrusive, Izzy."

"Meaning you would have thought of that yourself? I suppose you would have. I worry about you, though, Speed. You lack an attorney's inculcated sense of self-preservation."

What friends I have always feel free to discuss my flaws. I suppose I should be thankful. I thumbed through my boxes. Evie's mother's name was on the paperwork somewhere. Body released to. An address in Lakeside, a hard-drinking cowboy town snuggled up against the foothills.

I hit Lucky Liquor again, this time for a bottle of bourbon, having a premonition it might be useful. The Buick was smoking again by the time I had traveled east one more time, so I parked it at the garage and paid off the Cadillac. Hector assured me it would now run impeccably. I tried to sell the LeSabre to him, but he would have none of it.

Chapter Ten

The address on the coroner's report was in a trailer park. The modular itself did not look like much. The white aluminum siding was dark with the dust that precipitates out of the Southern California atmosphere, the crystallized smog that coats everything here. A splintery picket fence set it apart from its neighbors.

But parked out in front was a big Chevy dually, with a custom paint job, extended cab, a CB antenna sprouting from its roof and the dealer's sticker still glued to the windshield. A fifty-thousand dollar truck, built to haul a passel of cowboys and tow their horses in comfort. A Lakeside Cadillac, in the local patois, because it cost as much, if not more, than a brand new El Dorado. I held the bottle in the crook of my arm as I tapped on the screen door.

The blare from the television burst out the door before she did. All I saw of her was a hand on the edge of the panel, before she swung it open and came into full view, clenching her freshly lit cigarette between her lips.

And a view it was. Her hair was pulled haphazardly up into a bun, which hung crookedly to one side of her scalp, so that it looked like a furry asteroid about to crash into her head. She wore no makeup except lips painted the background red of a Stop sign. She was dressed in an object that was either a very fuzzy muumuu or an extremely colorful bathrobe. Wooden clogs wrapped around toes painted to match the lips completed the ensemble.

According to the coroner's report, her name was Gail Fortenwood. The last name didn't match Evie's and probably hadn't since a few divorces back.

"Mrs. Fortenwood?" I asked politely.

"Come in," she said right away, as if strangers bearing bourbon were always appearing on her steps. She took the bottle out of my hand and stepped across to the kitchen cabinet, where she stocked it in with a good number of its fellows. The place was small enough that I could see the bottles and read the labels. Not all were bourbon; the white liquors were generously represented as well. Mrs. Fortenwood's tastes were more catholic than I had imagined.

"Never drink that stuff before dinner," she said, speaking of the whiskey. She clinked ice into a glass and poured.

"Here."

"What is it?"

"Vodka and homemade lemonade," she said, pronouncing the 'homemade' with unmistakable domestic pride. I sipped it delicately. It wasn't bad. Go back two generations along Gail Fortenwood's family tree, no doubt the vodka had been homemade, too.

"What are you?" she said suddenly, as if the simple question were a trap she had unexpectedly sprung.

"I'm here as part of an investigation into the death of your daughter Evie."

"I knew you weren't no cop. Cops don't bring you bottles. Are you private?"

"I beg your pardon?"

"Investigator. A private dick. A renta-cop."

"I'm a lawyer, Mrs. Fortenwood."

She didn't seem disturbed. "Good. I been thinkin' about suing somebody."

She didn't say who it might be.

"Have a seat," she offered. "Cops didn't ask me too many questions about Evie. They had it all figured out. 'Bout all they wanted me to do was sign for her body."

"It must have been very hard for you."

"You got no ideer what it's like, losing a child."

"I can imagine."

I tried to, and failed. My son seems to me to have an implacable grip on life. I am certain he'll have them rolling at my funeral with dead lawyer jokes.

"Not that she was much of a daughter to me. I never hardly seed her. Once she hooked up with that little slut what stabbed her, she never had no time for me."

"Before she met Angel Pisaro, did she live with you?"

"God, no. She left home when she was fifteen. Didn't get along with her stepfather."

"Mr. Fortenwood?"

"Naw. That was Escher. He was a no-good bum. I useta catch him lookin' up Evie's skirt all the time. Not that he had too far to look, with what Evie useta wear."

"Did you suspect him of molesting Evie?"

"Molestin'? Naw. I tole you, the girl was already fifteen. He just wanted to get his hands on her. He was too much of a candyass to make a move, though. Matter of fact, it was me that told Evie to hitch on down the road. Thought maybe if Escher wasn't starin' at her ass all the time, he'd pay some attention to his marital duties. What I get for thinkin'. A month later he was gone too, with some skinny tramp useta work at the auto parts store. That's when I met Fortenwood."

I didn't bother to ask what happened to Fortenwood; it didn't seem likely to be relevant.

"What happened to Evie when she left home?"

"Well, she moved right away in with a black man. Just to break her mother's heart. I mean, what's a black man going to do with a fifteen-year-old white girl?"

"Did he turn her out?"

"Turned her every which way, I expect. Then all of a sudden she's got a job dancin' naked. That a promotion or not? I don't know."

"What happened to Evie's father? Her natural one?"

"Dead."

"How did he die?"

"Ask Evie. She was there. And now she's here. You wanna see her?"

Without waiting for my answer, she flung open the liquor cabinet. Stashed in with the bottles was an urn.

"Guess she's not talkin.'" She sighed. "Seems disrespectful keeping her in there, I know. But I don't know what else to do with her."

"How did her father die?" I asked again.

"I don't know what to do with her," Gail Fortenwood repeated herself. "Same problem I had when she was alive. As for him, he runned himself over with a lawnmower, the stupid piece of shit."

"Evie was with him?"

"Doin' her visitation with him. Not that he'd paid a scrap of attention to her when she was a baby. We was divorced when she was about two. I shoulda figured out what was going on."

"You mean he was molesting her?"

"I wouldn't call it that. Molestin's a one-way street, isn't it? Couldna happened more than a couple times, but she went along with it, sure enough. Leastways she never complained when it was time for her to visit him."

"You knew what was going on and you let it happen?"

"Suspected, mister. I suspected what was goin' on. I didn't *know*. And it was mostly on account of Evie. She was a forward child, if you know what I mean."

"No. Tell me."

"Kind of little girl that would always sit on a man's lap, whether she barely knew him or not. Kind of girl that would squirm her little bottom all over him while she was doing it. Kind of little girl whose underwear was always showin.' I tried to raise her with some manners, but it never would take."

"What happened when her father died? What do you mean, ran himself over with a lawnmower?"

"I told you, I don't really know. Got himself underneath it somehow, and managed to turn it on. Else he left it running while he lay down in the grass to have a smoke or a sleep an' didn't put the brake on. Ran over him an' he bled right out before Evie could get him help."

"How was that?"

"He was mowing some rich man's lawn. Guess it was a long way to the house for a little girl to run. By the time she got there and had him call an ambulance, it was too late."

"You said you were divorced from Evie's father when she was just two. Hard thing, for a woman and a toddler to be alone. Why did you get divorced?"

"That's personal, mister."

"Did you have any other children with him?"

Maybe Evie had an older sister who had paved the path for her father's affections.

"No. Evie was my only child."

For the first time she seemed on the verge of sorrow.

"I tell you what, it was my fault. I took to running around a little bit. A woman gets married and she thinks it's going to solve every little problem in her life, but it don't always happen. What was that man ever going to do for me anyway? What kind of a job is it for a white man, mowing other people's lawns? I ran into a crowd with a little money and partied with a few of the guys. Went on for a couple of years. It wasn't whoring, but there were some presents involved. Tokens of appreciation. Well, old Stupid Ass figures out what's goin' on and, instead of being grateful for me getting some of the stuff I want myself, decides he's too proud to be sharin' his woman and wants a divorce. I was a looker back then. Where do you think Evie got her looks? You want to see a pitcher?"

"That's it? On the mantelpiece?"

"No, that's Evie."

"Mind if I look at it?"

The only picture of Evie I had seen before had been the coroner's. She stared back at me flatly from the frame. It was a glamour shot, the kind women paid a hundred dollars for and gave to their men for a birthday or a Valentine, not the usual high school graduation portrait. From the content of her biography, Evie had probably been too busy to finish school. She had eyes so blue they looked like the photographer had touched them up.

"I shoulda just took the money," she said bitterly. "Like my little girl did. That way he never woulda known."

"Did you have insurance on Evie, Mrs. Fortenwood?"

"Naw. What makes you think that?"

"The nice truck in your drive."

"Didn't have nothing to do with Evie. I won the lottery. I get forty-four thousand dollars a year. For twenty years. Ain't that something? Finally got lucky."

The kitchen cabinet was still hanging open, exposing Evie's remains.

"Why don't you put her urn up there?" I asked. "Next to her picture?"

"Naw. She's fine where she is. I want to be able to shut the door on her. Would've buried her, but this is all her rich man would pay for."

I decided I'd had enough of her company. I had another vodka when I went back to my house, but I didn't drink enough to keep me from dreaming. I dreamt of a little girl with an uncomfortable wet spot between her legs, watching her father sleep off his exertions on the fresh mowed grass. I dreamed of her releasing the safety brake on the riding mower that was still roaring, because someone would wonder why it wasn't running if he turned it off to take his nap. I dreamed of it gathering speed slowly before the front tires rolled over his chest and the blade bit into his torso. And I dreamed of her running, screaming, forever, over a lawn so vast that it had become the world itself, and a father dying in its center just the tiniest drop of blood upon a continent of green.

The phone rang. "What's the difference between a lawyer and a rooster?"

The sun was just clearing the horizon. It was the rooster time of day.

"What?"

"When a rooster wakes up, its primal urge is to cluck defiance. Hey, can you give me a ride to work?"

"I've got to go to work myself."

"Clue in, Dad. It's fucking Saturday."

"It is, huh?" I was disoriented by my sudden awakening. I hadn't even gotten the lawyer joke yet, let alone checked my internal calendar. Fuck the clients. That was it.

"Why can't you drive yourself?"

"My piece of shit car is broke down. Keeps overheating. One of the guys at school says it's either the radiator or the thermostat."

Jesus. "We'll let Hector put in a new thermostat."

If life is so short, why do we spend it doing the same things over and over?

"Why can't your mother give you a ride?"

"She's busy. Going to Palm Springs with Otto."

"It's almost on the way, for Christ's sake."

"They got a tee time on Fuzzy Zoeller's new course, or something like that. Mom said you wouldn't want to do it. She said you'd be selfish about it. She sure knows your ass."

"Fuzzy's too, probably."

"Hey, they're just friends."

"What time do you have to be at work?" I was resigned.

"Forty minutes, dad. I'm running late."

Didn't even have time to put on socks. I threw on a pair of jeans and flip-flops and hurried out to the Seville. Holding down a part-time job was a condition of my son's probation. Naturally he couldn't pick a weekend occupation that was convenient for me. He had to work at a surf shop. And he had to work at a surf shop in Encinitas, thirty miles north, because all of the shops in town were too conservative for his rarefied tastes. Only a shop within trudging distance of Moonlight Beach would do.

I suspected him of using the job as a cover for inhaling epoxy and thinners. After a day of repairing and repainting boards, he would exit work giggling and red-eyed.

I picked him up at my former home. My ex was just departing. She and Otto were dressed in matching magenta golf outfits.

"Thanks so much," she said, swinging herself into the passenger seat of Otto's Infiniti. Otto waved at me distractedly. No doubt his mind was really on his backswing.

"Though it's really your fault he's stranded, for buying him that heap in the first place."

I don't get much unalloyed gratitude, I notice, as I get older, not from my family or anyone else.

"I'll have Hector take a look at it."

"Why don't you just buy him a new Nissan?" My ex wanted to give me a chance to bond with Otto. He had a dealership.

"Not this week."

"I heard you were having problems." She eyed me suspiciously. Wondering if the support was going to stop flowing.

I chose to let her wonder.

"Besides, I prefer American makes. Give my regards to Fuzzy."

"You know him?" My ex-wife frowned.

"Used to have a half-interest in a massage parlor I defended."

"Oh, my Lord." She looked at Otto askance. His connection with the famous names of golf was suddenly as ashes.

"Well, I knew Speed didn't know him from *golfing*," she said.

That had to be true. My schizophrenic upbringing manifests itself in my unfamiliarity with any sports other than team ones. I ran track and played hoops. We didn't swing golf clubs or tennis racquets in East LA.

"Know how he got the nickname Fuzzy?" I offered.

"I really don't care," she said frostily.

Otto was in for a long day.

My son came hopping out of the house when the Infiniti rolled away.

"What, trying to *blend in?*" he sneered, pointing at my feet.

He wore flip-flops too, but there was no doubt something about his that made them palpably more stylish than mine. He matched them with baggy shorts in a dense, chaotic print that seemed deliberately contrived to be as ugly as possible, and a tank top inscribed "Pipeline."

"Is that a tattoo?" I said, spotting an inky blur on his shoulder blade that was poorly concealed by the strap of the tank top.

"Yeah. Fuckin' rad, isn't it?"

"You have to be eighteen to get a tattoo."

"Will be in a month. Mom gave me permission. It's a tribal."

"What tribe do you belong to?"

"Get up on it, Dad. Tribal means it's a pattern, not a drawing. Not something crippled, like a heart with an arrow through it."

"Crippled?"

"Crippled. As in, beyond lame."

"Maybe I'll put in a call to the City Attorney."

Danny Akami would be surprised to find me on his side.

"Tattooing minors is a misdemeanor."

"I told you, I had Mom's permission."

"You need both parents. In cases of joint custody. Which is what yours is."

"Not what the tattoo guy told me."

"I'm a lawyer. He's a tattoo guy. Take my word for it."

"Hey, you're his lawyer, too. Says you got him off tattooing a minor once. He liked you a lot."

"Doesn't mean I like him."

Maybe some day Marvin Maeger would be a big fan of mine, too. Hell of a cheerleading section I was cultivating.

"I told him how you really were, man."

While we were arguing I had exited the westbound freeway and soared up the interchange north. Traffic was sparse and moving fast.

"What do you hip surf dudes think of guys like Big Daddy O'Toole?"

He cringed. "Don't talk like that. You have no idea how crippled you sound."

"Just answer the question."

"He's a *longboard guy*," he said with loathing, as if he was describing a species so alien to normal humankind that their right to life was barely tenable.

"They're bad?"

"They're roach food."

"Worm food," I corrected him.

"So I heard. Well, he was old."

"Ever listen to his music?"

"You're not going to, like, put it on the stereo?"

"No. Don't have any of his greatest hits."

"Thank God."

"I think I have something by the Butthole Surfers."

"Just put on the radio. They're nearly as crippled as Big Daddy."

The shop was called the Surf Shaq. A life-size, which is to say large, caricature of the basketball player was painted on the outside of the cinderblock wall. Other than that the place was decorated with the usual pictures of tiny surfers mastering huge blue swells. The relationship of the establishment with the sports star was not obvious from the decorating scheme.

"Let me off at the corner," my son said. "I don't want anyone to see me getting out of this car."

I did as he asked, as glad to be rid of his company as he was of mine. I doubted the basketball player had licensed out his image to the Surf Shaq. Possible grounds for legal action there, if he cared. If not, plenty of other businesses could use the publicity boost. Like Marvin's.

The Waq Shaq. Now, that had style. It was modern, both because it was misspelled and because it gave customers a false sense of identification with a celebrity who didn't even know they were alive. Marvin's customers could relax in the afterglow of their efforts, knowing that they were contributing not only to the tissue, but also to the hoops millionaire.

Other idle, that is to say non-legal, thoughts drifted through my consciousness as I pointed the car south. It was Saturday. I was entitled to give the law a rest. My son had not asked to be picked up; whether this constituted evidence of other arrangements or was just an oversight on his part was irrelevant to me. I wasn't about to volunteer.

The phone buzzed just as I hit the interstate split, south of Del Mar.

"Speed?"

"Who else, Izzy?"

"You want to come to the office? I got something for you."

The picture was of a boat called *Baby Blue*.

"One of his songs," Izzy explained. "Top Ten, I think."

"I expected a bigger boat." I didn't expect it to be a sailboat, either, but it was, maybe twenty, twenty-two feet long. It made Angel's story more plausible, though. The engine on a sailboat would be relatively small and attached almost as an afterthought. Easy to sabotage.

"Where did you get the picture?"

"Only a couple companies do small craft insurance. I lucked out. First one I called had the file. See the surfboard?"

I did. Painted a glowing yellow, with *Big Daddy* printed on it in letters big enough to read in the Polaroid. It was attached to the side of the cabin in a cradle arrangement, to hold it fast not matter how much the boat bowed to the wind. Even a non-surfer like myself could see it was a longboard. It was half the length of the boat.

I found I was holding my breath. I didn't realize how important the truth of Angel's story was becoming to me, until that moment. If I cared to think about it, it was clear it was important to me that, in my first homicide case since Willie Washington's, my client be innocent. Desperately important. A matter of redemption.

I forced myself to ask. "Is the surfboard still on it?"

"We don't know."

"Why don't we?"

"Because it's still at the bottom of the ocean, like you said. As you noticed, it's not that big of a boat. Probably not worth salvaging, from the insurance company's point of view, even though it's lying in only about thirty feet of water. Right off the kelp beds. You want to go see?"

The yacht club was humming with Saturday trade, mostly at the bar. About every slip in five was empty, as weekend sailors took their craft out to ply the bay and the near ocean waters. The one Izzy led me to looked empty, too, from the dock, but when we got to the edge I could see six feet beneath us an outrigger canoe, tarped over against the weather. Izzy clambered down the ladder and made the canoe ready to sail. He put a waterproof bag between the two slats that served as our seats and we pushed off.

"Paddle much?"

"Never before."

"Doctor tells me I have to get some exercise, so I bought this. Nothing looks funnier than a fat man jogging, don't you think? The yacht club lets me keep it at a free slip. Professional courtesy."

"How far do we have to go?"

"Couple miles. Put your back into it. The tide is slack right now. It starts coming up, it's going to get that much harder."

My back already felt like it was dissolving. Izzy paddled in big, productive strokes. The canoe shot into the main channel.

"We could've hired a boat."

"I need to do this anyway. And if we don't find anything, we can keep it to ourselves."

"And if we do find something?"

"Probably best to keep that to ourselves, too." He glanced back at me. "Snowball's chance you'll be doing that, I guess."

"Why are you helping me, Iz? You're the one that warned me about the heat on this case."

He shrugged. "Can't tell you one reason, really. Good to see you back in real law, for one."

"For two?"

"You have a client who might be innocent. That'd be a thrill for me. I'm living vicariously through you. Aren't you getting winded yet?"

"Some." I was breathing deeply.

" 'Some' means you're not paddling hard enough. Put some arm into it. Being on the ocean in a boat like this is serious business."

I paddled. The water of the bay streamed by, twelve inches below my elbows as I dipped and stroked. This close to the water the connection with it was almost intimate. I popped the rainbows of little oil slicks with my paddle. I saw the flash of mackerel beneath us, chasing anchovies that broke the surface ahead of the canoe, panicky to escape the mackerel maws. Seals squatted drowsing on the harbor buoys. The wind blew cool from the ocean, but my back in its lee was damp with sweat.

When we rounded the point and entered the ocean proper the change was profound. The water blued out as we got deeper. I could see ten or fifteen feet down the strands of giant kelp.

"We can't get into this stuff too thick," Izzy ordered. "Paddle around."

"Okay. But tell me now, how are we going to find one spot on the open ocean?"

Izzy reached into the waterproof bag and produced a hand-held Loran.

"Never go out without it. This isn't Hawaii, my friend. They have fog here. The coordinates are on the insurance report."

The sea was flat; a few brave water-skiers had ventured out of the bay to slice across the sluggish Pacific itself. Izzy propped the navigational device in the prow of the outrigger and ordered me to paddle right, left or stop according to the changing numbers on its face. The rock of the point shrank from a cliff face we paddled beneath to an outcrop at our stern. "About here," said Izzy finally. He grasped an anchor, a cinderblock tied to a piece of rope, and frowned at the depths.

The direction of the current was apparent by the way it bowed the stalks of the kelp. Izzy ordered a few more strokes of the paddle then threw the cinderblock overboard. He made the rope tight against one of the forward slats. From the bag he took a mask, fins and an underwater camera and light.

"You're going to free-dive it?" I asked, astonished. "No wetsuit?"

"Can't stand to breathe through a tube. Never could. And they don't make wet suits in my size, at least not off the rack. I've got my own insulation." He slapped his hands against the blubber of his sides. "Keep an eye out for anything big. We're right on the outskirts of the shipping lanes. That was one of the theories the cops put forth about how Big Daddy drowned himself, that his boat was swamped by the bow wave from a carrier or a big tanker."

I glanced at the horizon nervously. The only vessel of any size was a rusty freighter laboring to the south. The rest of the traffic consisted of cabin cruisers and Saturday sailors in search of a breeze.

Izzy slipped under the water without much of a splash, considering his size. He guided himself down by the rope of the anchor. He stayed under until my lungs would have been bursting. He surfaced by the stern of the outrigger, surprising me.

"Move up front and pull the anchor," he said. He hauled himself over the stern and paddled quickly out and north about twenty yards. "Try again. Thought I caught a glimpse of it."

He was under even longer the second time, so long I was beginning to entertain visions of kelp grasping at his bulk, trapping him underwater. He didn't bother to re-enter the canoe when he surfaced.

"Underneath the tarp," he gasped. "Another cinderblock. Don't hand it to me yet," he said, shifting the light and camera to hang from his neck. "Now."

He sank quickly into the purple of the deep water. A few sea birds investigated me and decided I was not a promising food source. The rusty freighter began a slow eastward turn toward harbor. Izzy popped up like a breaching walrus.

"Got it," he said. "Help me back in."

He covered himself with a sweatshirt and threw a towel over his legs, but he was still shivering. He raised the anchor and then untied the cinderblock, tossing it into the ocean to join the one he had used for ballast.

"No sense hauling them back in," he said. "Come on. I've got to row off this chill."

We dipped paddles again, this time pulling for the harbor.

"There's no surfboard on that boat," said Izzy. "I'm sure there's not. It's lying starboard side up, which is the side it was attached to. I could see the cradle clearly. But the board is gone. I'm pretty sure I've got a good picture of it, but no matter. You can have the boat raised. Insurance company will claim it once it's floating again, so you can send them at least part of the bill."

"How do we know it was on there to begin with?"

"It always was. Big Daddy never surfed the beach. Claimed the experience wasn't pure enough for him. Said he used to sail to San Clemente Island, where he alone knew a break that always produced perfect sets. Where he could surf with only the company of the ocean. It was all bullshit, of course. The skinny was that Big Daddy couldn't surf at all. Sang a surfing song and got stuck with the image. The board was just camouflage."

"How do you know this? Were you a fan?"

"Do I sound like one? My people invented surfing. Do you think we need some millionaire *haole* to sing to us about it? I surf, that's all. The local boys all respect a *kanaka maoli*, so I hear things. Hey, what's that guy doing?"

I looked behind me. The rusty freighter had belched out a black cloud from its funnel. The distance between us had shrunk out of all proportion to the time that had passed. "He's turning it up."

"Can't wait to be on the beach. Miller time for the old rummy that's piloting it, I expect. Steer back towards the kelp. He won't want to run through that."

We paddled. The marine breeze was to the stern now. The sweat evaporated cold off my back. Rivulets of seawater ran from Izzy's hair and soaked into his sweatshirt. Beneath us I noticed only clear water. Izzy glanced back. "Shit," he said, and dug harder.

"Where's the kelp?" I asked.

"In back of us. The tide is carrying us straight toward the harbor mouth. We're going to have to paddle across in front of him. Don't look behind you."

I did, immediately, and saw only a wall of rust. "Pull!" Izzy ordered, and I did. Minutes of hauling at the paddles passed. I expected momentarily to see the freighter's bow in my peripheral vision and hear the crunch as it bit the outrigger in half. Izzy only glanced back once.

"Hold your paddle right!" he yelled, and paddled right himself. The outrigger swung about and we caught the freighter's bow wave. Safely, on the starboard side of it. It dropped us within a hundred yards of the harbor entrance.

"Shit," Izzy said. "I thought I was going to go down in my canoe while I was still breathing."

"You got plans for it when you stop?" The muscles in my arms were as cramped as the back seat of the Hyundai.

"When I go, I plan to go in this. Hawaiian funeral. Have my pallbearers row it out to sea. Cast my ashes overboard. Though the way my friends paddle, I'll be lucky to make it out of the inlet."

"I'm a track star, not a weightlifter. Didn't know you had all your plans made, for when you cash in your chips."

"It's all on paper. I'm a lawyer, for Christ's sake. I wouldn't have a will?"

I kept my mouth shut, because I don't.

"Actually, I'm planning on a combination Viking-Hawaiian funeral. Don't just sprinkle my ashes over the ocean. Leave them in the canoe, and set the whole thing on fire. Put my weapons by my side. Let my friends put any possessions that remind them of me or they'll not be needing any more in the hull, and send me off to Valhalla. They need a good Hawaiian there, I expect. And I'll do. Won't be the first time for me. They needed a Hawaiian at UC Berkeley, so off I went."

"Why didn't you ever go back to the islands?"

"Always meant to. But you know how it goes. Got married here, had a kid here, got a divorce here. Got a booming practice here. Now it's too late to start over again. Lucky if I get to spend two weeks a year in Hawaii, holed up in a Waikiki hotel like a fucking tourist instead of a *kanak*."

"Always retirement, Iz."

"Doctor says I'll never live to see it. The white man's food and drink is no good for my Hawaiian heart. You think *I* can make an outrigger move? My people paddled all over the ocean. We were blown off course and sank in storms and when we survived we ate seaweed, poi and dog. Do that for a thousand years, you really build up an appetite for cheeseburgers."

I thought of Vampire Eddie prowling the morgue. "Get a transplant."

"Could never live with a *haole* heart, Speed. I paddle my canoe and I surf when I can, but I spend too much time sitting in front of a computer screen and going to lunch. I have kept too much of the white man's world, too close to my heart."

He slapped his chest for emphasis.

"Sorry, Izzy."

"Not your fault, Speed. Mine, for listening to my teachers tell me 'You one smart Hawaiian boy. Get off the rock Go to Punahou, go to USC, go to Berkeley. Make something of yourself in the big world.' And you're all right, Speed. I would live with your heart, if I had to. If you didn't need it any more."

"Thanks, Izzy. I guess. Could've had it for half price, a minute ago."

"Your little murder suspect was lucky she didn't get cut in half herself by the *Nimitz* while she was making her way back to shore. Ship traffic depends on the tides, not the time."

"I still find it hard to believe she paddled all the way back."

"Why not? We just did. And a board is easier to move than a canoe."

"What if she slipped off? Or got caught by a wave?"

"She either finds the board again, or dies. Fear of taking a risk wasn't a problem for her, according to you."

I looked at the piled stone of the harbor entrance. "Where would she land?"

"Current runs south. Would give her a boost right past these rocks, onto the beach at Coronado or the Silver Strand. She's wearing a wet suit, she's just another surfer on Dawn Patrol. Her biggest problem is ditching the board."

We were in the quiet water of the harbor.

"We're going to have to shoot across the entrance again. Eyes left. Some fucking guided missile cruiser comes steaming in, it's not going to stop for us any more than that freighter did."

The rising tide bore us kitty corner across the bay, so that we only had to paddle a half mile or so to reach the yacht club. By the time I pulled myself up the ladder to the surface of the dock, I was shaking from fatigue. Even though I was on land, my inner ear still swam in the rhythms of the waves. I staggered up the ramp.

"Speed! You look like hell."

Jill Congliaro looked magnificent, in a gold sheath dress, made up to slay, with every hair of her head disciplined into place. She held a flute of champagne in one hand while with the other she held fast to a man of about fifty for whom the word dapper was coined to describe. "Have you been drinking again? And Izzy, what a surprise. Didn't know you were a member. This is Dr. Verlace."

Izzy waved a greeting.

"Not guilty to the drinking charge," I said. "Just a long afternoon's work."

"Well, you'd better get started." She snagged champagne off a passing tray and handed one each to me and Izzy.

"I don't think we really should," the doctor said, but Jill dismissed his objections with a wave. "Go find us some food, sugarbun. Can't be drinking on an empty stomach. God knows whose arms I'll end up in if I do."

The doctor scurried off in search of the canapés, clearly serious about not giving Jill any excuse for wantonness.

"He probably thinks you're two of the maintenance men," Jill explained. "He's such a befuddled dear, sometimes. You are a little underdressed. Did you have the impression it was going to be a beach party?"

"Here on unrelated business," I said.

Izzy was silent. It was my case. Up to me how much of it to reveal to the Public Defender's office. The way I had been getting my ass kicked lately, I figured, not a syllable.

"Clam-digging, huh?" She laughed again, then she leaned in confidentially. "You wouldn't mention the other night in front of the doctor, would you?"

"Naturally not."

"I knew you were a gentleman."

Maybe so, but jealousy prodded at me anyway. "The doctor, he's a long term prospect?"

"Absolutely."

"So tonight, you plan…"

"Not to be spontaneous."

I felt relieved to know that Doctor Verlace would not be following so quickly in my wake, then I felt angry with myself for investing emotion of any kind in Jill Congliaro.

"You catch on so quickly."

"What kind of doctor is he?"

"Plastic surgery, the lamb. Perfect. Elective only. None of those nasty emergency calls in the middle of the night."

"Sounds like the ideal mate. Marriage?"

"He already is. I don't mind. I like them to stay busy. If I decide he needs to get a divorce, paying for it will keep him even busier. Is this all you could find?" she demanded of the doctor, who had returned with a plate of nachos. "I saw smoked duck when we came in."

"They were re-stocking the buffet. I'll go again in a minute," the doctor pleaded.

"So how did the rest of the working week go for you?"

I let Izzy answer first.

"Same old. Dope dealers, my bread and butter. Walked one, got another off with two to four when he was looking at career status. Oh, and I'm under threat of death by a crazed transvestite."

"How's Desiree?" I asked.

The Ethics Committee hearing was in six days. I might have to squeeze in another date if she would have me.

"Miserable. Been hell all week on the staff. Caught a cold from being stranded in the rain so she's hacking and blowing her nose every two minutes. Doesn't make it any more pleasant when she's bitching you out. How about you? Any progress on the Pisaro case?"

"I'm still working on mental," I lied. "Too bad you're not a psychiatrist," I added to Dr. Verlace. "And I had a nice chin wag with Frank Manus."

"Manus!" Dr. Verlace said unexpectedly. "There's a guy that needs a psychiatrist."

"You know him?" Manus hadn't looked to me like he'd had a facelift.

"Did the augmentation for his little girlfriend. In a hospital setting," he said distastefully. "Wouldn't trust me in my own office. Hyper-controlling lunatic, if you want my opinion on him. I've had my hands on more tits than George Clooney," he boasted. "What, I was going to lose a patient? It's basically a simple procedure. Didn't need an anesthesiologist and a frigging pathologist, for Christ's sake, standing by while I did her boobies. Did he think she was going to go septic on me?"

"Lambchop, must we have all this *boob* talk?"

"He paid for everything, of course. That's one thing he's got no problem doing."

"You know I hate it when you talk shop. It's far too gristly for me. Be your charming self. Do you think they've put out the smoked duck yet?"

"I'll check."

He leaned over and pecked Jill on the cheek, then went briskly to once again survey the buffet.

"You look like you've got him trained pretty well." I observed.

"He's a doctor, not a lawyer, so he's not the argumentative type."

"I notice he's a white male."

"It's rare that I find a non-Caucasian that really shares my recreational tastes. No offense, Mr. Kahauolopua. The lesbian option is not for me. It's politically unfortunate, but there you have it. Much as I am aware of the edge white males unfairly enjoy in the society they have built with violence and stealth, I find myself inevitably in their company."

It was hard to feel sorry for her, as she sipped Moët from the flute. "It's sit-down time," the doctor announced on his return.

"Oh, dear. I suppose you two really can't crash dinner dressed like that."

"What's the occasion?"

"Some real estate thing. They're condemning a block by the airport to put up a parking structure. Nice party on behalf of a parking lot, huh? But somebody's going to get cured doing it, so they're celebrating. White males at work and play. Although I partake, I do retain detachment enough to be amused."

By virtue of arriving while the sun was high, we had one of the prime parking spaces in the yacht club's lot. As I pulled out, Frank Manus arrived, in the rear of a Town Car. Mrs. Ambergast was his escort. Probably feeling too puny from his operation to squire a friskier female. Our eyes met, and he glared at me. He followed it up with a scowl at Izzy.

"I think you just made an enemy."

"Not the first time. He had a problem once with a fatality on his workman's comp. Was using his building landscaper to work at his home. Some poor Joe got killed, and the insurance company's position was it didn't have to pay the claim. We won. But Frank and I made up later on. I got him off on an environmental beef. Had some valley land that the EPA wanted for the California Least Tern. Filed his statement after he'd started driving piles into it for a shopping center. The EPA held hearings and found that the least tern wasn't likely to resume nesting at the site, since it was now the jewelry counter at Neiman Marcus. We settled by donating a half-acre of fill dirt out by the mall's exhaust fans as a nesting spot for the least tern. Don't know if any of them ever settled there. Do know that if they did, every time they turn up the air-conditioning at the Broadway, those fans blow 'em right into the bulrushes."

It was only a half-mile to Izzy's office. I followed him upstairs.

"How does Evie get the surfboard off the beach?"

"What, you want co-counsel on this?"

"Witness. Who else is going to testify that the board is missing?"

"Salvager. When you have the boat raised. But I doubt it's enough that it's missing. Yeah, you want to introduce. But the prosecution is going to point out that it's a big ocean. None bigger, they might want to mention. There's the possibility it became detached when the boat sank, and drifted off."

"I thought you said it was unlikely."

"It is. Like I said, the surfboard would have come to shore, or been spotted from the air, although remember that nobody was looking for Big Daddy too hard. If it happened the way we think it did, though, Evie's biggest problem was getting rid of the board. It's dawn. You've had a hell of a night, killing a guy by sinking his boat at sea and then hand-paddling your way in from the ocean deep. You've gotten clean away with it, except you're carrying a bright yellow surfboard with your victim's name emblazoned on it in letters big enough to read from Palomar. What do you do?"

"I don't know, Iz. I don't surf. I murder somebody at sea, it's going to a personal first, too."

"First thing, you got to get off the beach. Chances are, you didn't park your car too close to where the tide brought you in. You unzip your wet suit so you're showing a bit of cleavage and stick your thumb out in front of a passing truck. You pick your ride carefully. Locals in a surf wagon would recognize Big Daddy's board. Maybe some illegals in a pickup. People who wouldn't know Big Daddy from Vladimir Putin.

"You're off the sand, so you've solved problem number one. But you've still got the board, and you don't want it lying around, just in case they mount an energetic investigation of Big Daddy going overboard. You can take it home, break it up into pieces with a hammer, bag it in Heftys and throw it away. That's a lot of work, a lot of noise and a lot of fiberglass dust blowing around, so it's not something you want to do in the den. These girls, did they have a garage?"

I shook my head negatively.

"You're a pretty little stripper, you want something physical done, what do you do?"

"Get a man to do it for you."

"Yeah. Trouble is, it would have to be a pretty dim man. People buy and sell used surfboards all the time. You get a new board, you want it painted your own colors. Lot of surf shops survive on just refinishing boards. But Big Daddy's longboard was unique. Almost anyone would recognize it. When he turned up dead, they'd remember who'd brought it in. It'd be a problem. You sure it wasn't anywhere in their household possessions?"

"If it was, the cops ignored it."

"Not beyond them. But not likely. They have a yard?"

"No."

"I'd've buried it if I was her. Look for a fresh surfboard grave. Bet there's one somewhere between the Silver Strand and Evie's home."

"That's just about hopeless."

"Yeah. You ready to rinse that nasty champagne taste out of your mouth?" Izzy plucked the vodka out of the freezer.

While I sipped, I checked out Izzy's pictures of an idyllic Oahu. A brown-skinned clan on a sun-bleached beach underneath Makena Point. Kailua Town. Chinaman's Hat. One picture was not of palms swaying. It was a desiccated corpse lying in an ice field.

"Nice contrast on this one, Iz. Did you get the guy off who did this?"

"That one happened five thousand years ago, so even if the statute of limitations hasn't expired, the perpetrator surely has. That's the Iceman.

Found him years ago in the Tyrolean Alps during a drought. The layer of snow he was buried in hadn't seen daylight in five thousand years."

"What's he doing on your wall?"

"To remind me not to end up like him."

"Going to be another Ice Age before it snows that much here."

"Figuratively. To remind me not to get so close to the edge. Here's a guy, leaving his Neolithic village in the fall. Who knows what for? Maybe his people needed some medicine, or some juju powder, from the people on the other side of the ridge. It's a long hike, and the weather's closing in, but he figures he can make it. He pushes his luck just a hair too far, and nobody sees him again for five thousand years."

"What's it have to do with you?"

"I already live too far from my home. It's a male thing. Women will always be at the center of life. They are when they are children. When they grow up they have children, and when they are old they are the center of attraction for their children's children."

"Not always." I was thinking of Gail Fortenwood.

"Generally. It's a position that's theirs to lose. But a man is always tempted by the outside of the circle. Fine to walk along that ridge, but beware the avalanche. And don't be surprised if no one comes after you when you're missing. For example, Big Daddy."

"Yeah, but he was a miserable, middle-aged phony."

"People who have lived who were too good to die. There's a short fucking list." Izzy slopped some more vodka into or tumblers. "I don't see your Angel getting bail set on the strength of what we've got now. You need that surfboard."

"You just said it was hopeless."

"Couldn't be that many places she could conceal it, between the beach and her house. Or maybe she did get someone to take it and repaint it. It would have to be someone completely clueless. Someone who didn't even know, or care, if Big Daddy was dead or alive."

It came to me just as the vodka had completed its comforting invasion clear out to my extremities.

"I know someone just like that," I said. "Mind if I take that picture with me?"

Chapter Eleven

I was already awake and had a cup of coffee in me when my son called on Sunday morning.

"They have no guts, no hearts and their mouths are interchangeable with their assholes," I replied, in answer to his question, which was why surgeons found it easy to operate on lawyers.

"What, are you looking these things up on me?"

"You want something?"

"A ride, man. Your buddy Hector says it's not the thermostat. Says the car needs a new radiator."

Déjà vu in the auto repair sector.

"Your mother can't give you one? A ride, not a radiator."

"She and Otto must've stayed out in Palm Springs."

Get those off-season hotel rates. It was still hitting a hundred and ten every day in the Coachella Valley, but my ex could never resist a bargain.

"Twenty minutes," I said.

"Can you make it ten, man? They get all browned off if I'm late."

Before I could make it out the door, the phone rang again. It was her.

"Can you give our boy a lift?" she asked without preamble.

"Already set up."

"Thanks. Otto and I spent a little too much time at the nineteenth hole to drive back last night. And Palm Springs is quite reasonable before Christmas."

"How come the hell you told him he could get a tattoo?"

"I didn't," she said, in the injured tone that only the chronically guilty can affect when they are, for once, unjustly accused. A criminal lawyer is familiar with that tone. She sounded just like Marvin Maeger when the subject of sperm on his floor was brought up. "He's got a fake ID. How do you think he gets the cigarettes?"

"Why don't you rip it up?"

"Then I'd have to buy them for him. I couldn't do that. I'd feel guilty."

Pure ex-wife logic. There was no refuting it. I put on shoes and socks, since the flip-flops had been such a fashion foul the day before, and found my son waiting on the curb.

"When someone buys a used surfboard, do they usually have it refinished?"

"Is this about Christmas? Are you trying to cheap out on me? I got all the surfboards I need, man."

"Just answer."

"Sure, man. You don't want to ride on someone else's design."

"And if the board is hot, or of other questionable origin?"

"Then you gotta get it done."

"How much of that do you do? Up where you work?"

He shifted in his seat uncomfortably. "Hey, they're just boards, man. They don't have titles, or nothin'. Somebody comes in with a board and wants it re-done, we figure it's theirs."

"Refinished any longboards this year?"

"A course, man. We do them all the time. Where we going?"

I pulled onto the tarmac at Hector's and handed my son the keys to the LeSabre. "Drive yourself," I said. "It's over there."

"You got to be kidding."

"Perfect beach car."

"What about school, man? I can't drive this thing there."

"That's tomorrow's problem. I'll follow you up the freeway."

"You better, man. Doubt this heap is going to make it."

The LeSabre started right up. My son looked disappointed.

The solitary ride on a Sunday morning was soothing. My son pushed the LeSabre up the highway at about eighty-five, on the forward edge of the traffic flow, but the Seville kept up easily. The ocean appeared on the left when we hit Del Mar. The racetrack had just closed for the season. On Batiquitos Lagoon, a few jet-skiers made use of the still waters and the early autumn sunshine.

My son exited in Leucadia, turned right, and then doubled back to reach the Pacific Coast Highway. Probably trying to lose me. Moonlight Beach had surf in the one- to two-foot range. Longboard waves, if my secondhand knowledge of the sport was accurate. A few wave riders sat idle on one of the breaks, hoping for better swells. I counted four other surf shops, apart from the Surf Shaq, in the commercial clutter of downtown. I would be paying them a visit, if my interview at the Shaq was fruitless.

"You're not coming in here, are you, man?" The tone in my son's voice was near panic.

"I need to talk to your boss."

"What for? This is work, man, not school."

"That him on the phone?"

"Don't be hassling him, man. What other kind of job do you expect me to get?"

The man behind the counter hung up the phone. He looked like an older version of my son. Same stringy hair, same perpetual sneer.

"Yeah?" he said to me, not bothering to veneer his greeting with anything approaching courtesy.

"I'm looking for a surfboard."

"Yeah? Well, look away."

"This is a particular surfboard."

"You a suit?"

"What do you mean?"

"Cop. Building inspector. Landlord. A suit."

"I'm a lawyer."

He shot a satisfied smile at my son.

"See? I told you I can tell a suit. Even when they're not wearing a suit. What kind of advice you got for me, Mr. Attorney?"

"Offhand, I'd say repaint your exterior wall. Or else change the name of the place. You can call the place the Surf Shaq, or you can have a picture of Shaquille O'Neil on the outside, but you can't do both. Not without Mr. O'Neil's permission. That's good legal advice, at no charge. Now, you seen this surfboard?" I had the picture in my hand.

He looked across at my son again. This time he looked like he wanted to cuff him.

"I told you you should've left that board alone."

"So you have seen it?"

"Hey, man, she said he gave it to her."

"Guess she made his dick as hard as she made yours. Maybe she just fucking swiped it, though, since lawyers are coming around looking for it. Who is this guy, anyway? I saw him follow you in."

"He's my dad," my son mumbled, his voice hollow with humiliation.

"Even better that you should deal with him, then. Talk to your kid," the owner said. "It was all his doing."

"I'm going to need to talk to both of you. It was a girl that dropped off this board? When?"

"Fucking weeks ago. I told him she'd never be back."

"She leave a name, or an address?"

"No. The paperwork was pretty minimal on it. There wasn't any. Whole thing happened when I was out of the store. Came back. Board was here. She was gone. Your boy had stains on his shorts, and the look of love on his face."

My son looked paralyzed by discomfiture. The owner was still talking.

"She left a design she wanted on the board. Said she'd be back in a week. No deposit. I still let him sand off the top of the board, on my time. Thought he was going to die of a broken heart if I didn't."

"Hey, man, she took my cell number." My son tried to rise to his own defense.

"And has she ever used it?"

"So the board," I interrupted, "it's still here?"

"Naw. Sold it as it was. Maybe two weeks ago. Some old lady. Said her grandson's hobby was refinishing surfboards. Actually asked if I needed any more help around here. I didn't then." He looked at my son balefully. "She wanted one I could make her a deal on. That piece of shit came right to mind."

"Did you know the original owner of the board was dead at that point?"

"Naw. Don't read the papers much."

"He was a surfer."

"Not on Moonlight. Didn't know him."

He would have me believe that since Big Daddy moved outside of his perceived circle, the tiny world of the ultra-hip, his death would be unremarked upon in the Surf Shaq. I chose not to believe.

"Could be trouble for you, helping dispose of evidence in an unnatural death."

"Hey, man, he drowned. Happens all the time."

I said nothing. I just gave him the what-have-we-here look I'd seen cops use on suspects. He shut his mouth with a grimace.

Having the board in my hands would have been too easy.

"Your cooperation at this point is essential. To avoid any legal problems yourselves. Got a phone book?"

He threw one at me. I didn't bother to ask to use the Surf Shaq's phone;

I just picked up the receiver and dialed. Four calls later I had a magistrate that was willing to come out and do a deposition on a Sunday morning. I didn't want to issue a subpoena for a bail hearing. I had a pretty solid hunch it would be tough enough to get the owner to show up for trial.

I drove back south and east. Traffic was starting to pick up, as people strove to obey the primal urge of the Californian on a weekend, which was to be someplace other than the place they woke up. Fishing boats on trailers were towed towards the bay, while quadrunners lashed in the back of pickup trucks were bound for the desert. Having already satisfied my need for travel, I went home and watched the local football mercenaries get pretty well roughed up by the Broncos. The cat sat in my lap. After all the ugliness between us, he still expected to have his ears scratched.

In the morning I filed a motion for a new bail hearing. I attached the depositions from the Surf Shaq. The new court calendars were posted for the week. I noticed my preliminary for Marvin Maeger and Raquel Bumgarden was scheduled for Tuesday in Barry Appenzeller's court. I quickly scribbled a request for the new bail hearing to be scheduled for then as well, hoping Barry would think well of me for using his remaining time efficiently.

Judge Rheinhart's name was posted. He must have cut his vacation short. Again in longhand, I filed a request for a hearing on the restraining order. Schuckelgruber might not know that the judge was back in chambers. I might catch him unaware with a served notice.

Everything was clicking. I thought about idling in the courthouse lobby, hoping to run into someone I'd like to see, like Schuckelgruber or Jill Congliaro. Then I thought of all the people who might be milling between the fake marble of the walls that I'd rather not meet, like Desiree Mason or Jimmy Donnelley, so I guided the Seville over to my temporary quarters at Izzy's.

I don't know why I decided to take the steps. Maybe it was because my arms still ached from paddling Izzy's outrigger, a steady pain that reminded me of how out of shape I was getting to be. Ten floors of walking up wouldn't hurt me. The fire escape was a skeleton of a staircase made of painted black metal. The walls were bare concrete. I heard the clatter of someone else coming down. Another exercise buff, I assumed, running the stairs instead of having a Danish at coffee break. She passed me on the fifth floor landing, a black woman with boxy shoulders. As I turned the corner at the next landing, I saw a green scarf lying on the steps. She must've dropped it.

"Hey," I called after her, but she was making time. I felt an interior scorn; anybody can run *down*stairs. Then I noticed her shedding her vest.

I ran the remaining four flights up without regard for my buckling knees or my thumping heart. There I found the scene I feared; a corridor full of shocked and weeping people in front of 1001, a few collapsed against the walls and floor, racked with crying or nausea. Take-charge types were screaming loud and contradictory advice at each other.

"Don't touch anything!"

"Give him CPR!"

"Anybody call the cops yet?"

"Anybody know CPR?"

"Give him air!"

But Izzy had no further use for air. No blood ran from him, although he was soaked with it. His heart had ceased to pump. There were bullet holes in his head, his neck and his torso. Nine of them, I guessed, from the empty ammunition clip on the floor. Izzy would have presented a tough target to miss. His hands and forearms sagged at his sides, mere stumps, shattered by the shells passing through them to do their fatal damage. Defensive wounds. The expression on his face was peaceful, and I hoped it was because his dying eyes had seen the light they say awaits us all, but I noticed that his dead pupils were locked not upon the pictures of paradise, but on the photo of the Iceman.

"We're gonna get him," Pennofrio said, speaking of Double Delicious Didi.

"Frank Manus did this," I said.

"Fucking three-time loser transvestite did this."

"He should've been in jail."

"Thanks to your dead buddy, he wasn't."

"Not so, Sergeant. He was literally supposed to be in jail. He had a contempt-of-court sentence that had not been served. A judge had to dismiss the remainder of that sentence. A Judge Rheinhart would be my guess. Look it up."

"You look it up, Counselor. I got a corpse. I got a suspect dead to rights. Witnesses, of which you're one. Lucky for you he emptied the whole clip at your buddy, otherwise you'd've never made it up that stairwell. I got a mop-up murder here, is what I got."

"A judge, who's supposed to be gone for two weeks, shows up at the courthouse and releases a prisoner with a stated vendetta against the deceased, and you're not even going to investigate?"

"Lil' ol' homicide cops like me don't investigate judges. We don't have enough juice. Call the FBI."

"Want to bet Rheinhart's back on vacation? And he'll stay that way, until he finds out you've collared Didi? He's on his hit list, too."

"Don't you find it ironic that you, as a member of the defense bar, are upset with me, a dedicated civil servant, because some puff-brained judge let a he-she gunslinger loose here in Dodge City, a legal action you would ordinarily applaud?"

"My best friend is dead."

"And wasn't he, even more than you, dedicated to the summary release of every form of scum that we skimmed out of the municipal pond?"

"It was his job. His part to uphold, in the machinery of justice."

"Irony, irony, irony."

I shoved Pennofrio with the flat of my hand, in the shoulder. "Don't just stand there chanting at me like some kind of plainclothes Hare Krishna! He was a human being!"

Pennofrio frowned and brushed at his shoulder, as if an insect had alighted there.

"Yeah, he was a human being," he admitted. "Trouble was, he thought Jerome Putnam was a human being, too. Guess we can consider that mistake all paid for. You gonna ID?"

"He's got relatives."

"Only his ex-wife and her daughter here. The ex won't come down. The girl is only ten. Technically, we should use her, but…"

"Consider him ID'd, then. Israel Kahauolopua."

"No, you got to go over to the cooler. Sign the coroner's papers. You know the drill."

"When?"

"A few minutes. Not much crime scene work necessary. You specialize in this wham-bam stuff, Counselor. How's your defense of the little snatch-matcher coming?"

"Got a new bail hearing coming up."

He shook his head. "When are you going to learn?"

"The right to bail is clearly stated for those who have not been convicted of a crime. In Angel's case, any crime. It's fundamental."

"I'll tell you what's fundamental. A big carbon-steel blade slipping through your ribcage, that's fundamental. Bullets exploding your wrists before they bury themselves in your brain, that's fundamental. Bail, or the lack of it, is just a flourish."

"Murder is more fundamental than justice, Sergeant. No argument there.

It's primal. But justice is the framework we use to deal with murder. Otherwise one killing only begets another. And freedom is the heart of justice."

"Since when does justice have a heart?"

Pennofrio was right. Justice isn't a living thing. Justice is a steel and concrete cage. People get dropped into it like BBs. They rattle around for a while. Some bounce out, some sink to the bottom and stay there. Sometimes a judge or a lawyer gets to shake the cage and a few pellets fall out through the cracks. It's all artificial. Murder, though, is organic. It has a heart. And it's a heart that never stops beating.

"What's justice doing about Jerome Putnam?"

"What, not opposed to the death penalty on this one, Counselor?"

"It wasn't even supposed to be Izzy's case. He got it on a farm-out. Public Defender was too busy."

"Those poor boys and girls must get sick of dealing with the dregs. Big blowhard attorney like your dead friend, he's got to put his money where his mouth is once in a while. Take time out from stuffing his pockets with drug money to champion the cause of a poor armed robber slash crossdresser. Slash killer now. Culmination of a career. Didi's, not your friend's."

"Good thing I don't need your sympathy."

"That's fine. Because you won't get it. I know the arguments you champions of individual rights put up. That freedom taken from the guilty is freedom taken from the innocent, too. That it's better that ten guilty men walk free than one innocent be jailed."

"If you're that one innocent guy, you're in favor of that speech."

"We don't buy it down on my watch, because we never meet that guy. You ask the clerks at the 7-11s Jerome robbed if they feel their rights have been enhanced by him walking the streets. Get a Ouija board and see if you can raise the deceased. Ask him if he's for lethal injection now."

"I told you, he didn't spring Putnam. Frank Manus' pet judge did."

"Got any evidence for that, counselor? That Rheinhart runs in Manus' kennel? I'll listen."

"Circumstantial."

I related the story of the lawsuit, the restraining order, and Mikey's redevelopment woes.

"Not enough, you know."

"I'm working on more."

"Even if you get it, you'll never tie it together. No one did anything illegal here, except the perpetrator. Even if Manus is running this judge, it's perfectly legal, as long as there's no quid pro quo. Just favors between friends. And a judge is perfectly within his rights to reduce a contempt sentence. And if the reduction in that sentence caught Jerome Putnam's parole officer by surprise, so he wasn't waiting at the jail door with the electronic anklet, well, that's one of those bureaucratic snafus that happen because we on the enforcement side are tired, cranky human beings, too. And if Frank Manus found himself a weapon like Jerome Putnam, then he's lucky. A bit harder to aim than a sidearm, but once you turn them loose, there's not a damn way we can trace them back to you."

Pennofrio's hand-held squawked. He held it to his ear. A broad smile spread across his face.

"One thing I can tell you that's good news," he said after he signed off. "You won't spend any sleepless nights re-thinking your position on the death penalty on account of Double Delicious Didi."

"Least of my worries, but why?"

"Because when we got him, we really got him. Pulled the empty .45 on the patrol unit that caught him flinging away his *bustier* on Tenth Avenue. Got more holes in him than your friend Israel. Some shit stains in trousers sustained by the patrol officers but, with the help of their drycleaners, they're expected to make a full recovery."

All the rest of it was perfunctory, but it still took hours. I rode with Pennofrio, welcome again in the front seat of his unmarked, while an ambulance took Izzy's remains first to the hospital, to be officially pronounced dead, and then to the morgue. Second time in a week I'd been there. Went with the territory of being a big-league attorney again. Already I was nostalgic for my misdemeanor cases. So far in my first-degree case my client was still in jail and my only reliable ally had been killed.

The high-powered talent for vengefulness that Frank Manus possessed had been exposed, but that hardly counted as a triumph since I was the only person who saw the connection. Izzy murdered just for being seen with me. Since I hadn't taken Manus's first warning seriously enough, it was possible Izzy had died just to serve second notice. No doubt Frank would have preferred that Double Delicious Didi would have had homicidal intent beating beneath his padded brassiere for me, but that made it even more chilling that he had Izzy plucked out of life. Just because he could. I searched my memory for maniacs behind bars that might be spring-loaded for killing me, but I couldn't think of any. Nobody wants to ice their lawyer because they got convicted of a misdemeanor.

A straight-out hit had now to be regarded as a possibility. For a moment I cringed away from the thought, not out of fear but embarrassment. Who was I, to contemplate a melodrama of paid-for murder, with myself as the lead corpse? I had the solemn view of the coroner's wagon, just a white panel truck with the county seal emblazoned on the sides and rear doors, winding down the freeway ahead of me and Pennofrio, to force me to take it seriously.

After a few minutes' analysis, I came to the conclusion that it was unlikely. Manus wasn't set up like that. He knew judges, politicians and prosecutors. He didn't rub shoulders with guys who knew how to wrap a gun barrel to silence it or how much strychnine you could put in a tuna salad sandwich without killing the creamy mayo taste.

He killed Izzy because he could; he spared me because he couldn't help it.

Or was I deluding myself? I sat in the front seat of a police car, guest of the city, and felt profoundly unsafe.

Pennofrio told me I could go when the paperwork was complete.

"How long will it take? For the whole autopsy?"

"I don't know. Not long, probably. Cause of death not in doubt. It just has to be formalized."

"I'd like to wait. To take him out."

"It'll be a couple hours at least. And that's if the medical examiner gets right on it. But he should. Been a light weekend for murders. Right, Eddie?"

"Don't remind me," Vampire Eddie said. "I should've gone to Vegas. This is even a waste of time. By the time the doc finishes with him, I'll be lucky to pluck his eyeballs."

"That's vulture talk for removing the deceased's corneas. Eddie's a real sensitive guy."

"Don't call me a vulture. I'm a medical professional."

"Why didn't you finish med school, then, Eddie? Way I hear it, you wanted to spend all your time in the cutting room, instead of boning up on how to keep people alive."

"I save people's lives in here, Pennofrio. When was the last time you did that? All you do is catalogue one stiff after another."

"Without me, you'd be out of business."

"Not so. I get the good stuff out of hospitals. Brain dead. They're still hooked up to the machines, so the organs are still alive. Fresh," Eddie said, uttering the word with a thespian passion, like a TV gourmet describing a plate of sashimi. "Out of here I get corneas, mostly. By the time the ME's done with these stiffs, they're mostly starting to rot. Like the fat one in there."

"Mr. McKeon's best friend?"

"Best friend?" Eddie looked at me. His lip curled up at me as if I had just asked him for spare change. "Only next of kin can sign. What am I doing here? Does the moke have a signed card?"

"I guess. Otherwise we wouldn't have called you, right?"

"Wish you hadn't. Corneas are barely worth switching off the tube to clip. Dime a dozen. All the good stuff is just turning into Spam while the doc figures out which bullet wound killed him."

"Might've taken a bullet through all of his vitals, Eddie."

"I could get lucky. Heart's gone, sure, but maybe a lung's still good. Thirty K. A liver, the same. I get ten grand for a kidney, and there's two of them. More, sometimes. Money, that is, not kidneys. But nothing that good comes out of here. Accident victims, sometimes, they get pronounced dead on the scene. The coroner will let me have them. Proximate cause of death ain't that important, when you got a whole drive shaft up your ass."

"Got a real style, doesn't he, McKeon? And then he bitches when we call him a vulture."

"Fuck you, Pennofrio. I don't need your respect. I got the respect of my peers. You ever hear of cryptopreservation?"

"Ain't that one of the puzzles in the newspaper?"

"That was a fine display of total ignorance, Pennofrio. Cryptopreservation is the latest in organ transplant technology. Black Ice. Keeps the donated organ fresh for weeks, instead of hours. And who's got one of the first units approved for use by the FDA? Me, that's fucking who. So-called Vampire Eddie. So I don't need your approval. I got the approval of the FDA."

"They approved that Vioxx shit that blows up people's hearts, too."

"Up yours, Pennofrio. You know what? You can just take me out of your friggin' Blackberry. With what I got sitting at my house, I can't afford to waste my time cutting out corneas. Only time I remember getting anything worth keeping out of a call-down here in the last year was that stripper murder. Cause of death was so obvious, the coroner let me have liver and kidneys before they turned into mystery meat. You," he said.

"Me?"

"Here's my fucking card. Next of kin gets here within a half hour and want to give up any organs that aren't on the donor card, give me a call. I don't want to hear it from your cop buddy Pennofrio."

"Just doing my job, Eddie."

"Fuck your job. If you were doing your job, would the fat guy be dead? I'm doing my job. Being a mother-fucking Angel of Mercy. Kiss my ass." Vampire Eddie strode off to sit at the far end of the corridor, alone with his angst.

"Strain appears to be getting to him," I observed.

"You an organ donor?"

"No."

"Me neither. Department strongly encourages it, too. But when I got to know Eddie, I tore up my card."

About ten o'clock another snag developed. Two teenage boys had been shot by the sheriffs. One was critically wounded, the other dead. Neither was armed, but they had been "behaving erratically," as the cops like to say, which covers any sort of behavior that the police don't like, from giving them the finger to crashing through storefronts. The dead kid was immediately boosted to the front of the coroner's list, as the forces of law and order wanted to make damn sure that, as they suspected, he had some illegal chemicals in his bloodstream. He was a corpse in a hurry. They told me Izzy's inquest wouldn't be finished until morning.

"Didn't even get fucking eyeballs," Eddie groused. "Tell the bald wop that, next time you see him."

Pennofrio was long gone to a late dinner.

I took a cab back to Izzy's office. I found a legal messenger waiting for me.

"Been here two hours," he complained. "That's after I drove out to your home address."

"You could have left it."

"Obtained by the court," he replied tersely. Which meant it had to be returned to the court. And court was closed for the night. Only one judge would direct out evidence that meant some kid might have to shiver in a hallway until sunup. Broad Appeal Barry. The inconvenience of dying slowly of cancer gave him his own perspective on subjecting other people to inconveniences.

I signed for it. The videotape was marked Polar Security Services. A subsidiary of ITA, Inc. Manus employed an outside security firm. Just another corporation. Probably let his security contract out to bid every three years or so, and gave it to whatever firm lowballed it. Polar Security obeyed the subpoena because it had to obey. If Manus ran his own security, which I had half expected, the tape would never have been found. Some loyal Manus soldier would have destroyed it, and claimed blandly that it had been lost. Or it would've been found with the crucial parts blotted out by someone's bar mitzvah.

If Manus wanted to act like a real mobster he needed real wise guys, not rent-a-cops. The fact that Fortress Manus was secured by mercenaries gave me more confidence in my own safety. It was doubtful Polar Security would bid out on a contract hit.

I wanted to view the tape right away, but Izzy's office was not a fit place to sit. In a shooting death, or a death of any kind that they are forced to attend, the police are strictly interested in the removal of the victim and obtaining of all possible evidence. After the chalk lines have been photographed and the police barriers taken away, someone has to clean up the actual detritus of death. In the case of the death of Israel Kahauolopua, that was me. I broke into a hall closet for a bucket, mop and ammonia to attack the pools of blood. So much of it; blood congealed on the desk and floor and spattered drying on the walls. I broke the tacked-over surface of the pools with a sponge, exposing the liquid still gleaming red underneath the skim of the dried hemoglobin. I trudged back and forth to the janitor's closet to empty pink-tinged buckets and spill in more suds and fresh water. I got down on my hands and knees and washed bits of Izzy's wrist bones out of the drapes and off the baseboard.

All the while I wept, incoherent with grief. All the deaths I have seen, my own father's, the friends and family I have lost over the years, all the state funerals with the world mourning its favorite princess or President I have watched on the news, weren't nearly as sorrowful as sponging up scraps of my friend's body like an accidental spill.

The stains on the walls defeated me. They would have to await the painter. I flicked on Izzy's computer, hoping to find some instruction there. It demanded a password. After a moment's thought, I typed in "Iceman."

It came right up. He kept his last will and testament on his desktop. I printed out the instruction for his funeral, for distribution to his friends. Then I tried to play the tape, but by that time I was too tired to find the crucial moment. I fell asleep in front of the blank blue TV screen, in a room that still stank faintly of murder.

Chapter Twelve

"Are you still asleep?" Marvin Maeger was fairly screaming over the phone line. "I'm already down here!"

"Course I'm not asleep," I mumbled, not even convincing myself. The TV was still the only artificial light in the room, but it was now washed out by sunlight spearing through the mini-blinds. My watch read 8:45. "I'll be there in half an hour."

"These papers say to be here by nine!"

"That's just in case they call our case first, Mr. Maeger. Chances are they won't. If they do, just say your lawyer isn't there yet."

I felt an apprehensive jolt as I contemplated Marvin facing off with Barry Appenzeller. My mind shunted yesterday's tragedy aside in favor of today's first potential disaster. I tried to avert it.

"If that should happen…"

"A grand I give you up front, and I have to talk to the judge myself?"

"All you have to do is politely tell him that your attorney is somewhere in the building."

"Meanwhile you're still trying to match something up out of your fucking sock drawer?"

"Politely tell him. Remember politely," I said. God only knew what kind of toxic pharmaceuticals Barry had taken for breakfast. Given a chance to let his personality shine forth, Marvin could be towel boy at the half-court game in the yard at Soledad by the time I got to the courthouse.

"What, I ain't got enough couth to be one of your fucking customers?" Marvin bristled.

"Sure you do. You're right up in the ninetieth percentile, etiquette-wise.

Just be careful with this particular judge."

"What, you've got some psycho judge for me?"

"An attorney does not get to pick his courtroom, Mr. Maeger."

"Is that a yes? What's this crazy fucker going to do to me?" Marvin's voice was rising into a panic pitch.

"Nothing, Mr. Maeger. Not today. It's only a preliminary. We just have to show up, let the City Attorney say his piece, and be bound over for trial."

"Whaddya mean, bound over?"

"Just a term, Mr. Maeger. You've already been released on your own recognizance. Is Raquel Bumgarden there?"

"Who?"

"Opal."

"Yeah, she's here. She's the only one who did anything wrong, as far as I can see. They want me to, I'll testify against her, if they give me a deal."

Marvin. Not cut out to be a *capo* in the mob, that was for certain. What to say? I chose the route of honesty.

"It's your ass they want, Mr. Maeger."

"That's bullshit! All I do is rent fucking cameras!"

My watch had ticked around to six minutes to nine.

"The longer I talk to you, Mr. Maeger, the longer it's going to take me to get down there. Why don't we go over the case when I get to court?"

It was the gentlest way I could think of to hang up on Marvin. He was still bitching inarticulately when I cut the connection. I didn't even have time to scribble a note to charge him for another quarter-hour for the phone call. I would probably forget it. I glanced around Izzy's chambers and remembered him telling me he had a computer program that would automatically charge his clients every time the phone connected, so he would never neglect to record a billable moment. Part of his attorney's inculcated sense of self preservation. See what good it had done him.

One of Izzy's walls was mirrored. I glanced in it and saw that sleeping in the chair had wrecked my suit and wrinkled my shirt. I shaved in the hall bathroom with a razor I snuck into the lady's room to buy out of a coin-vended machine. It had a plastic daisy embossed on the handle. I smoothed out the wrinkles in my shirt by splashing water onto my hands and running my palms over the fabric as a substitute for ironing, an old slob trick my ex-wife had taught me. Dampness patched the cotton-poly blend. Hopefully, the air was dry enough to evaporate it on the short run over to the courthouse. The suit jacket was hopeless. I decided to sling it over my shoulder as I entered Judge Appenzeller's fiefdom.

"Mr. McKeon," he greeted me. "So nice of you to make it."

I grimaced. One of my cases must have been called first. Twelve on the morning's docket, two of which were mine. Only one in six against, but already the odds were beating me. Which case? Marvin glared at me as if I had run over his dog. Question answered.

"Is the prosecution, at least, prepared to proceed?"

"Absolutely, Your Honor," replied an attorney whose face was unfamiliar.

Terence Chichester, no doubt. He was as young and earnest as I had imagined him. He was trying to exude confidence but the bray in his voice betrayed him. Every courtroom attorney remembers the first time he leaves the theory of law behind and enters its practice, when he abandons the lofty castle of academic argument, where every case is decided on its merits, and enters the gamey arena of real law, where irritated judges and ignorant jurors regard his carefully constructed arguments as mere barriers to be overcome on the way to an early lunch. This would be that day in Terence Chichester's memory. It appeared that Danny Akami was going to duck me until I was safely disbarred.

I had lied to Marvin Maeger. It was my ass that was wanted.

"Your motion?"

Barry looked bad, worse by far than he had appeared at Angel's last bail hearing. One glance in a mirror should have been enough to persuade him to relinquish his grip on life. It was entirely inappropriate for his skeletal appearance. His skull seemed too large for his skin, so that it stretched his mouth into a rictus. His lips were pale to the point of invisibility. The chemical metronome was beating again as his head twitched uncontrollably a degree or two to the right every few seconds.

"In the matter before us, to schedule a trial for the people versus Marvin Maeger and Raquel Bumgarden."

"Mr. McKeon?"

"The defense wishes to apply for separate trials."

"Mr. Chichester? Do you object?"

"Naturally, your Honor. The people wish to spare the state the expense of separate trials in what we assure the court can be demonstrated to be an interrelated series of offenses."

"The charges against my clients are entirely different."

"But all stem from the same incident."

Terence Chichester was doing fine. Danny had coached him well. I was the main target, but they weren't going to let Marvin walk if they could help it.

"Alleged incident." I paused. "I do not see Detective Pullman in this courtroom."

The only cops in the room wore uniforms. Undercover vice always wore civvies.

"Detective Pullman is on vacation."

Who wasn't?

"I move that this hearing be delayed until the officer's testimony can be secured."

"Detective Pullman has already testified at arraignment."

"Denied."

"Your Honor, I urge you to reconsider. My client, Raquel Bumgarden, is charged with soliciting, committing a lewd act in public and disorderly conduct. My client Marvin Maeger is charged with pandering, operating a house of prostitution and a violation of the health code that, while not specifically the concern of this court, will nonetheless be impacted…"

"Do not use the word 'impact' as a verb in my courtroom, Mr. McKeon."

It was a bad day guaranteed when Broad Appeal Barry started correcting your grammar.

"Will nonetheless be *affected* by the credibility of Detective Pullman's testimony."

"This hearing is merely to set a trial date,"

"Two trial dates, Your Honor. My motion."

"Denied."

"You're doing crappy," Marvin Maeger said, standing by my side and whispering in my ear like the voice of conscience.

"The individual rights of each of my clients can only be protected in separate trials."

"The defense only wishes to detach the trials to confuse the jury. Without considering the actions of defendant Bumgarden, the jury might conclude that defendant Maeger committed no illegal acts."

"Wouldn't that be hell?" I said.

"This is my courtroom, Mr. McKeon. I'll handle the sarcasm. I have already denied the request, in any case. Are there any other motions?"

"Move that the charges against Mr. Maeger be dropped."

"You may amplify."

"Mr. Maeger has been directly connected to no illegal acts. He merely operates the business under whose roof the alleged disorderly incident occurred. He experienced no personal contact with Detective Pullman except to be arrested by him. Ms. Bumgarden, the other defendant, has offered no evidence that she was directed or coerced to perform any illegal acts by Mr. Maeger."

"Such testimony would be extracted at trial!" Terence Chichester yelped. "The purpose of this hearing is to set date for trial!"

"Trial is set at the discretion of the court."

Acknowledge Barry's omnipotence; that was one way to stay alive in his courtroom.

"What about the sperm on the floor?"

"Alleged sperm. Even if proved to the court's satisfaction, not, per se, illegal. A violation of the health code, not a crime."

"Evidence of ongoing criminal activity!"

"Not in the least. For example, whose alleged discharge was present on the floor of Mr. Maeger's business? No person has been identified as its source. If it was Mr. Maeger's sperm, what crime could that be called?"

"Did I just hear you right?" Marvin whispered furiously. "Did you just let them think I was jerking off on my own floor?"

"Only presenting a hypothesis, Mr. Maeger."

"Do you want to consult with your client?" Broad Appeal Barry snapped. "Does he wish to claim ownership of the criminal clot on his premises?"

"I object to the court's use of the word 'criminal.' The court is obviously prejudiced against my client, or possibly both my clients. I request that this hearing be transferred to another court."

I was begging for an afternoon sentence for contempt. Barry's eyes popped wide, a physical effect that must have cost him every milliliter of blood pressure his wasted body could exert.

"Denied!" he squawked.

"I submit that the court cannot deny. The use of the word 'criminal…'"

"Strike it!" he ordered the stenographer. The court reporter blanched. I came to her rescue.

"Your Honor is not permitted to strike his own remarks."

"Strike it! Strike it! Strike it and be damned!" Barry frothed. The court reporter paused over her transcript. "Should I strike Mr. McKeon's use of the word?"

"Goddam, yes. Fix it up."

The stenographer hurried to obey. No one under the authority of Broad Appeal Barry's courtroom was immune from a contempt sentence.

"Any other motions?" He hurried past the point without waiting for a response. "Good. Trial for both defendants is set three weeks from today, in this court. Requests?"

"Request that bail be set for both defendants," Terence Chichester chirped.

"I move request be denied. Both defendants are free on their personal recognizance. Both have appeared for this hearing. What purpose would bail serve, except to arbitrarily punish the defendants?"

"How much?" Barry asked.

"I repeat, the defendants have demonstrated by their presence in this court that establishment of bail is unnecessary. Bail is set to assure the defendant's presence for trial..."

"Don't lecture me on the law, Mr. McKeon."

"Considering the seriousness of the offense..."

"A combination of misdemeanors, Your Honor!"

"And the easy access of both defendants to cash generated by their sordid business..."

"I object to the characterization!"

"Ten thousand each."

"Granted. In the case of Mr. jizz-on-the-tile. The girl is free on her own recognizance again."

Then Judge Appenzeller had to retire to chambers. I had never been inside his private sanctum but it was said by those who had to be set up as a hospital room. Two or three times a day the judge would feel his cancer cells multiplying disrespectfully and would stop proceedings to get injected with chemotherapeutic toxins. A nurse stood by in his court at all times ready to drip creosote into his veins. These sessions seldom improved his mood or increased his adherence to law but often affected his political orientation, so that the ideology that governed his rulings would midday sometimes switch from right of Judge Roy Bean to left of the Politburo. It was my only hope for Angel Pisaro.

Marvin Maeger hopped angrily at my side, spitting his words at me loudly and liquidly, like a drunk trying to win a bar argument.

"That was fucking great! Now I've got to pay another thousand bucks!"

"Pay the whole thing, Mr. Maeger. You don't have to go through a bondsman. You'll get it back at the conclusion of the trial."

"You think I'm going to trust that nutso judge with ten grand of my money? What the hell is wrong with him, anyway?"

"Cancer."

"What, and he's allowed to work?"

"Who's going to stop him?"

"How come I got to pay bail and Opal gets to walk for free?"

"Must be something about you."

"It ain't fucking fair. She's the only one did anything illegal. I'm innocent."

Sad thing was, Marvin was technically right. Raquel Bumgarden walked silently on my opposite side. Marvin turned his snarling her way.

"Ain't you going to work today?"

"It's still early."

"We been open for forty-five minutes. Get over there and show somebody your ass."

Raquel Bumgarden squeezed my hand. "Thanks," she said. "For getting me out of there. Without having to pay money."

"It's not over yet."

"You'll do fine." She smiled her approval.

It was apparent Raquel Bumgarden had her private opinion of how guilt and innocence worked at the whack shack. She clacked off over the linoleum in her work shoes, four-inch spikes that she hovered over like stilts.

"You got something going on with her?"

"I didn't even touch the tissue box, Mr. Maeger."

"You ain't going to turn over on me to save her butt, are you?"

"I'm not turning over on anybody, Mr. Maeger. If she walks, then you walk. There can be no pandering if there was no soliciting."

It occurred to me that the regions of Marvin's brain that control the emotions of suspicion and self-pity must be marvelously well developed. He should end up under a researcher's knife, on the day his earthly concerns cease, as a scientific curio.

We passed the stairs to the holding cells; somewhere beneath our feet, Angel Pisaro awaited her new bail hearing.

Putting Angel on the stand was a decision I had come to reluctantly. Before a tolerant court it would be a highwire act to shame the Wallendas. In front of Broad Appeal Barry it was a potential career-crusher. Not to mention that it could be legally fatal to Angel as well. Putting the damage to my reputation before my client's existence was very Marvin-like. It was apparent I had to ditch the Phantasy Photography owner before his whini25 infected me with full-blown symptoms. No pity to be had in Broad Appeal Barry's court. Keeping company with his carcinomas left him with scant sympathy for those whose problems were of their own making. I tried to dismiss Marvin with an optimistic observation.

"Chances are we won our case on appeal today, Mr. Maeger."

"Appeal! You got to get convicted to appeal!"

I had underestimated Marvin's grasp of the law.

"In the event of a conviction…"

"Don't talk to me like that! In the fucking event! Like it's something that's happening on TV! We're talking about my business here!"

"You could always go back to the video trade."

"Fuck that! I'm paying you to keep Phantasy Photography open!"

There it was, and thanks for saying it, Marvin. That's what I got paid for, so the naked ladies could gyrate and the men masturbate. What was wrong with that? The newest plateau in carnal satisfaction. Sex for the new century, perfectly safe as long as you didn't slip on someone else's passion puddling on the linoleum.

"Chances are good, Mr. Maeger, but nothing is certain."

"For a grand I want better thinking than that."

"Speaking of that grand, and I notice *you* never stop speaking about it, your retainer is just about exhausted, Mr. Maeger."

"We ain't even been to trial!"

"A hundred-sixty an hour can dissolve a thousand in no time."

Marvin should be able to figure that out. He had pretty good math skills when it came to camera rentals.

"A hundred-sixty an hour for every minute of the trial?"

"You betcha."

Did I want less to pick my way through the killing field of Barry Appenzeller's courtroom, daring the fusillades of his rulings, skirting the remains of unluckier advocates? To war in a cause as cheap and puny as Marvin Maeger's? A hundred-sixty an hour was a bargain.

"No wonder you wanted separate trials," Marvin said bitterly. "You can double-dip my wallet."

"Best legal strategy. And not necessarily more expensive. We win acquittal for Raquel, they'll drop charges against you. Moot point now. Chances are it's going to be a short trial, too, at the rate the judge is denying my motions. That ought to cheer you up."

"Only until I start thinking about appeals," Marvin said. "Ain't no special homeboy rate for appeals, is there?"

"No."

"I never hated lawyers before I met you," Marvin said, with un-Marvin-like eloquence. He turned away from me and out the municipal doors, to his working day, I supposed, to exhort his staff and watch his TV screens and keep vigilant against the protein hazards of his floors.

I sat in the courthouse cafeteria, sipping a cup of coffee brewed from beans that the commissary contractor had selected especially for their lousiness, and contemplated the effect I had on people. My own blood led the list of individuals for whom the sight of me was a special abhorrence. I wondered if my son knew Marvin Maeger. Could be. I wasn't kidding myself that Evie had presented him with Big Daddy's telltale longboard out of sheer coincidence. Maybe they had met at Phantasy Photography. Eighteen and over. My ex had a Puritanical streak that manifested itself always in public and occasionally in bed; she might not be so sanguine about the fake ID if she knew that our boy was not using it merely to char his lungs but also to manage his hormone surges. I paid child support, out of which my son got an allowance; he shelled it out at Phantasy Photography, and Marvin Maeger in turn handed it over to me when he got clipped for pandering. It was an Economics 101 model of cash circulation.

No one offered to sit with me, although the table had chairs for six. My pariah status had not been negated by the death of Izzy. It seemed rather to have been intensified. Now my company was not only ethically tainted, but potentially fatal. Jill Congliaro sat at the far side of the room, in the center of a male circle of courthouse regulars, a couple cops and a few fellow counselors, all pretending to cherish her conversation, all sneaking sly glances at the distance her skirt had traveled up her thigh. She didn't see my gesture of greeting, or chose to ignore it.

A chair scraped the floor as it was reversed. Terence Chichester sat in it backwards, sticking his cherubic face in mine.

"The people did pretty well this morning," he observed.

"Congratulations."

"It's like anything else. You get a feel for it, a rhythm, and everything just flows."

"You'll be on Danny's A-team in no time."

"Every task has its own inner logic. I firmly believe that. There are no mysteries. Anything anyone else can do, you can do." Terence Chichester talked as if he had a shelf full of self-improvement manuals on his nightstand.

"I was a little intimidated by having to go up against you, my first time out."

"Absolutely unwarranted trepidation."

"You've got quite a reputation around the office."

"Again, undeservedly so."

"Lot of those sleazeballs like Maeger would have been shut down years ago, if it wasn't for you."

"Merely protecting my clients' First Amendment rights."

"Bosh. The First Amendment doesn't provide legal justification for public masturbation."

"Masturbation is its own justification, is it not, Terry, babe? Or do you search for a precedent every time you beat off?"

Terence Chichester's hairless cheeks went red as fast as Ho Chi Minh City.

"That's just the sort of thing I expected from you this morning," he confessed. "The underhanded style. A bushwhacking."

"I was off my feed. Promise you better when Barry reconvenes."

"I'll be there. Got a whole slew of arraignments today."

Danny Akami was letting his protégé handle all of the business at Broad Appeal Barry's rather than run into me there.

I left Terence Chichester sitting in the cafeteria. He was still glowing with quiet pride at having scratched out a hit in his first at-bat in the league, sipping at his crummy coffee, too self-satisfied to notice the high sign a friendly bailiff gave me. Judge Appenzeller was back in court.

I checked the docket before I re-entered and discovered Terence Chichester was right. Apart from Angel's bail hearing, the remainder of the cases were misdemeanor arraignments. DUI's, mostly. A sign of wisdom being displayed by the assigning judge. Tough to appeal a misdemeanor conviction. No matter how bone-jarring an injustice had been done, the higher courts were not likely to grant it hearing. They had more important cases to ponder. Let Barry Appenzeller punish the slurry of minor criminals for the encroachment of his cancer. Less chance of a highly publicized reversal than if he was given sway over felons.

Angel Pisaro being in Barry's court was an anomaly. Could be the chief judge had seen my name next to it and automatically assigned it to Barry. The sheriffs had rounded her up from downstairs. She sat in her jail smock under their close supervision. When the bailiff called out "State of California versus Angel Pisaro" they marched her to the defendant's table, next to me.

"Am I getting out today?" was her first question.

"No telling, Angel. You understand this is another bail hearing, not a trial?"

She nodded. "If they set bail, I can get out?"

I nodded. "If it's an amount you can afford to pay."

"Mikey will pay it."

I had my doubts about that, but I let them go unspoken.

"I assume the defense is ready? Or do you want more time to confer with your client?"

"Conference is complete, Your Honor."

"Where is Mr. Donnelly?" Barry Appenzeller stared out over his courtroom. "Mr. McKeon? Have you seen the District Attorney?"

"Not today."

"Probably at some damn lunch or another. It's all he's good for. Him and his goddam perfect digestion."

Barry Appenzeller looked disgusted to the point of dysentery himself.

"Is the District Attorney's office represented here?" he called, loudly enough to still the conversation among the gaggle of lawyers that were shooting the breeze at the rear of the courtroom until their cases were called. None of them owned up to being with the DA's office.

"This presents a problem."

"Since my request for bail is unopposed…"

"Denied, Mr. McKeon. I am not granting bail without opposition in a capital murder case. Perhaps the District Attorney's office is just running late. You," he said to the bailiff, "find me a DA someplace."

The bailiff returned after five minutes of scouring the corridors, empty-handed. All members of the office were engaged in one courtroom or another.

"It seems the question of Ms. Pisaro's bail does not concern the District Attorney greatly, so I move…"

"I already said no. I'll deny bail myself without further argument if you interrupt me again before I resolve this problem, Mr. McKeon. It's your fault for demanding this hurry-up hearing in the first place. I should not have granted it."

But you couldn't help yourself. Warned into silence, I kept myself from even grinning. Barry must get sick of those DUIs. Terence Chichester re-entered the courtroom, still wearing his self-satisfied smirk, innocent as an early Christian. The lion lurking in the catacomb leapt.

"You!" Barry Appenzeller fingered him.

Terence Chichester blanched.

"This is a hearing for bail in a capital murder charge. Represent the state."

"Sir, I represent the City Attorney, not the District Attorney."

"So? The government pays your salary, doesn't it? Give them something for it."

"Sir, I am completely unfamiliar with this case."

"Just object to everything McKeon says. That way you'll be borrowing from the style of the people's elected advocate," the judge snorted. "Mr. McKeon?"

"Move that the court consider additional exculpating evidence for Angel Pisaro in the matter of determining her bail."

"Objection," Terence Chichester said weakly.

"Objection to what?" Barry Appenzeller snapped.

"Objection to..." Terence Chichester hesitated.

"Objection to the evidence itself? Objection to its being presented? Or objection to bail being reconsidered in the first place?"

Multiple choice test, Terence. Can't be that long since you've taken one.

"Objection to the evidence."

One third of the time, the answer is "A."

"How can you object to the evidence? We haven't even heard it yet! Denied! Proceed, Mr. McKeon."

"The defense calls the defendant."

"Objection!"

"What?"

"Sir, I am not prepared to cross-examine this witness. If the defendant wishes to testify in his own behalf…"

"Her own behalf. The defendant is female."

"…the proper forum is at trial. State of mind testimony…"

"Are you going to elicit state of mind testimony, Mr. McKeon?"

"No, Your Honor. I am merely seeking to lay a factual basis for the introduction of additional evidence."

"Then proceed."

Barry Appenzeller glared at Terence Chichester. The twitch in the judge's neck had reversed itself sometime during the course of the morning's break to poison his cancer cells; his whole head now bobbed perceptibly to the left every few seconds.

"What is wrong with you?" he said, with seemingly genuine curiosity, to the kid attorney.

Terence Chichester was floundering. He had lost his rhythm completely. Nothing was flowing for him anymore.

Angel was sworn in.

"Tell the court everything you know about the death of Father Howard Canto," I said.

"Objection," Terence Chichester gurgled, giving the impression of a man being forced to speak while under torture.

"Grounds?"

"Irrelevant."

Terence Chichester evidently hoped to minimize his danger by choosing one-word replies.

"Mr. McKeon?"

"The defense will argue for acquittal on the basis of self-defense. It is our position that the defendant was in imminent danger of being murdered herself, by the so-called victim. Ms. Pisaro has information about the death of Father Canto that will not only prove intrinsic to her defense but should interest the law enforcement agencies of this county, who have mistakenly identified Father Canto's death as an accidental one."

"Sounds damn interesting to me. The witness may answer the question."

And Angel spoke. She was perfect. If she had a dollar for every point of her IQ she'd have less than a Franklin, but it's geniuses who make poor witnesses, not dolts. The flat tone and the matter-of-fact recitation made the witless ends of Father Canto and Big Daddy O'Toole even more scarifying. The court, even the gossiping lawyers in the back, grew quiet as they recoiled from the tale of the priest's last ride off the edge and the singer's final mouthful of brine. Only Barry Appenzeller seemed blackly amused. Even an unexpected end must seem sweetly sudden to him, compared to the ongoing mutiny of his organs.

Terence Chichester objected to the hearsay nature of the testimony only once, when he was firmly told that hearsay testimony is permissible when the teller of the tale is deceased. Evie qualified. Thereafter he too seemed shocked into silence by either the stories themselves or Angel's complete lack of empathy for the victims. He looked only to the door of the courtroom for someone from the DA's office to burst in and rescue him, but none appeared. Monumental screw-up by Donnelly. If I managed to get bail set for Angel, Danny Akami would martyr him for it in their still-hypothetical electoral match-up.

I entered the insurance company's picture of the *Baby Blue* as evidence, without a peep from Terry. I also entered the picture taken by Izzy, whose skill with an underwater camera showed through in the clear image of the empty cradle.

The moment came. I had set up beautifully, but the hearing could end exactly as the previous one had if the judge refused to accept the depositions as evidence. I read the names of the witnesses and the magistrate, thanking whatever cynical spirit watches over the fortunes of lawyers that my son, as part of his ongoing project to spite me whenever possible, had changed his surname back to his mother's maiden one when she had done the same with hers. I summarized the contents and noted that the witnesses would be subpoenaed for trial. I held my breath.

"Objection," Terence Chichester said. The depositions were in his hands.

Another morning shot to hell, if Chichester detected the problem with the depositions. No opposing attorney had been present to cross-examine. I had put in a call to the DA's office before the magistrate arrived, but naturally no one had answered on Sunday. Entering the depositions anyway was a fast one, and I was pulling it.

"Yes?" Barry Appenzeller leaned forward, ready to slam Angel back behind bars. He wouldn't have missed the error.

"The magistrate failed to sign both copies," Terence Chichester said.

"My mistake. Xeroxed them too quickly. The originals," I said quickly, passing the documents, sealed and signed as ponderously as the Constitution, over to the bailiff.

Barry Appenzeller looked like he was about to explode. Could happen, too. Be a better end for him than the relentless withering, but it wouldn't suit my purposes. I urged him silently to contain himself. I was almost home. I continued my telepathic plea. You're going to give me this one, Barry.

"Is that all?" he roared.

There is a certain type of land mine called a Bouncing Betty, I am told. It does not explode when you step on it. But it is immediately fatal when you remove your foot. Terence Chichester looked like he just discovered a Bouncing Betty under each instep.

"Bail will be set," Barry Appenzeller said. "Amount?"

"I move that the defendant be released on her own recognizance."

"Absolute nonsense. No. The people have a suggestion?"

"A large amount, sir. A million dollars," Terence Chichester said, still lost.

"An amount equivalent to bail not being granted at all."

"Which so far has worked just fine."

"I need Ms. Pisaro free. To aid in her own defense. I am certain she cannot post a large bail."

"What's your suggestion?"

"Ten thousand dollars."

"No. This isn't drunk and disorderly."

"Ms. Pisaro welcomes trial. Ms. Pisaro is eager to prove her innocence. A large bail will assure her presence at trial no better than a reasonable amount. Twenty-thousand dollars."

"You sound like an auctioneer, Mr. McKeon."

"May I interrupt?" Terence Chichester asked. He was waving the depositions. It wasn't his fault, really. He had only had a few seconds to glance over them. "These statements…"

"Have been admitted by this court. The court was given no choice, since the people failed to object in a meaningful way. We are now setting the amount of bail."

"I urge the court to reconsider the admissibility of these documents."

"Urge all you want. We don't backtrack in this court."

"This is a travesty, sir."

"What?"

"Or collusion. Between yourself and Mr. McKeon."

Terence Chichester's stance had abruptly been transformed from confusion to foolhardiness. Easy, Terry, babe. This isn't moot court.

"Collusion!" Barry Appenzeller hissed.

"It gives the appearance of collusion," Terence Chichester said, backpedaling a step.

"Feel free to explain yourself," the judge said. Handing him the noose.

"The hurried nature of this hearing meant I had no time to examine these documents. The nature of my own appointment a reflection of the unseemly haste with which this hearing was conducted. That alone should render the proceedings invalid. In fact I so move."

"Denied. You find me unseemly, then, young man?"

"Personally, no. I…"

"I am not a well man. Not at all. Perhaps I should wear a wig." Barry touched his gray-skinned pate with a palsied finger.

"It is not Your Honor's personal appearance that is unseemly. It is this court's proceedings."

"Like my own appearance, my court is bare of cosmetic touches. We find the law, we make our rulings, we move on. You are preventing me from moving on. Do you have a date for tonight?"

"Huh? No."

"Not planning to visit your aged mother, are you?"

"My mother lives in Nashville," Terence Chichester said, utterly confused.

The inner logic of the situation was escaping him completely. Everyone else in the courtroom was hiding a snicker. If you went through the pockets of all the attorneys in the room, in most of them you would find a toothbrush. We all knew the hazards of appearing before Appenzeller.

"Just going to sit at home, crack a sixer, watch some cable?" asked Barry, winking in mock camaraderie.

"I have to go back to work."

"No you don't. After you have finished with your scheduled arraignments, you are sentenced to serve the remainder of this day, and until six o'clock tomorrow morning, in the county jail for contempt of court. Collusion, my ass. Bail for the defendant is set at fifty thousand dollars. Next."

I was on the line to a bail bondsman before they could take Angel back to jail. I didn't want her released in public, where the press could get their hands on her. Lucky for me, reporters avoided Judge Appenzeller's court. Journalists hate natural deaths as much as they love splashy murders or spectacular accidents. Watching Barry Appenzeller slowly dying was neither edifying nor newsworthy.

There were going to be a lot of people who wanted to ask a lot of questions of Angel Pisaro. The notion that the cops, both city and county, had let two murders go unsolved, unnoticed even, was going to attract media of every stripe. The DA would want to talk to her, not really out of a sincere desire to investigate Evie's crimes but because, if they lacked basis for a direct murder charge, they would love to find her guilty on an accessory beef. Even the cops, when they were forced to re-open the cases of Father Canto and Big Daddy O'Toole, would need Angel's statement.

I wanted nobody to talk to her. I sat her next to me in the Seville, still in the jail smock. "Angel, do you have five thousand dollars in your bigger boobs fund?"

"Mikey will pay it."

"We're going to leave Mikey out of this for now if you have the money."

For certain. Would Mikey finger Angel for Frank Manus, to save his club from demolition?

"Do you have it?" There must be some kind of money in doing the little girl act.

"Yeah. I don't want to spend it on this, though," she whined.

"Maybe Mikey'll pay for your surgery."

"He *should*," Angel decided. "If I have to pay my own bail."

I needed to put Angel someplace. Not my place, it was sure to be watched. Any address she'd previously had, the same. It came to me as we cashed out Angel's savings at a local bank. Someplace where, even if anyone saw her, they couldn't admit it. I dialed the number on my cell phone.

"Phantasy," Marvin answered.

"How would you like to earn some slack on your legal bill?"

"I'd like it."

"How are you set for girls?"

Then I returned to Izzy's office. I cracked open a beer. The alcohol made me emotional before the can was half gone. Tears formed in my eyes when I looked at the photo of the Iceman. At least the hunter-gatherer had a few moments to compose himself, to look back on the world he was leaving behind, before the cold numbed him forever. More than Izzy had.

But I was doing my late friend proud. I was playing in the bigs. I wondered if Gehrig had lived long enough to see DiMaggio bat. I didn't think so. But the dynasty went on. I had taken my first swing today in a long time.

And hit it right out of the park.

Chapter Thirteen

Pennofrio was haranguing me on the phone. This had happened every one of the three days Angel Pisaro had been free on bail.

"Just a few words. A little conversation. You can be present."

"Thanks, but I'd like to point out that's not overly generous of you, since it's covered by Miranda."

"Don't you owe me a favor?"

"First time I ever had to buy a car to get back from a ride offered by the cops. A guy gets out of Chico, he at least gets a bus ticket."

"After our picnic in the junkyard, I assumed you were a guy with a sense of humor. Sorry if I was wrong. Now, how about just a little coffee talk with Angel?"

"No can do."

"Goddammit, you opened this bucket of shit! And now you're walking away with the lid!"

"My client's interests come first."

"Don't talk like a lawyer to me!" Where had I heard that before? "I got the press all over me. Did you see the editorial in the Trib yesterday?"

"Yes."

"Wasn't that a piece of crap?"

"The one about how every suspicious death deserves more than a perfunctory investigation? No matter who the victim was? That everyone who hasn't been convicted of murder has a right to life and to the protection of the law?"

"That's the one."

"Sounds remarkably similar to something you said to me, once."

"So? We don't need to hear it from a goddam newspaper! All I want is a chance to question Angel about her girlfriend's date with Big Daddy O'Toole. The pervert priest was out of my jurisdiction, thank you, father. Just an hour or two, you, me and Angel, so I can tell the congenital ass-biters upstairs that I'm moving on it."

"You had her in custody for more than a week. Why didn't you talk to her then? All you wanted her to do was shut up and keep her arms swabbed down for the bye-bye needle."

"Circumstances change. I now wish to be her friend. Or else I'm going to recommend to the DA's office that they re-file the charges as accessory to murder and plant her ass back in Las Colinas."

"As her attorney, I promise to advise Angel every day to be grateful she has friends like you. But I'm not giving her up. The DA would have to drop the murder charge in order to file accessory-after-the-fact and I don't think Jimmy Donnelly's ready to do that."

"Maybe not. In fact, after the week he's had, Donnelly probably has to warm up, maybe do some stretching exercises, before he can find his ass with both hands. But I can find Angel Pisaro. And when I do, I'll talk to her whether you're there or not. I'm just giving you a chance to be there."

"You're threatening an attorney with an illegally obtained statement. Don't you have more coherent things to do?"

"No idle threat, counselor. Remember, I've taken a statement from your Angel before. She'll waive her right to counsel as fast as she'll waive her right to wear panties."

I doubted Pennofrio could find Angel, but I scribbled a note to call her and reinforce my advice to her not to say a word to anybody but me before her trial convened. She hadn't been too entranced with working at Phantasy Photography, and Marvin Maeger had been just as unhappy to have her back, but so far my plan for concealing her seemed to have been inspired.

The only picture that the media had of Angel was her mug shot; a little deft work with makeup and a new hairstyle rendered her pretty well unlike it. Apart from that, the customers at Phantasy didn't come to the whack shack to look into the girls' eyes.

Of course Pennofrio had already checked out my address, Izzy's office, Angel's old apartment and Terrifically Titanium, all the obvious places Angel could be keeping a low profile. I thought about calling Mikey and asking him if the cops had come by but decided against it because he, like Desiree Mason, was remaining a stalwart member of the not-speaking-to-Speed club.

The only real danger that Angel would be discovered came from the vice squad, and even they weren't likely to pop Marvin again as long as his current case was pending.

Danny Akami liked to spread his enforcement talent out and around. Didn't want the voters to perceive him as picking on an individual scumbucket business when he'd rather be seen as conducting a campaign against the lot of them.

Spread out on the desk before me were the paper files of Izzy's cases, abstracts of unlucky moments in the criminal careers of the people whose names the folders bore. Drug dealers for the most part; the name of Search And Seizure Izzy had glowed for them like a shaft of daylight piercing the roof of a cavern in the subterranean moment of their capture. Most of them had already, although reluctantly and suspiciously, transferred their legal woes over to me, and I had agreed to represent. Not such a bad client list, for my re-entry into real criminal law. Taking care of people's illegal recreational needs. It was not much different than Marvin Maeger's or Bandit's business, although the legal penalties were astonishingly higher. Under the three-strikes law, unloading a bag of weed on an undercover cop was a swing as much as sticking a loaded pistol in a grandmother's face. There were plenty of lives to be saved, or at least dealt down.

And it would give me the time and resources to deal with cases like Angel's, the legally bereft, people the justice system tossed away like marbles down a manhole, to pop and rattle only briefly before becoming entombed in the mire. It was like a plastic surgeon installing row after row of silicon breasts for the chance to operate *pro bono* on the truly deformed and the accidentally maimed. Careful not to end up like Dr. Verlace, though, gossiping about my clients at the yacht club while keeping a weather eye out for my high-strung date.

I wouldn't have minded getting back into the competition for Jill Congliaro myself. I wondered if I could re-qualify for her attentions, now that I had upgraded my practice. I was certain it was the client list of peep-show operators and whack shack habitués that had made me an unfit prospect for steady dating. Although Jill, shrewd girl that she was, had perhaps discerned my lack of wealth. That could be the criterion for making the final cut. In that field I was no better off than before. Most of my new clients had already paid substantial retainers to Izzy, which he had already banked. That money now belonged to his estate. Could probably stay there if I got disbarred in the upcoming week, but if I survived the Ethics Committee I would have to prepare a polite letter to his ex-wife, along with an accounting of the fees, requesting their return. I could already guess at her reply, which would put me in the morally fragile position of having to sue my friend's estate if I wanted to obtain the funds.

It was a task that promised minuscule returns for my self-esteem, so I put it off. Instead, I inserted the tape obtained for me by the court from Polar Security Services into Izzy's VCR. I had the dream catcher and Pennofrio. I had the *Baby Blue* with its missing surfboard and the testimony of my son and his boss at the Surf Shaq. The video of Rainbow Valley cab dropping me off at the Manus Building, along with all that evidence, should add up to reasonable doubt even if the jury impaneled in Angel's trial was composed entirely of overweight women who hated strippers viscerally.

The video was time-stamped but fast-forwarding it made it impossible to read the numbers. I punched the FF button for a few minutes at a go, then had to slow the tape so I could see how far that day and night had progressed toward 9:55 PM.

At the point in the tape marked 4:07, with the sun still shining on Frank Manus' asphalt, I saw a figure I recognized. She was bundled up in an overcoat instead of a housecoat, but the hairstyle was unmistakable. The cosmic-looking hair clump threatened to crash into the opposite side of her head than the one I remembered. The face had been painted to match the lips, a concession to her formal appointment.

I abandoned my search for Rainbow Valley Cab and flicked on Izzy's computer. A quick tooling along with one of the search engines produced a list of California Lottery winners. So many of them! The state ran more games than Caesar's Palace. Even at far worse odds, the list of recent winners still caused the computer to spit out five pages of fine print. I ran my finger alongside the column of names beginning with "F" once. Then I remembered Escher, and checked "E." I folded the paper into my pocket.

I pointed the Seville east. Even though Izzy's office was only a few blocks away from my old one, the most convenient route east was now the interstate, instead of the Dr. Martin Luther King Jr. Freeway. No more rolling down the slum road for me. Another subtle indication that I had arrived.

The only difference in the homestead in Lakeside was the angle at which the dually was parked. Gail Fortenwood answered the door with a sour glance at my empty hands.

"Mr. Attorney." She led the way inside. "What brings you back here? Drink?"

The afternoon's vodka and lemonade stood melting on the coffee table.

"Not right now."

"I'll pour you some of your bourbon, if you prefer. The seal's been broken on it. Rocks? Ginger? Coke?"

"No." Why was I refusing a drink like a cop? "On second thought, the vodka and lemonade sounds fine."

She poured with a heavy hand. The yellow of the lemonade was a mere aurora in the icy upper reaches of the drink. I put my hand around my glass. She clinked hers against it before I had even raised it off the table.

"Yo," she said, and took a productive swallow.

I took a tongue-numbing sip myself.

"So, what brings you back?" she repeated herself. "Found someone for me to sue? Or you just know where there's a single woman now?"

She crossed her legs, and the unbuttoned housecoat slithered away from her thigh, revealing a wall of white dimpled flesh. At least Desiree knew how to dress. And undress, probably. After dark would be a good idea, both for her and Gail Fortenwood.

"I want to ask you about winning the lottery."

She snorted. "Making sure I can afford you?" she asked.

"What game did you win?"

"What do you mean? I won the lottery."

"Yes, but which game?"

"What does it matter to you? It's enough to have plenty of fun on."

"Was it the Big Spin? You get in it on a scratch-off?"

"I never buy them things."

She looked annoyed, as if I was a novice gambler eyeing the chips of the high-roller at the next table.

"Then it was the big game? Pick Seven? You win on a Wednesday or a Saturday?"

"I don't remember."

"You don't remember? Biggest day of your life, and you don't remember?"

Lot of people would mention the birth of their child as being the biggest day in their lives, especially if they had only one, but I was betting Gail Fortenwood wasn't one of them.

"I did a lot of celebrating. Come on, let's have some fun. You act like you think they're gonna repossess the water bed before we're done."

"You didn't just hit it big in keno, did you?"

Keno was the state's bid to keep hooked the hopeless gambling junkies. They played it every forty-five minutes, on color monitors at convenience stores. Stand in front of the pastry rack and piss your money away all day long.

"Fuck keno, honey."

Maybe she was thinking a little dirty talking would jump-start my libido.

"Or the Daily Number? Because there isn't that much money in winning those games. You'd have spent it all on that truck."

"Goddam, you ask a lot of questions. And funny ones, too. Most guys would ask if I was on my period, or takin' birth control. You want a different drink? You need to get a little happier 'cause you're the nervous type? I told you, I still got some of your bourbon left."

"This is fine."

I took a healthy slug of the vodka-lemonade. Didn't want the cabinet door open. Could get sidetracked into a discussion of Evie.

"You see these papers, Mrs. Fortenwood?"

"Oh, shit. Lawyer with papers. And you still calling me Mrs. Fortenwood. What kind of shit am I in?"

"This is a list of all the California Lottery winners for the last two years. Everybody that won five hundred dollars or more. Lot of names, you can see that. Every game the state plays, from scratchers to Lucky Seven. Your name isn't on here."

"I told 'em to leave it off," she said, lying smoothly. A valuable talent for a faithless wife. "A woman, especially a single woman, needs her privacy."

"You might have asked, but they couldn't do that, Mrs. Fortenwood. It's a state law that they have to publish the names. You don't have to give them your address, your job, or talk to TV or the newspapers. But you have to give them your name, and they have to publish it. Yours isn't on here."

Gail Fortenwood glared at me, a you-son-of-a-bitch stare that she had probably perfected on Escher, when she caught him looking up her daughter's dress with interest in his eyes. "I think you'd better leave," she told me.

"Who bought you the truck, Mrs. Fortenwood?"

"You better go now."

"Was it Frank Manus?"

"Old man who lives in back has a gun. He's sweet on me. He's got an artificial leg," she added, as if I would need to know why she had offered herself to me instead of him.

I left the papers on the coffee table.

"I won the Arizona lottery," she said. "So there. I visit my sister in Gila Bend every two or three weeks. I bought my ticket there. Now you know, so get your nosy ass off my property."

I did, but I stopped at the truck to check the odometer. Less than six hundred miles. Gila Bend sits on the hundred-nineteen-mile marker east, and the Arizona border at Yuma is a hundred sixty miles from Lakeside. Hadn't driven the dually over after she cashed her ticket, that was for sure.

I stopped at Nubie's right before sunset. A cinnamon glow reflected from the windows of the cars in the Santa Claus lot. Sully put down his rag as I sat at the bar.

"Vodka and lemonade," I ordered.

"Ain't got no lemonade."

"Just vodka, then. Chilled."

He swirled a shot of Popov desultorily around with some ice before draining it into a shot glass that he took pains to demonstrate was polished with the same rag as the bar. Luckily I only had time for one sip of the awful beverage. Bandit came charging out of the pool room. A pimp like Bandit made no concession to sundown in the matter of wearing his sunglasses. I knew my own eyes craved a lot more light since I had passed forty. Bandit must be nearly blind behind his shades. Maybe that was the infirmity that was forcing him to contemplate his retirement prospects.

"What the fuck now, Speed?"

"You ever work a girl named Fantasy, Bandit?"

"I don't recall. What's it got to do wit' you and me?"

"Nothing. Nothing with the City Attorney, either. You'd remember her."

"Nobody named Fantasy. You know I name my girls after flowers." That was true. Bandit's girls were generally named Rose or Daisy or Violet. It was one of his business's service marks. Apart from Nubie's and its immediate environs, Bandit would usually venture out only to Home Depot, where he would wander the aisles that displayed seed packages, looking for fresh names for his flock. Probably a working girl named Zinnia walking the streets for him right now.

"You know who I'm talking about. She was one of your success stories, if she was yours. Spent the last few years of her career dancing naked for the high and mighty."

"Oh, her."

"What did you call her?"

"I don't know. Was a while ago. Maybe Fantasy. She like that name."

"How did she leave your employ?"

"Girls move on."

"Without getting chain-whipped?"

"She was no good, nohow. Got so she hated to fuck men."

"Who really loves their job? You didn't let her walk out on you because she had a bad attitude. Somebody paid you for her, didn't they?"

"Man's got a right to a ree-turn on his investmen.'"

"His name was Frank Manus."

"I don't have to tell you nothin.'"

"Buying and selling human beings is illegal."

"Motherfuckin' shit. I needs a white man to tell me that?"

I got back downtown in a snap. Freeway traffic was all moving the other way, Friday night traffic, the lanes packed not only with regular commuters but peppered also with the trailer rigs hauling ATVs and dune buggies out to the desert and jet skis out to the river, heavy machinery for despoiling nature. In Izzy's office, I dug through my cardboard cartons until I came up with the Rolodex. Izzy no doubt had a program on his computer with the number I needed in it, but I hadn't made myself literate in all of his software.

Pete Winam sounded surprised to hear from me. He also sounded like he'd already had a few drinks.

"Speed," he gurgled. "How's your dad?"

"Doesn't have a problem in this world, Pete."

"That's good to hear."

"Need a favor, Pete."

"Anything," he said expansively.

Pete had his own tuxedo, of course. We had to make a quick stop while we rented mine. Luckily, it wasn't prom season. My size was on the rack.

"Don't know why you want to tag along on this," Pete said.

It wasn't really a question, so I didn't answer. Pete's natural lack of curiosity made him a bad reporter but a perfect society columnist, I guessed. His newspaper didn't want the social elite riddled with embarrassing questions while he covered their cotillions. Could hurt advertising dollars.

I was about to play hell with that strategy. The Radisson was once more my destination. This time the ballroom was packed for the Downtown Businessmen's Association, a gathering that emphatically excluded owners of ground-level businesses like newsstands and burger joints, but would certainly include a valley mogul like Frank Manus. I looked around for the You Make My Snout Wet woman, but hotel security must have run her off. Bunch of lightweights like us defense attorneys didn't merit so much vigilance on the part of the Radisson, but the Downtown Businessmen's Association, despite the catholic-sounding name, only admitted power hitters, Fortune 500 guys and their sycophants, politicians currently holding office and their retinues. No bag ladies were going to be permitted to disturb their appetites. Invitation only, but they expected Pete to make an appearance and I breezed in on his coattails.

Pete was picked off right away; the mayor wanted to introduce him to a pop singer passing through town. The singer's band was lighting up the arena tomorrow night. He had probably slithered into the open spot on the schedule courtesy of His Honor, and the price was standing by the mayor's side letting the old crook bask in his charismatic aura. Impress the youth vote. Never mind that the mayor had gotten his political start in the construction unions, and was three-quarters deaf from working a pile driver when they sank the foundations for downtown.

Hearing-Impaired Old Pol Sucks Up to Millionaire Junkie.

Nope, Pete was not going to get any help from me writing tomorrow's column. I just didn't have the right vision for the society page. I made a sweep around the perimeter of the room. Lot of talking heads there, the president of one of the TV stations, the guy that still liked to put himself on for an editorial once in a while. The chairman of Gas and Electric. He got his face on TV every time they hiked the rates. The owners of the football and the baseball teams. Everyone else in the room looked camera-ready, too, perfectly dressed and coifed and tanned. The women, too. The trophy wives glowed and the old battle-axes that had refused to be ditched were inlaid with enough stones to hide their wrinkles.

I spotted Manus from behind. His date was still Mrs. Ambergast. He looked like he had aged considerably since the last time I had seen him. His tux was not cut well enough to conceal the droop of his shoulders, as if he had wasted away between wearings. The skin of his face was dry and gray. Barry Appenzeller's twin, if he shaved his head.

"What?" he spluttered, as I moved into his field of vision.

"Frank," I said. "Mrs. A," I added casually.

"Here to gloat?" he asked. "Not that you'll be here for long."

He craned his wattled neck out of his collar, as he looked for someone to evict me.

"No, Frank. Let's be buddies. Life's been treating me well, lately. Big break for me, getting Angel sprung on bail. Kind of legal deed that makes a legend. And Israel Kahauolopua, the attorney that was unfortunately murdered? Looks like I'm going to pick up the majority of his caseload."

"You had your chance with me," Manus warned.

"People might say that makes me look like some kind of vulture, benefiting from my friend's death like that. But I figure you'd understand. Izzy would have wanted it that way, don't you think?"

"I got no ideer what your goddam friend would've wanted."

Stress was causing Manus to lapse back into a Midwest twang.

"Just like Evie would've wanted you to have her kidney."

Manus looked as though I had just stuck my finger in the plate of shrimp he was holding.

"You heard me right, Frank. Her kidney. The one that's sewed tight up inside you right now. As we're having this little chin wag. Of course, you had to do some legwork for that. Her mother had to be paid off, so she'd sign it away. 'Just tell people you won the lottery,' was what you said for her to say, if anybody asked why she was suddenly rich."

"You are outta your mind."

"Am I, Frank? What else are you doing, buying her a pickup truck that's worth more than her home? She might've looked good twenty years ago, but she's just a beat-up old tramp having vodka for breakfast, now. Not that your personal odometer hasn't turned over, too. You're old, Frank. Rude of me to mention it, but it's a fact. Way too old to be a good candidate for an organ transplant, so my guess is some doctors and hospitals had to be fixed up so the job could be done. The whole thing had to be real hush-hush," I said loudly. A few people started to stare.

"But Evie would have wanted it. Or else you just figured you owned the damn thing anyway? Buying Evie away from that pimp like you did, you figured you had dibs on any parts she might be able to spare. Or do you go back even further than that, Frank? What kind of comfort did you give her, the day her father died on your lawn? What kind of help, with the police and the coroner? Because even then, little Evie knew how to get a man to do things for her. How long did she squirm around on your lap before you unzipped your fly?"

Unzipped your fly. I said that loud enough. Probably the first public mention of a fly being unzipped in the conversational history of the Downtown Businessmen's Association annual bash. A guy who needed to rent his ruffled shirts with nineteen-inch collars started moving my way.

"You got everything wrong. There'll be a suit for slander," Manus said.

"I doubt that, Frank. Suing's not your style. And it would play hell with the bubble you've managed to stick over the whole thing. But let's make it libel. I'm willing to talk to the media. I know a reporter here right now."

I was bluffing.

Gray-market organ donations top topic at Businessmen's Ball.

Couldn't see Pete writing that headline.

"Besides, you sue, I get to subpoena medical records that would otherwise have to remain confidential."

"I know what kind of slime you are."

Manus was spitting at me. I guess my career defending peep shows and dirty bookstores will forever haunt me.

"You're casting it in your own dirty light. Whatever that girl did for me, she did out of love. I would have done the same for her."

"What organ were you going to donate to her? Even the one you gave her on a regular basis wasn't working so hot, right? Besides, what about people who could've used that kidney? Someone might've died waiting for it, while you shoved yourself into the head of the line. You weren't that sick. You weren't even on a kidney machine."

"I wouldn't have lasted a week on the machine," Manus said.

I got it. Manus suffered from a fear of dialysis. An Okie horror. *Don't put me on that dang machine.*

Security was at my elbow.

"Come on," he said.

Even the hired muscle wore name tags at the Downtown Businessmen's Association chicken fry. My captor's read *Pullman.*

Shit, they were using off-duty vice for security.

"So, how was your vacation?" I said conversationally as Pullman dragged me out the emergency exit. Being yanked across the dance floor like a car in tow caused me to collide with a full tray of cocktails. People were staring. That didn't bother Pullman; he opened the emergency exit by slamming me against it.

The stairway was as drably cemented as the ballroom was opulent. The grayness of it was regularly pockmarked with the inch-wide depressions left in the concrete when they cut off the ends of the rebar. Pullman dangled me over the drop, holding my arms back and keeping his leg crossed over mine, so I'd have no way of breaking a fall, if I took one. He had a brutal, fleshy face with a single black eyebrow that did the job most people needed two to cover. I couldn't imagine why Raquel Bumgarden thought he was cute. What women find attractive about men will forever remain a mystery to me.

"Who do you think you are, bothering people here?"

"I think I'm Ted McKeon. I think I'm an attorney. I think you better let me put my feet back on the ground."

I get paid for thinking, I nearly added, but thought better of it.

He thrust his fingers down the back of my borrowed collar. The starched edge cut into my neck. If my shirt-buttons popped, I was going down the stairs, headfirst.

"You got an invite?"

"Choke the suspect out first, then check to see if he might be guilty," I wheezed. "You're a cop of the old school. I can see that."

He shoved my head toward the ground, so I could see the cheap crisscrossed vinyl the builders had used to cover the edge of the risers. I wondered how much of the pattern would end up stamped on my chin or my forehead if I fell.

"You're getting the fuck out of here."

"Fine. The canapés suck anyway. I got a suggestion for you. One word, but it's a four-syllable one, so listen carefully. Elevator. You got it? El-e-va-tor. Let's go down the elevator."

"Speed?" said Pete Winam, peering in through the exit. Not like Pete to be first at the scene of a ruckus. He must have been close by. The exit was fairly proximate to the bar. I twisted my afflicted neck. Pete had a split of champagne in one hand and two glasses in the other.

"Come on in, Pete. The view is great, and the company is lively."

"What are you doing with him?" Pete demanded. His bloodhound reportorial instincts were rising to the fore.

"Who are you?" Pullman countered. Pete pulled back, so he could pretend to look at Pullman from a height, although the vice cop was half a foot taller than the society columnist. The height of his fame. Easy, Pete. Dangerous ground here. Detective Pullman doesn't read the funnies.

Pete affected all the dignity a little pot-bellied man half-lit on free champagne can muster. "I'm with the Tribune," he said.

Pullman had a reporter *and* an attorney at his mercy in a deserted stairwell. Best day he'd had all week. "*You* got an invite?" he snarled at Pete.

"I?" Pete yelped, startled into grammarian affectation. "You don't understand…"

"I understand pretty good. I understand that the people at this party intend to enjoy themselves. I understand they probably don't enjoy getting bothered by shysters and pestered by newspapermen."

Pullman obviously wanted to at least plant a boot in each of our asses by way of starting us down the stairs but it occurred to him that he was now outnumbered. Plus a number of gape-mouthed bon vivants had appeared in the emergency doorway. None of them looked inclined to rescue us, but they'd serve as witnesses.

"Give me that!" Pullman demanded. He released me to snatch the champagne and the glasses out of Pete's hand and elbowed him downwards. I was already on my way toward the ground.

Pete's hands grasped uselessly at the air now that they had been deprived of their task of holding the drinks.

"I never," he said breathlessly, as I led him towards the ground floor exit.

"When was the last time you got kicked out of a shindig?"

Pete's eyes narrowed. "I *never*," he repeated, this time with conviction.

Probably true. Pete was the epitome of refined celebration. Had doubtless always been so. I could imagine the emerging Winam at a college party, the first wisps of the goatee twirling about his chin, monopolizing the attention of the homecoming queen with civilized banter while the rest of his fraternity brothers drooled over her and drank themselves sick with lust.

"Whole new angle on things for you, then."

The paragraph headings unrolled themselves in my mind.

Your Reporter Cut Off, Eighty-Sixed Down Stairwell.

"I've a mind to go right back up there."

Frank Manus' Hired Gorilla Does A Number On Local Attorney, Columnist's Egos.

"You go right ahead, Pete. You mind dropping me off, first?"

Sealed Windows Prevent Defenestration Of Investigative Pair.

He didn't mind at all. Izzy's building was deserted. I treated myself to the elevator ride, having had enough of stairwells for the week. The red light on my telephone glowed, indicating a saved message. I punched it up on the speakerphone.

"You better get your ass over here," Marvin Maeger's voice grumbled into the empty air. "Your little Angel's flown the fucking coop."

Chapter Fourteen

At ten o'clock on a Friday night, the parking lot at the strip mall was given over entirely to the customers of Phantasy Photography. The matron in the Security t-shirt had fled and the other shops had closed and barred their doors against the Phantasy overflow. Guys parked their cars, made the dash across the lot and whipped aside the velvet curtains of the whack shack in a steady stream, lured by its pink neon pulsing. A few lingered behind their steering wheels, taking a snort or two off a flask or a bagged bottle, either loosening their libidos in anticipation or relaxing in the afterglow.

No girls lounged in the waiting room. All were modeling for the sightless eye. Five or six men sat on the couches, staring straight ahead, waiting for one of Marvin Maeger's staff to come take them by the hand. I followed the same etiquette, not looking at anyone else in the room, although I don't know whether I wished to avoid embarrassing them or myself.

Marvin saved me by cracking his concealed door and letting me into his office.

"See how busy it is? Last time the little tramp split on me was a Saturday. Now Friday fucking night. Friday nights are big for me."

"How long ago did the tramp decamp, Mr. Maeger?"

"First she said she wanted the morning off. Then she called in and said she'd be back by six. No fucking show."

"Maybe she just needed a little time out. She'll be back by lights out."

Angel had been sleeping in one of Marvin's studios.

"Or maybe she's out doing a little private whoring."

I shrugged, but I was worried. Not about Angel turning a trick or two on the side; you can't take the stink off a skunk. Or about Marvin's proprietary interest in every spouting that one of his girls inspired. Angel was on the loose. Pennofrio or the vice cops could run across her, or Manus could grab her off. It was an unsafe place for her and, consequently, her case.

"Got any idea where that would be, Mr. Maeger?"

"I was going to ask you the same thing. Anyhow, you find her, tell her she's through."

"She'll be back."

"Then I'll put her out on the street myself. I got a problem with that girl. You know what that problem is?"

Marvin Maeger was going to supply an insight. I put my fingertips together and awaited it.

"I'll tell you. It ain't that she's a dyke, or that she likes to cut deals for herself on the side. Shit, half these girls lick each other's boxes. What do you expect them to do, the number of pricks they see all day long, they want to have a little clit under their eyeballs when they're trying to have fun. And all of them would cut me out, if they were smart enough to figure out how to do business themselves. Angel ain't no different than any of them that way. My problem with her is fucking deeper. She don't take this business seriously."

"Easy mistake to make, Mr. Maeger. That doesn't look like the boardroom of General Dynamics, out there."

"Fuck you. You're the same. Maybe that's why you take care of the little twat so good. You know what I tell these girls when I hire them?"

Marvin's business philosophy. About to be revealed to me.

"This is an acting job, " I say. "Up to you to act like you want their company. Up to you to make 'em enjoy themselves. The customer don't owe you a damn thing. Above all, don't laugh when they pull down their pants. Angel's a fucking laugher."

"Happens to all of us. Happens to presidents, from what I hear."

"It ain't supposed to happen here."

I wished Angel would walk through the door, make Marvin look bad, make it an early night for me.

"The point being that I tell my girls to treat every customer the same. No matter what kind of wang he's pointing at you. You giggle, you ruin the moment for him. He's got to get hard again, and that takes time. And time is money, their money and mine. Fucking so obvious, but you'd be amazed how long it takes some of them to catch on. Some of them never take the business serious. Angel never did."

"So she's been chuckling her way through the working day?"

"Probably. Actually, I don't monitor her so much. Can't stand to look at the little bitch."

"Lucky your customers don't have such discriminating tastes, Mr. Maeger. My bet is that they like to look at her just fine. And I need to look at her again, too, since she, like you, is my client. I'm still guessing she'll be back here by lights out, but in case she isn't, I have to go find her. You can help. When I brought her in, did you do any paperwork on her? Apart from the contract they sign that they're not going to do exactly what they're paid to do?"

"Sure. I got to do that. In case one of them drops dead of an overdose, or has a heart attack out of sheer fucking ecstasy because Brad Pitt comes in to whack off on her, I got to know who to call. Got to check that they got a friggin' Social Security card, too," he groused.

"Where is that piece of paper?"

Marvin flipped through a pile of bills and invoices on his desk. "Could have filed it already," he muttered. "Naw. Here it is." He glanced at it. Suddenly his eyes bulged and his skin flushed hypertensively. "You see what I mean?" he exclaimed. "You see what I mean? Look what she wrote here."

Marvin shoved the paper at me. It had *Application For Employment* printed boldly across the top.

"Name," I read. "Address. Educational Level Attained. You need to know Educational Level Attained, for a girl that's just going to get naked for strangers?"

"I use the same form I used for the clerks when I had the video store. I still had a case of them left over. Don't worry about that shit. Further down. This box here. You can tell from that, she thinks the whole job's a big joke."

I looked at the box Marvin's pudgy finger was poised over.

"Big laugh, isn't it?" he said. "The little bitch was just fucking with me again. This guy ain't even alive. And what's she doing, putting his name here? Trying to make me feel like I'm some kind of slimeball, like he was? Everything I do is legal! I ain't laughing!"

I wasn't laughing, either.

In fact I felt a cold quivering shoot up from my prostate through my guts and into the back of my head, where it spread out and became an icy palm cupping the contents of my skull. Maybe someone having a stroke feels this way, I remember thinking, as my whole frame of reference regarding Angel was abruptly flipped over.

In small print in the corner of the box were stenciled the words "Emergency Contact-Relationship. Under "Relationship," Angel, in a small, determined hand, had written "Father." Equally precisely, in the space under "Father" she had written *Chessie the Clown*.

One more panicky dash to Izzy's office. One more rooting through the boxes of my effects. This time truly frenzied, scattering papers everywhere, throwing things, leaving bits of office trash, paper clips and sticky pads, perched in my friend's potted plants, like odd birds gone to roost. Finally I found the envelope from Gladys Bernheim, the one I had never remembered to have Amy answer.

The late Frank Fernando's apartment was south and east of downtown. It wasn't a bad little building. Fresh paint and landscaped grounds set it apart from its neighbors. Made it a beachhead of respectability driven into the slum environment. A few graffiti scrawls on the walls showed that the neighborhood was working on repelling the invader.

The key in my hand wouldn't work the security gate. I stood irresolutely before it.

"May I help you?" A woman inside the complex noticed my discomfiture.

"My key won't work."

"That's an apartment key. You need a security key. Who are you?"

She was a tall, self-possessed black woman. She had the air of a civil servant, an administrator for the city or a high school principal.

"I'm an attorney. My name is Ted McKeon."

"Mr. McKeon? I'm Gladys Bernheim."

She let me in the gate. "I'm afraid you're too late. There's already someone in there."

"Rented out? Are you the resident manager?"

"No. I just try to keep an eye on things while Mr. Kroll is on vacation. With the owner's permission," she added, not wanting to give the impression she was a freelance busybody. "Someone from one of the owner's other properties stops by every day, but it's not enough. You can see that."

She gestured disparagingly at the graffiti.

"Maybe they'll let me take a look around."

"Do you want me to come with you? I can vouch for who you are."

"I'd better go myself. It's more a matter of persuasion than legal preeminence."

"As you like, Mr. McKeon."

I fit the key into the door. I thought about knocking, but decided having surprise on my side if I was right was worth the embarrassment if I was wrong.

I let myself into a room lit only by a single fluorescent lamp over the sink. It was a one-bedroom apartment. The room I was in combined the functions of kitchen and living room. Spread out over the sink were printouts from Family Planning Services. A vial of Percodans, half full, was capped next to them. On the table were twenty vinyl sheaves marked *Visa*. I unsnapped one. Traveler's checks, in one-hundred-dollar denominations. Ten of them in each sheaf. Unsigned.

Angel wasn't pregnant anymore. And she was leaving town.

The tiny sound the snap made when I unbuttoned it must have alerted her. She appeared in the doorway, nude except for a massive pad between her legs. The painkillers made her eyes hollow and her legs unsteady. She leaned against the frame. She pulled the front of the pad away and peered down it.

"The bleeding's almost stopped," she said. "What are you doing here?"

"That's my question for you, Angel."

"I'm getting better. How did you find me?"

The answer to that question wasn't going to improve this particular attorney-client relationship, so I didn't bother with it.

"Going somewhere, Angel?"

"I'm going to leave, as soon as I feel better. Then you won't have to worry about me anymore. Down through Mexico. Then over to Cuba, and over to Europe. Then Japan the long way. They won't be looking for me there. I can get my boobs done in Mexico, too. I'll be like Evie, then. I can quit doing the little girl act. They're cheaper down there, too. Someone told me it's because you can't sue if they screw it up. That's okay with me. Can you imagine me suing anybody?"

She let out a short laugh like a bubble popping.

"Suing them is better than killing them, Angel."

"You mean Evie? I told you, I didn't have any choice. She would have killed me."

"I don't mean just Evie. The man that lived here is dead. Cops thought it was a suicide. This is starting to seem familiar to me. Sounds like something Evie might have thought up. This man molested you, didn't he, Angel?"

"Evie only ever wanted to kill strangers. People who were famous."

"This guy was famous, too."

"For a while. And that was after. When it happened, my mom took me away. She said God would punish him. God never did a damn thing. Even when he was caught with some other little girl, he didn't even go to jail. But my mother never did anything, except take our old name back."

"So whose idea was killing Frank Fernando? Yours?"

"His own. He killed himself," Angel said defiantly.

"How do I know you didn't set him up with Evie? You promise him a little more of what he craved? A little more of the little girl act? That why he was naked? Then, when he was completely nude and unresisting, probably with his eyes shut in fantasy, your girlfriend held his own gun to his forehead and killed him. Put the gun in his hand while it was still smoking, so the cops would think it was suicide. That about right?"

"No. You don't know what you're talking about. Evie couldn't do the little girl act after she got her big boobs. The guys who like that, they didn't want her any more. She didn't look right for it. It was a big mistake for her. Money-wise. A big mistake."

Wasn't much of a mistake compared to some of the other ones that had littered Evie's life was what I was going to say, but then I experienced the same cold jolt to my nerves I had felt when I saw *Chessie the Clown* written on Angel's job application. It was worse this time. The icy shock I felt inside my head was so intense I really thought I might be suffering some untimely health event. I'd be shit out of luck if I decided to have that stroke in the presence of Angel. For sure she didn't know CPR, and the chances of her calling 911 were as remote as Mars.

The feeling passed, but I sent a prayer winging skyward before I asked my next question. I don't pray often, but when I do it's with utter sincerity, and the words of my prayer are always the same: *Jesus help me, for I am a fucking moron.*

"When did Evie get her boob job, Angel?"

"I dunno. A while ago. I remember last Valentine's day, she was so sore I couldn't touch her. I was sad. I was really in love with her, then. She bought me some earrings, to make up for it."

"So Evie was out of the little girl business last February. But Father Canto fell off the mountain in April. Who was doing the little girl act then, Angel?"

Angel was quiet far too long, even for someone in a painkiller stupor.

"I need to sit down." She put herself in one of the chairs.

I needed to sit down, too, but I stayed upright. Even drugged and suffering the aftereffects of an abortion Angel didn't put me at my ease.

"I'm thinking it was you, Angel. How long do you think you'll need to sit there, before you think of a story that'll convince me otherwise?"

She rocked back and forth for what seemed like an hour, although it really couldn't have been more than a few minutes. She opened her mouth to speak, and then shut it, a couple of times. She folded her arms and knees together and pressed her hands to her face as if that might help her concentrate.

"Well," she finally said, and then didn't add anything else, for another ungainly silence. Wasn't even a clock ticking in that room. I could hear people barking their food orders at a fast-food drive-thru a street away.

Then Angel actually smiled. It was a sad smile, small and loopy and defeated, but a smile nonetheless. "A long time," she admitted.

"But you were smart enough to implicate Evie. You planted the dream catcher, just in case?"

People want to confess. The longer they wait to do it, the more likely they are to hold nothing back. It's a human tendency that has ruined many otherwise perfectly winnable cases for those of us in the defense bar.

"That was just luck. I thought the dream catcher was stupid. What would I ever want to dream about? I meant to wear my crucifix, but Evie had borrowed it. She was in one of her Madonna moods," Angel said. A faintly critical smile crossed her face. "So I borrowed a piece of her jewelry. It really did happen just like I said. The priest said it ruined the effect, but I could tell he was afraid of it."

"You had the cabbie drop you off at the Manus Building. You were trying to implicate somebody."

"I didn't want to go straight home. It was the only other address I had memorized."

"Why Mikey?"

Angel had already killed Canto when they met, by my calculations, with more murder on her schedule. Funny time to strike up a fresh relationship.

She sighed. "I don't know. Maybe it was because he was a regular guy. I'd never had a regular guy, really. Maybe it was because he was a good father. I never knew one of them, either. I let myself get pregnant, too. I was going to maybe try a regular life. But then everything else happened, and it never worked out."

She stared out the tiny kitchen window. Only a lonely street light glowed outside it, a big fuzzy spangle to her sedated vision.

"You killed two men because Evie wanted you to?"

"They deserved it," she said flatly.

"Nobody deserves to die like that. And then you killed your own father?"

If I had the chronology straight.

"That scared Evie, too. She didn't think I could do anything on my own. But I just kept right on going. Why not? She was right. It was people like him that ruined girls like us. They don't deserve life. I'll never have a life, a normal life. What man would want me, for more than a night, after I've been what I've been? I never knew why I was mad all the time. I never knew why boys my own age never made me happy. Evie told me why."

"Psychiatrist would have told you the same thing, Angel. And you wouldn't have had to kill anyone."

"I went to a psychiatrist. He tried to fuck me."

A look of apprehension must have crossed my face.

"He's still alive," she added. An opiated giggle shook her from the inside. "You're so sweet. Worried you were going to have to get me out of jail again?"

"You're a worrisome girl, Angel. But you don't have to run. They'll never convict you." Rock solid case, now. Knowing the truth meant knowing all the potential pitfalls. Even as I spoke, I felt my gut tightening up with self-loathing. The only ethical thing for me to do would be to walk my little killer right out the courthouse door. Pin Father Canto's and Big Daddy's deaths on deceased Evie, who had never killed anybody, at least with her own hands. Had merely pointed Angel at them, just like she had let that riding mower roll. Killer by default, Charlie Manson all silked out and siliconed up. There was another question I had to ask.

"What about Evie and her father?"

"She never killed her father. I found that out. I killed mine. Like everything else I did, nobody knew. Now you do."

Her consciousness seemed to click up a stop. The Percodan film over her eyes lightened a little.

"You can do anything you want to me," she said, in an entirely different tone. I thought she meant I had power over her existence, but then I realized the invitation was sexual. She fingered the pad, suddenly aware that her most formidable weapon was useless.

"I'll do it for you with my mouth, for now."

"You don't have to do anything for me."

"I want to."

Like hell. I pictured myself concentrating on the oral pleasure of Angel, while her hand slithered toward the knife drawer.

"Angel, listen. I can't do anything to you. I can't tell anyone what you've told me. It's called lawyer-client confidentiality. You understand?"

"You can't tell?"

"I would be breaking the law if I did."

Not true, but I didn't know any other way to convince Angel I was bound by my promise.

"I know you don't break the law."

A wan smile. Maybe she was reflecting on how much of an overachiever she was, in the field of breaking the law. She focused on me suddenly, doubtfully, and I realized she was determined to force silence on me in the way she was used to.

In the way she had forced Evie's. Never mind she had no weapon. She'd find one. Homicide had become such an easy habit for her that she probably thought she could, in the stupor brought on by the painkillers.

She put both hands on the table. He forearms shook as she tried to rise.

"I can't get up," she said numbly. "Stay. Until I feel better."

"Angel, I've got to go."

"Stay," she said. "I'll be all right in a couple of hours. I've had the operation before. These pills wear off in a little bit."

I backed toward the door, considering that she might be faking the paralysis.

"Stay," she moaned. "Don't call the police," she added, when she saw my hand on the doorknob.

"I won't," I said.

Then I fled, fast, through the gate, out to my car, not wanting to run into anyone. Anyone at all, especially anyone like Gladys Bernheim, anyone who I might have to explain myself to. Anyone not drenched in second-hand gore. Anyone who was not, like I had become again, counselor to the bringer of death.

Ally to the paws of murder.

My house was locked up tight. Must have left the cat inside all day. The air was thick with his smell, but that was the least of my worries. I went straight to the freezer and twisted the cap off the bottle I found there. Belarus to the rescue.

I didn't bother with a glass. I had none frozen and didn't want to take a chance on the spirits warming even a degree before I gulped them down. I took swallows straight from the bottle, replacing it in the pile of freezer snow between drinks.

I could have called 911. Should have, but I thought I had time. Instead I rang Pennofrio and left a message. Friday night. The valley was awash in pink-collar flesh. The police sergeant was probably squeezing a knee at that very moment. I wandered in a circle around my kitchen between the freezer and the phone, a circle whose circumference became more erratic as the level in the bottle got lower. All the while I tried to think of differences between the case of Willie Washington so long ago and the problem of Angel Pisaro in the present day.

I knew Angel Pisaro had killed someone the day I took her case. The same for Willie Washington. No difference.

I knew Angel was a soulless little bitch, a paid-for fuck that hated nearly every man alive. I knew Willie Washington was a convicted stick-up artist that walked a high wire across the pit of homicide every time he stuck a weapon in a salesclerk's face. No difference.

I knew Angel Pisaro's most heartfelt desire after her capture was to make it out onto the street. Willie Washington's to be free to put a gun back in his hand. No difference.

I thought Angel Pisaro was a mindless little toady, a mere accessory tramp to a real king-hell bitch, who struck out in fear of her life. I thought Willie Washington had the makings of a family man, who killed only to protect his own. In both cases I was dead wrong.

No difference.

If life is so short, why do we spend it doing the same things over and over?

I stumbled over a chair and came close to falling. I paged Pennofrio again when I realized it had been an hour and a half since I had done so the first time. I decided to give him five minutes, then it would be 911. I took the bottle out of the freezer and uncapped it again, then paused. It was a complicated story I was going to relate to whoever answered at the emergency switchboard. Friday night it was as busy as a roadhouse. I wondered if the emergency operator would know I was drunk.

I knew I was drunk.

"He's drinking again."

At first I thought it was my inner voice, commenting on my actions. Then I realized it had been real sound. I turned around. Standing at the window, horror of horrors, Angel Pisaro. How? I had left her naked and busted, and notorious, with every cop in town looking to bring her in for questioning. Who was left in her circle of acquaintance idiot enough to come to her aid without considering the consequences?

That would be my son. He was standing beside her.

"How about you let us in?" he said.

Angel was squeezing his neck. Affectionately. For now. I wanted her hands off of him, fast.

"My mom said she left him on account of the drinking."

Easy, kid. You're not going to impress a girl like Angel with our family secrets. They're seriously lightweight by her standards. I opened the door, unable to think of anything else to do. Could I yell at my son to get away from her, as quickly as he could? Why would he start taking my advice now, just because his life depended on it? He would only sneer.

The LeSabre was behind them in the drive, visible in the porch light.

"Just her," I said. "You wait in the car."

"Hey, no way."

"Go ahead and wait," Angel told him.

"What do you want to see *him* for?" my son asked whinily.

"Lawyer stuff. Just listen to your music. It won't take long."

"You're not going to, like, *do* anything with him?"

Angel, smiling, shook her head no. Not a reassuring negative, not to my son or me.

"I'm going to be right outside," he warned her. Then he leered at me. "And thanks for getting her out of jail. Really, thanks."

"Close the door."

Angel spoke as soon as the doorjamb clicked.

"It's true you can't tell anyone what I told you. I found that out. But you can't let me run. You're an officer of the court."

Her eyes fell on the silver hand-axes, still sitting next to the sink. I was at the apogee of my orbit around the room. She was closer to them than I was.

Available weapons. Make use of them. Evie's combat philosophy. She had lived barely long enough to regret having such an able student.

Angel was still slowed by the Percodans, but I was crippled by the grain. She had one of the axes in her hand before I had finished my lunge for the counter. She took a backhand slice that connected weakly with my forearm. I didn't even look at the wound, I just felt the bleeding start. She brought the ax around again, this time a double-handed swing that whistled for my head. I fell back and scrambled away. I put one of my mismatched sofas between us, feinting escape around it one way and dodging the other. Fooled her enough that her next chop missed me by a foot.

I was already completely winded and dizzy from the booze. The more fatigued I became, the more lithe Angel seemed. Where was my son? Angel would have to kill him as well. A fight that would pit a slobbering mass of juvenile hormones against an accomplished serial killer. Easy to figure out how that one would come out.

Angel was still between the door and me. She held the blade in both hands, trying to herd me around, corner me up against the clutter of my living room. She was breathing hard, too. None of her other victims had put up this much resistance. That'd be a point of pride for me, if she opened up my guts instead of caving in my skull and I got a few minutes of flashback while I bled to death.

I backed up against the banister. Turning, I fled up the stairs. I felt as if I had no choice, even though it's always a mistake, in crime melodramas. Angel had me in a confined space. She threw the ax. It landed with a fatal-feeling thump right between my shoulder blades. I fell and it clattered to the carpet next to me. No blood stained its blade. Must have hit me with the haft instead of the edge. I put my hand on the weapon, practically weeping with gratitude.

Angel saw me and backed away. I slid down the steps, not regaining my feet until I reached the bottom, holding the blade high with both hands over my head like Attila the Hun in full sacking form. Angel backed to the counter as I advanced, and grabbed the other ax. Then she screamed. Battle cry of the father-killer, I thought. Revenge scream of the molested child.

The ax slipped out of her hands. I was so startled I hesitated. She looked at the cat shit dripping from her fingers. She let out another cry of rage and loathing. I jumped, ready to swing.

The door was behind her. She fled outside. I followed with my weapon. My son snatched off the I-Pod he had been wearing to kill time while Angel tried to kill me.

"Hey, what are you trying to do to her?" he yelled. "Hey!" He punched open the door of the LeSabre and ran after us.

"I'm a fucking adult!" he screamed. "Who I hang with is my own business! What, you're going to kill her for being with me?"

I ignored him. I had no breath to argue and no time to explain. We were out on the road now, heading downhill. I concentrated on my sprinting form, trying to remember my track coaching. Angel was lighter and faster and younger than me, and I had always been a lousy sprinter, but perceptibly I was gaining. Angel was bleeding, too, I realized. The violence must have started her hemorrhaging again.

Another hundred feet and I would overtake her. Whether it was caused by adrenaline or need for revenge or relief at my own escape, I was filled with the lust to kill. It made the desire I felt for Jill Congliaro's naked body seem a paltry and transient emotion by comparison. I drooled to sink the ax into Angel's head. I could not imagine myself stopping until I had hacked it from her body. I longed to see her die. I would celebrate her limbs' final twitch and the rattling of her last breath. I would dance around her corpse like a barbarian in a victorious horde, chanting thanks to the war gods while her blood still misted in the air.

The heart of murder and mine beat one and the same.

Then I hit the wall. With my head. It was a funny wall. It shouldn't have been there, and it was loud. I was unconscious before I fell to the asphalt.

I could hear before I could see. There were sounds of a lot of people moving around me, feet crunching through gravel, vehicle doors being opened and shut. One voice was nearby.

"Guy running with an ax in his hand, what did you expect me to do?"

"Maybe shout halt, huh?"

"He was almost on top of the girl."

"Too bad you didn't hit her instead of him, you fucking idiot. Too bad you didn't hit her *and* him."

Pennofrio had finally responded to my page. In person.

I blinked. I could see now. Orange light flashing, lighting up the interior of the place I was lying. Bottles and tubes and packages of gauze. The inside of an ambulance. I moved my arms and legs, just to see if I could. The pallet I was lying upon was soft and unbelievably clean.

"I didn't know it was him," the voice was pleading. "People in this neighborhood don't do things like that. And the kid was chasing them both."

I couldn't see or hear my son.

"He's a lawyer," Kenny whimpered. "Sure as there's fish shit on the bottom of the ocean, he's going to sue me."

"I'm gonna sue you, too, man. For pointing that thing at me. And I'm going to sue the cops, too. For putting me in handcuffs."

"Shut up, you little asshole."

My son. Always inspires the same reaction in people. At least he was okay. Gratitude buzzed inside me, like an anesthetic. Then I blacked out again.

Chapter Fifteen

They kept me in the hospital for a day and a night after they picked all of the neoprene out of my head, giving me every neurological test they could think of, making sure that Kenny's shotgun blast hadn't permanently scrambled my egg. The tests were boring and repetitive, but pleasant compared to my interview with Pennofrio.

"She fucking hauled out of here. Stuck out her thumb and was gone before the first unit responded," he said at the conclusion of it.

"She's heading for the border."

"She's already across it, Counselor. Tried to cover it, but you can't close the road to Tijuana on a Friday night. Physical impossibility."

"You checked the apartment? She must have had some kind of baggage."

Painkillers? Pads? Clothes? Six month's income in traveler's checks? She hadn't left her belongings in the LeSabre.

"Nothing was there when we checked it. Attractive female doesn't take much time to hitchhike anywhere, especially if she's willing to pay for the ride with the sex coin. Which was no problem for our Angel. First guy picked her up probably took her to the apartment, helped her pack, drove her to the border, got a second helping of oral joy and then went home and told his wife he had to walk three miles with a gas can, must be something wrong with the gauge, honey."

"You got a shit-sour view of human nature, Sergeant."

"That's because people lie to me and conceal things from me and dither around paging me when they ought to be speed-dialing 911. What, I'm your personal confessor?"

"When I saw her, she was in bad shape. I never thought she'd get out of that apartment last night, let alone try and kill me."

"One of our main problems last night was your thinking end was on the fritz. I figured it was the gunshot wound, but from the way you've been acting, maybe you'd been suffering from the problem all week. Took us a half hour to get the address out of your boy, too. Angel had him pretty well convinced there was a malignant conspiracy, probably the same one that killed Kennedy and Princess Diana, to fry her innocent ass. Kid watches too much TV, and he's too stoned while he's doing it, you ask me. He held out pretty tough until we clicked on the bracelets. Aiding and abetting, you know."

"He isn't in Juvenile, is he?"

"Naw. Pretty easy to see what happened. Hell, you opened the door of that old car, you could smell what happened."

"What about Kenny?"

"Pretty much depends on you. He's released on personal right now. He ain't going anywhere. You want to press, assault with a deadly or ag assault. Not a sure conviction by a long shot, though. You were chasing her with a hand-ax. Your friend Kenny had an inaccurate perception of the situation, but when his attorney starts exploring state of mind, intent to commit a crime may be found to be lacking. I learned to talk like that from lawyers. Ain't you proud? Just sue the bastard, is my advice."

"And get what?"

"Maybe get him to stay home at nights, catch up on his beer drinking and ESPN watching, huh?"

I was being discharged that afternoon. My ex-wife had brought some fresh clothes. They hung in the tiny hospital room closet. The ex had groused about the chore, but with Izzy gone, Amy suing me, and Jill Congliaro just not the kind of girl you asked to go rooting through your underwear drawer, I didn't have anyone else to cover it for me. I had a little project planned for the afternoon. Pennofrio could be of help.

"You remember when Evie got killed, Sergeant?"

"Wasn't that many cold people ago. Of course I remember."

"Did you put in the call to Vampire Eddie?"

"No, I didn't."

"Which meant Evie didn't have a donor card."

"So? Next of kin can okay a donation. And Eddie's always there, there's not any good brain death happening in any of the local hospitals."

"You know who got Evie's kidney, Sergeant?"

He listened when I told him. Then I hit him with the proposition.

"No."

"Right under your nose," I reminded him.

"No," he said. "It's Sunday afternoon. Barefoot Bar. The reggae band starts at three-thirty. You ever go there? Not that it's the best day for you personally to mingle, but for those of us who haven't been wounded this weekend, it's paradise. Tourist women, looking for a vacation memory. Local girls showing off the latest creations in silicon. Beach babies whose loser boyfriends are serving every weekend in jail from now until Easter. I plan to be at my regular table, guzzling down two-fifty Mai Tai's, until the sun goes down."

"It won't take long."

"Monday. You ever hear of Monday? Start of the working week."

But I knew Sunday would work better. Sunday, when Polar Security turned on the alarms at the Manus Building and put its feet up on the couch until the morning. I just guessed Frank Manus would be in. What else was there for him in life now, except work? There was an emergency exit conveniently propped open. There was a slow banging noise from one of the loading docks nearby. At least one worker labored on the Sabbath. I walked away from it.

Upstairs, the tank full of snails bubbled peaceably in the anteroom. I went in without knocking. Frank Manus was just sitting, touching the desk lightly with his fingertips, looking at his reflection in the surface. Waiting for it to dissolve before his eyes, most likely. It didn't take an MD to see that he was not a well man. But his hatred for me was still healthy.

"You, again?" He treated me to a pop-eyed glare.

"So rudely interrupted, last time we were talking."

"It's going to happen again," he warned, reaching for the phone. "This is trespassing."

"Door was open. And the cops have had enough of me this weekend already. Do you think I'm going to put my hands on you? I'm not in real good shape, myself."

I touched the bandage wrapping my skull, with my stitched-up arm.

"It serves you right. You were warned about her."

"Yes. I know. Believe me, I'm not feeling so smart today. The head wound doesn't help."

"You're here to apologize, then."

"Just to commiserate, Frank. You don't mind, I call you Frank? Because I feel much closer to you now. We're both medical miracles, you and I. I survived a shotgun blast to the head. And you, a kidney transplant at your age."

"I don't regard it as a miracle. I had every confidence in my doctors. I don't trouble myself employing the second rate, McKeon. I only use the best. Medical science is a modern wonder. You'll find out yourself, when you start feeling your age."

"Almost quit getting older last night, Frank. So I don't know if I'll live long enough to need spare parts. How long had you known about your kidneys, Frank? It can be a slow disease, nephritis. Months, maybe even a year before you had to go under the knife, you knew your kidneys were failing."

"How long I was sick doesn't have anything to do with anything."

"Yeah, it does, Frank. It's why you had Evie tissue-typed when you bought the breast augmentation for her. Just to find out. That's what the pathologist was for. Dr. Verlace's still fuming about him, by the way."

"I don't take chances."

"That's not right, Frank. You take some big ones, I think. You've led a full and exciting life. So full and exciting that it's difficult for you to get excited about anything any more. You just about admitted that to me. So you leap at the chance for a thrill. It doesn't have to be a sexual thrill.

"Just say, for a minute, you knew about Evie and Angel's little project. Killing father-molesters. It could be a great secret for the three of you to share, when you're lying naked together, after the girls have put on one of their special shows for you. The girls want to do a little freelance purifying of the gene pool. You don't disapprove. Maybe you even fingered Canto and O'Toole for them. I don't know how else the girls could have found out about them by themselves. They were pretty busy to keep up with the news. And Big Daddy O'Toole, especially, was ancient history from their point of view.

"What did those guys ever do to you, Frank? Let me guess. Big Daddy could crack your social circle, on the strength of his recording career. He get loaded at some party and insult you? Because I know how you view that. Negatively. And Father Canto, he was an embarrassment to the Church. You're not Catholic, Frank, but big landowners stick together. The Cardinal bitch about Father Molester running free? Don't touch that phone, Frank."

I swept it off the desk. It landed unhooked on the floor.

"This is all speculation of course, Frank. Stuff I'll never know for sure. Of course, if you didn't know about it, why did you pay off the Rainbow Valley cabbie? He would've identified Angel, not Evie. If you were innocent, a good thing. But if not, if Angel knew she was going down for any murder in addition to Evie's, she'd have no incentive to keep her mouth shut about you.

"One thing I do know is when your disease got critical, you asked Evie for a living donation. They're much more likely to succeed. She owed you, Frank. You got her out of the life. Wasn't for you, she'd be turning tricks in East town and getting the money slapped out of her every night by her pimp. You set her up in her own business, a lucrative one, at least by stripper standards, and you were her best customer. You bought her breasts. Two for one organ deal, from your point of view.

"But Evie turned you down. Pretty little dancer girl doesn't want a scar. Maybe she goes to a doctor privately, Verlace or some other, she knows plenty of rich fucks besides you, and he advises her against it. Just for medical reasons. It's a long life ahead, when you're twenty-three. A future best faced with both kidneys.

"That pisses you off, Frank. After all you've done for her. Selfish little bitch. Lucky for you, and your life has been filled with luck, Evie gets into a spat with her murderous roommate and gets herself killed."

"There's no doubt about what happened there."

"No doubt about what, Frank. Lot of doubt about why. Why did Angel, as slick a killer as any that ever cut a wider path through the public eye, kill Evie so she had to be found out? She knew she was never going to be Evie's next victim because she was Evie's hands and eyes for murder. Not that Angel couldn't make a desperate move. Nobody knows that better than me.

"And the girls were angry with you, Frank. Far angrier than they were at each other. They'd figured something out. Maybe that doctor blabbed a little bit too much about the biology of organ donation. Must've made you mad again. I'm surprised he's still alive. Maybe he isn't. I'll have to ask my friend, Detective Sergeant Pennofrio, whether any prominent physicians were iced by angry ex-patients this past couple of weeks. See, Frank? I'm beginning to figure out your style."

"You're beginning to figure out nothing. You have no facts to support these preposterous speculations."

"Glad you asked for facts, because here's some. What are the odds, a man and his mistress's kidneys matching? We're not talking about finding your soul-mate, Frank, or something amorphous like that. We're talking hard biochemistry. I was talking about it this afternoon, while I was taking some neurological tests. Boring tests, Frank. Stuff like, does this feel hot or cold? Am I touching the top or the palm of your hand? Is the green spot above or below the red spot? But the conversation was very interesting.

"Two people, picked at random, what are the chances one could donate a kidney to the other? Fifty or so to one, Frank. Plus Evie was AB negative. A rare blood type. It's in the coroner's report. As Angel's defense lawyer, I got to read it.

"More than blood type has to match up, but AB negative makes it really long odds. More like a thousand to one. You're a lucky guy, but you're not that lucky.

"Angel told me Evie never killed her father. I thought she meant the riding mower accident was just an accident, that Evie merely took credit for it, so she could be the senior killer. But Evie probably did it, didn't she? Took off the brake and let the machine roll. You know, Frank. It was your first secret. Followed five minutes later by Secret Two. But Angel wasn't talking about that. She meant Evie never killed her father, because that's you.

"Evie was your little girl, Frank. Your biological daughter. Otherwise the kidney never would've fit. You and Gail knew it could be, all along. She never could come after you on it—the guy that died on your lawn signed the birth certificate—but you two *partied*, as Mrs. Fortenwood likes to call it, together. Twenty-three or so years ago. Little sex action—there was plenty of that going around, and by now I understand your tastes well enough to know that you wanted in on it. Gail Fortenwood, or whatever her name was then, turns up pregnant. Conveniently for you, she's married, so hubby takes the credit for hitting the bullseye, but you kept an eye out for Evie, in your own way. Gave her so-called father odd jobs. Plucked her off the streets. Salutary, at least by your usual standards. Then came the day you couldn't keep your hands off her a second longer."

"I hope you're a good lawyer, son, or else you know one," Manus said, setting the tone of his voice low to affect sincerity.

"Both, I think, Frank. So the girls figured it out. Had it explained to them by some eager medical Joe. Just to impress a couple of little hardbodies, maybe, no better reason needed. Little irony for Evie and Angel. Just after they figured out that all the problems of the world were caused by fathers molesting their daughters, their main benefactor turns out to be the biggest daughter-molester of them all. Because you'd known for certain since Evie's implants were done, and that didn't slow you down. No love like West Virginia love, eh? The biggest thrill of all. Made it even better for you, didn't it?"

The phone had long since ceased to make the off-the-hook beeping. Frank Manus stared at me with his white trash eyes. Blue as cornflowers. Evie's eyes.

"Plenty of hostility in the little triangle now, but that's an environment you can work in. You blackmail Angel. You've got the serial killings, enough for the needle. And Evie would go down, too, so Angel has to figure her life is already lost. You promise Angel you've got enough influence in this town to get her off light. Angel kills her lover so you can have her kidney. Like I said, a lot of irony, but Angel isn't the type of girl to be paralyzed by irony.

"But then you turn over on Angel. Your habit is to extract the maximum advantage out of any situation, and it's a tough one to break. You use your friends to turn up the heat on her. Let her think about lethal injection for a month. Then you'd get Donnelly to offer her a deal. Even a good one, where she could be out in twenty. New kidney or not, Frank, in twenty years your problems in this world are over and from the way you behave, I doubt you believe in the next.

"Angel would have to take the deal. She never gets a chance to open her mouth in court, except to say *Guilty*.

"But Angel still had Mikey, and Mikey had me. She couldn't tell the truth, about Evie or about you, but she could flip the story so the frame fit Evie instead of her. Once she started looking good, thanks to me and Izzy, you reversed course again. I should have figured that out as soon as Jimmy Donnelly didn't show up for Angel's bail hearing, that you were back on her side. My own stupid fault, because I'd been warned how you did business. Friends become enemies, enemies friends, and back again. It's the way business gets done. Too bad if they get square in your sights when they're on the opponent side of the cycle, though.

"Israel Kahauolopua was a hell of a lawyer, Frank. He was a hell of a friend of mine, too. But that's not why I'm going to see you pay. Last night you primed your little weapon again. I know who Angel called when she disappeared Friday. Through Cuba? Who's going to tell Angel that the only way to get a flight to Europe without going through a US airport is through Mexico and Cuba? 'Officer of the court'? Only kind of officers Angel knew were vice cops. Someone a lot wiser in the ways of the world than Angel was whispering in her ear.

"I slap some subpoenas on your bank accounts, I bet we find you bought a lot of traveler's checks sometime Friday."

He reached inside the desk drawer. I slammed it shut on his fingers with my good hand. He screamed, a quavering sound, not loud, but it conveyed the essence of pain. In the drawer was a nickel-plated Colt Python .357 Magnum.

As good a revolver as a man can buy. I clicked the cylinder open and pocketed the shells.

"You broke my fingers," he moaned. "I was reaching for my checkbook, not that thing."

"This one's not on my fee scale, Frank." I put my face an inch from his. "Angel almost got my kid, too. Trying to wipe out my whole family—that's tough to look away from."

"It's you that's assaulted me. It's you that's going to pay."

Manus had decided to tough it out.

"There's no evidence for anything that you've said. It's just a cock and bull story."

"There's evidence. We live in wonderful times, Frank. You mentioned the miracles of modern medicine yourself. Know what DNA is, Frank? Know what a modern paternity test consists of? Don't need the whole person, Frank. Just a swab from the inside of the mouth will do."

"Maybe you don't know, but she was cremated."

"But I did know, Frank. I know it was your idea, too. You think any possibility of finding out the truth went up in her smoke, don't you? You're wrong. We both know part of her is still alive."

He shrank away from me, clutching his flank, as if he feared the kidney would burst out of its own volition, telltale as Poe's heart.

"That's not what I mean. That'd be a hell of a subpoena to get, permission to go inside a man and clip a piece off a borrowed organ. There's an easier way. You know Vampire Eddie, Frank? Of course you do. And you're aware people have two kidneys? Without a doubt, because both of yours weren't worth a crap. Where's Evie's other kidney, Frank? Vampire Eddie still holding onto it? Just in case you need it? Because he's got the latest in organ transplant technology. Cryptopreservation. Black Ice. Keeps an organ fresh for weeks, instead of hours. Evie's cold, but she's not gone."

Frank Manus let out a gurgle from the bottom of his gut. It was neither a cough nor a retch but a combination of both and more, as if every organ in his chest cavity needed to expel something at the same time. A sound that could only be made by a very sick man.

"Your fault, Frank. You had to have the best. It's our habits that destroy us, more often than not."

I replaced the phone on the desk and the receiver on the hook before I left. I threw the revolver down the trash chute. It made a tremendous clatter as it banged against the metal. The thumping from the loading dock stopped momentarily, then resumed at a more rapid pace. I followed it to the far side of the building.

Mrs. Ambergast was wielding a masonry hammer against the remains of a surfboard. Half of it had already been reduced to unrecognizable chunks of fiberglass. Only the upper portion remained. The underside was still epoxied in brilliant yellow. The top had been sanded off. On the stark white of the bare fiberglass someone had used a carpenter's pencil to draw the outline of a dream catcher. A gift Angel never got to give to Evie.

Mrs. Ambergast wore a mask and gloves. Her forearms were covered with white dust. Her eyebrows flared when she saw me.

"I'm taking that," I said.

She tried to get me with the hammer, but her movements were arthritically slow. She was no trouble for an opponent that had sparred with Angel. I grabbed the haft with my good hand on her backswing, before it acquired any momentum at all, and pulled it away from her. I shoved her backwards onto the floor with the elbow of my bad arm. She fell sprawling, so that her hem rose above her support hose and the skin of her thighs, pale and varicosed, was exposed to daylight. I dropped the hammer between my feet. I stuffed the fiberglass chunks into one of the trash bags she had intended for their disposal. I hefted the filled bag in my good hand and, wincing, wedged the unbroken half of the longboard under my armpit with my bad one.

"You wouldn't do this if you really knew him," Mrs. Ambergast hissed. "You don't know all the things he's done."

"I sure as hell know enough of them," I replied.

I kicked the hammer sixty feet across the floor, far enough so that I had no worries that Mrs. Ambergast would be able to shuffle after it and blindside me before I got outside.

Pennofrio was waiting in the car, wearing the headphones. I displayed the surfboard triumphantly. He unlocked the trunk and we stowed it away. I unbuttoned my shirt and peeled the tape away from the wire on my chest.

"Did you get all that?"

"All what? He didn't admit anything."

"Yes, he did. You should've seen the look on his face."

"The wire is only good for audio, Counselor."

"He offered to bribe me."

"Not in so many words."

"Never mind, then. We got the surfboard."

"A thousand ways it could have ended up there."

"Name a hundred of them."

Pennofrio was silent.

"Okay, name ten."

"I am fucking thinking here, okay?"

"Name one."

"It's almost four. I don't think so good on Sunday afternoons at four. The reggae band in my head starts playing and the tourist women start swaying before my eyes. Nine o'clock tomorrow, I'll give you an innocent explanation for that surfboard being there. Call me then."

"The only reason that surfboard was there was to make sure Big Frank kept his iron grip on Angel. Showed it to her before he sent her off to collect a kidney for him, I'll bet. Nice choice he gave her, Sergeant. Kill your lover and get life in prison, or let her live and you both get the needle."

"Nice girls like Angel deserve nice choices."

"Let's go see a judge. And then your buddy Vampire Eddie."

"Oh, that beats the crap out of the afternoon I had planned."

"You know you have to do it."

"Fuck."

Pennofrio swirled the car angrily around a corner, barely missing a bicyclist whose face blanched in terror.

"Why do you hate me?"

"I don't hate you, Sergeant. I like you."

I scratched at my chest. The tape Pennofrio had used to wire me up had left big, itching, red welts. Another addition to my weekend's collection of injuries.

"Tell you one thing, though. I pretty much can't stand reggae."

Barry Appenzeller was more than happy to stop dripping resin into his veins long enough to sign a warrant. We picked up a med tech to take the actual sample but by the time we got to his address Vampire Eddie had destroyed the kidney. Turned out he had a little oven at home, a miniature crematorium. Told us that the organ went bad and had to be incinerated, but his records showed that he made that decision four minutes after I concluded my interview with Frank Manus. Lucky Frank. Eddie had been home. Not the kind of message you could leave on someone's voice mail.

We buried Izzy at sea, exactly as he had wished. We modified the Viking portion of the funeral so that only his ashes were in the center of the outrigger canoe when we set it ablaze. I put a few of his law books in its hull, along with the pictures of Oahu and one of his tailor-made suits, hand-crafted to dignify his bulk. Others added their mementos of Izzy's life, things that made the big Hawaiian special to them, photos, jewelry, letters. Not all of the mourners were legal professionals. Izzy was something special to his customers as well. I expect a couple crack pipes and glassine bags were burned in that canoe, his client list being what it was.

We poured lighter fluid in it to the gunwales and set it off, watching from two rented cabin cruisers. Probably completely illegal, from the points of view of the Environmental Protection Agency and the Coast Guard, but with all the lawyers present, it would have been insane for them to protest.

The outrigger burned to the waterline, but then floated just at the surface for the longest time. We bobbed on the ocean until nearly sunset. It seemed to all of us disrespectful to head for shore. Finally the canoe absorbed enough water through its charcoaled hull to slowly drift out of sight in the depths.

Detective Pullman proved to be a lot better in a stairwell than he was on a witness stand, and Raquel Bumgarden was found innocent of soliciting. Likewise Marvin Maeger was found innocent of pandering, but the Board of Health had him cold on the sperm situation on his floor and locked Phantasy Photography up tight for twenty days.

Amy, at the advice of her counsel, Ernest Schuckelgruber, withdrew her suit against me for sexual harassment. The restraining order was lifted as well, but I declined Ernie's offer to resume sharing office space with them.

Frank Manus died. He suffered complete renal failure the day after Izzy's funeral. His body rejected Evie's kidney, although I like to think it was the other way around. Another matching donor could not be found. Just as he predicted, he didn't last a week on the machine.

Now I let my son spend any night he wants to at my place, and every Sunday afternoon. Mostly he spends them criticizing every facet of my life and every decision I've ever made, but every once in a while we have a quiet moment in which I realize we're a family, and maybe he does, too. Anyway, it gives his mother a break.

I deal with my new client list as best as I can, keeping in mind Izzy's observation that no one is guilty in their own mind. He was close to being a hundred percent right. The dope dealers and the armed robbers, the domestic squabblers and the aggravated assaulters I represent now all claim with a single voice that they had no choice but to dirty their hands with dope or guns or blood. All self-serving deceptions, of course, but I am more generous in my thoughts toward them, now. What would I be telling myself, I wonder, if I had succeeded in bringing my weapon down on Angel's head?

Not to mention I bluffed a man into burning his own paid-for kidney. Bluffed, because I knew there was more of Evie left than her preserved organ. The coroner would have kept something of her, at least the vials of blood he tested to discover she was AB negative. Blood that could have convicted Manus of murder and incest, of keeping his own flesh captive to his sex and then depriving her of a half-century of her life so he could have a few more years of his. But he was an old, sick man with a fortune to spend delaying justice, and the town prosecutor in his pocket as well. Even with Evie's other kidney, chances are he would have died naturally before he was ever found guilty. So I sped up the process. Gave him the death penalty. Me personally, just like a preening DA playing for the voters by ramrodding some murderous dimwit into the execution chamber. My apologies to my departed father.

I imagine I was large in Frank Manus' thoughts as his blood was filtering through the dialysis machine for the last time, and I don't feel guilty about it at all.

I feel worse about the cold Desiree caught from me leaving her out in the rain. It turned into walking pneumonia, and then pleurisy. She got so sick she was unable to attend the meeting of the Ethics Committee at which Danny Akami's complaint against me was read.

Jill Congliaro sat in her place. She decided that the testimony of Warren Porter Wallace, aka Bandit, was insufficiently reliable to merit the attention of the Committee, and I walked. A reward for my discretion in dealing with Dr. Verlace, I'm sure.

Low Rate Auto Rental rewarded me, too. They made me a Gold Card customer for keeping the Hyundai for eleven days and only putting seventy-eight miles on it.

And Angel's loose in the wide, wide world. My fault. Beware Osaka. Don't think she's coming back this way, but, just in case, I left those damn axes in the bottom of Izzy's canoe.

About the author

Richard Cahill was born on the East Coast of the United States but moved to Southern California in his twenties, Hawaii in his thirties, and returned to his native state of Pennsylvania in his forties. He attended the University of Pennsylvania in his extreme youth. Not ha   ving any talent for academia, he has since worked as a carpenter, cabdriver, agent for nightclub acts, comic, emcee, disc jockey, bouncer, nightclub manager, and salesman.

During the course of these several careers Mr. Cahill claims to have encountered more libidinous drunks, irate cops, scheming attorneys, erotically adventurous showgirls (and the poor souls obsessed with them) than anyone deserves to meet in a Buddhist cycle of lifetimes. Voices like theirs echo through the pages of *Truth or Bare*.

Shorter works by Mr. Cahill have appeared in *The Pebble Lake Review*, *Writer Within*, *Firstwriter Magazine* and *The Quiet Feather*. This is his first novel.

Provocative. Bold. Controversial.

Kunati Fall 2007 titles

Available at your favorite bookseller

www.kunati.com

The Last Troubadour
Historical fiction by Derek Armstrong

Against the flames of a rising medieval Inquisition, a heretic, an atheist and a pagan are the last hope to save the holiest Christian relic from a sainted king and crusading pope. Based on true events.
■ "A series to watch ... Armstrong injects the trope with new vigor." *Booklist*

US$ 24.95 | Pages 384, cloth hardcover
ISBN-13: 978-1-60164-010-9
ISBN-10: 1-60164-010-2
EAN: 9781601640109

Recycling Jimmy
A cheeky, outrageous novel by Andy Tilley

Two Manchester lads mine a local hospital ward for "clients" as they launch Quitters, their suicide-for-profit venture in this off-the-wall look at death and modern life.

US$ 24.95 | Pages 256, cloth hardcover
ISBN-13: 978-1-60164-013-0
ISBN-10: 1-60164-013-7
EAN 9781601640130

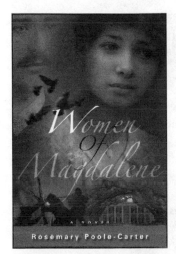

Women Of Magdalene
A hauntingly tragic tale of the old South by Rosemary Poole-Carter

An idealistic young doctor in the post-Civil War South exposes the greed and cruelty at the heart of the Magdalene Ladies' Asylum in this elegant, richly detailed and moving story of love and sacrifice.

US$ 24.95 | Pages 288, cloth hardcover
ISBN-13: 978-1-60164-014-7
ISBN-10: 1-60164-014-5
EAN: 9781601640147

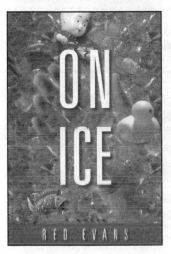

On Ice
A road story like no other, by Red Evans

The sudden death of a sad old fiddle player brings new happiness and hope to those who loved him in this charming, earthy, hilarious coming-of-age tale.

US$ 19.95 | Pages 208, cloth hardcover
ISBN-13: 978-1-60164-015-4
ISBN-10: 1-60164-015-3
EAN: 9781601640154

Truth Or Bare
Offbeat, stylish crime novel by Richard Cahill

The characters throb with vitality, the prose sizzles in this darkly comic page-turner set in the sleazy world of murderous sex workers, the justice system, and the rich who will stop at nothing to get what they want.

US$ 24.95 | Pages 304, cloth hardcover
ISBN-13: 978-1-60164-016-1
ISBN-10: 1-60164-016-1
EAN: 9781601640161

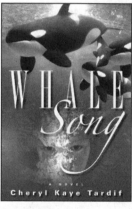

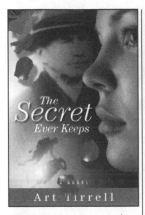

The Secret Ever Keeps
A novel by Art Tirrell

An aging Godfather-like billionaire tycoon regrets a decades-long life of "shady dealings" and seeks reconciliation with a granddaughter who doesn't even know he exists. A sweeping adventure across decades—from Prohibition to today—exploring themes of guilt, greed and forgiveness.
■ "Riveting ... Rhapsodic ... Accomplished." *ForeWord*
US$ 24.95
Pages 352, cloth hardcover
ISBN 978-1-60164-004-8
EAN 9781601640048
LCCN 2006930185

Toonamint of Champions
A wickedly allegorical comedy by Todd Sentell

Todd Sentell pulls out all the stops in his hilarious spoof of the manners and mores of America's most prestigious golf club. A cast of unforgettable characters, speaking a language only a true son of the South could pull off, reveal that behind the gates of fancy private golf clubs lurk some mighty influential freaks.
■ "Bubbly imagination and wacky humor." *ForeWord*
US$ 19.95
Pages 182, cloth hardcover
ISBN 978 1 60164 006 6
EAN 9781601640055
LCCN 2006930186

Mothering Mother
A daughter's humorous and heartbreaking memoir.
Carol D. O'Dell

Mothering Mother is an authentic, "in-the-room" view of a daughter's struggle to care for a dying parent. It will touch you and never leave you.
■ "Beautiful, told with humor... and much love." *Booklist*
■ "I not only loved it, I lived it. I laughed, I smiled and shuddered reading this book." Judith H. Wright, author of over 20 books.
US$ 19.95
Pages 208, cloth hardcover
ISBN 978-1-60164-003-1
EAN 9781601640031
LCCN 2006930184

Rabid
A novel by T K Kenyon

A sexy, savvy, darkly funny tale of ambition, scandal, forbidden love and murder. Nothing is sacred. The graduate student, her professor, his wife, her priest: four brilliantly realized characters spin out of control in a world where science and religion are in constant conflict.
■ "Kenyon is definitely a keeper." STARRED REVIEW, *Booklist*
US$ 26.95 | Pages 480, cloth hardcover
ISBN 978-1-60164-002-4 | EAN: 9781601640024
LCCN 2006930189